Falling Under the Stars

ABBEY FALLS SERIES

ALSO BY KAREN DEEN

Time For Love Series

Love's Wall

Love's Dance

Love's Hiding

Love's Fun

Love's Hot

Defining Us

The Chicago Boys Series

Gorgeous Gyno

Private Pilot

Naughty Neuro

Lovable Lawyer

New Year's Eve with The Chicago Boys

Cherished Moments Series

That Day

Better Day

Hotel Temptations Series

The Craving

The Desire

The Passion

The Attraction

New Beginnings Series

Never Forgetting You

Falling Under the Stars

ABBEY FALLS SERIES

KARENT DEEN

The characters and events portrayed in this book are fictitious. Any similarity to real persons, living or dead, is coincidental and not intended by the author.

Published by Montlake, Seattle

www.apub.com

EU product safety contact:
Amazon Media EU S. à r.l.
38, avenue John F. Kennedy, L-1855 Luxembourg
amazonpublishing-gpsr@amazon.com

ISBN-13: 9781662540554
eISBN: 9781662540561

Cover Design by Allyse Karam
Cover image: © underworld © Maurizio Milanesio © Hafid Firman
© Olexandr Ostrovyi / Shutterstock; © Wander Aguiar Photography

This book is dedicated to my mother

You encouraged me to read books,
and in between those pages,
I fell in love with words.
You believed in my stories and
encouraged me to keep writing.
You taught me how precious love is and raised me to dream big.
That nothing was out of my reach and to never give up.

Today, I live these dreams, Mum, all because of you.
Words are only words, until they become a story.
A story is only enjoyed if there is someone reading it.
Thank you all, for being my someone.

Chapter One

Ashley

Mirrors don't lie, but some mornings they're just too brutally honest.

"You look like hell this morning," Tiffany says in greeting as I walk through the door of her teahouse.

"Wow, love you too, but could you be a good friend and lie to me, just this once?" I bite back as I slump onto the stool in front of her.

I mean, she's not wrong. I caught sight of my face in the rear-view mirror this morning and I look as exhausted as I feel. But I didn't need reminding, again.

But that's what friends are for, to be blunt, even when you don't ask for it.

"Surprisingly, a lack of sleep will do this to a person," I say, waving my hand in front of my face.

"Please tell me that the sleep deprivation is due to some big hunky man with a huge dick that took you to pound town all night long."

"Tiff, seriously, you can't say things like that in here. What if someone heard you?" Looking around the teahouse, there is only a couple of older women sitting at a table in the back.

"Why? Old Gertrude is as deaf as a post and so wrapped up in that book she's reading. And I can see that Mary doesn't have her hearing aids in." She chuckles to herself as she pulls my teacup down from the top shelf behind the counter. The one where she keeps the special cups. She has individual ones for all her friends and no one else gets to use them.

Going about her ritual, Tiffany makes me a special tea mix from her jars that are lined up along the back wall. I've given up asking what I'm drinking each time.

All I know is that whatever she makes me always tastes good, and I feel better after drinking it.

"What if I wanted a coffee this morning?" My elbows are now on the counter with my head resting in my hands. Not because it's comfortable, it's purely to keep me awake.

"Pfftt. Since when do you know what you need more than I do? Now, you didn't answer my question about visiting pound town." She starts to fill the teapot with hot water and raises her eyebrows.

"Yeah, right. The only huge appendage I've seen in the last few years is on Old Man Cochran's prize bull that he proudly wants to show all the girls in the pasture at Hindmarsh Farm on a regular occasion."

I stifle another yawn. Last night's callouts kept me from getting more than two hours' sleep at a time. First, twin calves stuck in a cow that was calving for the first time, and just as I thought I could finally put my head down and pass out, Mrs. Bradley called because her pet pig had been attacked and needed to be looked at right away.

Then there was a poor stray dog that was hit by a car out on Manor Road and needed surgery to fix some internal injuries. She doesn't look like she has eaten for a while and is in desperate need of a good wash, a new home, and a whole lot of love to nurse back to full health. But I'll worry about that later.

Seriously, why can't these things happen during the day? Or at least only one emergency a night would be manageable.

"Oh wow, Old Man Cochran is out shaking his schlong around in the pastures?" Her giggle tells me she knows the answer, but I can't help but bite back with a reply.

"No, the bull!" I roll my eyes at her.

"Thank goodness. Nobody needs to see that." She winks at me as she does her usual ritual with the teapot.

Two circles to the right, three circles to the left, and one last circle to the right again.

The scent wafts from the cup as she pours my tea and tells me this one has jasmine in it.

"I thought we agreed to give up on the jasmine?" I ask, knowing that I get no say in what tea she makes me.

"You wish. Jasmine is known for attracting romance, and you, my friend, need it. As someone who spends more time with males of the furry variety, you need all the help you can get." Tiff walks around the counter and plonks herself down on the stool next to me.

"Umm, I'm a vet, remember? That's kind of my job," I say, lifting the tea to my lips and taking the first sip.

"Yes, your job, not your life." Tiff looks at me like she's peering into my soul, trying to remind me that I'm not just a vet, but a woman who's lonely at times too.

"Ashley, you know I love you, but it's time to stop hiding behind work as the excuse for why you haven't been on a date in over three years, not since dickwad Jeremy left town for that bimbo he met online."

"Mmmm, this tea is so good. What muffin do you have that can substitute for breakfast?" I smile innocently at her as I take another sip. I mean, I'm not lying. This tea tastes just perfect this morning.

"Yeah, yeah, change the subject." She stands and kisses me on the top of the head as she returns behind the counter and places her famous carrot-walnut muffin on a plate in front of me.

"It's not healthy to only eat a muffin for breakfast." Walking back around the counter to me, Tiff sits back on her stool next to me and looks at me like she's getting ready to lecture me about looking after myself.

"I disagree; this has a vegetable in it," I reply as I sink my teeth into it for the first bite, and it doesn't disappoint as per usual.

"Seriously," she scolds, throwing her hands in the air.

"Don't you have other customers to lecture?" I lean my head in the direction of the two ladies, who are oblivious to our conversation.

"You wish. Now please tell me you have placed that advertisement for another vet to work in the clinic and take a bit of the load off you. You can't keep this kind of workload up. Not only did Jeremy break your heart, but he fucked you over by leaving you as the only vet in town. I mean, he was never as good a vet as you, but at least he let you get some nights off so you could sleep. When you bought the clinic here after college, it was never meant to be run solo."

And this is why I love Tiffany. She truly cares about me, and I wouldn't have gotten through the last three years without her.

"Yes, Mom, I did it two days ago, but there hasn't been any interest yet. I mean, being a small-town vet is not for everyone."

For me, it's all I ever wanted when I qualified.

Move to the country with Jeremy, leaving the confines of a soulless large city to live in a small town where people actually care about their neighbors and talk to you as you walk down the street. Not like San Francisco where I grew up.

Then establish ourselves, pay off our college debt, and then buy some land to live happily ever after on.

Four out of those five dreams came true.

And I'm starting to think that the happily ever after is meant to be me with all my stray animals. They're more faithful and complain less than a man anyway.

So maybe it's a win-win situation after all.

Conversation between us turns to this morning's town gossip, because if there is anyone who's going to be all over it, it's Tiffany. I mean, she gets all the early risers in for their coffee or tea and a pastry or muffin while they share morning reports of what's happening around town. I have to say, despite wanting to live in a small town, I was never so happy to get my ten acres of paradise and privacy away from the local busybodies and their gossip two years ago after I picked myself up from the state Jeremy left me in.

It's not perfect and still needs a lot of work, but it's mine and it's home.

A place I plan to be for the rest of my life, living the dream.

Customers have come and gone while I've been sitting here drinking my tea, with Tiffany topping it up a couple of times. I love my pale pink teacup that's covered in a floral pattern. She says it's her way of giving me a bunch of flowers every day so I know I'm loved. This cup was a new one she gifted me the first morning I made it out of bed and into the teahouse after Jeremy left me. It's not huge, petite like me, she said, and also, because I like my tea black and hot. If the cup is too big, it goes cold too quickly.

Just as I'm about to push off the stool to visit the bathroom, because tea always makes me want to pee, Tiffany's gasp stops me in my tracks.

"Holy shit," she whispers, which freaks me out because Tiffany never whispers.

"What, what's wrong?" I look at her staring into my teacup.

"He's coming."

"Who's coming? What are you talking about?" I'm so confused.

"Your man." Her eyes sparkle as she lifts them from looking into the teacup.

"Oh, for fuck's sake, not more of your woo-woo visions again." I sigh, guessing at what I'm about to hear.

"Oh shush, it's not my vision, it's yours. These are your tea leaves, and they don't lie. In all the years I've known you, nothing has appeared in the leaves, until today. Oh, Ashley, this is so freaking exciting. Look, oh lordy, he's going to be everything you dreamed of in a man."

"No thanks. I had one of them and he turned out to be a douchebag, and that's being polite." My left leg is now bouncing on the stool because my need to pee is getting more urgent.

"Forget about Jeremy. He was just the preshow entertainment for the main event. This one is tall, broad shoulders, big hands." Which brings out a giggle from her. "You know what they say about big hands—oh, and he knows how to use them too. Boots, water, and trees."

I dare not ask, but it just slips out. "What the hell does that mean?"

"I don't know. I'm just telling you what I'm seeing. A dog, big dog. Oh, and a cute dimple on him, the man that is, not the dog. Just one dimple, but it's hidden."

I'm cracking up at the load of crap that Tiff is rambling on with and cross my legs. I can't wait any longer.

"I've got to pee. I shouldn't have laughed." As I jump off the stool, my elbow catches the cup and knocks it out of Tiff's hands, and the last little bit of tea spills onto the counter.

"Sorry," I yell behind me as I run toward the toilet that is out back of the teahouse.

"Nooooo!" I can hear her screaming at me. "I've lost it."

Oh, she's lost it alright.

I have no idea what goes on in that head of hers, but it's nothing normal, that's for sure.

The relief I feel walking back into the shop from the bathroom is short-lived when I see Tiff smiling brightly at me.

"Don't even start. It's just tea leaves in a cup, not some portal to the future." I reach down and pick up my bag.

"Say whatever you like, but you can't stop the universe when it decides it's your time to shine." She waves her hands in the air at me. "Big hands that he knows how to use, yeah, baby."

"You are ridiculous, you know that? But I'm not going to lie, my own hand is getting a little tired of being the only one I get. Now go wash my cup and make sure you use plenty of soap to scrub away whatever spell you cast in it. I'm perfectly happy in my own little place of bliss."

The bell above the teahouse door rings as I walk outside, and I can't help but shake my head at what just happened.

I hope the rest of the day is quiet and a lot less crazy than the last twelve hours.

The last thing I need is a man to complicate my life when I've finally found the place where I belong.

Which is happily being all on my own.

JAKE

I almost made it.

Pulling into the gas station in Rocky Cedars, I'm only twenty minutes from Gran's house in Abbey Falls, but I remember Gramps always complaining that you can never guarantee old Jed's garage in town will be open. So, better to be safe than sorry.

Walking to the counter to pay, I see the old guy behind it eyeing me up and down.

"You're one of Noel and Betty's grandsons, aren't you?" he says. "Yeah, I recognize you from the funeral. Noel was a good man. God rest his soul." And his words stab right into my heart.

It's been ten days since he passed, and it still feels so raw.

"Yes, I am and thank you." I indicate that I don't want to talk about it, but this guy isn't taking the hint. I'm stressed, tired, grumpy, and seeing this guy getting ready to wind up into a lengthy discussion about the man I loved unconditionally and who was my ultimate hero . . . I just don't think I can do it. Not that I don't want to hear how Gramps was beloved all over the area, I just can't bear it today. Not until I have had some more time for the grief to settle. It's all just too fresh.

Before he opens his mouth, I cut him off.

"Sorry, buddy, I'm in a hurry to get to Gran's. She's waiting for me. Just paying on debit, thanks." Holding my card near the machine, I cross everything in me that it goes through.

He cracks a crooked smile at me and I feel a little ashamed for using Gran's name that way. "Well, we can't have you late to Betty's place. We all know how that woman runs a tight ship on Heatherbrae Vines, and in Abbey Falls too, for that matter. She may as well be the mayor."

I tap my card and hold my breath. The word *approved* shows on the screen and I start breathing again. I know there is money in the account but there's always that fear of the bank freezing my account.

"What's the plans for the vineyard now Noel is gone? Guess you'll be selling."

It's a question that really bugs me, but I could hear all the old people at the funeral muttering it among themselves as well.

"Business as usual," I reply as I grab the receipt from his hand and walk out to my truck.

"Sort of," I mumble to myself as I head out of the gas station.

My mind wanders back to the morning after the funeral where Gran had us all together, and she was sitting eagerly awaiting the lawyer to start reading out Gramps's will. She already knew what it contained but seemed keen for us all to hear it together. It was the regular stuff—most of it went to Gran and all the kids got some mementos, keepsakes. Mine was his wood-carving knife he used to whittle little things out of the fallen branches from the big white oak tree on the farm that we buried him under. Something I will treasure forever.

Then he started on a letter that Gramps had left for us boys.

> Heatherbrae Vines was bought to be a family legacy for my grandchildren. My age and health never saw my dreams come to fruition. Although I know this is a lot to ask, I want my four grandsons, Beckett, Declan, Jake, and Chase to move to Heatherbrae like we always planned and bring it to life. I wish for them to live with their grandmother for the twelve months following my death. Build our vision. The one we mapped out so many times when they all visited over the years while sitting around the firepit. Life always got in the way, but time is a precious thing which can be taken away easily, so now I'm relying on them all to do it without me. The time for this is now. Once they have completed this task, then their grandmother will sign over the ownership of Heatherbrae Vines to the four of them, with the stipulation that she continues to live in our home until she passes. This is my dying wish.

Shock settled over all of us. It went on to say the girls would inherit a cash equivalent if the letter's wishes were fulfilled. But more than anything, the four of us boys were suddenly the center of attention.

There was no way I wasn't packing up my life and moving to Abbey Falls for a year out of respect for the man I idolized. And the more I thought about it, the more it seemed like perfect timing. I could do with putting some temporary space between me and my problems, and Heatherbrae's not what it used to be when Gramps was in his prime.

Only five minutes down the road from the gas station, I cross the county line and see the sign that greets every visitor.

Welcome to Abbey Falls
Population 2902

And that's when it hits me. Someone better get out here with their paint because there is about to be a change in that number, Gramps may have left this town, but they are about to get four more just like him. Well, three, because there is no way my brother Beckett is like Gramps. Far from it. And I'm not even sure if he will show up, unless it's to be the boss of the remodel. Beckett deserves an award for being a controlling asshole—just like he aced all his grades in school and business college, it's something Beckett excels at. I doubt he's failed anything in his life. I swallow down the bitter wish I could say the same.

Rolling down my truck window, I rest my elbow on the door and let my hand fall out with fingers spread and allow the cool air to run through them. It may be April, but the spring air still has that crispness to it. Leaning over, I take in a deep breath and the scent of Abbey Falls fills me. That distinct pine aroma reminds me of all the years I spent here on school break with my cousins.

I can almost feel my shoulder tension releasing as I look toward the hills full of pine and fir trees that border the town. Abbey Falls feels more like home than Sacramento, despite living there for twelve years. That place I'd hoped to build my life, family, and future feels more like a prison.

The roads here are nothing like in the city. You feel every single bump and pothole, and in some places, the roads aren't even wide enough for two cars to pass without going off onto the grass on the side. But the slow pace of living here means that no one is in a rush, and with a smile and the friendly wave of a hand, you both maneuver past each other.

I'm close to Heatherbrae now, and with a grin I press Answer as my phone rings in its holder.

"Hi, Declan," I say happily.

"Jake, you there yet?" Declan's voice fills my cabin.

"How did you know? Just driving up to Heatherbrae now."

"And will be getting a delicious Gran special for dinner, while I'll probably be grabbing a pizza on my way home from basketball practice." Declan groans and I can't resist a smile, Gran's cooking really is second to none. "How has it only been a week since we were all there? I'm already missing her cooking. I'd forgotten how good it was." He chuckles to himself.

"Not sure how Gran fed us all, but she never complained and there was always plenty to go round." It was chaos when my siblings and all my cousins arrived at Heatherbrae for our holiday stay with them. So many of my best memories of my childhood happened on Heatherbrae.

"I know, and sitting around the firepit last week with you boys smoking Gramps's best cigars really brought home how much we will miss him. He will be sitting up there, looking down on us, chuckling at us sneaking in to get his cigar box like we were kids again."

We both start laughing.

"Remember when we stole those cigars and climbed that big old white oak and then Chase coughed so hard he fell out the tree and broke his arm in three places?" I can still hear Beckett's lecture the whole way back to the house, how it was a bad idea and "that's what we get for doing something we weren't supposed to." My brother has always been old for his age and a controlling know-it-all, even as a kid.

"Yeah and how Gramps covered for us but then spent the next few weeks giving us extra chores as our punishment," Declan replies, sending me back to those memories of Gramps's secret smirk as he sent us off to walk the vines and count grapes—which was a useless exercise—or rake the gravel driveway that he would then drive his truck down at speed and fling it all over the place again, and all sorts of random chores that really didn't need to be done. I mean, who rakes a gravel driveway on a working farm.

"It's going to be strange being there for twelve months without him. I can't seem to shake the guilt that I haven't been back in five years. Except for one night where I was just passing through. I had no idea that things had deteriorated as bad as they had. I feel so guilty." My voice is a little more somber now.

"I know Beckett told us all that Gramps's letter is not binding in any way, it's just his wishes, but they are kind of hard to ignore. He meant so much to us all it was like a slap in the face when I looked back and realized it's six years since I was there too. Where the hell did that time go? The guilt level is high for me too, cuz."

"I knew the moment I drove through the gate for the funeral that I was coming back to fix it up. I didn't need Gramps to ask me to do it. But it's easy for me. I'm a contractor, it's what I do. But like I said to you guys, it doesn't mean you have to do this too."

I can't tell him that I also have other reasons to be leaving Sacramento. That's a mess I'm not ready to share yet, not even with the people closest to me. It will be a kick to my pride and with losing Gramps, I'm not sure I can take another gut-punch right now.

"Like Chase said, stop trying to be the martyr and making us look bad. Of course we were going to want to help you. You might be a builder, but you can't do it on your own. It's eight weeks until the end of the school term and I'm just waiting on confirmation for my one-year sabbatical. Once the school board have approved and my school can find another basketball coach, I'll be there."

I feel a knot of unease unravel in my stomach. Eight weeks isn't too long to wait.

"Chase says he has a couple of photo shoots to do and then he can join us. He's not sure he can do the whole twelve months straight. He may have to come and go." And as soon as the words leave my mouth, Declan is guffawing. "You know him, always got some sort of excuse to get out of work but more than happy to come in at the end to claim the glory. Cheeky little shit."

No matter how old we get, Chase will always be the youngest and the one we love to give crap to.

"I'm impressed you could leave Sacramento so quickly. I mean, I know you don't have anyone holding you there anymore, but I thought you'd have jobs lined up."

"Just wrapped a big job, so I was able to pass the future contracts that were booked in to another builder. Family first."

I try to pass it off quickly and like my heart isn't threatening to escape my chest, but the words sound like acid on my tongue because I haven't been putting family first and look what's happened. I'm barely talking to my brother, and I missed that last chance to see my gramps one last time. It's not like we had any warning. His heart just gave out one night and when Gran woke in the morning, he was gone. But in a way that's the best way to go, no pain and next to the love of his life for sixty-two years.

"Fair enough. Just checking you are okay. You seemed a bit quiet last week."

I can hear the concern in his voice, and I love him for it.

"Yeah, I'm all good. Guess I've had enough working for entitled people who have no idea what it takes to build something, and then there's all the crap that goes into running your own business. It will be nice to get some fresh air and build for the fun of it again."

The vines of Heatherbrae come into view around the corner and I sigh in relief. It will be heaven to work all day on restoring the vineyard and then head up into the woods that surround the property for a hike.

Gramps gave me the gift of finding my love of the great outdoors. And it's just one of the many things he taught me and that I'll always be grateful for.

"Darn, the troops have arrived for practice. I have to go. Don't smoke all Gramps's good cigars before I get there!" He chuckles as he hangs up and I grin.

It's good to be back in touch with my cousins, to be back here. Maybe twelve months at Heatherbrae and a hearty dose of Gran's cooking is just what I need.

Pulling around the circular gravel drive, I sigh in relief. There's Gran out waiting for me . . . but the scene in front of me is not quite the welcome I was expecting.

"Gran, what's going on?" I call as I leap from the truck and race round the back of the house toward her as she tries to shoo a white goat from her prized flower garden. Only for my raised voice to startle a brown and white cow that was at the side of the house and now sets off toward a vineyard of young grapes.

"Hello, Jake!" Gran shouts out to me with a smile that makes me feel like I've come home and been given a hug all in one go. "Don't worry, it's just Daisy and Gerald. They managed to get through the neighbor's fence again, but they'll wander home soon. They always do." She sounds so calm while the stupid goat continues attacking her azaleas.

"How often does this happen?" I ask after I've grabbed a rope from inside my truck and storm toward the goat I assume is Gerald, because everyone knows cows are called Daisy.

"Every day for the last week," she mumbles as she tries to gently shoo it out of the garden, but it doesn't move an inch.

"Well, today is the last day!" Keeping my voice as calm as I can, I loop the rope around its neck and start dragging it behind me. "Which neighbor?" I bellow behind me as I start dragging the now loudly complaining goat, chasing the cow away from the grapes.

"Windemere Farm." She points to the west boundary that is hidden over the hill and behind a row of bushes.

After capturing the cow and keeping the whining goat on its rope-leash, I have to walk a few laps of the fence line before I finally manage to push them through one of the many holes in the boundary and then keep walking until I get to a run-down barn of some sort. It figures—the farm is in just as bad a shape as the fences.

"No point just putting you in your pasture with no fucking gate on it. I'm tying you to this fence, Gerald, while I put your partner in crime in the yard that I hope to God will hold her."

The sweat is pouring off my face as I finally pull the gate closed, which of course doesn't lock.

"What kind of farmer has animals that they can't fucking look after?" I mumble to myself when a large Toyota SUV comes racing up the gravel drive. Dust flying everywhere, it comes to a screeching halt beside me.

As the dust cloud starts to disperse, the door is flung open and a smallish woman jumps out, her eyes flashing as she storms toward me. Her brown hair is pulled back tight in a bun and she's wearing dirty overalls.

"Great, a wannabe farmer." A comment I should have kept to myself but too late now.

"Who the hell are you and why is Daisy tied up?" the woman snaps and I find myself noticing the smoldering fire in her flecked brown eyes.

I take a step forward, refusing to give ground as I snap back, "She's not. She's in the yard, if that's what you call it, with the broken gate."

Without even acknowledging me, the woman huffs past me and goes straight to Gerald.

"Last time I looked, this is rope, and oh shit, it's tied around Daisy's neck. Are you blind?" She doesn't even look at me as she delivers her angry comment and starts to untie the goat. "I swear, if you have injured her in any way, you won't hear the end of it."

"Wait, you called the goat Daisy and the cow, that is obviously female, Gerald? Oh, this just keeps getting more ridiculous."

She stands up as the damn goat runs off, heading straight for the broken fence again. With her hands on her hips, she looks like she's ready for war.

"One more time for the dummies. Who the hell are you and what are you doing on my property?"

"Wow, feisty, aren't we." I can't help but poke the bear. No matter how intense she looks, she's a full head shorter than me, but there is something about her face. Maybe it's those long lashes framing her eyes, and not in a way they should when she's glaring at me as if she'd happily tear me apart.

"You have no fucking idea. Now answer the question." She's not giving an inch, and I've got to give her points for confidence.

"Your new neighbor, who's here to tell you to fix your shit fences. If you want to play happy farmer with your ridiculously named animals, then at least have the decency to keep them on your own shit farm."

"New neighbor." She pulls in a little gasp. "Noel only died a week ago and his family is kicking Betty out of her home? What a bunch of assholes." Her hand lands on her heart, obviously worried about Gran, which I guess is kind of nice, but the rest of her sentence has pissed me right off.

Knowing I'm about to lose my cool, I need to walk away. It's been a long week at the end of a long year and I'm tired.

"This family you think you know so much about? Well, I'm one of them and I've just moved in." Turning, I march back to my new home—or least home for the next twelve months.

"And fix your damn fences. Because if you want to play farmer, you need to take the responsibility that goes along with it."

And even though I'm already halfway across the pasture, I can hear her screaming at me. I picture her with those hands on her hips, a gesture that she doesn't realize also pushes her chest out, leaving me with plenty to imagine. *What a perfect handful.* Not that I was looking . . . well, maybe not the whole time.

"If the rest of the family is anything like you, then I was right, a total bunch of assholes!"

"Well, farm girl," I mutter to myself as I step over the broken fence, "your life is about to get a whole lot more interesting, because it's going to start raining asshole men around here."

Chapter Two

Ashley

It's been two days since that arrogant jerk stepped foot on my farm, and I'm still seething.

How dare he be so patronizing.

He has no idea about me or my farm. Where does he get off questioning if I even know how to repair a fence? Of course I do. I just need the dear animals of Abbey Falls to stop getting injured and sick. How the hell am I supposed to find time to fix the fence that was like that when I bought this place when I can't even find the time to fit in the recommended eight hours of sleep? I'm tired. Correction, I'm exhausted. And with this type of exhaustion, I have no patience for men who think they can puff out their chest and dish out orders.

I haven't had time to stop by Tiff's Teahouse since his little visit. She's been blowing up my phone, asking if I'm eating properly and getting enough sleep, do I need her to find me a new vet, and the best text was telling me she can feel it in her waters that the earth is about to shake for me.

I wanted to reply, *Does it count if the earth is shaking with rage?* But I know that will just result in my phone ringing nonstop.

Sighing, I note that my schedule is full today, but I can call the rural store and have them deliver some fencing wire to the farm. Until then, Daisy and Gerald are stuck hanging out together, because on top of everything, I do not have the energy for another showdown with the dickwad next door.

I'm still yet to get to the bottom of the "new neighbor" label he used. Should I be worried about Betty having to put up with living with him? That woman is the sweetest thing and wouldn't even know how to raise her voice.

Maybe he came home for the funeral and is just staying for a few days to keep her company. I felt so bad that I couldn't be there to send Noel off, but I was caught up thirty minutes out of town helping deliver piglets to a prize-winning sow, and the farmer didn't want me to do a caesarian and leave her with a scar. So, it meant I had to stay for five hours and assist the poor momma as she struggled to birth the sixteen piglets.

I called Betty and apologized, telling her I would come around for a cup of tea soon, but now I'm not going anywhere near that house just in case I run into Mr. Patronizing. While I don't even know his name, I can think of a few choice ones.

"The little Addison twins are so adorable with their twin rabbits." Adi, my vet nurse, beams like she always does when we have kids in the clinic.

"I know, right? But let's see how happy mom and dad are if the rabbits turn out to be a boy and a girl. Overnight, two become ten." We both start giggling as we clean down the table and counters in the exam room.

"Got anything planned for tonight?" she asks me as I pack the last of the instruments into the sterilizer.

"Pray for me that I get the chance to sleep. Knowing my luck, I have now jinxed myself by saying that, but fingers crossed I get at least six hours." On cue, the moment I mention sleep, the biggest yawn overtakes me.

"Yeah, I'm praying for you, but my biggest wish is for someone, anyone, to reply to your job ad. You can't sustain this, Ashley."

"Maybe so, but no matter how desperate I am, I'm going to be picky. Look at the last vet we had. What a mistake that was, in more ways than one. If I could choose, it would be a woman. I've decided men are the worst, period." I lean back on the counter.

"Ah, but they are useful for some things." Adi looks down at her watch, seeing it's past her knock-off time. "Like cooking me dinner. Time for me to head home to my hubby."

I'm so blessed to have Adi work for me. She never complains when she works late or if there is a big emergency and I need to call her in during the night. I don't do it often, but there are just some things I can't do alone. I haven't told her, but I have also advertised for a new vet nurse, so we can lighten her workload too.

"Yes, go, please. Tell Tim I'm sorry you are late . . . again." Luckily he's such a great guy that he never complains, or so Adi tells me.

"Grab your bag, we can lock up together," Adi says sternly and fixes me with a glare. I know that look. It's the same worried one she's had for a while now.

"It's okay. You go. I'm going to spend a little bit of time with Rosie while I catch up on some paperwork." I look down at the stray dog that's recovering from the hit-and-run the other night and is now curled up on the bed I've given her to hang out on during the day.

"I can't believe how quickly she's recovered. It just goes to show what a little love can do." Adi swings her bag onto her shoulder as she nods and starts heading toward the back door of the clinic.

I crouch down in front of Rosie. Her head lifts for a pat and I run my hand over her, scratching under her chin as she starts nuzzling into my chest in appreciation.

"Love, a good bath, and some food, hey, my gorgeous girl?"

Rosie lets out a little playful bark, which has both Adi and me laughing.

"See you Monday," I tell her.

"Sleep," she yells over her shoulder as the back door closes.

"If only it were that simple, hey, Rosie? I think you like your new name. It suits you. You reminded me of a rose bush that night you arrived in the clinic. You looked rough and spiky, but really are as sweet and beautiful as a rose." With another playful nudge in my chest, I land on my ass on the floor, losing track of time loving up this very affectionate German shepherd.

Her burst of energy now dwindling, she lays her head in my lap as I rest my back against the wall and slowly stroke down her long-haired coat while she begins to snore softly.

"What happened to you, Rosie girl? Did someone just get sick of you and dump you on the side of the road? It hurts to be thrown away like you meant nothing at all, doesn't it. Life can be cruel sometimes."

The longer I sit here, the lower my motivation is to get up off the floor.

"I wish I could take you home to Windemere Farm with me, sweet girl, but I know it would just bring more chaos. My menagerie of strays isn't going to cope well with you trying to round them up and keep them under control. And I'm not sure my heart could take it if something happened to you. I've only had one dog in my life, Sally, and she was my whole world, and when she died, part of me did too. I wouldn't have made it through my childhood without her. She was the only one who didn't want to leave me, but it was her time to go."

I take a deep breath because memories of that time in my life are always hard. I keep stroking over Rosie's head as I push those thoughts out of my head. "But don't you worry, I'll find you a good home. You deserve to be loved. We all do." I sigh as my head drops back against the wall and my eyes start to close.

Just five minutes . . . that's all I need.

◆ ◆ ◆

"Ughh, I hate that noise." I try to drag myself out of the sleep coma at the sound of my phone ringing.

"Go away," I mumble as it starts ringing again, and I know I need to get up because my pillow is moving under my head.

"Shit," I chide myself and sit up straight. "Crap, sorry, Rosie." I realize I have been lying on the floor with her, snuggling and resting my head on her warm body.

Her sleepy brown eyes look at me, pleading for me to shut up that annoying noise that is disturbing her sleep too.

"Hello." I don't even look at the phone screen as I accept the call.

"Are you avoiding me?" Tiff's voice screams down the phone. "I haven't seen you for days, and I know you are still at the clinic when you should be at home."

"Can you stop yelling? I love you, but tone it down for a hot minute," I reply, falling into the chair at my desk.

"Right, that's it. Get in your car and drive home. I've spoken to Wade over in Rocky Cedars and he's going to cover any callouts tonight and all day tomorrow for you. It's his weekend off, so he's doing it as a favor to me, and you too, I guess."

I sigh. "Tiffany, you can't just butt into my business and Wade doesn't need to be working his days off to help me. And let's be honest, he's only doing it because he can't say no to you. That poor man has been crushing on you for years."

"Well, someone has to butt in before you work yourself into an early grave. And don't you worry about Wade. I'm not the right woman for him, and he certainly isn't enough man for me. I need a man who knows how to handle my big personality. Wade's too sweet for me." Tiffany starts cackling to herself.

"Maybe so, but can we get back to the part about you meddling in my life? I'm calling Wade right now and apologizing for wasting his time."

"Too late, he's arriving in town in the next thirty minutes. I've booked him a room at the bed-and-breakfast. All you need to do is transfer your calls to his number and drop the spare key for the clinic into the B&B on your way home. Then you're going home, showering, putting on some makeup, and doing your hair so you look like a hot single woman for a night instead of a hardworking vet. I'll be there to pick you up at seven thirty, and we're heading to Grizzly's bar and grill for a night of drinking and forgetting the world around us."

She's talking so fast I can't seem to get a word in.

"No, no, no," I interrupt. "One drink and I'll be passed out on the bar, drooling out the side of my mouth and snoring so loud you'll hear it over the band." Alcohol and a lack of sleep are a bad combination.

"Who gives a damn! At least you will get a nap. Or you might find some sexy-as-sin guy and take him home, let him fuck you within an inch of your life, and then have the best post-orgasmic sleep of all time."

"You really believe that's possible," I scoff, laying my head down on the table. "There hasn't been any new talent at Grizzly's for a long time. Same old guys who are either nearly seventy and holding up the bar, or in their twenties and looking for a quick one-and-done for the night. This thirty-five-year-old woman is not interested in guys with a small dick and a big ego. I'll pass, thanks."

I groan at the way everyone thinks the life I live is so tragic that I'm somehow desperate for a man.

I'm not.

"Alright, we'll pass on the sex, but you are coming out drinking and forgetting about all your troubles. You are either dressed and ready when I get to your place, or I will drag your pretty little ass into my car, wearing your overalls that are probably still covered in blood and guts."

The determination I can hear coming down the phone tells me I have no choice, because she means it.

"You know I hate you, right?" I mumble into the phone.

"Yeah, yeah, love you too. One hour, time's ticking, Ash, go get your dancing shoes on. See you soon." Tiff hangs up, and I'm left pushing myself up off my desk and shaking my head at Rosie, who's snoring peacefully on the floor.

"I'm so jealous." Leaning down, I give her a pat on the head and get her into the cage for the night, then make sure she has water and food until tomorrow, when Susan, our high school helper, comes in and cleans out the cages and spends time with all the patients who are still here over the weekend.

Dragging my sorry ass out to my car, I know this is a bad idea, yet I'm doing it anyway. After driving to the B&B and dropping off the spare keys for Wade, I call and thank him, apologizing profusely for my pushy friend. Finally, I'm standing in my bedroom, looking at the vision of myself I don't get to see very often.

I'm wearing a long, flowing ankle-length brown skirt with flat sandals because I doubt I could handle heels tonight, and a floral shirt in all shades of autumn colors. My brown hair is down, hanging loosely around my face, which has just a touch of makeup to give me that feminine feeling I miss most days.

"Okay, you don't get these nights off very often, so don't waste it," I tell my reflection, then pull my shoulders back, pick up my bag, and make my way out to the car as it crunches over the gravel.

Seeing Tiffany in the passenger seat and her brother driving, a little sigh escapes before I get to the door.

Tonight's about to get messy.

◆ ◆ ◆

"You look hot tonight. Ready to let your hair down?" Tiff says as she links her arm through mine and we walk in through the back door of Grizzly's, the band already in full swing.

"Yes," I reply but shake my head signaling no, which only brings laughter from both of us.

"I'll take that answer." Stopping at the edge of the room, Tiff spots an empty table near the bar and starts dragging me over toward it.

The bar is busy, but then again, it is a Friday night.

Plenty of people wave to us as we pass and, looking toward Tiffany, I ask, "What are you drinking? I'll get the first round." At least I can start out slow that way.

"Let's start with a tequila shot, followed by a margarita." She flashes me that devilish look she gets when she's ready to let loose and slides into a chair.

"I don't know if I'm going to survive tonight." Rolling my eyes at her, I head to the bar and run into a solid wall of muscle. Arms wrap around me to stop me from falling as I wobble on my feet. I can tell he's tall, because my face is buried in his flannel-shirted chest. I can't help but take a deep breath of that mix of man sweat and cologne with a spicy hint of orange and sandalwood.

"Shit, sorry, I didn't see you there." His voice rumbles through my head as I realize I have been resting there longer than I should have.

Then suddenly my brain catches up to the rest of my body as I register I've heard that voice before.

Pushing back hard, I immediately put distance between us.

"Whoa, steady there," he says as I look up from under my hair that has fallen across my face. "Oh, it's you, the little farm girl."

I'm so not in the mood for this tonight.

"Just leaving, are you?" I won't give him the satisfaction of reacting to his comment, even if it has me seething on the inside.

"I was, until someone clumsily fell into me." He smirks back. Jerk.

Don't react, don't react, don't react, I repeat over and over again uselessly in my head.

"Well, the door is clear now, so I suggest you use it." I gesture to the old wooden door just to my left.

"I hope you aren't the town welcoming committee, because you'd suck at your job." The smile on his face just got bigger, and goddamn it, a little dimple appears on the right side of his lips.

Ughh, why does he have to be so good-looking but have the personality of an asshole.

"Oh, I'm the head of the committee, and it's my job to scare off the trash that comes into town." I stand up straight to give off the confidence that I don't actually have, but *fake it till you make it,* they say.

"Nice try, but I'm here to stay in Abbey Falls. By the way, how's that fence repair going?"

That's it, time for him to leave.

"Fuck off," I reply, pushing open and signaling for him to walk through the front door.

"That's what I thought. Maybe if you spent less time socializing and more time working, those broken fences would be mended by now. Have a nice evening." He brushes past me as he walks out, and I'm left with my mouth hanging open in shock staring after him.

Watching his perfect ass in well-worn jeans, with his shirt stretching across his broad shoulders, and his medium brown hair that's curling just a little over his collar as he strides across the parking lot. His looks fry my brain and that's a problem.

His quick turn as he pulls open the driver's door on his big maroon truck has him facing me, and he catches me staring at his ass.

Then he winks.

Fucking winks—who the hell does he think he is!

I spin around, pulling the door closed behind me and stomp to the bar. "Four tequila shots and two of the strongest margaritas that you can legally make." I slam my card down on the bar, and Regina, the barmaid, just smirks at me.

"Coming right up."

When I set the tray of drinks down on the table, Tiff beams up at me.

"Want to tell me what the hell that was all about? Because that tension between you two was vibrating the air like I've never seen before. And I'm all here for it."

Lifting up a shot glass, I just glare at her. "The only energy you saw was the one that had me wanting to knee him in the balls . . . hard."

I clink my shot glass against hers. I toss my drink down my throat, and the burn has my body shaking all over.

"Let's do this." We both pick up our second shots, slamming them down too, and the buzz has my muscles starting to loosen up and my head spinning already.

Good, that's what I need to erase the last ten minutes.

But instead, all the alcohol does is make me spill every detail to Tiffany about my not-so-cute meetings with him, and that's the worst thing I can be doing.

Because the more I talk, the bigger her smile gets.

I knew I would regret tonight.

JAKE

"Fuck me," I mutter, running my hand through my hair as I pull up to Heatherbrae.

Who the hell is that woman?

The first time I saw her, she had me so furious I kicked every rock on the way back across the pasture.

But watching her stand up and take me on in our little verbal spar tonight triggered me in all the wrong places. Which I shouldn't be interested in.

I'm here to take care of Gran and get the vineyard back to its prime. And I can already tell that woman is going to be a thorn in my side.

"Did you have a nice time down at Grizzly's?" Gran asks as I slump onto the sofa across from her.

I want to ask her about our little fiery neighbor, but I'm not that stupid. I might not have grown up here, but I know how small towns work. The minute I ask Gran, she will be on the phone to Lesley and Margie, her best friends, and before I wake up in the morning, half the town will know I asked.

"It was good. Ran into Anthony that we used to hang out with when we were kids. I didn't know he moved back home after his mom got sick." I kick off my boots and stretch my legs out in front of me. My body sinks deeper into the sofa and relaxes for the night.

"Yes, I'm glad she's all better now, and that Anthony and his family loved it here so much they decided to move home permanently. So much better for the kids than living in one of those big, stuffy cities."

Watching her crocheting, starting a new blanket for some lucky soul, it always amazes me that she can do it so fast and without looking at her hands. Instead, her eyes are fixed on me, as if she's trying to tell me I should do the same as Anthony and make this a permanent move.

"Now, I have something to talk to you about. Well, I need to talk to all you boys, actually. Can you do one of those video things on your computer so we can see them and I can talk to everyone at once?" Her hands start waving around in the air like a FaceTime call is some kind of mystical magic. I suppose at seventy-nine years old, trying to understand technology is hard.

"This sounds serious, Gran." I glance at her, trying to gauge her demeanor, but she looks just as happy as usual.

"No, I just don't want to have to repeat myself." She smiles, continuing to weave her crochet hook in and out of the blanket on her lap.

"Okay, give me a minute and I'll grab my laptop and set it up." Pushing myself up from the sofa, I head to the bedroom I'm staying in until I can get the barn fixed up and message the group chat as I walk.

JAKE: You guys around for a FaceTime with Gran? She wants to talk to us all together, won't tell me what it's about.

DECLAN: Is she okay?

BECKETT: I knew you were all upheaving your lives for nothing. Bet she has changed her mind and wants to sell.

JAKE: You can be such a dick sometimes.

CHASE: Just sometimes? I'm free now.

DECLAN: Me too.

BECKETT: I'm working, but I'll stop for Gran.

JAKE: That's so gracious of you, big brother. Call coming now.

Positioning my laptop in front of Gran, I place a dining chair next to her so I'm in frame too.

As the connection starts and the guys' faces start popping up on the screen, I notice the twinkle in Gran's eye at seeing everyone at once.

"Oh, even Beckett is joining us. Hello, my sweet boys."

And the rest of us try not to laugh out loud as he looks a little hurt that she thought he wouldn't.

The first few minutes of the call Gran spends catching up with everyone, like she hasn't just seen us all together a few weeks ago.

Then Beckett cuts in. "Gran, do you want to let us know what was so important that we had to do this call tonight?"

"Always in a hurry, my little Becks, but yes, yes, let's get started." She puts down her crocheting so she can give the call her full attention.

"I figured if we were going to do this, we should hold meetings every few weeks, so we are all on the same page. So, welcome to your first Heatherbrae Vines board meeting, and of course, I'm the chairlady, aka boss lady."

This time no one can hold back the laughter.

"I still love that you named the vineyard after the town in Scotland you both fell in love in." I smile as I give her shoulder a little squeeze. "Even though he isn't here, I can still hear Gramps calling from the kitchen that he's the boss around here when you're not home. It was his favorite joke."

All of us nod, remembering fondly the way they used to banter with each other. It was one of their love languages.

"Oh, pfft. We all knew that grumpy old man wished he was the boss around here. Which brings me to point number one of this meeting. Now that you have all agreed to come home and help me."

I look straight into Beckett's eyes. He hasn't agreed to do anything yet, but he doesn't even flinch at my stare or Gran's words.

"I have a little surprise for you." She pauses a little and looks at me, then back to the others. "I don't just want to get the vineyard up and running. We are also going to build a restaurant and small art gallery as part of the vineyard."

There is a stunned silence, and just as she's about to continue, Beckett can't help himself.

"Gran, I love your idea, but that takes a lot of capital investment, and none of you know how to run a business. It will take experts in those fields, staff, and a long time to make it a success. Most new businesses fold within a year. Do we really want to put you in financial hardship at your age?" His stern boardroom voice is booming through the speakers of the laptop.

Although I tend to agree with him, I bite back at his comment.

"So, running my own business for the last ten years obviously doesn't count, you bast—" I catch my swear word at the last minute, knowing my grandfather would strike me down in this seat for swearing in front of my grandmother. But Beckett has no idea how much his comment stings, especially now.

I know how to run a successful business, and have done for years, until the moment Danika walked out and then the clusterfuck of things that followed brought me to my knees. But then again, I don't think anything I have done in my life has lived up to Beckett's standards of "success," including Danika.

"You know what I mean, you don't run a restaurant," Beckett mumbles, but I know that's not what he meant. He works in the big corporate world, and my one-man-show business has never really rated highly in his eyes. "Plus who's going to look after the vines while all this building is happening? It's not like Gran has the money to keep paying contractors to come in and do it."

"We will. Gramps taught us all what to do. We are not useless," I bite back while Chase and Declan both nod in agreement. It will be tough because there will be a lot to do in a year, but I'll be damned if I fail at this. "Time to turn Heatherbrae into a full functioning winery instead of selling off the grapes. Plus you could always come and help in picking season." And that's when I see the same annoyance on his face he gets when he has to be around me.

"Now, Becks, I understand your concern." Trying to soothe out the discussion, Gran steps in and I can see him cringe at the nickname. No one is allowed to shorten his name except Gran. "But just because I'm old, that doesn't mean I'm stupid. This is something I've wanted to do since we purchased this place. Your grumpy gramps just flatly refused. And after he struggled to get the vineyard operational so we could make our own wine instead of just selling off the grapes every year, I didn't push the point. But I never gave up on my dream or his, and now it's my time to live it, for however long I still have on this earth."

My heart aches a little hearing that she has had to wait until he passed to do something she wanted. Knowing Gramps, though, he would've given Gran the world, so there must've been a reason.

"Gran, we are obviously very grateful for the gift you and Gramps are trying to give us, but I just want you to know we would be here doing this regardless. It's not in any way conditional on our inheritance. It's important you know we don't expect anything from you. We all want you here for a lot longer yet." I place my hand on hers and give it a loving squeeze as all the others agree with what I said.

"Oh shush, it's already done, so let's move on. And just so you know, there was one thing your grandfather was good at, and that was accumulating money. He left me with a nice tidy nest egg. So, the capital you talk about, Beckett, I think I've got that covered. I just need people to do the work, and I'm looking right at them. Four big strong men. Because the first step is to get building." She beams, reaching across and patting me on the knee. "And aren't I lucky that I have the best builder around living in my house right now."

"Thanks, Gran." It wouldn't matter if I were shit at my job, she would still be my biggest cheerleader. There is something about the love of your grandparents that gives you a warm, soul-deep hug. "But there's a lot of background work that's needed, construction plans, building permits, etcetera."

"Which you can sort out, and don't you worry about the building permits. Mayor Johnson will look after me, I'm sure," she declares with a cheeky smile on her face.

"Gran, you aren't going to pay off a public official to get your way?" Chase laughs.

"No, of course not, but he does love my cupcakes." She's looking at us all with the face of a saint and I can't help but remember what the guy at the gas station said, how she may as well be the mayor of Abbey Falls. Obviously Gran gets what she wants around here.

"Oh, fantastic, we're going to bribe the mayor with cupcakes! This is just getting better and better," Beckett mutters under his breath, but the microphone picks it up just loudly enough.

I shoot him a glare. How are we brothers?

"I just have one question to ask you, Gran," Declan, who's always the calmest of us all, asks. "Is this what you truly want us to do for you, to bring your dream to life?"

And in that moment, as his words float around the room, I see Beckett roll his eyes, while Chase leans forward a little closer to the screen.

Gran takes a long, deep breath, sits up in her chair a little taller, and replies with just one word. "Yes." She clasps her hands together in her lap like her mind is made up. "I'll provide food, living quarters, and all the building materials required. All you boys need to bring is the muscle."

"Then that's what we will do," Declan declares. "We will build your restaurant and gallery at the same time as the cellar for the vineyard. Right, guys?"

"Absolutely." Chase smiles in agreement.

Leaning over, I kiss her on the cheek and pull her sideways into a hug. "We will make it happen. Just give me time to get the barn livable, and then by the time the boys get here, we can start your project." And that's when I hear the tiniest little hitch in her breathing and notice a stray tear in her eye.

We owe so much to our grandparents, and I let the opportunity to repay Gramps slip through my fingers. I'm not about to do the same with Gran.

"Okay, I have to get back to work but keep me posted." Beckett's gruff voice brings my attention back to the screen.

"That's okay, sweetie, we will call you for the next meeting. Make sure you eat something. You looked too skinny when you were here." Gran blows him a kiss, and the rest of us swallow our laughter.

Beckett spends every morning in the gym working out, and he's solid and toned within an inch of his life. So being told he looks skinny would have just topped off his frustration.

While Gran is saying her goodbyes to everyone, I send a quick message to Declan and Chase to tell them I will call shortly after Gran is tucked up in bed.

There is plenty to discuss, including my brother.

After talking to the guys, my head is full of checklists, the required supplies, and figuring out a schedule to get the barn ready for Declan and Chase. But as I finally fall into bed, the vision and voice of my sassy new neighbor keeps interrupting:

"Oh, I'm the head of the committee, and it's my job to scare off the trash that comes into town."

She might think she means it, but her flushed cheeks and the feel of her pebbled nipples against my chest told me a whole different story.

While I don't have time for anything other than working, especially after the bombshell Gran dropped tonight, it doesn't stop me from wanting to know more about the intriguing little farm girl next door.

Chapter Three

Ashley

"Gerald, if you moo that loud again today, you are going to end up as prime rib steak."

Those first two tequila shots seemed like such a good idea after Mr. Opinionated pissed me off, but then I made the big mistake of following them up with more. I can't even tell how many shots we had.

I'm sitting on my porch steps in the warm sun, sipping on a strong coffee and nursing a head that feels like Satan himself is inside with a hammer, banging my dehydrated brain over and over again.

I suppose I should be grateful because I slept the longest I have in years, missing the entire morning and surfacing after lunch. And that was only because Tiffany called to check that I was still alive. I told her again for the umpteenth time how much I hate her. She just laughed and offered to drive out a batch of her hangover cure tea, but I refused. I told her if she put one foot on my property, I would shoot her at first sight. Instead, she had her brother, Douglas, leave the package on my doorstep, with him yelling out, "Don't shoot the messenger," as he knocked before howling all the way back to his car.

There is a reason I don't drink often, and that's the morning-after regret, which makes me question every time if it was even worth it.

And the worst of it is that when I messaged Wade after I woke, he told me he slept through the night with not one callout.

Seriously! Why is the universe so cruel? I've almost been begging on my hands and knees for time off, where I can sleep through a whole ten hours without a phone call. And the moment I take a night off, Wade gets the golden ticket of the perfect evening.

Wade, being the gentleman that he is, has offered to work for me again tonight because he feels like he didn't earn the money that I paid him. And I can't say I was in any shape to argue. It will take the rest of today to recover and probably tonight too. One day I will return the favor to him.

The warmth of the late-April sun is seeping into my bones and helping soothe my tense muscles as I try to piece together the night. Tiff tells me we danced the night away, joining the band on the stage at one point to sing, which apparently sounded like the worst karaoke anyone has ever heard. I'm sure it was not my finest moment. It's normally only the poor animals at home that have to suffer through my singing. It's part of the deal. I give them a place to live the rest of their days, feed them, and keep them happy, but in return, they have to listen to my ridiculously bad singing.

Thank goodness the longer I sit here, with my back now resting against the wood post and my legs stretched out, the Tylenol I took with the coffee is starting to kick in.

I look toward the broken fence and know I should be doing that today, but I just can't manage to summon the energy to get up. Instead, I'm just scrolling through my phone. As I open my email app, my eyes widen at an email with the subject line Veterinary job application.

"Holy shit, finally someone applied."

I sit up straighter and open the email, almost expecting it to be a prank or just some spam reply from a scammer in a faraway country. Tiff doesn't know it, but the job has been advertised for at least two months, with not even the slightest bit of interest. I'm sure it's because small-town vet clinics are not everyone's cup of tea. There are usually two types of people who work in the country: people who were born and bred here and come home after they gain their qualifications, or people who are running from a life that they no longer want to be in. That could be as simple as wanting out of the rat race, or fleeing from a relationship gone bad, or maybe something bigger, but at this stage, I don't care what the motivation is. I'm desperate enough to take anyone, within reason.

Applicant: Beau Robinson
Age: 38
Qualifications: Bachelor of Veterinary Biology and Doctor of Veterinary Medicine – University of Sydney, Australia

"Oh, he's Australian, hmmm, interesting. What in the world is he doing applying for a job up here in an out-of-the-way small town in the hills of Oregon?"

I continue to skim through the application, and it all sounds too good to be true. He has had all kinds of experience working in different parts of the US. The only strike against him is that he's male. I know I shouldn't be picky. I mean, it's the first application I've had, and if last night showed me anything, it's reinforcing how truly exhausted I am. I'm not one to ask for help. Ever since Jeremy left me running the clinic on my own, I wanted nothing more than to prove to him, and the rest of the world, that I could do this without the help of a man. But it took a gargantuan hangover to realize the only one that I'm hurting in this process is myself.

I put my phone face down on the porch next to me and run my hands up and down my jean-covered thighs. I'm not in shape to make any big decisions today. However, the nervous energy coursing through my body tells me that it's the first shimmer of hope I have felt in a very long time.

"Sleep on it, Ash, don't rush this." Taking a deep breath, I finally push up from my place in the sun and slip my feet into my old farm boots.

The barn and the yards full of animals are calling me. There are no days off from being a farmer and the constant feeding and cleaning up after them. Especially on this farm where there are so many different species living together that I should hang a **Noah's Ark** sign on the front gate.

I can't help it. I come across animals that are in need of love, and I give them a home. Sometimes it's because they have a health issue that their owner can't take care of, or just won't. Or sometimes they are abandoned and if I can't find them a new home, they end up living on the farm with me. That's why in the barn there are nine different breeds of chicken, five ducks, two sheep, a miniature horse, two pigs (who happen to be mom and daughter), three full-grown horses, and of course, Gerald the cow and Daisy the goat. But the most demanding animal here, that is also the cutest, is Herb, my donkey. He makes the most noise on a regular basis, but as soon as you pay him the slightest bit of attention, he's like putty in your hands. Kind of like a man, really.

My heart wants to add Rosie, but I know it just can't happen. Not with me working such long hours. An energetic German shepherd could be the straw that breaks the camel's back in this delicate ecosystem.

Another fun discovery today is that cleaning up manure is not great with a hangover. While the smell doesn't normally worry me, right now I am dry retching, and it's the worst. Because of my new annoying neighbor, Gerald and Daisy are now contained in the yards that are attached to the barn with wooden rails held together with rope. This makes the job of cleaning up after these animals that much bigger. Normally they are out roaming so where they shit wasn't my problem. Until now. Another reason to hate Mr. Perfectionist.

Next time Tiffany decides we need a night out, it better be drinking tea, munching on some of her delicious treats while sitting around the fire. No alcohol involved.

◆ ◆ ◆

As I started traveling into town early this morning, my hangover is now a distant memory. Thank goodness. I'm approaching the outskirts of town and looking around at the cuteness of it, which always puts a smile on my face.

I'm sure when they planned out towns in the early days, it was almost compulsory to have the main street with a town square in the middle of it. A park with the old bandstand at one end and beautiful trees with wooden benches underneath them, where the older generation sit and talk most days. Or more to the point, where they gossip about every single small thing that is happening in Abbey Falls.

It's too early in the day for them to be there yet, but I'm still picturing the seats full later today. Driving past the bakery now, I can see it's full of customers getting their coffee and breakfast. The florist next door is just opening up, moving the potted plants out onto the footpath for the day. The lawyer and accountant's shared office is still shut up tight, blinds down and the CLOSED sign in the window, because it's too early for them. Oh, how nice it must be to work office hours five days a week and then have a life after the door is closed each night.

Next is the post office and then the doctors' clinic, and right on the corner is Tiffany's teahouse. It also doubles as a gift shop, and if you ask her, she will tell you it's also a spiritual hub, but I'm not even sure what that means. So, I just play along.

I pull into the perfect parking spot out the front of her shop and jump out of my car. Mr. James comes to a stop next to me in his truck, winding down his passenger window.

"Morning, Doc." He's already chewing on his gum for the morning. I don't think I've ever seen him without a piece in his mouth.

"Morning, Mr. James. Shaping up to be another day of great weather." I smile, leaning my elbow on his door in the open window. "How's the stitches holding up on that horse's ankle? She learned that trying to jump barbed wire fences is not much fun yet?"

"Well, I hope so, silly old thing. I think she's forgotten she's getting on in years and can't do what she used to when she was a young filly. But thanks to you, I checked the bandages yesterday and she's just about all healed up. So, I just wanted to let you know and say thanks." He reaches his hand out to pat the top of mine.

And that's what I love about being a small-town vet.

You know your clients and all their animals, but more than anything, it's the kindness and appreciation you get from them for just doing your job. Besides, life is interesting with the variety of animals I work with. I don't think I could take being stuck in a big-city vet clinic where all you see are spoiled dogs, cats, birds, and the occasional reptile. To be honest, I'm thankful I've never had to deal with a snake on my own, only when I was in college, and even then there were other vets there to help or at least watch out. Snakes are not really a small-town type of pet because there are enough of them in the wild, which I do my best to avoid. Give me a large smelly pig over dealing with a venomous snake any day.

I turn my attention back to Mr. James. "Good to hear. I'm guessing that bale of sweet-smelling hay on the back of your truck is a little treat for her."

Mr. James lifts up a small clear bag off his seat and gives me a big grin. "That, and a few juicy apples that Mabel at the grocery store kept aside for me before they got thrown out."

Both of us are laughing now.

"Well, she's one spoiled horse today. You have a good day and give her a nose rub for me. I'll stop by later in the week and check in."

He gives my hand another pat before I pull back off the truck. I give him a wave and head inside to grab my morning cup of tea from Tiff.

"Well, don't you have a little pep in your step this morning. Want to share what has you smiling like that?" Tiff looks up from the coffee machine where she's busy making a couple of cups for the customers standing waiting to the side. They must be travelers passing through. We might not be a huge tourist destination, but we do have campgrounds about forty minutes out of town at the base of some small mountains, usually attracting hiking enthusiasts. It's like a pit stop on their way to the bigger mountains or on their way back, a nice spot to enjoy that mountain air before heading home.

Shaking my head at her, I take my spot on my favorite stool and pick up the local paper that is sitting folded in half on the counter. So much of our life has become electronic, but Abbey Falls still manages to keep a local newspaper in production once a week. It's mainly just human interest, local town gossip, with a crossword, the kids' joke section and coloring competition, as well as a recipe of the week, and of course what the town council has been up to. Occasionally, a proper newsworthy article is published and that becomes the talk of the town for weeks. My aim is to never make it into the newspaper.

The bell over the door clangs as the couple leaves, and as soon as it's just the two of us, Tiff starts talking fast.

"Before anyone else comes in, I have the tea." She's almost running around the counter to get closer to me.

"Yes, lots of tea," I reply, waving my hand at the copious jars with tea leaf blends in them.

"No, not *that* tea, the gossip tea. Keep up, woman." She gives me a playful smack on the arm. "So, your hottie new neighbor from the bar, his name is Jake Davis, a builder, and he's thirty-nine years old. And most importantly he's single and living with Betty for the next year to help her out. He's one of her grandsons, which you already worked out on that first day."

I roll my eyes at her. "Christ, how did you find all that out? No, wait, actually don't tell me. I don't want to know if you saw it in the tea leaves or by looking at the moon."

"You can mock me all you like, but one day you will be sitting here thanking me and apologizing that I was right. I told you he was coming and, hey presto, in walks the new guy in town, who conveniently lives next door to you, and has a dimple. Coincidence? I think not." She taps my nose with her finger and heads back around the counter to start brewing my tea.

"Even if I did believe in your woo-woo powers, there's no way it's this guy. He's an asshole. You saw the way he acted in Grizzly's on Friday night. You can strike him out. I doubt I could even spend more than five minutes in a room with him." Folding the newspaper back in half, I cross my arms across my chest and place them on the top of the counter.

Tiffany smiles and says, "Mhmm, you might think that now, but just you wait. What I saw on Friday night was like fireworks exploding. It was magical." She looks like she's about to break into a full-on happy dance. With her hippy-looking long flowery dress flowing around her ankles, her long wavy brown hair, and, of course, a flower tucked behind her ear. This woman is so carefree and happy in her life that she loves to spend time trying to find that same happiness for me.

"Oh, there was an explosion of annoyance. That was all you saw." I wrap my hands around my teacup that she's just placed down in front of me.

"That's not what his cheeky smile told me as he walked out the door." She laughs as she grabs the tongs and a paper bag. "Now, what treat are you taking with you today?"

"No, I don't need one today. I ate breakfast," I say, trying to bluff my way through, because the more I keep eating her treats, the bigger my hips are going to get.

"Excuse me, an apple in the car on the way here does not count as a full breakfast. You either pick something or I will just put one of each in the bag for you and Adi to share at the clinic." Her hand is on her hip, and she's looking at me like my mother would when I was about to get a lecture.

"It was a banana, actually." The words come out before I have time to stop them, and the look on her face tells me there is no point choosing anymore. I'm getting one of everything, and if I complain, she will turn up at the clinic and force-feed me later.

"Seriously."

Her huff makes me laugh.

"You love me, just admit it." I'm trying to make light of the situation.

"Most days, but today it's still up for consideration." She pushes four paper bags at me at the same time the bell over the door signals more customers, and I just smile at her as I lift my cup to take another sip of tea. I can't even work out what is in today's brew, but it's strong and punchy, and I can feel it perking up my energy and getting me ready for the day.

I finish my tea as quick as I can because I have a lot to do today, and Tiff has been busy the whole time, so as I stand, grabbing my paper bags of treats, I just lean over the counter and say quietly, "The reason I was smiling this morning was because I replied to a job applicant and asked for more information. Bye." I watch her eyes widen with excitement.

And then as I reach the front door, she calls out to me, "Okay, it's been decided—I do love you today."

I smile as I close the door behind me, knowing it will kill her that she can't ask more questions with a shop full of customers.

Walking to my car, I'm trying to juggle all the bags of treats and my takeout iced tea for later when one bag starts to slip and before I can do anything about it, it's on its way to the ground. Leaning down to try to grab it, I hear a deep voice at the same time.

"I've got it" are his words as our heads hit and I fall backward onto my ass on the sidewalk. The rest of the bags land in my lap and luckily my hand's still clutching tight to my tea that has barely spilled.

"Lucky save," Mr. Annoying says as I just glare at him from the ground.

"Good to know that you were more worried about the food than me. Checks out!" I exclaim grumpily and try to get myself back up, which is proving more difficult than it should since both my hands are full of bags and my takeaway cup.

"Let me help you." He's showing restraint from cracking up at me in my mess.

"No. I'm fine. I can manage," I snap back as his hands are wrapping around my biceps and pulling me up before I even have time to attempt to juggle with what is in my hands.

"Mhmm, it looks like it. Sorry about that."

Looking at the smirk on his face just enrages me.

"You should be. Watch where you're walking next time." I snatch the bag that he caught out of his hand and don't look back as I walk past him to my car. Opening the door and loading everything, I then climb in and start it up. Pulling out of the parking spot, all I can see is him standing there, arms crossed and the most gorgeous smile plastered across his face.

"Don't smile at me, asshole, it's not going to make me like you, no matter how hot you are. Ughh," I mumble to myself as I drive toward the clinic, trying to forget about Mr. Tall, Dark, and Handsome, because I do not need any other complications in my life. And I'm not letting him ruin my day.

◆ ◆ ◆

"Morning, Rosie girl, how are you on this fine Wednesday?" I ask, opening her cage to let her out. We keep cages in the back of the clinic for any of the animals who are with us for a few days. It keeps them safe and my clinic clean.

Her tail is wagging, and she rubs her head against my thigh as I give her a big good-morning pat.

"Let's give you a check over before things get crazy in here today. Because I think you're nearly ready to leave soon." Which earns me a happy bark from her.

Rosie passes her checkup with flying colors, and after a quick run around the little yard we have outside, she comes back in and settles herself in her soft bed and looks up at me, watching as I set up for the day. Now all I have to do is find her a new home. The right home.

The rest of the morning goes smoothly, and just as I sit down at my desk to eat a little bit of lunch, Adi sticks her head around the door from the front of the clinic.

"I know you are on lunch . . ."

Closing the wrapper over the sandwich that I haven't even taken one bite out of yet, I'm already standing.

"It's fine. What's wrong?" I ask, walking toward her.

"Oh, it's not anything bad, it's just that Betty has called in to have a chat if you have five minutes."

Both of us laugh quietly because a chat with Betty is never for five minutes. But at the same time, I feel awful because I promised I would visit her after not making it to the funeral and I still haven't got over there. I mean, it might have a lot to do with avoiding her house now that she has a certain man living with her.

"Of course, bring her on back. I'll make her a cup of tea, and she can eat one of these cakes that Tiff made me take."

Adi just nods as I head to the electric kettle, flicking it on.

"There's my sweet Ashley. Sorry to bother you when you are so busy."

Adi guides Betty to the chair at my desk and leaves us to it.

"Betty, it's so lovely to see you. I'm so sorry I haven't been over to visit like I promised," I apologize, leaning down to give her a hug and a kiss on the cheek.

"Oh shush, don't you worry, poppet. I know how hard you work to keep all the animals in Abbey Falls safe."

She's always so kind, but it doesn't make me feel any less guilty. I mean, this is the woman who never complains when my naughty pets end up in her gardens. An image of her irate grandson raging about the same animals flashes into my head, and I try to shake it off, because I don't want to upset Betty by letting on what an arrogant jerk he was.

"I try, but sometimes it would be nice if they would give me a few quiet days." Grabbing a tea bag and placing it in the cup, I look over my shoulder at her. "Two sugars and milk, if I remember correctly?"

"I can't believe you remembered. That would be lovely, Ashley, but only if you have time."

"I've always got time for you, Betty." I place her cup of tea down in front of her with a lemon cake, courtesy of Tiff.

"Oh, you spoil me." She smiles but also picks up the spoon straight away and takes a bite. "I know that's one from Tiffany's store. One day she will give me the recipe."

I know she won't, because she doesn't make them. There is a lady in town who bakes them but wants to remain anonymous. Tiff is just trying to help her out with a bit of extra income.

"Now, did you just call in to see me or is there something you need help with?" *Like getting rid of your pesky visitor,* I think but would never say it. I'm sure she thinks the sun shines out of her grandson, like all grandmothers do.

"Yes, sweetie, I do have something I thought you might be able to help me with. Since I've lost my Noel, it gets lonely in bed at night. I think I might like to get a puppy to keep me company."

My heart is breaking for her. But I'm not sure this is the right thing for her at her age.

"I'm sure this is a really hard time, Betty, and I want to help you as much as I can, but puppies are hard work and need a lot of training. I'm not sure this is a good idea." I don't know how to say to her that I think she's too old to cope with the crazy energy that a puppy brings to any house, without offending her.

"Don't you have one of your grandsons staying with you? Isn't he keeping you company?"

"Jake is adorable and spends time with me as much as he can, but I have put him to work, and I don't want him to think he has to give up his life to babysit his old gran twenty-four hours a day."

I'm not sure I would use the word *adorable* to describe him, but I can see the love in her eyes as she talks about him.

"Has he moved here for a while?"

"That's right, and don't tell him I said this, but the truth is, I don't want him hovering over me all the time. I don't need a babysitter. I've managed in this world for a long time, and will continue to do so, even without my Noel. It will be different, and I will miss him like crazy, but I don't need a man to survive. I can do it on my own." There is a mixture of sadness and determination in her eyes, something I recognize.

"I don't doubt that for one minute. You are one of the strongest women I know. And that won't change. You will still be bossing us all around and looking after yourself just fine." I reach out and squeeze her hand as the tears dry.

The loud laugh Betty lets out is enough to wake Rosie from her slumber, and she pulls herself up from her bed. As she walks over, I get ready to settle her next to me so that she doesn't scare Betty. Some people take one look at a big dog like Rosie and worry that she's either aggressive or over-the-top excitable. Neither could be any further from the truth with Rosie. She just wants to be loved.

But before I have a chance to grab her collar, Rosie walks straight past me and places her head in Betty's lap.

"Oh, who's this friendly one?" Betty starts stroking the top of Rosie's head, over her ears and down onto her back.

"This is Rosie. She was hit by a car a few nights back, and I've been nursing her back to health."

The more Betty pats her, the more content Rosie seems, her tail swishing back and forth on the floor.

"Her family must be very grateful to you for looking after her." Betty looks up at me from where she has been transfixed on Rosie.

In my head I'm trying to decide if I should play along and not admit that Rosie is a stray, because I can see what is happening here. But then again, who am I to step in the way of two friends meeting and giving each other the one thing they are both craving?

I decide to answer truthfully. "Sadly, she's on her own, so I need to find her a forever home."

"No, you don't, she's the perfect solution to my problem. She doesn't need training, she'll keep me company, and she's big enough to scare away any unwanted strangers that might turn up at the vineyard. Plus, look at her, she's already in love with me. I mean, who wouldn't be. She can see that I'm a perfect match for her. Looks like it's you and me, Rosie. Enjoying a few lazy days in the sun, while I sit crocheting and bossing around my grandsons. Sounds kind of perfect to me, what do you think?" Betty asks, leaning down closer to Rosie, who then reaches up and gives her a lick on the face.

"Are you sure about this, Betty? Rosie might seem nice and quiet in here, but I haven't seen her out in open spaces yet. Maybe you should talk it over with your grandson first, and then we can see how Rosie will transition to living with you." I'm not really worried about how Rosie will be, it's more that I'm not sure Betty has thought this through. Ten minutes ago, she was after a puppy, and Rosie is a lot different to that.

"Nope. I just told you I don't need a man to make decisions for me. Rosie will be fine, so I'll take her home with me now. Jake will love her. I'm sure you can get everything into the car for me, her bed, some food, bowls, etcetera. Whatever you think I might need. And of course, a lead so I can take her for a walk, or when I don't feel like it, Jake can take her on one of his long hikes up to the falls."

All I can think about is how unimpressed Jake will be when his grandmother turns up with a large dog that is going to be living with them and then tells him that he's now responsible for walking her each day. Because as agile as Betty is, there is no way she intends on walking Rosie. I could tell in the way she got a sly little grin on her face when she mentioned it would be Jake's job.

I know it makes me look unprofessional, but the thought of how annoyed Jake is going to be has me now agreeing eagerly with Betty and sorting out everything she needs to take Rosie home today. I know Rosie will be loved and looked after by Betty, so I'm not concerned for her welfare in any way, otherwise I wouldn't let her adopt her. I wish I was going to be there to see his face, the moment he sees Rosie arrive.

Well, Jake did ask if I was the welcoming committee for Abbey Falls, and this is the most perfect "welcome to town" present I can think of.

We load everything into the truck, and Betty gets in behind the wheel. I'm not sure why she's driving Noel's truck instead of her own car, but my guess is that it keeps him close to her, and who am I to judge how people get over their loss.

Seeing Rosie sitting up like a good girl on the passenger seat in the front of Noel's old Chevy has my heart squeezing. They will make a great match. They both need someone to love, and I know that Rosie will be well looked after.

As I watch them drive away, Betty gives me a huge wave and Rosie barks, then lets her tongue hang out like she's so happy, and I know it will all work out fine.

The next hour goes by so fast that when Adi tells me that we are on the last patient, I'm silently cheering because it's a simple annual vaccination. Just as I place Mr. Moggie into his carrier and his owner heads back out to the reception area, I hear shouting coming from the front of the clinic, and I don't even have to see him to know whose voice that is.

"I'll wait! I want to see Doctor Alleyne. He has some explaining to do."

I'm cracking up behind my hands from inside the exam room. Then composing myself, I pick up the phone and buzz Adi. "Send the raging bull in so he can meet the very female vet who he has a problem with. This is going to be so much fun."

"Are you sure about that?" Adi sounds worried, but I know that man out there is all bark and no bite. I've seen it enough times now to get the sense that I'm safe around him. Plus, it's time for a little payback.

"Doctor Alleyne is through here, Mr. Davis." Adi's voice gets closer, and as soon as she opens the door to the exam room, Jake storms through, and the look on his face is priceless.

"*You!* I should have known. As soon as there is chaos, you show up." His chest puffs out, and he's still steaming.

"What can I do for you, Mr. Davis? I hear you think I have some 'explaining' to do. Care to elaborate?" The calm tone of my voice seems to only exacerbate his anger.

"One word. Rosie!" His voice is loud and echoes around the room. "No way, no how. She has to go, and you have to convince my grandmother that you made a mistake."

Watching him standing in my domain and trying to tell me what to do just makes me laugh. He might have caught me off guard in our first and second encounters. But not this time. I'm ready for him.

"Oh, is Jake too scared to stand up to his granny? I'm not surprised. I figured out what kind of man you are the first time I met you."

"And what kind is that?" he blusters in frustration.

"A delegator, great at giving orders, but when it comes to doing the hard work, you're nowhere to be seen." I turn my back on him and continue cleaning up the room.

"You don't know one thing about me." His voice vibrates around me.

"Let's keep it that way, shall we." I turn to look at him, meaning every word of it, but there is something annoyingly sexy about this man who I can't seem to have a conversation with without it being an argument.

"I wish, but I have a feeling that's not going to be possible," he replies.

And it's probably the only thing we agree on.

Chapter Four

Jake

Damn Gran and that dog! I'm pissed, and my head is still reliving the events of the last thirty minutes back at Heatherbrae, when instead of my gran and some grocery bags, she unloads a German shepherd of all things. A dog that is half the size of a cow, with the brains of one too . . . she doesn't sit, stop, or fetch. Just races around unchecked across the vineyard while I holler, making myself look ridiculous.

Then I walk into the vet's and who should it be but that damn farm girl! She doesn't seem any happier to see me, but I can't seem to stop getting distracted by her. Maybe it's because for some reason, despite the fluorescent lights, she might have the most beautiful eyes I've seen in Abbey Falls . . . no, scratch that, ever.

I've tried to tell myself I'm here in Abbey Falls purely to help my grandmother and to take a break from the problems I left back in my normal life, but the more this fiery little thing opens her mouth and yells at me, the more it turns me on. Even the insults she's hurling my way about what kind of man she thinks I am don't seem to change the way my gaze is fixated on her.

She shows no indication of backing down and as she turns away from me, I can't help but notice her tight little ass perfectly sculpted in those body-hugging jeans. And even in work boots and a dark green shirt, she can't hide her femininity.

Turning back to face me, I see that same little flash of hesitation I saw on Friday night, as though she's trying to decide whether to hate me or to accept there's something about me that she wants to know more about. I hate to admit it, but I'm having the same thoughts . . . damn, I know I'm about to regret this.

Pulling back my aggressive attitude, I take a deep breath and start again. "I know we didn't get off on the best start, but we're neighbors, so I have a feeling we're going to keep bumping into each other. Now, about Rosie." My tone is a little softer this time, which I can tell catches her off guard. She's ready to throw the next insult at me, but I don't give her the chance.

"Look, we got off on the wrong foot the first time we met. Well, actually, every time we've met, but can we maybe put that aside and talk about my elderly grandmother and that huge dog she just arrived home with?"

"What's the problem?" She's still standing her ground but drops her hands from her hips, giving me the first sign that she might also be backing down a little.

"Firstly, Gran has never owned a dog in her life. Like me, my gramps wasn't a big fan of them." As the words slip out of my mouth, it's like a light bulb goes off in my head—maybe that's where I get it from? "Anyway, she has no idea how much work is involved in caring for dogs. Secondly, Rosie is going to need walking, because from what I've already seen, that dog has plenty of energy. Gran might still be very mobile for her age, but it's a recipe for disaster; Gran falling as she tries to keep up, or getting tangled in her lead as Rosie starts running around her legs."

Taking a deep breath, I voice something that I don't even like to think about. "And I don't want this ever repeated. But we don't know how long we have left with Gran, so what happens if she goes before Rosie does? Who looks after her then? Or worse still, what if Rosie dies before her? Gran is trying to look like she's coping with the loss of Gramps, but we all know she's not."

And I want to add that we are all struggling with his passing, and that might have had something to do with why I have been such a jerk.

Sighing out loud, I realize that I just unloaded a lot on this woman, and I still don't even know her first name.

"Jake." The way my name rolls off her lips is the softest I've heard her voice sound since meeting her, and something in my stomach unfurls. Fuck I want her to say that again. Slower.

"What's your name?" I ask to distract myself, and it brings a smile to her face for the first time. "I mean, other than Doc, or Doctor Alleyne, which was all Gran cared to share with me." I shrug a little as some sort of apology for assuming she was a man.

"Ashley. Ashley Alleyne, aka Doc, town vet." Her body relaxes a little as she leans back against the exam table that she was pretending to clean a moment ago.

Taking a few steps toward her, I hold out my hand. "Jake Davis, nice to meet you, Ashley. Well, properly this time. I think I might owe you an apology for being a bit of an asshole that first day." Feeling the softness of her hand in mine reminds me to step back and keep my distance. No attachments. That's not why I'm in Abbey Falls.

"You think?" She laughs easily, like it comes so naturally to her.

"Yeah, okay, I deserve that," I admit, feeling my lips curving up into a smile.

An awkward pause descends between us, like we are both trying to navigate where we go from here. Do we keep being hostile, or can we find some common ground and actually behave civilly toward each other?

Seeing as I was the one who started us off on the wrong foot, I think I need to be the one to move things in the right direction.

"So, you aren't just a farmer. You also moonlight as the local vet too," I say, pointing out the obvious.

"Ha, more like the other way around. Being the town vet keeps me so busy that trying to fit anything else in is too hard. But I wouldn't exactly call myself a farmer. More like an animal lover who can't stand to see them being mistreated or neglected. People can be so cruel. So, when I can't find an animal the right home, I end up taking them in."

"Ah, so Rosie needed a home, and you thought Gran would be a good fit?" I'm keen to hear her answer.

But I'm caught off guard by the slight blush appearing on her cheek and the little dip of her head.

"Partly. I mean, Rosie took to her straight away, and they bonded in front of my eyes. I think she can be good for your gran. But I do have to confess there was a little part of me that hoped it would piss you off. Because I know a lot of the care is going to fall on you. Sorry about that."

She lifts her head a little to look at me. I can see she doesn't regret it that much, though, and I can't help but laugh. "Well, at least you're honest."

And as the tension eases between us, she joins in with a laugh that makes me feel lighter.

"Well played, I have to say, but I've got to admit something that is going to make you think less of me than you already do." I'm hoping I'm wrong as she looks at me with a puzzled face.

"A few minutes ago, I probably would have answered *that's not possible*, but you've been making an effort here to redeem yourself.

Don't wreck it." Her smile and the way it lights up her face makes me want to see it more often.

"Damn it, this could wreck that." Taking a breath, I try to play on the fact that it is something more major than it is. Well, in my eyes anyway. "But here goes: I'm not an animal lover. I've never owned a pet and would prefer not to start now."

Ashley's eyes widen, and I can tell that is not what she expected.

Her mouth opens and closes a few times before she finally gets some words out. "What . . . how can you not like animals? Everyone loves animals." There is no frustration there, just confusion.

I hold my arms out wide. "I'm proof that's not always true."

"But why? What happened? Did you get attacked or something?"

I can tell the only way she can rationalize it in her brain is if something has made me dislike animals.

"No, nothing like that, and it's not like I hate them. I've just never really been around them and have no deep desire to change that. Plus, I'm only here for twelve months, so then who walks Rosie after that?"

Shaking her head at me, I can tell she doesn't understand, but at least she isn't yelling, calling me an asshole. We must be getting somewhere.

"Well, you won't have to worry about that because Rosie is Betty's dog, and by the time you leave Abbey Falls, she will be perfectly trained. I'll make sure of it. Just think how comforting it will be knowing that your grandmother has company and is being kept safe."

"Why do I feel like I'm swimming against the tide here?" Linking my hands together and resting them on my head, I try to think of another angle.

"Because you are." Not a scrap of empathy shows on her face. "Betty has been my neighbor since I bought the farm a couple years ago, and I've known her since I moved here. She approached me looking for a puppy, which in my opinion would have been far more dangerous and hard work."

I can tell she has her vet persona in full operation as she reasons with me.

"Look, Jake, animals have a special ability to choose their person. Rosie picked Betty, and as soon as Betty ran her hand over Rosie, the bond was sealed. Who am I to get between that?"

"Sounds like there was encouragement from you, though. Surely you could've dissuaded Gran. I mean, any person in their right mind would understand this is such a ridiculous idea. A big dog and an old lady. Just because you needed to offload her doesn't mean you should've ignored the obvious." I can't help but still be frustrated, even though I'm supposed to be trying to play nice.

"No, that's not what I meant before." Ashley arches up at me. Her hands are back on her hips and that glare is staring me down. "Once Betty decided she was taking Rosie home, I just enjoyed picturing the horrified look on your face when she rocked up in the truck with a big hairy dog."

There is a wicked sense of humor hidden behind the tough vet facade she has while in this office.

"Well, you were right. But Christ, Ashley, don't you think it's a bit irresponsible?"

"Wow, how dare you call me irresponsible! Might I remind you that this doesn't have anything to do with you. Rosie and Betty are my clients, not you. So maybe you should just go along with your gran's wishes. Damn and you almost had me fooled that you weren't really the asshole I thought you were."

Fire snaps in her eyes as I wish I had just kept my damn mouth shut.

But now I'm on a roll.

"Oh, don't be fooled. I can be a great guy. It's just you that brings out the asshole in me. Now stop playing games and take Rosie back. Find some other home for her, just not Heatherbrae!" I'm losing it again and I have no idea why it keeps happening around this particular woman. Other women have called me charming, even attractive, but I just can't seem to keep it together with Ashley.

"I think it's time for you to leave, Jake." She walks to the door and opens it for me.

Stalking out, I can't help but think there is something weird about how this woman is constantly showing me the door.

Now standing in the reception area, I can feel the judgmental gaze of the receptionist as she looks me up and down. I seem to have a habit of giving very bad first impressions in Abbey Falls.

"Tell *my* client Betty I will call out and see her in a couple of days to check on Rosie. I recommend you aren't there at the time." Standing next to her receptionist, both of them are now giving me the death stare.

"Noted. I would say nice to see you but we both know that would be a lie." As I open the front door of the clinic, I can't help myself, "Oh and about that fence? I see nothing has changed . . . sometime this year would be great." Turning and walking out, I refuse to look back. I can hear her ranting loudly to her receptionist.

Ashley Alleyne might be jaw-dropping gorgeous, until she opens her mouth, when she becomes nothing more than annoying, annoyingly attractive that is. Damn this is going to be a problem.

◆ ◆ ◆

Slouched on the sofa after dinner, I'm listening to some of Gran's music, taking me back to our holidays here as a kid. All of us knew the rules then. Dinner, showers, and then grab our own special blanket that Gran had made us, ready for quiet time, which was to either play a board game or a card game with Gramps. The only other option was to read, but that was never my favorite pick.

Tonight, though, it's much quieter with just the two of us in the house. And the big elephant in the room, the hairy one that we haven't discussed since I got back, because Ashley was right, I don't want to upset Gran. Looking over at Rosie lying on the floor at Gran's feet, snoring peacefully, she's looking like she belongs here, like she's been part of the family for years. Gran's hands are moving freely with her crochet hook and wool, and I can't believe how much of the new blanket she has added since yesterday.

"She's a lovely girl, that one." Her words break the silence.

"Who are you talking about, Gran?" Looking over at her, I see a dopey grin on her face.

"Ashley," she replies, like she was innocently just dropping the name in there.

"I'm not sure about the lovely bit," I mutter to myself before clearing my throat. "You mean Doctor Alleyne, the female vet you failed to mention was also your neighbor. All of which would have been handy information."

A sneeze escapes me, which has Rosie jumping a little, and she lifts her head to glare at me for waking her up before settling straight back down on the blanket at Gran's feet.

"Oh well, now you know."

And I figure since she has brought Ashley up, now is as good a time as any to find out a bit more. "She sounds like she works hard. Does she have a partner to help her?"

"No, she's single, and has been for a few years. Damn shame, though, because she's a good catch."

"I meant does she have a partner in the vet clinic, not her personal life." I try to keep a straight face as Gran glances sideways at me, knowing full well what I was after.

"Mhmm, yes, she's the sole vet, poor thing. Her partner was a vet also, but he left a few years ago, no warning, and she has been trying to manage on her own ever since. She works seven days a week and never leaves an animal without the care it needs."

Gran continues telling stories of different miracles Ashley has pulled off, saving animals all over the town, but I tune her out.

Things are starting to click into place and make more sense.

Ashley's farm is run-down and needs so much work. I would argue it needs even more work than Gran's place, and that's saying something. If Ashley is working so much, it wouldn't leave her much time for repairs. Why didn't she just say that? I would've offered to help.

Though Ashley's right, I was acting like an asshole when I marched over to her farm that first day. It's on our boundary line as well. Maybe as an apology I could help to get it back up and secure. I mean, I wouldn't be doing it because I feel sorry for her or anything. It would mainly be for our benefit. Keep the animals out of Gran's gardens and away from me.

It's the least I can do, you know, the neighborly thing.

Over the next few days, I'm up early to work on the sleeping quarters in the barn, and then after lunch, I work on a section of the boundary fence, making sure I'm gone by the time Ashley gets home from work. She'll know it's me, but I don't want her to feel like I'm overstepping or doing it to make her feel bad. So avoiding her seems like a better idea.

I've always loved being outside, working with my hands and having something to show for a day's hard work. But nothing beats working in the fresh mountain air. I had forgotten how clean and crisp it is up here, being so close to the ranges. On the edge of

Gran's property, the land rises into the dense woodland area where the amazing Rock River splits in two. The main river runs down into a neighboring farm, but we get the smaller Copper Creek. It's where we pump water from that helps to keep the dam full and plenty of water for the vines and Gran's gardens. She says it's her secret to the gold ribbon at the Abbey Falls Town Fair every year.

Wiping my brow with a bandanna, I step back and survey the barn. It's looking good, should be inhabitable in a few days, just need to finish off the bathroom and then I can move in. Live by myself for a little while, until the boys descend.

Draining my water bottle, I eye the woods. I've been dying to go for a hike to the falls. It's cooler in there and would be a great way to escape this heat. Hiking is one of my favorite activities back home in Sacramento. There's nothing like getting out there, breathing in the fresh air and pushing myself enough to enjoy the wind down from a busy week at work. It's been nearly a month since I stretched my legs properly like that. It's time. I can get on with the bathroom tomorrow.

Poking my head in the back door of the house, I call out, "Gran, I'm just going for a quick hike up to the swimming hole."

"Take Rosie with you. She'll keep you company. And remember to watch out for snakes. I don't want her getting hurt," she replies as I hear Rosie coming down the hallway at full pelt from the kitchen.

"Great, just what I need." I roll my eyes and swap my work boots for my hiking shoes that are still inside the laundry where I set them optimistically when I arrived.

Striking out for the woods, my good mood crumbling, I look down at Rosie, who's right beside me, tongue lolling happily at my annoyance. "I love how Gran is more worried about you getting hurt than she is about me. I rank lower than a stray dog in this house. And who said I wanted company? The whole point of a hike is to get time on your own!"

As we arrive at the tree line, I stop and look down at Rosie, trying to control my grumbling.

"Look, here's the rules, dog. If you get lost, I'm not looking for you. If you get hurt and I have to take you to the vet, where I'll be chastised for not taking good care of you, then I swear I'll put you back up for adoption myself. So, let's just get through this walk without any drama, okay? Then I might consider taking you with me next time I go for a hike. Deal?"

It dawns on me how stupid I must look, standing here talking to a dog. Seriously, how did I get to this point in my life? It's almost as embarrassing as admitting you are nearly forty and just moved in with your grandmother.

A loud bark echoes around me and Rosie wags her tail, as though agreeing with my proposition.

"Okay, let's do this." And before long, I'm lost in the thrill of seeking out the trail to the swimming hole I remember spending hours in when we were kids. What I hadn't thought through properly is that it's likely been at least fifteen years since anyone has walked these trails, so it's harder work than I anticipated.

After spending an enjoyable hour clearing part of the trail by hand, I decide it's time to turn back. Next time I'll come prepared. Peeling off my shirt and tucking it into the back of my shorts, I head out of the woods and back to the house for a shower.

Luckily Rosie has stuck to our deal and is walking calmly beside me, but as soon as we get halfway down the pasture, she takes off running at full speed. It's only then that I notice Ashley's car parked at the side of the house.

"Glad you waited for me, Rosie," I call out to her as I'm coming around the corner of the house, not wanting to give away that she has been so well-behaved with me the whole time.

"She can't help it if you are so slow." Gran pushes up off her porch swing, walking in the front door and calling Rosie in for some water. No offer to get me a drink, I notice.

"Hey there, are you checking to make sure I haven't gotten rid of the dog yet?" I stop at the bottom of the porch steps and look up at Ashley, whose head is moving around while she tries to focus on anything other than me. Oh, I'm enjoying watching her embarrassment at seeing my bare chest.

"Betty says she's doing well. So yeah, that's all I need to know." Ashley stands and walks toward me, heading down the stairs. She's trying so hard not to make eye contact that she misjudges the first step and starts falling.

My arms are out and around her before I even have time to think about it. But the momentum of her fall has me losing my footing too, and in one quick move, I'm flat on my back with Ashley on top of me, and her mouth has just brushed innocently against mine. My lips feel like they are on fire, tingling for another taste. Fuck, she tastes so good. Her hands freeze on my sweaty bare chest, her eyes level with mine, and I can see them getting wider the longer we remain there.

"Ashley, you should stay for dinner, oh . . ." I hear Gran as she comes out the front door.

"No, I need to leave." Ashley rolls off me so quickly I don't try to stop her. Jumping up off the ground, she's already on her way to the car before I can say a word. Slowly I push myself to a sitting position on the grass and watch her with amusement as she makes it to the driver's door. "Oh, and thanks for the fence repairs, but I can do the rest. I don't need you to fix it. But yeah, umm, thanks." And then she's in her car and leaving with just a little wave to Gran.

"Looks like she's allergic to half-naked men." Gran looks down at me still on the grass. "Either that, or she liked what she saw.

Might be something you need to look into, Jake." Winking at me, Gran heads back inside the house with Rosie at her heels.

I lie back on the ground and look up at the sky. "Great, not only do I have a semi after feeling Ashley fit so perfectly on top of me. Now I have my grandmother trying to do some matchmaking!" Pushing my hand into my crotch, I try to settle it down. This clearly has disaster written all over it, both for my cock, that is banned from seeking attention, and for Ashley, who Gran now has in her sights.

To be honest, I'm not sure who's going to be the hardest to control from chasing Ashley. Gran, or my now very awakened sex drive for the woman who drives me crazy every time I see her.

I haven't even made it through the first month living in Abbey Falls, and I'm already getting myself into trouble.

Who knew a small town could be such a dangerous place for a single man? Is there anywhere to hide?

But more importantly, do I really want to?

Chapter Five

Ashley

"Holy shit, holy shit, holy shit." I'm mumbling incoherently as I drive down Betty's long driveway to the road heading home. "That wasn't supposed to happen, but holy freaking hell." My heart is banging on my rib cage. I can't seem to settle myself.

I've sworn off men since Jeremy walked out on me, and have no intention of changing that. But if there was ever a man who would make me second-guess that decision, it's the bare-chested one who just set my lips and libido on fire at the same time. And he just so happens to irritate the hell out of me.

I can't believe I kissed him. The man I can't stand. And not like a proper kiss, but lips touching and breathing the same air for a split-second kind of kiss. My mind is spinning. Was it the fall that placed my lips on his or did one of us lean in those last few inches to make it happen?

Not me. I never even thought of him like that.

"Bullshit." I can't help but chuckle out loud.

That body has been appearing in my dreams whenever I get enough time to hit REM sleep anyway. As much as I try to ignore them, ever since that night in Grizzly's when I buried my head in his chest, the sexual tingles have been reawakened in my body. How can you feel like that for a man you can't stand?

These feelings have been dormant ever since Jeremy ran off with that little plastic-looking blonde. But if I'm honest with myself, I think my sex drive died a few years before that. That spark that was there in the beginning with Jeremy was dying, maybe on both sides, with him paying me less and less attention. Sex sort of became a chore, and nobody wants to be in a relationship where you are almost looking at the calendar to schedule times for an orgasm.

I turn my car into my driveway. My finger starts tracing my lips subconsciously, and all thoughts of Jeremy are wiped from my mind, because no matter how much I thought I loved him, even in the heat of a deep kiss, it never felt like that!

I can still taste Jake on my lips.

His salty sweat, mixed with the taste of pure man, is something that I can't describe and doesn't even make sense to me. There was something about how he tasted that makes me imagine what the rest of his body is like. If I accidentally fell with my tongue out and it swiped up his rock-hard abs and sucked on his nipples, would I get the same explosion of my senses? Or, God forbid, what if his shorts tore away from him as he toppled to the ground, and I just happened to gasp at the same time, so when I fell, my open mouth landed on his cock . . .

Oh, that would definitely be salty, and more man than I could probably handle.

Crunch.

"Shit!" I slam my foot on the brake so hard my whole body jerks forward and then back a little.

"You idiot." I stare at Gerald, who looks so confused as to why I have just driven straight through the fence and into the side cattle yard where he has been stuck for the last week. "As if I don't have enough to fix."

Climbing out of the driver's seat, I walk to the front of the car where I can see a few scratches and a cracked headlight, plus both the fence railings are now hanging in two off the post that they were barely attached to in the first place.

"I seriously need some sleep."

Gerald lets out a loud moo, giving her opinion on the mess before me.

"Or between you and me, big girl, a good fucking wouldn't go astray either. But don't tell Tiffany I said that."

Laying my arms down on the hood of the car, I rest my head on top of my clasped hands and pause for a moment to take a few deep breaths before pushing up again.

"Okay, no point in wasting time. Better find some wood to fix this and then go get some more fencing done before the sun goes down. The sooner you are out in the pasture again, the easier it will be on me. I can't let Mr. Macho Man do it all, then take all the glory for fixing our joint boundary fence."

At the mention of the animals finally being allowed back out of the barn and cattle yards, Herb sticks his head out of his stall.

"*Hee-haw, hee-haw, hee-haw.*" He's voicing his view like he always does when I'm talking out loud to myself, and the chorus of animals now starts to join in.

"See what you did now, noisy?" Walking to him and giving his head a pat, I soothe him before he starts a riot. Moving from animal to animal, until finally they have all had a few seconds of my attention, I get back to work.

I grab a bottle of water out of the old fridge in the barn, where I also store animal medication that needs to be kept cold for night-time callouts, and grab an apple that is all dented and I'm sure a bit bruised on the inside, but will sustain me until dinner.

Thinking of Jake's opinion that I would need to pay someone to fix the fence, I start giggling as I grab my cordless drill and circular saw and wonder how quickly his mind would change if he could see me in action now. Bold of him to assume I have enough money to pay a contractor to come in. I paid the deposit for this farm with my life savings and now have a hefty monthly mortgage, so there isn't much left at the end of the month to be shelling out for repairs. Owning a farm and a business is a lot, and I was probably stupid to take this place on alone, but I will never regret it.

Home is where your heart is, and my heart is here with my animals at Windemere Farm.

◆ ◆ ◆

Thankfully it's been a week since my little run-in with my timber fence and no one seems to have noticed the damage to my car.

"I love homemade Saturdays," Tiffany says as she links her arm in mine and we walk across the road to the town square.

Once a month all the shops close early and the town square fills up with stalls of people selling or trading their homewares. I'm a sucker for Mrs. James's fudge and the lemon butter from Lesley, Betty's bestie. Oh, and last time I picked up little hand towels with the button that you hang over the oven handle. It's so cute how everyone supports each other's hobbies here. I think it started as an excuse for the town to get together on a Saturday afternoon. There is usually someone playing live music, and tables to sit with friends to enjoy the food and drinks up for sale.

"Me too. But between you trying to feed me cakes every day and all the amazing cooks in this town, my waistline doesn't think it's such a great idea," I'm replying as we head to the corner of the square so we can start in the same spot we always do, at Mrs. Green's homemade ice cream, which is to die for. The honey crunch is my favorite but for Tiffany it's double choc chip, every time.

With ice creams in hand, we start making our way around the rest of the stalls.

"Have you had any more run-ins with Jake?" Tiff asks slyly, hoping for more gossip.

"No, thank goodness. I make sure he's nowhere to be seen when I head up to do any work on the fence. But you know what he did yesterday?" It's still irritating me. "He undid some of the fence I had done and redid it. Like it wasn't good enough or up to his perfectionist standards. I hate know-it-alls, seriously." I start licking my ice cream a little more aggressively. "Anyway, let's not talk about him. It will just wreck our perfect afternoon."

"Well, I think the amount you complain about him is a pretty good indication that you have a thing for him. I mean, the tea leaves don't lie." Tiff nudges my shoulder with hers and I just glare at her. She might be right, but I won't admit it to anyone, not even myself.

"Don't be ridiculous. We would kill each other. We can't even be in the same room without getting into an argument. And you know that is my greatest fear. Being with someone who I fight constantly with and end up like my parents." I roll my eyes.

"Yeah, but that was different and you know it." Tiff looks at me with sympathy in her eyes.

"Why, because my father had an affair, just like Jeremy? But instead of disappearing without notice, my mom and dad fought like crazy for months before he finally left. Seems to be a common thread in my life. Men who say they love me but don't stay. So why would I choose another man that will eventually just leave too." Crunching into the ice cream cone with more force than was needed, my teeth hit each other hard.

"Your father was a douchebag and Jeremy leaving had nothing to do with you, that was all on him. You can't give up on the chance of finding a good man. There has to be someone out there.

I know you want to get married, with kids and the perfect happily ever after. You told me that before, right?"

Tiff's words hit hard because I had. I even thought I had found it, my forever person to build that life with, but it all just slipped away. And I've been telling myself that I don't want that kind of life anymore, but the truth is I've been lying to myself.

"What about you?" We both look at each other and then immediately start grinning because Tiff is always on the lookout for the next man who's going to satisfy her free-loving ways.

"Time to change the subject." Tiff controls her giggles as she stops at the secondhand table. She loves to collect old teapots. Her shop is already full of them, but she always finds room for more.

With Tiff engrossed in the stall, I start looking around. Everyone in the town is out this afternoon with the weather being so great. And that's when I see him. Jake, swamped by the single ladies of the town. I should have guessed it wouldn't take too long before they would find an opportunity to pin him down.

When his eyes meet mine, it's like I'm in a vortex that I'm not sure how to break out of. And then he winks at me again. What the fuck is with these winks! It just reminds me of his arrogance. Standing there in his jeans, a white V-neck T-shirt that fits snug across his chest, showing off his abs . . . the same ones I pictured licking, and I hate to say it, but they are perfection. His sunglasses pushed up on the top of his head and, as annoying as it is, just the sight of him has my body tingling, reminding me how long it's been since I've been touched by a man—let alone one who looks like that.

"Ashley." The sound of my name snaps me out of my ogling. Dragging my eyes away from Jake, I turn to see Betty waving at me from her table about ten stalls up, all her beautiful hand-crocheted wares set out in front of her.

"Hurry, I need you," she calls out to me frantically.

Shit. My feet start moving quickly toward her.

"Betty, are you okay?" I take her hand that she's waving around at me and hold it to see if it's clammy or hot, then slide my hand up a little to try to feel if her pulse is racing.

"No, no, I'm not. I need Jake. Please can you get him for me. Now?" she claims.

Without even hesitating, I'm rushing across the grass toward him and the moment his eyes lock on me again as I approach, they look worried.

"Ashley, are you okay?"

I don't even speak to the women around him, who are all giving me the stink eye.

"Betty needs you urgently." I tug on his arm and pull him back in the direction of Betty's stall. Jake's long legs mean he outpaces me as he races over.

"Gran, what is it? Are you okay?" he asks, concern thick in his voice.

"Oh, nothing. You just needed saving from those crazy ladies. Ashley's here and I thought you might want to spend time with her," Betty nonchalantly replies.

"Gran." Jake sighs. "You can't scare us like that."

"Betty!" I exclaim.

"What? The vultures were circling. Now I got rid of them. So why don't you two go wander together. There are plenty of treasures to be found here." She's waving her hand around in the air toward the other stallholders with the biggest smile on her face. "What lovely weather to spend an afternoon getting to know each other."

"I think I have learned all I need to know about Jake, Betty. And it looks like he has plenty of people here to become friendly with."

Because the last thing I need is for the rest of the town to see Jake and me together. I love living in a small town and I moved here hoping to form friendships and find belonging and community, but the gossip chain that comes with this small town is a killer.

Growing up in a high-rise in San Francisco, all I had felt was isolated and lonely. Especially after my dad left, when my mom threw herself into her career and I was left on my own most of the time. I hated being alone. My dog, Sally, was my only companion, and she became my whole world, I loved her so deeply. I used to read stories that were based in small towns to escape my reality.

Which had me starting to dream of moving to a place where people knew your name. But what those stories never put in was the cruelty of the idle chatter—sure, being the new kid in town came with its challenges, but listening to everyone and their sister's opinion on my breakup? No! I was not entering the rumor mill of Abbey Falls ever again.

"Sorry, Betty, I have to go." I spin on my heel and stomp back toward Tiff, who's so engrossed in her teapots that she hasn't even noticed the commotion.

"I think she really is allergic to you, Jake," I hear Betty commenting from behind me as Jake the Jerk laughs with her.

"You could be right, Gran," he replies.

I want to turn around and have my say but that will just make things worse.

Instead, I walk up to Tiff and tell her I need to leave because I have a job to get to. She gives me a skeptical look but thankfully doesn't call me out on it.

Climbing back into my car, I realize I didn't get my fudge or lemon butter and I can't go back now. I'll have to wait another month.

Men! They ruin everything.

Why is it every time I turn around, I seem to be running into Jake? As much as I try to stop thinking about him, it's like the universe won't let me.

Before I can start my car, there is a tap on my side window that makes me jump.

Lowering the window, I scowl at the very man causing me all these problems.

"What?" Seriously, what do I need to do to get rid of him?

"Snappy, aren't we." I try to lean away from him as he rests his arm on the open window of my door.

"What do you want, Jake, I'm kind of busy." My pants should be on fire by now with the number of lies I've been telling.

"I just wanted to apologize for Gran. She means well but gets a little carried away."

I try to pull back my frustration that is partly from what just happened, but crazily enough it's also a little sexual frustration at having him this close to me. I can smell that same cologne he was wearing that night at Grizzly's, which seems to have branded me the moment I took the long deep breath in on his chest.

"I know. I adore Betty, but she's way off base here. There are plenty of eligible women in town that you can chase. And it looked like you were already taste-testing the menu back there. So, I suggest you head back and continue on with that." Why does Jake bring out the bitch in me.

"Not happening, Ashley. I'm not here to hook up. I'm in Abbey Falls to help my grandmother and that's it." He's crouching down a little and leaning his face closer to mine. "And I was hoping I could be at least friends with the neighbors, but unless you put your claws away, that's not going to happen either. Have a good day." He pulls back.

My breathing is shallow and my cheeks are warm. My heart is beating that bit harder and I'm wet in places I haven't been for years.

It can't be purely from Jake being around. It's just that I'm a desperate wrinkled prune who has forgotten what it's like to be touched.

Nodding at me, he takes another step back from my car and I'm quickly starting the engine. As I'm reversing out onto the street, I look forward out the windscreen, seeing him standing there smugly, hands in his jeans pockets. I slam the car gear stick into Drive with force. He lifts one hand and waves to me like we're best friends, with another damn wink.

"Uggghhhh!" I scream to myself in the car.

Jake

Since my run-in with Ashley at the fair and getting swarmed by those women, I've managed to avoid town for five days. But even that hasn't stopped the madness, as I've had two phone calls on Gran's house phone asking me to meet for a drink, and then some random woman turning up at Heatherbrae to drop some pie for Gran but asking if I was around to say hello. I'm not interested but I don't want to get a name for myself while I'm here of being an awful person and turning down every eligible female. Ashley already thinks I'm an asshole. I don't need the rest of the town joining in.

But when Gran says she needs some things from the store and is too tired to drive into town, I can't say no.

As I get to the road that passes Windemere, I see Ashley turning into her farm gate. I try to give her a friendly wave, and she waves back, but there is little emotion in it. Which gives me a good laugh—being nice to me must have almost killed her.

She's home early again so I'm assuming I'll find more fencing done when I look in the morning. I have to give it to her, she's doing a great job, even with the little adjustments I had to make in a couple of places. But for someone who didn't grow up on the land, she has learned quickly.

My phone starts ringing and the name *do not answer* flashes across the screen. My stomach drops as I send the call to voicemail. It will only be the bank, checking on progress of the payment of the overdraft on my business account. Even though my house is held as security, there is very little equity in it as we'd just bought it a year before Danika left. Like everything else, our first house wasn't up to the standard she wanted. So, we'd stretched our finances and upgraded, plus done some renovations to make it perfect for her. Looking back, there was nothing wrong with our home before that, but I would've done anything for Danika. And she'd said once we bought a bigger house, we could start trying for a family.

Pulling off to the side of the road, I throw the truck in Park and try to breathe. How the fuck did I get here?

Instead of living a blissfully happy life, married, children, a successful business, I'm drowning under two hundred thousand dollars of debt, single, thirty-nine, and living with my grandmother. I was already struggling after Danika cleaned out our bank accounts and left me with the mortgage and debt, but then came the client from hell who's arguing my workmanship is faulty and refusing to pay the one hundred and sixty thousand dollars that he owes me for the job I finished three months ago. I have lodged a dispute claim in the courts, but it takes months to sort out, and I don't have the money for any high-flying lawyer to sort it out quicker. And this guy knows it.

I could go to Beckett . . . but then I will have to live with the shame and embarrassment for the rest of my life when he keeps reminding me of this latest in a long fucking line of failures.

It's not like he has great people skills at the best of times, and I don't think I could cope with the lecture I would get, like I was some kid in the principal's office. Besides, we haven't really talked much since he told me a few years ago that he didn't like Danika and didn't trust her. I mean he was right, but love is blind and I couldn't see it at the time. So, I fought back and told him that just because his marriage failed it didn't mean mine would too. It was an argument that almost came to fisticuffs but luckily my father walked in, and everything stopped. We've never really addressed it since. He did try to call me when Danika left but I ignored the call. I couldn't take an "I told you so." So now I'm just going to have to fix it myself.

So far I've sold off all my furniture to raise as much money as I can to live off while I'm in Abbey Falls, and made an arrangement with the bank to pay them off over time with the rental income. They suggested I sell the house but at the time I was clinging on to it, hoping that Danika might change her mind and come home to me. That she would realize that the grass wasn't always greener on the other side. And with the market as it is, I'd be losing money.

"Shit!" I slam my hand into the steering wheel and instantly regret it as pain shoots up my arm. What are these things made out of?

I only ever had three goals in life: marriage, family, and a business. I've failed at all three. So as much as Gran thinks I need help finding a new relationship, I can't go there. I don't want to just add someone else to my ever-growing list of failures.

Taking a breath, I remind myself I've got a plan. I'm a good builder and have had a successful business for years, even if these last few have taught me that success can all turn on a dime. I pull out back onto the quiet road. At least I have one thing I can do today—get those items for Gran. Then I'm going to the woods. It's time for a proper hike. It's the only medicine when I get like this.

Alone and breathing in fresh air is the perfect way to end the day.

I pull into the parking space at the grocery store and take the first couple of steps toward the front door. I just need to get in and out without being spotted.

"Good afternoon, Jake," Mabel calls loudly from the counter and any chance I had has been blown out the window.

How quickly I can grab the seven things that Gran needs and escape is all I'm thinking as I smile back at her and say hi.

The woods are calling me. I can hear them. And I can't get there fast enough.

Ashley

Between the work Jake has been doing each day and the few hours I've been able to spend when I get home from work, the long boundary fence is almost completely repaired. If I keep going tonight until it's dark, I might just get it done. Which will be great because then there is no reason Jake will need to be on my land and there's less chance I'll run into him. Because every time I see him, he stirs something inside me. And that freaks me out. He annoys me and it's getting harder to ignore.

Pushing that thought from my head, I move my tools a little farther up the fence line to continue working, but before I can go back to grab my water, phone, and the bucket of supplies, I hear a loud grunting noise inside the edge of the woods that runs along the top of this pasture. I know it's a deer, but it doesn't sound normal. There is a distressed pitch in the call that keeps sounding out. Putting my hand up over my eyes to shield them from the light of the setting sun, I spot an older fawn standing looking at me. But her back leg is cut open and has blood running down it.

"Oh no, you are going to need my help, little one." Placing the tools down on the ground quietly so as not to startle it, I grab a short piece of rope that I had been using to tie tree branches out of the way while I fixed the fence. All my years as a vet have given me the skills of how to deal with a scared injured animal. Very slowly I edge toward the fawn as she keeps crying out in pain. Any sudden movement will startle her so there is no way I can go to my car, which is a good distance from the fence, to grab my phone and supplies. Otherwise, I'm running the risk of her taking off and injuring herself further.

"It's okay, little one, I'm here to help you," I say soothingly, but once I get within a few feet of her, she spooks and runs awkwardly on three legs into the woods. Then standing and listening out for danger, she stops not too far into the trees.

I knew I would jinx myself. I hate the woods at night, and I'm petrified of snakes of any kind, but I can't leave her out here, injured and alone. Taking a deep breath, I start walking past the tree line, my eyes adjusting to the dim light just enough to spot the injured fawn about thirty feet away.

You can do this, Ashley, patience is the key to gaining her confidence. Concentrate on the fawn and not what's around you. If I don't see a snake, then it doesn't exist. That's my motto, even though I know these woods must be full of them.

Step by step, I push tree branches out of the way ever so gently, but every time I get within a few feet of the fawn, she keeps moving farther into the woods. My full concentration is on her, and I keep one eye on her leg that still has blood trickling slowly down. The noise of water in the background breaks my concentration for a moment, because it triggers me to realize that I've walked a lot farther than I meant to. But the fawn is getting tired and is within a few feet. If I can just get hold of her, then I can get her to safety. Looking around, I notice the dim light isn't just because of the tree cover. I don't have my phone with me either and I think I'm lost.

I've been so stupid. I should have at least grabbed my phone and medical bag so that if I caught the fawn long enough to bandage her leg without bringing her back to the farm, then I could release her and hope for the best. But instead, I'm out in the dwindling light with absolutely nothing to help me except a piece of rope.

The fawn lets out a grunt that is so weak that I know it's now or never to grab her. *You can do this, Ashley.*

Inching forward and holding my breath, I take two quick steps and lunge for the fawn as my fingers clasp onto her fur, but she panics and shoots off, leaving me totally off-balance, holding clumps of fur in my hands.

As I lunge at her again, I'm horrified to notice that the ground beneath us starts dropping off toward where the sound of the water is coming from. Trying to stop myself from falling, I grasp for any branch to hold, but they all start snapping in my hands, and my feet are slipping on rocks like I have marbles under my feet.

"Ahhhhhh!" I scream as my foot slips into the crevice between two rocks and gets stuck there as I fall sideways. I land in an awkward position on the rocks, my body facing downhill.

Panting, I try to get my bearings.

It's then that I realize that I'm on my back and staring up at the treetops and the darkening sky. I try to look around to see if the fawn is still here, but she's long gone. Goddamn it!

The movement sends shooting pain up my leg and I screw my eyes shut.

"Shit, that hurts," I mutter quietly, tears running down my face. "Shit, shit, shit." My breathing gets quicker as I start to feel my panic rising.

I'm stuck, hurt, with no way to get help, and it's getting darker by the minute. I never noticed the noises before, but now they bounce around me as if they are in surround sound, confusing me further about where I actually am. There is no point screaming for help, because no one will hear me. I try to push up with my hands so at least I'm sitting and don't have sharp rocks digging into my back.

My head clears a little once I'm upright, and my hands fall to my ankle that is wedged between two rocks. I try to move it again, but the pain just gets worse. It's unbearable.

Panic and frustration explode inside me, and I scream as loud as I can, hoping it will scare off any critter that thinks I might look like some sort of snack.

"Arrrrrgggggghhhhhh." My voice echoes in the surrounding woods as I cling to the tiniest shred of hope that there will be a reply, but of course, there is nothing. Only the terrifying chorus of woodland creatures moving around me.

I burst into tears. And when I'm too exhausted to cry anymore, I sit, staring into the nothingness, telling myself I can do this. It's just one night in a dark, dark wood.

When I don't turn up at the clinic tomorrow morning, Adi will send out a search party. Surely.

I have to believe that's true. Otherwise I may as well give up now.

I hear a rustle in the leaves to the side of me that sounds suspiciously like the slithering of a snake, and it has my hands on these damn rocks and pulling as hard as I can. I'm not waiting for the morning.

I can hear Tiffany in my head, reciting the mantra she used to make me repeat when I didn't want to get out of bed after Jeremy left me.

"No one gets to keep you down once you decide you're ready to get up. So, choose to get the fuck up."

"Time to get the fuck up, Ashley!"

Chapter Six

Jake

"Time to head back, Rosie. We've done enough trail clearing for today. Well, not we, but me. I'm the one who's done all the work." She just lifts her head from where she has been lying, yawns, and then slowly gets up. "I don't know why you are even here. It's not like I invited you." Her bark in reply makes me snigger.

I'm still not sold on the whole dog thing, especially picking up the dog shit, but I do have to admit, Rosie has been easier to handle than I was expecting. And the look of love in Gran's eyes when she speaks to her has me trying a little harder to become an animal-tolerant person. I'm a long way from being an animal lover, but you could say Rosie is winning me over a little more each day.

"We can't be late, because Gran will have the back porch light on waiting for us." There are some things that Gran has been doing since I arrived here that make me feel like a child, but who am I to upset an old lady grieving the loss of her husband.

At least it won't be much longer until my cousins arrive, and just in time as I've now completed the renovations on the barn. Declan's sabbatical has been approved. School finishes in June, so he's aiming for late June or early July once he wraps up things at home, doing the handover to the new teacher and basketball coach that will relieve him. Chase is away working on a photo shoot but promised Gran that he will head straight to Heatherbrae once it wraps. Beckett, however . . . I mean, who knows?

I have put an intercom system in the house for Gran to contact the barn, so if she needs one of us when we're here, she just has to push a button. I'm pretty sure I'll regret that decision, and the guys will be ready to punish me. But surely the novelty will only last a few days, and then she will just use it when necessary. Or so I keep telling myself.

Today was another warm spring day, and you can tell we are getting closer to the summer heat, which I'm looking forward to. This late-afternoon temperature is the perfect time for the hike I desperately needed to clear my head and cool off after yet another call to remind me that my life outside of Abbey Falls is something I'm trying to forget.

The days are stretching out, and the afternoon light is great to be sitting on the porch after dinner, watching the sun slowly set over the mountains like Gran and I have been enjoying, and probably will again tonight after I'm back from my hike and in a better frame of mind. It's these simple things that I never really got to enjoy in Sacramento. Life moves a lot faster there than it does in Abbey Falls. It's definitely a benefit of spending some time here.

Now the barn is completed, I'll start drawing up some rough sketches of where the restaurant and art gallery should be built and some potential sites for the small cabins that Gran wants for the family to use when we come home to visit. It's her way of reminding us that when this year is over, she still expects us all back more often. Including all the girls and their kids too. It still makes me stop and think about how easily the word *home* already rolls off my tongue when I talk about Heatherbrae. I should be saying "home for now."

I readjust my backpack as I replace the tools and head back to Heatherbrae.

Walking back is a lot easier than the hike out now I've cleared a path, and I think even Rosie appreciates not having to dodge all the low-lying branches.

Stepping on a twig that cracks under my foot has Rosie letting out one of the loudest barks I've heard from her since she arrived at Heatherbrae.

"Really, it was just a twig. I made much louder noises when I was chopping with the machete before." I turn, looking at her as I try to explain, but her bark has stopped and she's standing rigid, looking intently into the dense woods heading toward the creek.

"What's wrong with you?"

Again, she barks and starts to lift her nose into the air, sniffing and moving her head from side to side.

Feeling a little concerned, I go to slip my pack off my back so I can grab her leash just in case, but I'm too late.

Rosie bolts off into the bushes.

"Fuck, Rosie, come back!" I shout, rushing under the rough scrub because Gran will kill me if her dog gets hurt, or worse, disappears.

"Rosie, come back, you dumb dog," I yell as I follow the sound of her constant barking.

"We had a deal, Rosie, if you get lost, I'm not looking for you, remember?" Yet it's exactly what I am doing and I get angrier the farther from the track she gets, calling out to a dog who I know is not listening.

As I break through the denser section of trees and bushes, I come to the creek where I can spot her a bit farther up the bank. Her paws are dancing up and down, her nose in the air, and she's sniffing like crazy.

"What the fuck is wrong with you? Have you gone mad? Is that why your last owner got rid of you?" I storm along the side of the creek, and as I get close, she lets out another loud couple of barks but then stops abruptly. I'm sure that she has scared away every piece of wildlife as the woods grow quiet.

And then I hear it. A faint cry for help.

"Is there someone out there?" I call as loud as I can.

"Yes, I'm here! Help, I need help!" A female voice is a little stronger now, and before I make it to Rosie, she's running at speed across the creek and up the bank on the other side. It's darker over there, so I lose sight of her through the trees.

"I'm coming. Keep calling and we'll find you," I shout as I'm running to where Rosie found the shallow part of the creek and the best place to cross. I jump from rock to rock, still trying to be careful because I'm no help to anyone if I slip.

As I clear the creek, I stop for a second and listen out for the voice, getting my bearings.

"Help . . . here." The voice is getting louder, but Rosie has found her and is now barking loudly and repeatedly like a homing beacon.

Bursting through the last clump of shrubbery, I see Rosie being hugged tightly by a sobbing woman. But not just any woman.

"Ashley!" I exclaim as I rush to her.

"Ja . . . ke." She's crying so hard it takes two breaths to get my name out.

"It's okay. I've got you." I crouch down until I'm level with her face, and without being told, Rosie backs away a few steps. With a sense of urgency to comfort her rushing through me, I wrap my arms around Ashley and hold her until her crying subsides.

"Of all people it had to be you who found me like this . . . a blubbering mess," she says into my shoulder where she has been making my shirt damp with her tears.

I pull back a little so I can see her face, although it's getting harder in the darkness. I try not to acknowledge her comment or fuel the embarrassment she's already feeling. "Are you hurt?"

"My ankle," she gasps. "I've done something. I can't move it. It's stuck in the rocks." Tears start welling up in her eyes again.

"Okay, let me take a look and we'll get you free, then we can assess the injury." I take my pack off my back and feel grateful all over again I remembered to pack a flashlight.

"Hold this, Ash." I pass it to her so I have two free hands and inspect the two rocks her foot is caught in. They are wedged tightly, but that doesn't mean I'm giving up. "Can you shine it around us? I need a large stick to use like a lever and try to pry one rock loose."

She does as she's asked, her hand steady, and I realize this is the first time we've spent any time together and she hasn't been yelling at me. Apparently, things do change. Though this isn't exactly the way I had hoped . . .

The moment I spot a stick, I grab it and am concentrating so intently on levering up the rock I didn't notice that Rosie is now beside Ashley, keeping her calm. She really is growing on me.

"Okay, once I get this rock loose enough, I'm going to lever it up. And when I tell you to, I need you to get your foot out as quickly as possible." I look up at her as she stares back at me, those molten brown eyes swimming in tears that make me want to gather her up in my arms again. "Can you do that, Ashley?"

She nods solemnly, and I continue to loosen some of the tightly packed earth around the rock before finally levering it up just enough for her foot to fit through.

"Now, Ash!"

She pulls her foot out as quick as she can, and the moment it's clear, I drop the lever and turn to check on her. The flashlight is now sitting on the dirt as she pulls her leg up toward her chest, feeling her ankle. I reach down and take the flashlight to press it back into her hands.

"Let me check it out. Stay still," I ask her as soothingly as I can.

"Good. Good. There are scratches but no cuts, which is a start." I gently feel her leg, starting at her knee down, and nothing appears to be too out of shape, and she's not screaming in pain. But when I get to the ankle, she whimpers.

"Can you move it?" I ask and watch her slowly try to rotate it.

Her breathing quickens slightly. "It hurts, but I have movement," Ash replies but winces as she continues.

With her having more idea about injuries than me, I let her lead the way.

"Do you think you will be able to put any weight on it?" I stand, trying to get myself into a spot where I can support her so we don't end up at the bottom of the embankment.

"I doubt it, but I want to try." She reaches her hands up for me to help her up from her awkward position on the ground.

"Take it slow." Digging my boots into the earth, I pull her up and wait until she's steady, but the moment she tries to put any pressure on her ankle, she collapses against me in pain.

My head is racing as I assess the situation.

It's fully dark now, Ashley can't walk, and there is no way I can carry her out of here. The terrain is too dangerous—even with a flashlight, our chances of falling are too high.

"Look, we are going to need help. Do they still have a rescue team around here we can call or maybe get help from the town—"

"No! Please no." She stops, takes a deep breath, and looks up toward the sky and then at me. "It's bad enough that you have seen me like this. I hate being the talk of the town. I'll manage. I can walk back on my own. Surely you know where we are. You can get us back with your flashlight."

"Ash, you can't even walk on that ankle, so how the fuck are you getting yourself out of here? And it's too dark for me to be carrying you on my back, because yes, I have a rough idea where we are if it were daylight, but in the dark it's not that easy. I could take a wrong turn and the next thing we are more lost than you are now." I give her the hard truth of the situation she's in right now.

"Should've known that you weren't the super-talented amazing man that walks on water like Betty portrayed you to be. I suppose you have some fantastic plan then."

I want to laugh at her throwing a tantrum like a toddler, but I know that's not going to go down too well right now.

"I think the *walking on water* was stretching the truth just a little, but I'll have to thank Gran for the accolades." I wrap my arm around Ashley's waist and ignoring the initial flinch from her, she eventually relaxes into me, so she can stand up properly.

"And you're right. Since you have refused to try Plan A, Plan B it is then." I knew she was stubborn but the reaction to people seeing her vulnerable surprised me.

"Okay, you aren't going to like what I have to say, but here's the situation. I'm going to find a flat surface at the top of this slope for us to camp the night. Because there is no way we can walk you out in the dark, not safely anyway, or without one or both of us injuring ourselves." I feel her shoulders fall in disappointment.

"You're right, your Plan B sucks."

But I can hear the defeat in her voice.

"I knew you would love it," I quip as I try to surprise a smile. "The good thing is we are surrounded by plenty of firewood, and in my pack, I have a fire starter, water, some dodgy food which may or may not be past its best-by date, and a blanket. So, it will be first-class roughing it, because only the best for you."

The tiny chuckle that is almost a laugh is a relief. Maybe we are getting somewhere.

"What, you didn't pack food for Rosie?" Ashley mumbles.

"That dog deserves a juicy steak for finding you today, but she's going to have to wait just like the rest of us. Now let's get you up to the top so I can get you comfortable. But there is one condition for this plan," I tell her.

"What?" She sighs.

"We agree on a truce from all this verbally attacking each other. We are going to be stuck with each other tonight so unless we can manage to make friends, then I'm calling in the rescue squad now."

"Fine, truce," she grumbles, and she twists her body a little away from me, brushing against me.

Shit! I didn't know how much a stubborn woman could turn me on as much as she does. But there is something about Ash that seems to be revving my engine higher and higher every time we see each other.

"So glad to hear the joy in your voice." This time I do laugh at her.

"Just shut up and let's get on with it. Nobody likes a gloater."

My plan sounds easy, but it's not. We are both puffing with the effort as we struggle up the embankment and then, finally, we make it to the top.

Once I have Ashley seated with the blanket wrapped securely around her, I collect some wood and light a fire inside the safe circle of rocks I have made.

The first crackles of the wood from the flames fill the air around us, and Ashley gasps.

"What about Betty? She will be worried about you."

I can't help but feel a pull on my heart that this woman in front of me is hurt and scared as hell but is worrying about my gran.

Pulling my phone out of my pocket, I lift it up, praying there is at least one bar of service, and I'm surprised to see I actually have two.

Not wanting to waste battery, and with no guarantee that those two bars will be enough to have a clear phone conversation, I shoot off a text to Gran, explaining what has happened and that we are all fine but will wait until first light to walk out. I know full well I'll be carrying Ashley, I'm sure with her protesting the whole way.

I'm relieved when I see it shows delivered, and the dots are dancing on the screen, albeit quite slowly, but she's getting there. Gran is not very tech savvy, but she does know how to text.

> **GRAN:** Oh, a cute first date under the stars, very smooth, Jake. Remember, what happens in the woods stays in the woods.

"Oh seriously, what is wrong with that woman?" I'm cracking up heartily, passing my phone to Ash, who can't help but join me. And in that moment, I can tell she's finally letting the tension she has built between us fall a little.

Looking across at her in the soft light of the fire, giggling when she really feels like crying, I can't help but see how beautiful she is. If only things were different, maybe this would be the ideal first date with Ash . . .

Wait—when did I start calling her Ash?

Oh no, as much as I have been fighting these feelings and pretending they don't exist, tonight all my guards are down, and my heart is thumping a different beat.

Maybe Gran is right. What happens in the woods stays in the woods.

Ashley

"Can you ask Betty to call my friend Tiffany? Just in case she turns up at my house and freaks out when she doesn't find me. Betty will have the number. Your gran knows everyone in town." I can feel my ankle starting to throb as I shift on the cold ground, trying to get comfortable.

"So you have other besties beside me?" He smirks at me.

"Umm, we only just agreed to be friends. You have a lot of hard work to put in to make it bestie level. And I dare you to challenge Tiff for that spot." I'm smiling at the thought of Tiff replying to that notion.

"Can't wait to meet the competition." He grins at me while his fingers fly over the phone's screen and once he gets the reply, he crouches down in front of me. "I'm turning the phone off now to save the battery just in case we need it."

Slipping his phone into the front pocket of his pack, he pulls out a compact red bag with a white cross on it.

I want to laugh at how prepared he is, because I've already got the impression that he's an attention-to-details man. Based on the quality in his part of the fence repairs and the way he sneakily fixed mine, I can tell he takes pride in everything he does.

Pulling out an alcohol wipe, along with a bandage, he looks at me. "Can I take your boot off so I can wrap your ankle in this bandage? We need to stop the swelling until we can get you checked out tomorrow."

A shiver runs through me as the adrenaline in my body starts to drop. "What if you hadn't found me?" I whisper.

"But I did." He reaches out and wipes his thumb to catch the small tears that are falling from my eyes again. His touch is so comforting, and a wave of calm settles in my stomach. "Well, technically Rosie did, but I'm not letting her take all the credit." In the orange glow from the fire, his brown eyes are captivating, and the attempt at humor works, with a small half giggle slipping from me.

"I told you that animals are amazing. You just had to give them a chance."

"Hmmm, the jury is still out on that, but I have to admit she has put in a solid effort today." I can feel him unlacing my boot and a sharp pain shoots up my ankle. Seeing me gritting my teeth, he keeps talking to distract me. "Now, can you tell me how the hell you ended up down an embankment, headfirst toward the creek, and your foot deciding it wanted to hide out in a little rock hollow?"

He peels off my sock and starts to wipe the scratches with the alcohol wipe, the sting making me suck in my breath each time. "Start talking, Ash, otherwise I'm going to assume it was all a ploy to get me to come rescue you. Have you been in cahoots with Gran?"

I can't help but laugh at that, even though I'm in pain. "You wish, big guy. I don't date, so that's not possible. But good try. Plus you drive me insane most days."

His eyes whip up from where he's concentrating on my ankle, and that piercing look has my mind racing.

Is it that he's shocked, or annoyed at me for admitting that he irritates me, or is he disappointed because, just like me, maybe there is some interest buried in a place he didn't realize, and that neither of us want to admit to?

"Why?" he asks bluntly.

But I don't want to share my inner demons right now, out here in the middle of the dark, when I'm already feeling so vulnerable.

"Story for another time," I mumble, to which he nods and continues to clean my scratches and then starts to strap the bandage around the already swelling ankle.

"Speaking of stories, stop trying to avoid the one where you tell me you were so clumsy you just fell while walking along the trail." Jake doesn't even look up this time but just keeps carefully wrapping.

"Oh, I won't deny I'm clumsy at times. That's why me and the great outdoors don't really blend together. And I know you are going to use today's adventure against me at a later date so I'll tell you the truth. I was trying to catch an injured fawn who ran into the woods." Sighing, I wait for the laughter that is surely going to come.

Jake's body starts bouncing up and down a little and still he isn't looking at me.

"Go on, let it out. Tiff tells me it's not healthy to keep laughter on the inside."

"Oh, thank goodness, because that was hurting my ribs." And he lets loose with the biggest belly laugh that has Rosie sitting up a little straighter and staring at Jake like there is something wrong with him. Trying to pull himself together, he finally looks up at me again. "Sorry, that was a bit mean. I shouldn't be laughing when you're hurt. How does that feel?" He finishes with the last wrap around with the bandage and secures it.

"Sore, but I know it needs to be wrapped. It will help with my recovery." And that's when it dawns on me that I'm going to struggle to work if this is anything serious. I try to push those thoughts out of my head because I can't be worrying about that until I know what the injury is.

Jake interrupts my thoughts. "You really need some ice, and I can't do anything about that, obviously, but I do have some Tylenol. It's probably not strong enough, but hopefully it will take the edge off." He reaches into his little bag of goodies that I'm so grateful for.

"I'll take it."

I swallow them with some water, just a few sips, because the last thing I need to do is drink so much that I need to go to the toilet during the night.

Jake then asks about the fawn and I tell him the sorry tale about how she kept drawing me deeper into the woods, until I ended up here. Sitting down next to me, he laughs along with me as I begin to see the funny side. While we chat, he continues to stoke the fire to a warm blaze. I'm beyond grateful, as the temperature will be dropping off steeply as we head into the middle of the night. It might be the beginning of May and beautifully sunny during the day, but the nights are still cold, especially out in the woods.

"Now, on tonight's menu, we have a variety of options. Would you like to hear the chef's recommendations of the two most popular selections by our dinner patrons?" Jake drags his pack onto his lap and digs down deeper to produce the rations.

And since dropping my instinct to always fight with Jake, I'm starting to see a different side of him and how funny he can be.

"I've heard varied reviews of the chef, so I'm not sure how much I can trust him, but please enlighten me."

Not that I'm overly hungry, but I'm hoping if I eat something, it will help the anxiety in my stomach settle. Jake is trying so hard to keep me distracted, but the constant throbbing in my ankle makes it hard to forget; plus, there is the fact that we are in the middle of the woods, with dangerous animals all around us, including snakes, and I have nothing to protect me from them. That's enough to keep my blood pressure elevated and my heart pumping a little faster than it should be.

"Oh." He places his hand on his chest. "I'm offended at the skepticism toward the chef. I know him personally, and he is a great guy."

"So I've been told by your gran, but I think she is a little biased." I think back to the chat we were having on her porch before Jake came home, how Betty filled me in on Noel's last wishes, and my heart swells before I firmly tell myself not to go there. Betty missed her calling as a used car salesperson. If I listened to everything she was telling me, I would be thinking that Jake doesn't have one fault and is an actual saint.

"I don't want to know." He breaks out of character for a moment, shaking his head. "And I'll just apologize in advance for her being pushy. It comes from a place of love, however misguided it is."

"It's okay. I think everyone deserves a gran like yours in their corner. You boys are lucky to get such a special year with her." I know they wish it would have been with their grandfather as well. "Now show me what you've got."

"Well, first on the menu tonight we have what some might say is a very appropriately named snack bar. It's a well-rounded trail mix granola bar, studded with a selection of roasted nuts that are guaranteed to keep you well fed and very regular." He pulls out the first bar from his pack and waves it around like it's some major prize, but the squashed and crinkled wrapping does not give it the gold-medal look he was trying to describe. My guess would be it's all broken into many pieces and will probably be best eaten poured into your mouth.

"Hmmm, sounds appetizing, but I would like to hear the other award-winning option, please." I pull the blanket a little tighter around me as we hear the howl of a wolf in the distance.

Jake reaches out and puts his arm around my shoulder as he moves a little closer. "It's okay, we are safe. They won't come near the fire."

He tries to instill confidence in me but forgets I'm a vet and know that a fire won't stop any animal if they really want to check us out or even attack us. But it is sweet of him to try, and I nod for him to continue with his big dinner description.

"Second on the menu tonight is hand-picked by the chef, an oat and raspberry bar, full of sugar and all those good preservatives that have random numbers attached to them, but of course, so good for your body. It is coated in drizzles of a brown smooth thing

I believe is called chocolate." He holds the other bar up in the air out of my reach as I lunge for it.

"You had chocolate this whole time and held out on an injured woman who's full of anxiety? Sorry, you've just lost some of the points you scored for rescuing me." I snatch it out of his hand while we both smile at the stupidity of our situation—battling over two small and non-interesting granola bars. It makes a pleasant change from trying to tear strips off each other.

We eat in silence for a few minutes and try to make something that tastes like cardboard last as long as we can.

"Are these rations supposed to keep you alive or kill you quickly to put you out of your misery? Plus, you lied about the chocolate; that was something brown, but it's blasphemy to use the word chocolate. This is not giving you any points in your race for bestie status." Taking another big mouthful of water from the bottle we're sharing, I pass it back with only a very small amount left. "Sorry, I know we should have been keeping that, but I needed to wash that terrible taste down."

Jake quickly drinks the last mouthful. "Same. But don't worry, I'll just walk back down to the creek and refill it."

"No!" I yell and grab hold of his arm like he's my lifeline. "Please don't leave me. I'm scared." So much for not sharing how I really feel. My fear has the words rushing out. My fingers are gripping his arm so tightly that even though he has a shirt on, I'm sure I'm still leaving indents in his skin from my fingernails.

"Ash, it's okay. I won't leave you. We can do without the water for now. If we get desperate, then we can worry about that later." His hand softly settles over the top of mine ever so gently, and his fingers start stroking over my hand. It doesn't take long before my fingers relax against his biceps. I don't pull away and neither does Jake. Instead, he takes my hand in his, slowly easing it off his arm and entwining our fingers together. He lays our joined hands on my leg without realizing he has given me an anchor for my anxiety, which confuses me, but I'll take it right now.

"Can I ask you something?" His voice is calm and full of warmth.

"Yes, but it'll depend on the question whether or not I answer," I cautiously reply.

"Can I call you Ash?" He's tentative as he turns to face me.

"Well, that wasn't what I was expecting, but yeah, if you want to. People around here usually call me Ashley, Doc, or Doc Alleyne, but Ash is what I used to get called at school growing up by friends, so that's fine. I'll answer to any of them. It doesn't faze me." I shrug.

"Okay, good. I mean, Ashley is beautiful, but I just think Ash suits you too. And your surname, it's different."

"Yes, it's of English origin, so not common here. I always forget it's not obvious how to pronounce it, but with new clients I usually need to go through sounding it out, A-lean, and then they get it."

"Well, I think it is just as pretty as your first name. And it's nice to be a little different, don't you think. Quite often we all just want to blend in and not be seen." There is no way he could blend in anywhere; my gaze would gravitate to him every single time, whether I like it or not.

"Thank you." The words slip quietly from my lips. His hand squeezing mine gently to reassure me, reminding me that he's still right here. My anchor.

"How about your family? Is it big and sometimes complicated like mine?"

I can see he's not being nosy or asking for small talk but is genuinely interested in getting to know a new friend.

"Nope, it's just me and my parents. And all my extended family are across the other side of the country so we aren't that close really, not like you and your cousins, it sounds like. You know, I made a birthday wish every year for a sibling, but it never happened, so if

I'm ever lucky enough to have a family, I want more than one child. Being an only child is a lonely life at times."

I wonder what it feels like to have that many people around you who care about you so deeply. Something I wish I had experienced growing up.

"Be careful what you wish for with siblings. I'm so blessed, but like I said, it's not always as perfect as it seems. My parents were great, although my dad could be hard on us, but only in a way he thought was good for us. I have a sister who's married and a brother that I have a very complicated relationship with."

And I can tell by the expression that comes across his face for a split second that there's deep pain there.

"Those weren't my questions, though." And he quickly changes direction away from talking about it.

"Well, you better hurry up. I have places to be and people to see." It brings a smile to his face.

"Sorry, I know you are in high demand." He shifts his body slightly, so he's now more face on. "Why don't you date? You are an extremely attractive woman, and from what Gran tells me, you have a lot to give, so how the hell are you still single?"

Crap, how do I answer this without sounding pathetic and weak? Do I just blurt out the truth that my heart was stomped on three years ago and left in tatters, or the stock standard answer I use for the town gossips?

Taking a long deep breath in and letting it slowly escape, I let the words out into the rapidly cooling night air.

"I'm just so busy being the only vet in town that I don't have time. The only males I spend the night with are usually of the four-legged variety." I can't look him in the eyes to say it, though. Fixating on the fire and watching the flames dance around, I try convincing myself that's the answer too.

But I've never been good at lying.

JAKE

Her words sound so hollow I know that's not even close to the truth.

"Is that your rehearsed answer, Ash? Because that's not going to wash with me."

She doesn't answer me, hoping I will just swallow her bullshit.

While she sits watching the fire, I look at her, and I can see the hurt that is sitting just under the surface. And the reason I can see it is because I see that same look in the mirror every morning I wake up alone, again.

"I can wait you out all night, Ash. Unlike you, I have nowhere else to be. I mean, you can tell me you don't want to talk about it, and that's okay, but don't feed me lies. I've been lied to by a woman before and hate it with a passion." I don't know what it is about being out here on our own in a place no one else can hear or touch us that I feel so free to say the words I haven't shared with anyone else.

"Maybe it will help if I tell you why I'm on my own and resigned to be that way for a while—well, at least twelve months, anyway."

Waiting for an answer, I can see her breathing a little quicker but still no words come out.

"Just over a year ago, my girlfriend, Danika, walked out on me after seven years. She pulled the rug out from under me with the words that we aren't the right fit. I mean, what the fuck had we been doing for all those years? I wanted to get married and settle down with kids while she just wanted to go off with all our money and travel and fuck every guy who would have her. Am I over her? Yeah, but does it still hurt? Oh yeah, like a fucking knife in the heart." Even saying it out loud brings that pain in my chest, although in time, it's now not quite so severe. More like a dull ache than the stabbing pain it once was.

Slowly her head turns toward me, and I can see the pity there. Yeah, it's the same way all our friends looked at me each time we would meet up.

"I'm so sorry, Jake, that sounds tough."

And I realize this isn't pity, it's someone who cares, someone who understands exactly the kind of pain I'm talking about.

"Who hurt you, Ash?"

"You don't give up easily," she murmurs.

"Not when it's important," I plead as something in my gut tells me if I don't get it out of her tonight, then there's no chance once we are back in our everyday life. "Just remember what Gran said, 'what happens in the woods stays in the woods.' That goes the same for words that are spoken. Tonight, there's no one but us here, but tomorrow, all the deepest secrets shared will float away with the rising of the morning sun."

Come on, just take that little step and share a part of yourself with me.

"I just can't look at you when you are being so compassionate and see that same arrogant man from the first day we met and every day since then. I'm getting the feeling that all that bluster you showed me is so far from the real you. How do you go from being an asshole to someone so caring and gentle? I'm still trying to work you out."

You and me both.

And I wasn't expecting you to be the person to help me possibly find out.

Chapter Seven

Jake

Shit, I know I'm in trouble now. If we keep talking like this, opening up, being vulnerable, I can't guarantee I can hold back. Because while I can control my physical attraction, this low thrum in my heart is anything but lust. I need to stop, but I can't seem to.

"I like to keep you guessing, but I can promise you, this Jake, the one here being raw with you, that's the guy I am. Do I always show that part of me? No, but you have some way of making me want to share it with you." I watch as my words sink in.

She raises her head from her knee though she won't look at me. She gazes off into the fire as she speaks.

"I met Jeremy when I was in college. I fell in love with his smooth words and our mutual love of animals. We made big plans. I'd always dreamed of moving to a small town, now I hoped we'd do it together—open our own clinic, work together, and settle into a slower, more relaxed life. I thought that was his dream too, but how stupid I feel looking back now. It was me who searched endlessly for the right clinic to buy. He just acted like he was being the great boyfriend by letting me pick everything. The town, clinic, the house we lived in—all of it, really. But I was too blinded by love to see that he just wasn't as into it as me."

I turn her head toward me and see the hurt I know so well in her sad face. She's past the anger but she still holds scars on her heart.

"Life was perfect, or so I thought." Stopping to take a breath, she continues, "Until I came home after a long day in the clinic, expecting dinner and a fire lit, keeping the house warm. It was Jeremy's day off. But instead, I walked in to darkness and it felt like all the warmth of our little home was gone. He'd packed up our future and taken it with him. He met someone online and had been talking to her for over a year, then spent a week with her in San Francisco when he was at a conference, while stupidly I was back here, holding down the fort, working my ass off."

She grits her teeth a little, and while I don't know this Jeremy, I already hate him. Watching her relive a really hurtful time makes me feel awful for pushing her to tell me. And as I'm about to apologize, the next words she says bring me to a halt.

"I guess I just wasn't enough." There are no tears, just a face that tells me that she believes what she's saying is true. That this is what she has been telling herself all these years.

"Have you ever said that out loud before?" Letting her hand go, I slowly raise both my hands to cup her face.

"No."

I barely hear her, but I can see her lips mouthing it.

"Don't you ever let anyone make you feel like that. He didn't deserve you, because the woman I'm getting to know is more than enough." I run my right thumb over her soft cheek, knowing I shouldn't. Knowing I can't stop. "To be honest, I'm having a hard time not kissing you right now, and I know that we hardly know each other and have spent the last few weeks annoying the hell out of each other. But you bring beauty and kindness to this world,

Ash, and as much as I'm trying not to let you get under my skin, I can't fight it anymore. No matter the number of times I tell myself we would be a really bad idea. That I don't plan on staying, but fuck . . . if I was, you would be in trouble, because I would be doing everything to convince you to break that no-dating rule of yours."

My heart is racing, and I can feel the air being sucked from my lungs. As we both lean into each other, I tell myself not to do this.

But it's getting harder to listen when her smooth red lips are just a breath away, almost begging me to take them.

"I want to taste you again. Once wasn't enough," I murmur. There are mere inches between us now. "Tell me you feel it too."

"That I'm about to make a mistake? Yeah, I feel it." But instead of pulling away from me, the blanket falls from her shoulders as she slides her hands up my chest and clutches my shirt.

And as I look deep into her longing eyes, she whispers ever so softly, "What happens in the woods stays in the woods . . . promise me." She bites down on her bottom lip, and I know I'm done holding back. I would promise her anything right now. I nod.

Then the two words I'm craving fall from her mouth.

"Kiss me."

You don't have to ask me twice.

The moment our lips touch is so gentle, an indication of how unsure we are. But as much as our brains are trying to put a stop to something that is going to complicate life for both of us, our bodies have totally stopped listening.

Because once we touch, the fireworks explode all over my body, and I can't contain my lust any longer. Especially once she moans into my mouth. I'm gone.

I slide my left hand to the back of her head and pull her tightly to me, tilting her to just the right angle that her lips open wider for me. With every inch of her mouth on mine, in this moment, I can show her that she is more than enough.

Trying to take it slow just isn't an option for either of us. Her smooth lips slide perfectly over mine. We start feeling more of the pent-up sexual tension between us. My tongue pushes past her lips and explores inside her mouth. Her hands release my shirt and reach into my hair, pulling, and the sting is the final straw of trying to hold back. In one swift motion, I lay her down, the blanket around her now protecting her from the cold earth underneath. Straddling over the top of her on my knees, I hungrily take her bottom lip between my teeth and bite down. Her body arches up at the same time she's releasing an erotic moan, which reverberates through me. The noise has my cock thickening to the point it's now pushing hard against her stomach.

It's been so long since I've had sex, but I'm not breaking that dry spell like this. Ash deserves more than a quick fuck on the floor of the woods.

If I ever get the chance, I will have her naked on a big soft bed, clean sheets that I will take great pleasure in dirtying all night long as I taste not just her lips but every inch of this sensual body. The way she's moaning and writhing under me as our lips mold together like they were made to fit just right, I know that sex with her would be like nothing I have ever experienced before.

It's then I realize the deep moan is coming from my mouth too. At the same time my hand starts to slide down the outside of her neck, I start to kiss along her jawline, wanting more.

"You are so fucking alluring, I don't know how to stop." Taking her ear between my teeth, I let her know how much she's turning me on just from tasting her.

"Don't stop." She digs her nails into my scalp.

"You are like the poison apple; one bite and I'm doomed." I slide my tongue down her neck, and she's panting as my hand skims down the side of her breast. I'm itching to take it in my hand, but I'm about to step over a line that I shouldn't cross.

"I need to stop. This isn't what you want." I try to use that rational thought to slow me down. *Be the gentlemen and step away. Don't make her regret this tomorrow.*

"You're wrong. I want more." Her hands drop from where she had them tangled in my hair to my back, where they are sliding up and down. She grinds her body up against mine to find some relief. "Touch me, Jake. Remind me what being touched by a man feels like . . . I'm desperate."

"Fuccckkkk," slips from my mouth as she pushes one hand between our bodies, reaching for my cock.

"Yes! Fuck me." I know she's totally lost in the erotic rush, and it's not what she really wants.

"No, I can't." But I sure as shit want to.

"I want to come. Please, Jake."

I can't say no to her begging.

Sitting up above her, with my legs on either side of her, the vision below me is so tempting. Flushed cheeks, mouth open, and her deep brown eyes fixed on watching my hand as it runs across her hard pebbled nipple poking through her shirt. I'm longing to feel her flesh under the clothes, her nipple in my mouth as I suck hard, making her whimper.

But this alone isn't enough. She needs more, and I move my hand to where she's desperate to be touched.

The moment I place my palm on top of her jeans and push down, Ash's head drops back and her mouth hangs open, panting.

"Jake . . ." she pleads and shocks the hell out of me by unbuttoning her jeans and pushing down the zipper.

A shiver runs through my whole body as I see the sweet pink satin panties with lace along the top. I tell myself what a terrible idea this is, but the moment she takes my hand and slides it inside her jeans on the top of the smooth material, I'm gone and can't resist her. I push my fingers down over the line of her slit, and finding her panties wet has me so fucking hard. I know I can't do anything to fix that, but I can sure as hell give her what she needs, even if it kills me. I start to circle my thumb on top of her hard clit that's hidden under her panties. Her loud moan echoes through the woods and it gives me a rush of satisfaction I wasn't expecting.

"You like this, don't you, Ash. Me rubbing your desperate little pussy."

"Yesssss. Mooorrree."

There is no stopping now.

"I wish I could taste you there. I bet you taste as sweet as honey."

She rocks her pelvis against my hand, trying to get that final release.

"Ooohhhh, fuck."

"I know you want that, Ash, my mouth feasting on you, and the moment you come all over my tongue, I'd push my cock inside you and show you just how perfect you are. Close your eyes and picture me fucking you, Ash. Hard, and making you come all over my cock."

And that's all she needs to push her over the edge, screaming out my name like I'm her savior.

But the truth is, I'm more like her devil.

What kind of man has a woman coming from his touch, knowing he can't give her any more the moment the sun rises?

But I don't regret one touch or taste. I just have to hope Ash doesn't either.

ASHLEY

Nothing will ever beat the rough yet gentle feeling of a man's touch on my body, sending my heart racing with unexplainable pleasure. I'm not sure if it's because it's been so long that I've forgotten what being touched feels like. Or is it purely because it's Jake touching me?

Here in the cold dark woods, scared of what could be hiding in the trees and with my ankle injured, I have been begging a virtual stranger to touch me. The way he spoke in that low timbre and told me I was enough made me desperate for him to take away my ache.

He met my needs in such a way that all the words he whispered in my ear felt like he was reading my mind. Creating a warmth that flowed through me like nothing I have ever known, taking away the chill and fear of the night from my body. He barely touched my skin as his hand pressed down over my underwear, making me want everything he was promising.

I know I shouldn't have let things get so far, but there was no holding me back once my sex drive took over.

I'm not usually the kind of woman to have meaningless sex with a man. Yet here I am, my body floating after being played like an instrument. Technically we didn't sleep together, but he made me orgasm harder than I have in a very long time.

The shifting of Jake's weight from over top of me shocks me back into the here and now.

"Oh shit." I quickly do up my jeans and try to push my body out from underneath him and back up into a sitting position. I can feel the burning on my cheeks as embarrassment starts racing through me. How could I have let this get so far out of hand? My quick movements almost make Jake fall sideways as he tries to give me space. My brain is scrambled, and I'm desperate to put distance between us, but as I try to get to my feet, putting the slightest weight onto my ankle, Jake reaches out to balance me at the same time as the pain shoots up my leg.

"Argggghhh!" I can't help but call out, loud enough it has Rosie shifting from her spot next to the warmth of the fire.

"Steady there. Let me get you comfy again."

I don't want to look directly at him, although it's more like I *can't*. Because I have no idea what I will see in his eyes. Will he be looking at me and just seeing a desperate woman? Or will he be shocked at what I just asked of him? Me, the woman who has been hating on him since the day he arrived, has flipped and was just begging him for sex. I'm so confused, but I don't want him to see that. And if I glance at him, I know that look in his eyes will confirm my thoughts one way or the other.

"I can do it," I mumble under my breath as I adjust myself into a sitting position on the blanket and pull it up tight around my shoulders. Like I'm putting a barrier between us.

"Don't do that," Jake whispers as he gently places his rough hand on my cheek, turning me to face him.

I still can't bring myself to look at him, so my eyes remain downcast, and that's when I see it.

I might have gotten my release, but the bulge that is still pushing against his jeans must be agony for him. A good woman would offer to do something about that, but I'm too busy over here freaking out.

"I'm scared of snakes," I blurt out like some crazy woman. My eyes are stuck staring at his crotch, and the awkward moment is broken by Jake's loud laugh. He continues to lift my face, so I have no choice but to meet his eyes.

"Good to know, and I can assure you I'll protect you from any out here in the woods." He leans forward and kisses me on the lips again, ever so gently in such a contrast to the steamy one we shared a few minutes ago. "And the snake you riled up, I can assure you it won't be coming out tonight either. So just relax."

His voice is not much more than a whisper as he pulls away from me, standing and walking over to the other side of the fire to give me the space that I'm obviously needing. Picking up a bigger branch he had left beside the fire, he lifts his left knee and snaps it over his thigh without flinching. He then throws both pieces onto the fire, and as he walks back toward me, he stoops and grabs the empty water bottle.

Before I can say anything, Jake looks at Rosie, who's now wide awake.

"Stay with Ash." The demanding tone in his voice makes Rosie sit up and lean so close to me that her body is now pressing against mine.

"No, Jake!" I know we need water, but the fear that he just washed away for me with his mind-blowing distraction is creeping back in again.

"I'll be quick, and I'll sing out loud all the way down and back so you can always hear me. The phone is in the backpack if something happens. Rosie will protect you." And before I can say a word, he's gone, moving through the trees and over the embankment.

"Ten bottles of beer on the wall . . ." I can hear him loud and clear, and it's awful. I didn't think it was possible, but his singing is even worse than my drunk singing voice. As he gets to the end of the first verse, I hear him yell, "Sing with me, Ash." I'm smiling, it's so hilarious and suddenly find myself joining in to the duet of terrible voices.

"Nine bottles of beer on the wall . . ." I start to giggle as the words fall from my lips.

"I can't hear you." His voice echoes through the woods, which just makes me laugh louder. Shouting my words, I'm now actually smiling at the stupidity of what we are doing, and by the time we are down to two bottles of beer, he appears out of the shadows. I stop singing when I see him, but his head starts shaking side to side.

"Nope, you can't stop at two. Keep going."

Starting off the next line, I feel obliged to finish with him. He has done his best to distract me, and it has worked. I laugh at him still singing and lifting his arms out to his sides as he finishes with a bow on the last line.

"I don't know if that was bow worthy." I give him a half-hearted round of applause anyway.

"So rude. I'll have you know that I performed for you in my best singing voice, one that has earned having food and shoes thrown at me in many a bar." He leans down and gives Rosie a pat on her head for staying where she was told, and then he sits back down on his patch of dirt next to me, passing me the bottle of water. The relief of having him back so close to me again runs through me, and I can't help but lay my head on his shoulder.

"Thank you, Jake." And he knows it's not just for the drink.

Taking a small mouthful, it's so cold, and the fresh water coming from the mountain springs tastes amazing. I wish I had more confidence in the woods because I'm sure it's beautiful at the top of the falls, where the water cascades down into the river. Tiffany described it as a place where magic is born.

Sitting together, I let the silence wash over me. I know I need to talk to Jake about what happened between us. He might be trying to do the right thing by me by not mentioning it, but we are both adults, and I can't settle until I say something.

"I don't know what got into me before." With both of us gazing straight ahead into the fire, it makes it easier for me to talk.

"Same. I shouldn't have done that. It wasn't right." Jake's quiet reply makes me realize that he's feeling just as embarrassed as me. But I don't want him to take all the responsibility.

"Oh, I can assure you, *it* was right," I say under my breath, which brings a small chuckle from beside me.

"Like we said, 'what happens in the woods stays in the woods.' But I just want to make sure that you understand you should never settle when it comes to a man. Unless he treats you like you are his queen, then he isn't enough for *you*. You deserve more than that Jeremy guy."

I can feel him looking at me.

I have a sense that if he wasn't leaving again, Jake might just be that guy. But that fantasy is not even worth thinking about. He has an end date in Abbey Falls, and that's enough reason to stop this before we let anything else happen.

"Yes, sadly I worked that out, just after the fact, and that didn't help." Letting out a small sigh, I continue, "Please, can we just forget this happened?" Turning to look at him was a mistake. The softness of his stare and the smile lines beside his deep brown eyes tell me that neither of us will be forgetting tonight anytime soon.

"I want to say no, but we both know that's not the right answer. So, it looks like we just get to be neighbors, and I hope at least friends too?" He shrugs, and I really like this other side of the man I thought was an asshole.

"Friends, yeah, I can do that. On one condition."

"Why do I know I'm already going to regret this?" He pulls his knees up to his chest and links his arms around them. "Go on, let me have it."

"You let me show you how amazing animals are. I mean, for someone who didn't want a pet, Rosie has already won your heart." I drop the blanket from around me, not feeling like I need a barrier between us anymore, and then pull Rosie close to show her some love with a big pat.

"Ughhh, see? I told you I'd regret it. What makes you think Rosie and I are friends?" The pretend scowl on his face does nothing to stop Rosie from trotting over to him at the mention of her name and pushing her nose between his knees so she's all up in his face, waiting to receive her pat.

"Gee, I don't know, maybe the way she sat where you told her to, protecting me until you returned, and, oh, maybe the tail that is wagging like crazy now."

Both of us laugh happily, and I can feel my shoulders relaxing a little more as Jake pretends to be reluctant as he shows Rosie some love. But I know better now.

Pushing Rosie away so she will settle down to sleep again, Jake looks at me again.

"So, tell me about this fear of snakes . . . the scaled variety." He smirks at his insinuation.

"I'm surprised you didn't say the line that I'm a vet, so I should love all animals. That's what I usually get from anyone who finds out my fear." I roll my eyes to signal the frustration I feel when people react that way. "It drives me insane. But if you must know, it's sort of complicated, but when I was growing up, just turned ten, the only child, my parents and I vacationed in a cabin in the woods of Russian River Valley near San Francisco. They were having marriage problems and thought for some ridiculous reason that it would be a great idea to go lock the three of us in a cabin for five days. Which of course it wasn't. All that happened is I sat around listening to them fight and it got worse each day. Until the last night I was in my room, getting under the covers, and a rattlesnake came out of the cupboard. I started screaming but they were too busy fighting over a text message from a woman that my mom had just found on my dad's phone that they weren't even listening to me freaking out."

I can feel my anxiety from that night, the breathlessness and fear that no one was coming pressing down on me.

"Shit, Ash, that would have been terrifying." Jake puts his arm around my shoulders to comfort me and it feels like something unlocks, a little.

"Yeah. It felt like forever until they heard me and finally came in to deal with it. I just . . . yeah anyway, that's the reason."

We sit in silence for a minute, Jake's arm still warm around me, before he asks, "Are your parents still together?"

"No. Dad left with the woman he was having an affair with after we got back from that trip. Just another man who has walked out on me." God, I need to stop talking. Why am I telling him all my deepest, darkest secrets, no matter how nice he's being? No one knows this much about me in Abbey Falls except Tiffany, and I trust her to take my secrets to the grave.

I need to change the topic, so I start asking questions about Jake's family and their plans for Heatherbrae and thankfully we fall into a less emotional chat.

Jake looks intently up to the sky now and I follow his gaze.

"Have you ever looked at the stars, Ash, like really looked? They hold so much wonder and magic." He takes my right hand and points it to one of the spots through the trees. "Lay your cheek on your shoulder and look straight up your arm. See that really bright star that feels like it's blinking brighter than the ones around it? That's the North Star. My gramps spent hours teaching us about the stars but he would always start with the North Star."

The emotion in his voice is so heavy it makes my heart ache for him.

"I've never even thought about that they have names. To me they are just part of the pretty night sky that I quite often am standing under with an animal. To me it's just been a notion of feeling like you aren't alone in this world. I don't think I've ever said this out loud to anyone before, but when I was younger I would sit at my bedroom window when I was lonely and look out at the night sky. It was as clear and bright as this, but I would think to myself that somewhere in the world there was another child out there gazing up at the same stars, looking for a friend."

Maybe it's because I'm tired but the emotions of that time float to the surface and I try to contain them before I let the tears flow.

"Show me more," I ask Jake as he then points out the Big Dipper we can see through the trees, along with a few other constellations. I'm not sure who's more comforted, him or me.

I've been trying to keep myself from falling asleep, thinking that pulling an all-nighter should be easy enough, but even with the throbbing pain and my anxiety of where I am, I'm struggling to stay awake. I'm guessing Jake can tell it's time for us to sleep by the way my eyes keep slowly closing for a few seconds, then opening and closing again, staying shut longer each time.

"Let's lay down the blanket and wrap you in it. I'll stoke the fire enough so it will hopefully last until daylight." His hands are already smoothing out the blanket, which is crumpled around me on the ground from where I had discarded it earlier.

Jake's plan sounds great in theory, but if I close my eyes, I won't see any snakes approaching. I shudder involuntarily and try to pass it off as if it's from the cold. But the other problem is there is only one blanket and I can't have him sleeping in the dirt. That's just wrong.

"No, let's spread it out flat, then there is enough room for us both. It's my fault you're out here, so the least I can do is share your blanket with you." I push parts of the blanket so it lies flat and then wriggle my backside to one side to give him some room. Looking down, I think I have severely underestimated how wide this blanket is.

"Are you sure about that?" Jake notices my uncertainty.

"Yeeeppp." The *P* pops as I reluctantly agree, knowing it's the considerate thing to do, but also sensing this is going to be a long night lying so close to him.

"Okay, I'm just going to put it out there."

I can't tell from the look on his face what he's going to say. His expression is soft, but there isn't any hint of his dimple that shows when he's smiling either. Oh my God, he has a dimple. I knew that, but it never really hit me until now. Tiff's stupid tea leaves. She said one dimple. Feeling a small shiver running through me and I'm already trying to deny there is any correlation between Jake and the tea leaves. Tiffany's words are just that, words . . . surely.

"You're cold." His hands are now on my arms, rubbing them up and down. Little does he know the shiver has nothing to do with the air temperature. "Which was what I was just about to say. As soon as we drift off to sleep, the fire will keep going until morning but eventually die down, not giving us enough heat, and it's going to get really cold. I don't want you to feel awkward, but I think we will need to share body heat."

My heart hits the front of my chest so hard I'm sure it just broke a few ribs. I can't do that. I mean, yes, it makes sense, but I've just let this man touch me in ways that I will never forget, and I'm now so embarrassed that I can't look at him. I begged him to make me come, for God's sake, and now he wants to cuddle all night after we just agreed to be friends.

"Ash, stop spiraling in that head of yours. It's just to keep warm, that's all."

How the hell can Jake read my mind? And he can pretend it's just about keeping warm all he likes, but the strained lines on his forehead and the way his hands are shoved nervously into his jeans pockets but still fidgeting as he looks at me are giving away his nerves too.

"So far we just have a swollen ankle. We don't want to add hypothermia to that list."

Everything he's saying makes sense, yet my internal siren is going off, warning me that this is just going to make things more awkward than they already are. If there is one thing I have found out about myself over the last few years, it's that I can be stubborn when I need to be.

"Thanks, but I'll be okay. We will worry about that if needed." I get myself settled on the blanket and try to take up as little room as possible by lying on my side and keeping my body as straight as I can, with my back angled to him. But Jake just walks to the fire and throws on a few more logs before coming back to stand in front of me, looking down so he can get his last say. Crouching beside me, he gently lifts my head and slides his backpack underneath to give me some sort of pillow, then stands up again to his full height, which from my point of view on the ground looks a lot.

"Okay, let's see how that works out." And there is that familiar little smirk on his face that I want to call his *asshole smirk*, but I can't see anything nasty behind it this time, just more like a know-it-all look. Which just spikes my determination to survive through the night on my own, no matter how damn cold I get.

Feeling him lie down behind me, he might not be touching me, but I can sense every inch of him. He chuckles slightly as he gets comfortable.

"Good night, Ash. I'm over here if you need me."

His smug voice makes it sound like he's such a long way away, when in reality he's probably less than a foot. How the hell have I gotten myself into this situation?

"Good night," I mumble, as I now realize I can't sleep on this side of my body because it's putting pressure on my ankle. Begrudgingly, I try to roll over as quietly as possible, hoping he won't hear me move, but the stupid smirk on his face while his eyes are closed tells me he knows I'm now lying on my other side and looking directly at him. It's also going to be a little hard to stop myself from checking out all the little details on his face when I don't plan on sleeping tonight.

Oh, that's a good point.

As tired as I am, if I'm not going to sleep, I can keep getting up and stoking the fire so I won't get cold. Well, I won't be getting completely up, but I can crawl over to the pile of wood that Jake collected.

The days might be warmer, but I can tell by the way he's dressed that he obviously knows what he's doing when he heads into the woods for a hike. Proper boots, jeans, and a long-sleeved shirt to protect his skin. But there is no hiding the shape of his arms under that shirt, and the moment he lifts his arms above his head, linking his fingers together and dragging them back under his head to lie on, his biceps bulge, and the vision of his naked, sweaty body glistening in the sun that afternoon at Heatherbrae comes flooding back into my memory. I can feel my breath hitch, and I need to close my eyes to stop gawking at his arms. I've already embarrassed myself enough tonight, I don't need to make it worse.

In a way, I wish I could curl up into a ball, but there isn't enough room on this blanket, so instead I cross my arms tightly over my chest and try to think of serene happy places. Isn't that what they say you should do when you need to stay calm? But instead, I find myself focusing on the sound of Jake's breathing. All the noises of the woods around us seem to disappear, and it's like his slow deep breaths in and out are my own personal white-noise machine.

The dull ache in my ankle is still there, but the more I concentrate on Jake's breathing, the less it becomes my focus. The fear of the night is slipping away, along with the sounds around me.

It's just him, and I feel safe.

And that should scare the hell out of me, except surprisingly, it doesn't. But I can't guarantee I'll feel the same in the morning light.

JAKE

I'm surprised to hear the first little snore coming from Ashley, lying beside me.

To get her to rest, I closed my eyes, hoping she would do the same, but I didn't think it would work as well as it did. She must be exhausted from the pain and panic.

Opening my eyes and ever so slowly turning my head to the side, I take her in.

This woman is gorgeous.

Even in her most vulnerable state, she still glows, reminding me that when I've seen her the last few times, her skin has a natural tan to it. You can tell she spends plenty of time outside in the sunshine. Taking my time, I really look at her now. She has three little worry lines on her forehead, and just on the top of her nose, there is a faint sprinkle of freckles that runs across both of her cheeks. I have never noticed them before, but now I can't unsee them, even though they are so light in color. Wisps of hair have fallen onto her cheek, helping to soften the slight frown on her face. But nothing could dampen her beauty.

As the minutes pass, I notice her breathing is slowing to a nice steady rhythm and the creases on her forehead ease. As much as I try, I can't get the vision out of my head of watching her come, just from my touch.

I should regret it, but I don't. Having her under me, giving in to her base desire to let herself feel, was something special.

I know I'm not in Abbey Falls to find love, or even to have a good time. But there is this spark running through my body that's suggesting I reconsider not wanting to get involved with Ash. And that's not helping my cock to settle back down one little bit.

Looking at my watch, it's now 1 a.m. and I have been watching over Ashley as she sleeps for more than two hours. She's starting to hug herself tighter with an occasional shiver, so I know she must be getting cold. Although I have been keeping the fire going, there is a chill starting to seep up from the icy ground. I can feel it myself and know that the temperature is only going to drop more before the sun rises.

Slowly sliding myself sideways, my body is now right beside her. I can feel her breath on my face, and even though I know she was too embarrassed to accept my body for warmth earlier, I don't think we have a choice now. The last thing we want is for her to get hypothermia too. Gently placing my arm around her waist, I pull her to me. A shiver runs through her body, and she partially wakes.

"Jake." Her voice is barely above a whisper, and I'm not sure how coherent she is.

"Shh, just keeping you warm." And without another movement from me, it's like she can feel the heat of my body, and that's all it takes for her to mold herself against me. Drawing what heat she can, her body starts to relax, and the sound of her breathing slows again to the soft lullaby I have been listening to for hours.

I've forgotten what it's like to sleep holding someone. Thoughts of Danika float into my mind, but surprisingly only for a few moments. Because the way Ashley is now snuggled into my arms—dirty, cold, and hungry, on the ground in the middle of the woods—it still feels more like home than it ever did with Danika.

In my gut I know this is one of those moments that I will look back on in years to come, where I'll know it was the right woman but the wrong time. And I'll always be left wondering, what if.

Chapter Eight

Jake

As I start to wake, Ashley's scent is still in every breath I take, and my arms are still anchoring her to my body. I might have been lying on the ground, but once I closed my eyes last night, it was peaceful having her so close to me.

Opening my eyes to the dim morning light that is starting to peek through the treetops, I see that Rosie has also been watching over Ashley during the night, lying right beside her, perhaps also sharing her heat.

"Morning, girl," I whisper to Rosie, at the same time I notice how full my bladder is, and it's all I can think about. I need to get up, but that means moving Ashley without waking her, and that feels like an impossible task.

I'm not ready to let go of Ashley. This will be the only time I ever get to hold her like this. Running my hands slowly up and down her back, I listen to the sound of her breath and inhale her beautiful scent. Last night I took liberties that I don't regret but know I probably shouldn't have. Despite Ashley pleading for it from me, I shouldn't have let my own desire overcome my rational thought. But this here and now, just holding her, is less about desire and more to do with how right it feels.

Taking one last deep breath of the sensual scent of Ashley, I know it's time to start waking her. I'm surprised at how solidly she has slept and that I managed to get a few hours too.

"Ash. It's morning." The sound of my voice in the still of the morning has Rosie moving and startles Ashley into trying to sit up quickly. I hold on tighter to stop her from hurting her foot while she's still half asleep.

"Whoa there, just take it slow. I've got you." But the fact that it's morning, reality has quickly broken the peacefulness she found in her sleep. Already she's pushing away from me. Giving in, I slowly release my arms from around her. "Don't try to get up too quickly. You need to watch your ankle."

Once she's sitting up and balanced, I slide to my side of the blanket a little and push myself to sit up beside her. I try not to laugh as she turns her head away from me and brushes the hair from her face before straightening her shirt twisted around her body while she was sleeping.

"Did I sleep on you?" she asks, her voice hesitant, and as much as I want to sit and reassure her, my bladder is not going to hold on much longer.

"Yep, like I said, we needed to share body heat. You got cold." I get up and walk toward the bushes behind us. "Back in a minute."

"Wait, no, don't leave me. I'll come too." I hear her moving behind me.

I stop and spin back toward her. "Don't you dare get up and try to walk on that leg." My voice is loud and stern and causes her to halt. "I'll be just there." I point to the bush that I'm about to step behind. "I'm in desperate need of a pee, so sit and put your hands over your ears if you don't want to hear it." Not the conversation I want to be having with her, but I'm torn between her fear and the piss shivers that are running through my body, leaving goosebumps on my skin from my desperation of holding on to go.

"Oh, sorry," I hear her mumble as I step away.

Returning feeling so relieved, I see her sitting with her arm around Rosie's neck and giving her some love. The morning sun filters through the trees and shimmers on different parts of Ash's hair, giving her an angelic glow.

Stop it. Friends don't look at friends like that.

"Okay, we need to get you out of here." I look down on her as I walk toward the fire, checking the last of the warm coals and stomping out the last lingering glow with my boot.

"And what is your plan for that, because from what I have learned, you always seem to have one." She smiles up at me like I have all the answers. Which I do, but I doubt she's going to like them.

"Well . . ." I start, holding both her and Rosie's attention.

"I can't believe you have piggybacked me the whole way without complaining once. What are you? Some kind of superhero with your dog sidekick?" Ash's voice is right beside my ear from where she's perched on my back.

"Hey, that dog is not mine in any way, shape, or form," I reply as I negotiate around the last few branches sticking out from the trees on the edge of the woods and then look out to see Ash's car sitting where she left it, next to the fence line. The sound of a bark beside me gains my attention, and Rosie looks up, unimpressed with my comment about her.

What I wasn't expecting is to see Gramps's truck parked beside Ash's car, with Gran leaning against it wearing a smug grin and holding a travel mug. The moment Rosie spots Gran, she's off running down through the field like her ass is on fire.

"I'm just going to apologize up front for whatever Gran is about to say," I tell Ashley, as I wonder how long she has been sitting out here waiting for us.

Ash's laughter has her bouncing on my back, and she buries her face into my shoulder. "Not sweet old Betty." She tightens her arms around my chest, and I hitch her a little higher onto my back again to carry her the last thirty or so feet.

"Yeah, right." I know full well that Gran is not just here to make sure we are safe. If there is one thing Gran is, it's a lover of gossip.

As we approach the car, Gran rushes over to us. "Oh dear, you poor thing, Ashley. I hope my Jake looked after you." As I lower Ashley down onto the back tray of Gramps's truck, I see Gran raising her eyebrows up and down at me.

"He was amazing. I'm so lucky he and Rosie found me." As I lean around Ash to relieve her of my backpack she had to wear, I take in what will probably be the last deep breath of her alluring scent.

"Oh, I bet he was amazing, especially if he takes after his grandfather." Gran is chuckling to herself as she heads to the front of the truck, opens the passenger door, and pulls out a thermos and two cups. I hope like hell it's hot coffee.

"Gran," I warn her with a tone that is not too sharp but stern enough that she gets the idea.

"Oh, shush, you. Here, pour these." She hands me the thermos and cups and then reappears with a basket full of muffins and sandwiches. "I was guessing you would be hungry, you know, with no dinner and after working up such an appetite."

Oh, for fuck's sake, why doesn't she just come right out and ask whether we fucked each other last night? Gran is as subtle as a sledgehammer.

"I don't know, your grandson had a snack for me, like I've never tasted before." Ash just smiles at me, proud of her comment and the reaction she gets from Gran.

"I give up." I throw my hands in the air. "You two women are impossible." Rosie then nudges into my leg, trying to get my attention. "Okay, sorry, you *three* women." She lifts her head, satisfied, and then heads back to Gran where she sits at her feet and gets fed some muffin.

Pouring the coffee and handing it to Ashley, part of me is glad she's here safe on the truck now, but I also feel a little disappointed that our time in the woods is over.

"Drink up, and then I'll take you to the doctors' clinic over in Rocky Cedars to get you checked out." I watch as a strand of hair falls into her face and resist the urge to lean forward and tuck it behind her ear.

"Okay, but not before I've had a shower and changed out of these clothes." Lifting the warm coffee to her mouth, she takes her first sip of caffeine, letting out a moan that should be against the law for what it's doing to me right now. It takes me back to last night, her lying underneath me, racing through that orgasm, but it's not a thought I should be having with my grandmother standing right beside me.

"Was it that good?" The words slip out before I can stop them.

"Good doesn't even come close to describing that feeling." Her cheeks are glowing light pink, telling me that she wasn't talking about the coffee.

Reaching into the basket, I take a muffin and hand it to her.

"Eat," I growl.

Because if I don't stop those lips from moaning like that, then I'll have to give her something to moan about.

I walk away from her before my grandfather strikes me down with some lightning for having dirty thoughts in the presence of his wife.

I know these two women are about to drive me crazy, and there's not a damn thing I can do about it.

ASHLEY

"I told you some hottie was on his way to sweep you off your feet, and you didn't believe me. Shame on you, Ashley," Tiffany rants at me as she places a dinner plate on my lap where I'm perched on the couch with my foot up on the coffee table.

The moment we got back to my car this morning and I checked my phone, I saw all the messages from Tiff, who had gone into crisis mode, getting Adi to take control of the clinic and calling in Wade to be the emergency vet in my absence. It seems like I owe Wade more than a few favors when I finally get back on my feet.

"Now tell me again about this horrible neighbor with the big hands." Plonking herself down beside me, she pulls her legs up and crosses them as she starts picking at the salad she made herself.

"I didn't say he had big hands. You just made that up." I roll my eyes at her.

"Aha, but he did know what to do with them, obviously." She giggles.

I slap my hands over my eyes. "I can't believe I begged that man to make me come. What the hell is wrong with me? He must think I'm some lonely old spinster who lives on her own in the middle of nowhere, and the first new man she sees, she wants to jump his bones. Or worse still, a member of the Abbey Falls Desperate Women's society like the flock of gushing vultures he had around him at homemade Saturday. I'm never going to be able to look that man in the eye again." I groan, wishing I could pretend the whole thing never happened. "And that's sad because they are such sexy eyes."

"Are you crazy! That man is at home reliving every moment while trying to keep quiet as he gets himself off in the shower with his gran in the room down the hall." Tiff elbows me with a stupid grin on her face.

"Oh far out, don't even say that. It's bad enough I can't even look at Jake without blushing, so please don't include Betty in that problem too." I take another mouthful of the beef stew that Betty insisted Jake drop over to me this afternoon. I was hoping to get through the day without having to face him again, but obviously, Betty had other ideas.

"Well, you better get over your embarrassment because I have a feeling you will be seeing quite a bit of the not-so-grumpy next-door neighbor. I can feel it in my waters." Tiff is clapping her hands together madly, like an excited child. And in some respects, part of me thinks that's what she is; a spirit child who has never grown up. Which is why I love her. She always sees the good in everything and everyone. I wish I could say the same, but life took that joy away from me a long time ago.

"Ughhh! Seriously, I don't want to know what your waters are thinking about me."

Tiff gasps at my words, faking shock with her hand on her heart, which just has me playfully rolling my eyes at her.

"Come on, Ashley, would it be so bad to have a little fling with Jake while he's here? It would get you back in the saddle and I bet the sex would be amazing." Tiff looks at me curiously.

"You know why," I grumble.

"I know you've been hurt plenty of times. First your dad left you, then your mom abandoned you by throwing herself into her career, forgetting her heartbreak and that she had a ten-year-old daughter who needed her too. And then Jeremy left, and you've convinced yourself that love isn't worth it, but you're wrong." She places her hand over mine and I can sense how much she cares and is trying to help.

"Who said I'm looking for love?" I bite back harsher than I mean to.

"Me. Come on, I know you." Now taking a more serious turn, Tiff looks at me patiently. "What are you scared of, Ashley?"

All my fears are racing through my head, and I want to keep them to myself, but I'm so tired and Tiff has this way of getting me to voice my thoughts to her, no matter what.

"That I will never find that person that will want to stay. Nobody stays. I wanted all the pipe dreams too, a husband, a family, our little slice of heaven here on Windemere, my vet clinic and a whole lot less debt than I have now. But I just don't think it's going to happen for me. I know you are going to say something positive about the universe working its magic when it's ready etcetera, but I'm just afraid to even try for that anymore. I've given up on that dream."

Laying my head on the back of the couch and looking at the ceiling, I try to remind myself that my life is simple. Just me and my animals. I don't need anyone else. Especially someone like Jake, who brings with him his own baggage and is not here to stay.

The thought of us two together is just a disaster waiting to happen, and I'm done with that in my life.

"You might have given up on that dream, but I haven't, for you or for me. What does the old fairy tale say, one day your prince will come." Tiff sits up straighter on the couch like she's manifesting her good thoughts to the universe.

"Pfft. We both know we are far from being princesses and I'm definitely past believing in fairy tales." My body is now so tired I'm struggling to stay awake.

"I mean, I'm not looking for some stuffy regal guy. I'll take a dark prince any day of the week." She raises her eyebrows up and down as we both giggle a little.

"Sorry, Tiff, I need to get some sleep. Last night was a lot." I lean my head on Tiff's shoulder. "But I do love you for trying to keep the dream alive. Somebody needs to."

After Tiff cleans up from dinner and leaves, I lie in bed staring out the window at the sky, wondering what Jake is thinking about tonight.

And as much as I shouldn't want it, I hope it's about me. Because no matter how much I try, my mind is full of pesky *what if* questions about Jake that I just can't seem to find magic answers to.

Damn Tiff and her reminding me to dream of a perfect life. It's just making things messier than they already are.

I should've known no matter what, it was never going to *stay in the woods*.

◆ ◆ ◆

As I look back on the last week since my fall, I'm surprised so much has happened in such a short amount of time.

Thank goodness there was nothing too seriously wrong with my ankle. It was just a bad sprain that I needed to rest and keep elevated for a few days, which wasn't easy, but I managed. I'm now walking around in this stupid moon boot for at least another week, but I'm grateful to be mobile again. I couldn't have done it without Adi's assistance in the clinic and Jake's offer to drive me around to all the farms who needed callout visits. Which didn't help with trying to keep my distance from him, but I didn't have any other choice. But it showed Jake a different side of me, and there is nothing more attractive than walking around in cow shit with a plastic bag tied over a moon boot.

The first day seeing Jake again was awkward as hell, but we managed to get past it and have moved into the friend zone, sort of, which suits me. We keep a physical distance from each other and don't talk about our private lives. Meanwhile, I'm trying so hard to bury the memory of our night in the woods.

But it hasn't worked or stopped me from waking up with an ache between my legs, reliving the way he touched me. Last night I almost took matters into my own hands, but I'm trying to ignore the longing, hoping it will just go away. Making myself come while I'm imagining the dirty—very, very dirty—things I would like him to do to me is only going to make things worse. I hear that deep, husky sex voice now in all my dreams. It's branded into my brain.

Thankfully, the Australian vet, Beau, agreed to come to Abbey Falls for an interview. He's just finishing up another job and will be here at the end of next week so we can sit down and talk about the position. I don't believe you can get a real feel for someone over Zoom. Call me old-school, but this is such a huge step for me, and I want to make sure I get it right. But, the truth is, if he has a heartbeat and knows how to treat animals, at this stage, the job is his, no matter how much I tell myself I want to be picky. If this injury taught me anything, it's that I need to slow down a little. I just don't want to hire another jerk, like my ex.

I can't believe I'm even thinking it but hopefully this Beau guy is like Jake, just without the first-impression-asshole part.

Giggling to myself at the ridiculous thought, it's almost like I have conjured him up when Jake's name flashes up on my phone screen.

"Hi, Jake," I say, trying to sound light and like I'm not affected in any way by his call.

"Hi, Ash. How's your Sunday been? Quiet, I hope."

I feel my heart beating a little faster in my chest, and my hands get a little sweaty the moment I hear his voice.

"It has been, but I hope you haven't jinxed me now." Both of us laugh. "How about you, have you been working on the barn?" Seriously, what is wrong with me? We sound like a couple of sixty-year-old people having a conversation in the grocery store.

"I finally put the finishing touches to the very basic bathroom today, so my cousins can now arrive whenever they are ready. Though I think Gran's been missing me—she's come up with some creative excuses for me to stay in the big house until I got all the plumbing signed off."

I love listening to the way he speaks about his grandmother. As much as he jokes around about her gossip, there is also so much love behind his words. A man who treats his grandmother like he does can't be a bad man.

"Poor Betty, it must be lonely in that house now. I'm sure she misses Noel terribly. Lucky she has you to keep her company, oh and Rosie too, of course. How is my favorite furry friend?" Hearing him groan at my question, I can't help but giggle. "Come on, you can admit it, you love her too."

"Love is such a strong word." An awkward silence falls between us. "With Rosie, I mean, of course . . . but yeah, she's okay, let's just say that." Listening to him stumble over his words has me grinning. "Anyway, I was calling to ask if you wanted to come over and celebrate me finishing the barn. I could really use a beer and thought maybe we could grab a meal at Grizzly's, if you are up for it? I can pick you up on the way into town."

My thoughts are racing. Should I say no, because that sounds like a date of some sort, or is he just asking as a friend, because that's what we are? Yes, friends, just friends. And he has been so kind helping me out this week, how can I say no?

"Ah, yeah, sure, but it's my treat for all the help you have given me this week." Yes, if I'm paying, then it's just a friend repaying another friend for his kindness. I smack myself on the forehead, knowing that I'm clutching at straws here.

"Not a chance. I'll pick you up in thirty minutes—does that work for you?" He sounds determined, but two can play at that game.

"Sure. See you soon." I end the call and start to spiral on what the hell I'm going to wear. I mean, it's just a beer and meal with a buddy, so I could just stay in my jeans and change my shirt. I push myself off the porch swing and hobble inside, knowing that I'm about to rummage through my wardrobe because jeans and a shirt was never going to be an option.

Throwing a few skirts and dresses on my bed, I realize it's been a long time since I felt the urge to dress up nicely for a man, even if he's just a friend. Deep down in my stomach, I have the flutters of wanting to feel more feminine. I want to walk into a room and have a few heads turn and think I look pretty for a change. Instead of just a few nods, waves, and chin lifts from the locals because Doc has walked into the bar.

Shit, I need to stop thinking like this. And I know a surefire way to make certain this does not end up as a date.

ASHLEY: Meet me at Grizzly's in an hour.

TIFFANY: Ummm, is that a request or a demand?

ASHLEY: It's a be there or I might kill you because this is all your fault!

TIFFANY: Oooohhh, I love a mystery. What did I do now that warrants murder?

ASHLEY: You and your stupid tea leaves have me freaking out right now.

ASHLEY: So, you are going to be my SOS and stop me from doing anything stupid.

TIFFANY: What, like taking him home and finishing what you started?

ASHLEY: Exactly! So be there and do not, I repeat, DO NOT say anything to embarrass me, especially about sex. UNDERSTOOD?

TIFFANY: Me? I'm your best friend. You can trust me . . .

ASHLEY: I mean it, Tiff.

TIFFANY: Best behavior. Got it. See you soon.

ASHLEY: I'm so going to regret this, aren't I?

TIFFANY: Absolutely . . . not . . . maybe

"Ugh." I groan to myself as I throw the phone onto the bed, watching it sink into the pile of clothes that's staring back at me.

"Don't be ridiculous, just pick something casual and get on with it. He'll be here soon." They say talking to yourself is the first sign of going crazy, but lecturing myself out loud I think cements that title for me. I finally choose a dark burgundy skirt and a fitted white top that has one strap over my right shoulder. At least the skirt will cover up most of the moon boot and it won't look so silly.

Pulling my hair out of its braided ponytail, it falls down soft and wavy around my shoulders. I part it down the middle, tucking it behind my ears, before turning to look in the mirror, and I'm happy. Casual but feminine. Perfect.

◆ ◆ ◆

After I finish putting on a little makeup, I find myself pacing the front room as I wait for Jake to arrive.

My phone starts ringing and I pray like hell as I pull it out that it's not a callout emergency. Surely the universe can't be that cruel. The first time I have had a *non-date* night out in years and it's about to be over before it begins.

Damn it, it's an unfamiliar number, which means my night is about to turn to shit.

"Hello, Doctor Alleyne speaking." My professional voice rattles off my tongue from muscle memory.

"Ashley."

I hear a voice that makes me freeze. My blood runs cold and I feel like I'm about to lose the contents of my stomach. I can't speak.

"Ashley, don't hang up, please. I just want to talk to you."

It's been three years since I've heard Jeremy's voice. One that used to whisper to me in the dark at night to soothe me, but now it's one that just brings pain like a punch to the gut.

"We have nothing to talk about," I barely manage to mumble.

"I'm sorry, Ashley," he rushes to say.

"For what!" I feel anger starting to rise in my body at his pathetic attempt at a blanket apology. "Breaking my heart, ripping my life out from under me, putting your dick in another woman while you were still fucking me, or just for being a pathetic piece of shit." I'm now screaming into the phone.

Silence is on the other end and as I'm about to hang up, he finally speaks.

"Yeah, all that."

I take a deep breath to try to calm myself down but then he says the words that blow me away instead.

"I need you. I need a job, and you need a vet. I saw in the job ads. We make a good team. You wouldn't have to do anything. I could just slot right back in."

The evil laugh that leaves me is like a part of me is being exorcised.

"Are you fucking kidding me?" I can't help but swear because it's what he deserves. "You are an absolute prick who not only abandoned me but abandoned Abbey Falls and you think that either of us will forgive you for that and invite you back so easily. Go crawl back into the arms of your plastic-looking bitch, or doesn't she want you now? Oh, that's it isn't it, please tell me, not only are you jobless but she kicked you to the curb too. That would just make my day."

My evil laugh continues as I'm back pacing my living room, as awkward as it is with a moon boot on. But my heightened emotions are running wild, and I can't stand still.

"We broke up six months ago and the job that she helped me get when I moved here has now asked me to leave, which I think she had something to do with."

As he pauses, I know it's malicious, but I feel like saying the words *karma's a bitch* but I'm better than that. Then his voice gets a little softer like he's struggling.

"You were never a cruel woman when we were together. What has happened to you?"

The audacity!

"You! You happened. You stripped me raw and I had to rebuild myself with the help of some of the most caring people in this town. And you're right, I'm not the woman you left. I'm the new and improved Ashley. A woman who will never . . . ever . . . let a man walk over the top of her again."

Deep inside me I am crying for all the pain he caused me but, in my head, I am being my own cheerleader as I finally get the chance to stand up to him and tell him what I think of him.

"Can I come and see you, so we can talk properly, face-to-face? If you can forgive me and move on, so will the people of Abbey Falls. I virtually gave you that clinic—you owe it to me to give me another chance."

The tone of his voice is changing and I'm done.

"All you gave me was debt after buying you out, and a workload that has almost killed me. You were happy to sign the papers the lawyers sent you and walk away to your new fancy life." I'm done with this. "Goodbye for the final time, Jeremy. Don't contact me ever again. I'm happy. I don't need you dragging me back down again. I've learned there are better men out there, better than you will ever be. I now know that you pissing off did me a favor. You aren't even half the man Jake is. So, I guess I'll say thank you for opening my eyes. Bye."

Pulling the phone from my ear, I can hear him screaming "*Who the hell is Jake?*" as I push the red button with more force than is needed.

My heart is racing and my blood is pumping so hard I can feel it. Sucking in air trying to take a deep breath to calm myself is easier than it sounds.

What the actual fuck just happened?

So many thoughts are running in my head.

The fear of him turning up in Abbey Falls, anger at him accusing me of robbing him of his share in the clinic, pity that his life has brought him to the point of begging, pride in myself for sticking it to him but most of all surprise that I brought Jake into it. And my stomach drops as I come face-to-face with the fact that I'm fooling myself if I don't admit how much I'm wishing that this was more than dinner and that Jake was staying after his twelve months are up.

When Tiffany started talking about our dreams the other night, I was afraid to voice my true dream aloud, that I will find a man who wants to be here in Abbey Falls, and not because I ask him to. A man who loves me for who I am and gives as much to a relationship as I do. My mom fought so hard to keep my dad and it made no difference because he had already checked out. I understand now that if Jeremy was off looking for someone else more exciting when he was with me, then he was never fully committed to what I thought was our shared dream.

I can feel the tears coming but I'm determined to keep them at bay.

"I will never shed another tear over that man. He has taken more than enough from me," I say out loud.

I take a deep breath and hold it for a moment, then slowly release it, along with the shock of what just happened that had every muscle in my body so tense.

Looking down at my phone that I'm still clutching so tightly the knuckles on the fingers in my left hand are white, a message comes through from that same number. Pressing Delete before I even open the message, I block the number. It doesn't mean I will be able to stop him, considering he called on a new number and caught me off guard, but it's something.

I want to call Tiffany but it's too late because I hear Jake's truck coming up the driveway. Putting my game face on, I grab my bag, walk out the front door, and hurry—as fast as I can in a moon boot—down the porch steps. I don't want him coming to the door. That would make it feel more like a date than it already does. I plaster a smile on my face because I'll be damned if I let Jeremy wreck this night for me.

As the truck pulls to a stop, I swing open the passenger door and climb in, not giving him the chance to get out of the truck and come around to open my door.

"Hey," I greet him as I pull the seat belt across me, buckling it up and then looking across at him. His eyes are locked on me, and the smile on his face tells me that he likes what he sees. And that makes me feel better than it should, sending Jeremy's unwanted call right to the back of my mind.

Jake wants me as much as I want him and although we both know it can't happen, that is enough to soothe me tonight.

"Hey to you too." He hasn't taken his eyes off me and looks like he's about to say something else but then thinks better of it, puts the truck in gear, and we start moving toward the front gate.

And I leave the upset of the last fifteen minutes behind me.

Tonight, I just want to relax and imagine what it would be like to be with Jake for real and let the fantasy drown out everything else.

But the reality is, that's easier said than done.

Chapter Nine

Ashley

Pulling into the parking lot of Grizzly's, there are plenty of vehicles, which means we won't look out of place having a meal with the bar almost empty.

I can tell Jake is still finding his feet in Abbey Falls by the way people are staring at him, curious to know more about this man. They would've all seen him at the town square that day and I'm sure the gossip mill has been running rampant ever since.

Waving to Regina behind the bar, she raises her eyebrows at me, giving me that smirk she wears so well, and we head to an empty table at the back. Heads turn in our direction as we make our way through, and I can feel the sweat prickle on my back from the anxiety of everyone's interest. I am so not looking to get back onto the Abbey Falls gossip chain. I feel myself tense up when I see women leaning across tables to their spouses or friends and then looking pointedly back to us. I want to stand up on a chair and get everyone's attention, yelling out the word "*Friends!*" just to stop the whispering, but what's the point.

"Is it just me, or do you also feel like we are in a fishbowl tonight?" Jake whispers into my ear as he leans around me to pull out my chair. Tingles rush down my body at the warmth of his breath on my skin and the familiarity of his body being so close to mine.

"Welcome to Abbey Falls, where everybody knows everything about you—whether you like it or not." I can't help but giggle as I sit down and he takes the seat across from me.

"I thought it was only the oldies, Gran's friends, you know, that era." Picking up a laminated menu from the table and passing it to me, he rolls his eyes. "Tell me what you want, and I'll go up and order. Are you a beer or wine drinker?"

Thinking back to the first night I saw him here and the amount of alcohol I had consumed, plus my adrenaline is still running from my phone call, I decide that sticking to a light beer tonight might be the right choice. "Just a light beer would be great, thanks. And I don't need a menu; I'll have the veggie burger with fries, please. It's one of my favorite things here, and as much as I always think I'll try something different, I never do." I shrug. "Creature of habit."

"Nothing wrong with that, and what better recommendation is a meal that you can't stop eating. I think I'll get one too. Back in a minute." He pushes his chair back from the table then stands, and I'm watching him walk over to place the order at the bar with Regina. I can see her smiling at whatever he said, which weirdly makes me feel annoyed. I'm not jealous. Who am I kidding? Even though I know I can't have him, that doesn't mean I'm happy for anyone else to have him either.

Shit, I really am in trouble here.

Jake's loud laugh has a few people in the room looking toward the two of them chatting at the bar. This is good, surely. They will see that he talks to many women, not just me. Jake flirting with Regina confirms to the room that we aren't together. So why am I still pissed?

Arriving back at our table, he looks so relaxed and still has that smile where his lips are parted and the corners of his mouth are pulled up, causing his cheeks to jut out a bit, with a sparkle in his eyes. “Regina has a wicked sense of humor,” he comments as he places the beer in front of me.

“Yes, she does. She’s great, until you piss her off and the tough bitch in her comes out. Be careful of that one.” I can’t help it, but I don’t want him getting too cozy with her.

“Oh, I don’t doubt it. You can’t run a bar and not have people scared of you in some way. But don’t worry, she’s got your back over there.”

He’s taking his first long sip of beer from his glass and I watch his throat flex with his swallow. Then his tongue is swiping the residual beer froth off his top lip, and the vision’s doing things to me it shouldn’t.

“What do you mean, she has my back?” My brain is now catching up to what he just said.

“She was commenting how the whole room is looking at me like I’m fresh meat for the poor, lonely vet. They already have us married off with two kids and driving a minivan. So, she told me if it looked like I was flirting with her at the bar, then it would throw them off the scent.” He looks at me, satisfied that he played his part well, and I can’t help but burst out laughing.

“Enough of the lonely vet, thanks. I’m perfectly fine on my own.” I don’t like that tagline when anyone is describing me and tonight it feels especially raw. Maybe I’m trying to remind both Jake and me that I am indeed okay being single.

“Seriously, though, this place is crazy, and the people that live here are next level sometimes.” Shaking my head and taking a sip of my beer, I didn’t realize how much I needed it until now.

“Yeah, I’m starting to learn that. But I did make sure Regina understood that we are just friends.” His face turns serious as he looks at me. And I know I should be happy about that, but I'm finding it harder and harder to turn my feelings off when I'm around him.

His face changes a little as he focuses intently on me.

"Are you okay, Ash?"

"Yeah, why?" I'm trying not to give away how much my stomach is churning from Jeremy's phone call earlier and that it's now mixing with the growing desire I have for Jake that I'm struggling to ignore.

"You just look a little preoccupied. Anything I can help with?"

I wish. I'm sure if I told Jake, then he would be ready to hunt Jeremy down, because he has already shown how disgusted he is with what Jeremy did to me. Although I could do with that feeling of protection if Jeremy does decide to turn up back in Abbey Falls. But it's not something I want to share with Jake right now.

Plastering a smile on my face, I reply, "No I'm fine, thanks. Just tired and you have already helped me plenty since my fall. So being here for a nice meal and good company is what I need and gives me the chance to say thank you for everything you've done." I lift my beer glass up and clink it against his. He seems to accept my response so I change the subject.

We fall into general talk about the barn apartment reno he has just finished, and Jake shuffles his chair around the table closer to me so he can show me the photos on his phone.

"They look awesome. I thought they were just meant to be temporary, but you could live permanently in those. The only thing missing now are your cousins." I don't know why I'm surprised the barn conversion is so good. He's a builder, after all.

"If I had the money, I would employ you to fix up my house. I have the vision, just not the time nor the budget." Handing his phone back, I see him looking agitated. "Sorry, I wasn't hinting for your help. You've already done more than enough with the fence and driving me around." Dropping my gaze to my hands where I'm suddenly so fascinated by my fingernails, I start picking at them.

"Ashley." His anger is evident in his voice. "Look at me," he demands.

I raise my head and try to act like I don't have anything to be embarrassed about, but I'm crap at lying.

"I'm not pissed at you. I'm sorry if you thought that. The asshole who left you in this situation, that's who I want to have serious words with. I know what it's like to be stripped bare when someone walks out and takes everything with them."

Reaching over and placing his rugged hands on top of mine, in such a gentle way, is completely in contrast with his demeanor right now. "He better not show up while I'm in town, because he won't like what I have to say to him."

Tingles run up my arms at the thought of Jake protecting me from Jeremy and making him pay for the douchey thing he did to me. Little does he realize that Jeremy is not as tall as him, and there are no bulging biceps like Jake's that constantly peek out from under his shirt sleeves. They are nothing alike, and I'm looking back now wondering what I ever saw in Jeremy, but of course, hindsight is a bitch.

"You don't have to worry. Jeremy drove out of town and never looked back. I can't imagine there is any reason for that to change," I reply, hoping that is the truth. Surely, after what I said tonight, Jeremy won't show up here. Instead of letting it get to me again, I concentrate on the warmth of Jake's hands on mine. It's so comforting, safe, but I know I need to move because this intimacy is enough to keep fueling the rumor mill.

"Well, isn't this cozy." Tiffany's voice makes me jump in my seat, and our hands separate instantly.

"Tiff, w-what are you doing here?" I stumble over my words, trying to sound casual, as though I'm not expecting her.

"You told me to come, or to quote your exact words *'be there or I might kill you.'* Yeah, that sounds about right." She has the stupidest smile on her face as she pulls over a chair from a spare table next to us.

I can feel my cheeks burning as Jake starts chuckling so loudly that people start turning around and looking in our direction.

"Ooohhh, I wasn't supposed to repeat that. Oops." Her hand hovers over her mouth, but I can still see the joy she's getting out of this.

"There is no *might* in that sentence now. I will be killing you tonight, the moment we walk out of here where there are no witnesses." I reach over and push her a little in the shoulder, which just makes her grin back at me.

Offering her hand to Jake, she says, "Hi, I'm Tiffany, the best friend. I'm sure you've been avoiding meeting me, or she's keeping you hidden. Either way, I'm here now."

Jake takes her hand and looks back at me, where I can see the amusement in his eyes. The frustration and anger from a few moments ago is gone, and all I see now creeping in is intrigue.

Before he even has time to blink, Tiff has flipped over his hand and is running her fingers across his palm.

"Good strong lifeline. Hmm, the heart line has a little kink, then comes good . . ."

Jake looks so confused at her words.

"Tiff, stop it! Put your woo-woo back in your pocket for tonight," I scold as I pull her hand away from Jake's.

"What the hell is woo-woo?" Jake's head is swiveling between us.

"The spiritual wisdom of the universe," Tiff replies profoundly at the same time as I say, "The weird shit that comes out of her mouth that she believes with her whole soul is a look into someone's future."

"Oh." Tiff gasps theatrically and her hand flutters over her heart. "Like a stab to my heart."

And I roll my eyes in response with a smirk. She might be a little crazy, but I love her.

"Okay . . ." Jake is looking between us, clearly perplexed.

"Ignore her dramatics. Jake, meet Tiffany. She's the owner of the teahouse, town woo-woo lady, and most days my friend."

"Nice to finally meet you, Tiffany. Sorry I haven't made it into the teahouse yet. More of a coffee drinker myself, and I've been kept kind of busy since I arrived." Jake starts to relax, realizing that this exchange is normal between Tiff and me.

"Oh, I've heard how busy you've been. Especially in the woods . . ." Tiff leans back in her chair as she settles into the conversation, and just like I predicted, I'm totally regretting inviting her. Glancing in my direction as I stare back at her in disbelief, she continues, "rescuing poor Ashley and all."

Before I can say anything, Regina arrives at the table with our food and places three veggie burgers with fries down in front of us.

"How did Tiff get food already?" I ask Regina, who's just grinning.

"She called ahead. You're crazy if you think she was going to sit here, third wheeling and watching you two on a date, without at least getting a free meal in." She also places what looks like a soda water in front of Tiff.

"Seriously, it's not a date," I mumble as Regina starts smirking and walks back to the bar, picking up empty glasses and plates on her way. "Remind me next time when I think it's a good idea to ask for your help that it's not." I take one of the fries off Tiff's plate while she and Jake chuckle at me.

"So, tell me more about yourself, Mr. Hero," Tiff says and takes the first bite of her burger.

"It sounds like you already know everything about me."

I'm not sure if I should be embarrassed or cheering on Jake for keeping Tiff on her toes.

"Touché, Jake. I think you and I are going to get along just fine. Friends, just not like *this* kind of friends," she says, waving her hand between Jake and me.

"I give up," I mutter and stuff more fries into my mouth.

The conversation between us all settles into a comfortable flow as we eat our dinner, and it's good to see Tiff and Jake bounce off each other so that nothing is awkward.

Just as I'm finishing my last bite, I see Mr. James making a beeline for us.

"Doc, good to see you out. I heard you hurt your foot." He stands over our table, holding a takeaway container of dinner for him and his wife.

"Hi, Mr. James. Yes, just a silly sprain. I'm fine. Have you met Jake, Betty's grandson?" I know he's standing there waiting for the introduction.

"No, not yet. Nice to meet you, young man. Now, you take care of our lovely little Doc here. That last one was no good, so I expect any grandson of Noel and Betty will treat her better." Patting his hand on Jake's shoulder to reinforce his point, it feels like Mr. James is warning him that the town will be after him if he doesn't.

"Oh, Mr. James, you are very lovely, but Jake and I are just friends," I say in my sweetest voice at the same time as Jake answers.

"You have my word, sir." Which results in an approving nod from Mr. James, and he's already waddling off toward the door.

With my elbows on the table, I drop my head into my hands in frustration and hear Jake and Tiff laugh.

"And this is the reason I don't live in the middle of town, not that it matters by the sounds of it. I'm still this week's top-ranking gossip topic." I suppose it could be worse. Oh, who am I kidding, it has been worse, and I survived it. I can only hope that this too will pass.

It's then that my brain catches up on what Jake just replied to Mr. James. He didn't rebut the insinuation or try to offer a different explanation of why we are here tonight. Instead, he pretty much confirmed the rumors are true.

What does that even mean?

My head is so tired from the craziness of my emotions swinging from one thing to another tonight.

I just need five minutes to clear it.

I push my chair back from the table slightly as Jake and Tiff look at me questioningly.

"I just need to go to the ladies'." I'm standing and getting my balance before I take a step with this awkward moon boot on my leg.

"Oh, good. Me too." Tiff jumps up from her chair and takes me by the arm as we start to move.

"Women and bathrooms." Jake is chuckling to himself as we leave him at the table.

As soon as we clear the door into the bathroom, Tiff starts checking all the stall doors to make sure we are alone.

"Okay, spill it. What's wrong?" Tiff asks.

"I need to pee. That's why most people go to the bathroom." Pushing past her into one of the empty stalls.

"Oh, I thought it was girl code that you needed to talk," she yells through the door. "But since we are here, I may as well pee too."

I hear the door to the stall next to me close and we both go about our business but as soon as I'm at the basin washing my hands and looking at myself in the mirror, even I can see the stress lines.

"Right. Now, I can concentrate. Enough of the bullshit. What's going on and I know it's not Jake, because that man out there is one massive green flag if ever I've seen one. So, something else has you wound up tight. Whatever it is, out with it." She's turning me around so I'm facing her. Tiff's now standing with her hands on my shoulders, staring me down.

"Fine." I sigh. "Why can't I ever get anything past you? You are such an annoying friend. You know that."

"I know. Go on."

"Now I don't want you to yell and scream and make a commotion when I tell you this." She nods. "Jeremy called before Jake picked me up and begged me for the new vet job at the clinic." I wait for the explosion but instead it's just pure shock.

"What the ever-loving hell was he thinking? I'm so shocked. I mean seriously, does he not realize the moment he steps foot in Abbey Falls, I will kill him and I'm not the only one? I will be lining up behind you and probably Jake if I'm reading him right, because he's falling for you big-time, whether you both care to admit it or not. But fuck me, Jeremy has lost it, truly." Tiff pulls me to her and wraps me in a hug, which is just what I needed without realizing it.

"Yeah, I know. But I still feel sick about it," I whisper into her shoulder. "And he said he wants to come and see me so we can talk it out."

My body is pushed off Tiff's shoulders.

"You better have told him no way, no how. That man is never getting near you again." Now with her hands on her hips, Tiff looks like she's quickly trying to come up with ways to protect me from Jeremy. "I don't own a gun and have no idea how to shoot, but I'll find every farmer in Abbey Falls to stand on the road into town and give him a message from all of us. He's not welcome here, simple as that. Don't you worry, chick, we've got you."

I can't help but start to laugh at the picture I'm imagining. Not just a giggle but a deep belly laugh has me now doubling over at the craziness of the idea, but I also wouldn't put it past Tiff.

"Did you tell Jake? Yes, that's what we need to do, tell Jake. He will protect what's his." And now Tiff is off in her own little world, solving the problem for me.

"Tiff." I try to gain her attention even though she's still muttering to herself about some spell she's going to cast on Jeremy.

"Tiffany!" I'm more forceful this time.

"What?" She looks at me, confused.

"We are not lining up guns at the city limit sign, and we are certainly not saying one word to Jake about this. Do you hear me? He's just a friend. That's it, end of story." I'm pointing my finger at her, making sure she understands how serious I am about her keeping this to herself.

"But . . ." she mutters.

"No 'but.' You keep this to yourself. Jeremy may have left me in a blubbering heap when he left last time, but I'm not that woman anymore. If he turns up here, I'm strong enough to deal with it myself." And for the first time since he called, I actually feel like I am. Because if there's one thing I've learned after Jeremy left, it's that you need to make your own way in this world.

"If you say so. I don't like that plan, but I'll respect it," Tiff says, crossing her arms over her chest.

"Um, who are you and what have you done with my meddling friend? She doesn't back down that easy." I step forward and put my arm around her as we head out of the bathroom.

"Yeah, well, I didn't promise not to put a dark spell on him, so there's that."

JAKE

There is something about Abbey Falls that I never felt as a child here on vacation because I wasn't looking for it.

It's a sense of family and belonging.

Everyone looks out for one another, and that's so different to Sacramento. I remember overhearing my mom say that she was glad that Gramps and Gran didn't move to Abbey Falls until after she had left for college. She said that hearing all the stories Gran tells her that she would hate the way people in small towns seem to poke their noses into each other's business. Mom prefers living in big cities because nobody knows anyone, so you can just live your life under the radar.

Which all sounds great until your life starts falling apart and you realize there is no one there to pick you up. Your buddies have good intentions, but then their partners are friends with your ex, so of course they start calling less often and your invites for those nights out for pizza as a group get lost in the mail. So, there is a small part of me that would be happy with the nosy nanas and opinionated old grumpy grandfathers involving themselves in my life.

"I think it's time to call it a night before any more of my lovely fellow Abbey Falls clients feel the need to come over and chat." I can tell by the look in Ashley's eyes that she's struggling with the constant attention and whispers. Even with Tiffany showing up, it hasn't really changed the vibe.

"I can get Tiff to take me home so you can stay and enjoy another beer." Ashley pushes back her chair and stands.

Not a chance.

"No need for that. I'm feeling a bit tired after a long day. Let's head out." I stand quickly and move the chair out of the way so she doesn't catch it with her boot. "Tiff, can I give you a ride home?" I offer, without knowing whether she drove or even where she lives.

"No, thanks, I'm fine. I live just down the road at the back of the teahouse. It makes the early mornings easier." Tiff also stands and then hooks her arm into Ash's, and they start walking toward the front door. Following them, I watch as they lean in close together and start whispering between themselves. I can only imagine the conversation but would guarantee it's about me.

Ashley and I say our goodbyes to Tiffany, and as we drive back out to Windemere in a not completely uncomfortable silence, I can tell that Ash is feeling a little uptight about the whole dinner and I kick myself. Tonight was supposed to be a bit of fun and relaxation over a meal.

When we turn into her driveway, I try to say something, anything, to prolong the evening.

"I know it's easy for me to say because I don't live here, but you need to ignore them." Reaching over and placing my hand on her arm, I give it a squeeze as her house comes into view.

"You're right, it's easier said than done. But thank you. I know you are just trying to help. It's not just tonight. I've just got some things on my mind."

"I knew the moment I picked you up that something wasn't right. Want to talk about it? Sometimes it helps. I know we aren't in the woods anymore, but the same thing applies. Whatever you tell me stays with me. I might not be Tiff but I'm a pretty good listener." I place my hand on her thigh and start rubbing it up and down in a reassuring way. I know I'm being a bit of a hypocrite because I am carrying my own problems that I haven't shared with anyone either. But I want to help her, however I can.

She sighs and keeps looking out the window, not wanting to look at me, so I guess that's the end of that.

"Jeremy contacted me tonight," she blurts out suddenly, "and he told me he wants to come and see me, and it rattled me, a lot." Her eyes are wide as she turns quickly to me and then throws her hand over her mouth. "God, I'm an idiot, I wasn't going to tell you, but you have this annoying habit of getting me to open up to you."

The rage inside me is building at the thought of her having to face the man who shattered her entire world and never even looked back or even cared about what he even did to her, until now. My protective instincts for Ash are roaring to life, and I'll be damned if I let him hurt her like that again.

"Ash . . ." is all I get out when she gasps and points to her house. "Why is my front door open?"

I sit up a bit straighter, seeing the worry on her face. My body is now on high alert.

"Are you expecting anyone, besides him?" I put the truck in Park and stop her moving before she has the chance to undo her seat belt. I watch her shake her head from side to side, indicating this isn't normal. "Okay, stay here until I go in and check who it is."

"No way. It's my house!" She glares back at me, and it's as though the meek woman who was worried about the town gossips at the local bar and grill is long gone and the warrior is back.

"Fine, but you stay behind me. Understood?" I demand and wait for her agreement before I let go of her seat belt.

"Okay," she grunts, and I'm out of the truck and around to her side before she manages to even take a step. Hearing her donkey braying loudly from the barn, it feels like something is not quite right here, and it has me on edge.

Stalking up the porch and toward the front door, I can hear Ashley shuffling quickly behind me as she struggles to keep up with me in her moon boot.

And now, standing at the open door to her house, I hear movement coming from inside; there's definitely someone here.

"If it's your ex in there, I'm warning you now, he won't be walking out on his own two feet. He will be getting what he deserves." I'm not usually much of a fighter, but for Ashley, I'll make an exception.

"Let's go," I mutter as I take the first step through the door. *Bring it on, asshole.*

Chapter Ten

Jake

Creeping down the hallway toward the noise, it's quiet for a moment before it changes to what sounds like something being dragged along the floor.

Glancing over my shoulder, I whisper, "What room is that?"

"The kitchen." Ashley glances back at me with a look of confusion.

I take a few more steps, and as I stand tall then turn into the room, what I see is nothing like I was expecting. I stare down the assailant and can't help but start to laugh as Ash gasps from behind me.

"Daisy! What are you doing in here? Look what you've done," Ash yells, and as she starts to step around me, I quickly jut my arm out to stop her.

"Don't," I tell her sternly while pushing her toward a small table and a couple of chairs. "Sit. We don't want you with any more injuries." Pulling the chair out, I place my hands on her shoulders and push her down into it.

"But I have to get her out of here." I know Ash's worry is more for Daisy's safety than her kitchen, which looks like there has been a food explosion all over the floor.

"Let me handle her. It's not like we haven't had this discussion once before." I turn back to look at Daisy, who couldn't give a shit that I'm in the room. She's already back to eating the box of Cheerios that she has chewed the corner out of, spilling them all over the place.

"Oh yeah, I remember that vividly."

I can't tell if Ashley is amused or thinking back to how pissed off she was with me the first time I had to handle this goat.

"Daisy, it's time to vacate the premises." Moving toward her slowly, I try to guide her to the door, but then it occurs to me that the doors of all the other rooms in the hallway are also open. So shooing Daisy out of the kitchen is only going to push her into another room and that will spread the mess.

The contemptuous way she looks up at me from her late-night snack and then goes right back to munching tells me that this might be harder than I initially thought. But I'll be damned if I let a goat get the better of me.

"That'll do it. She looks like she's ready to obey." Ashley sniggers beside me.

Daisy, I'm not letting you make a fool of me in front of Ashley. She might know I'm not an animal lover, but I'm not about to hand in my man card just yet.

"Right, we can do this the easy way or the hard way, Daisy, do you want to pick?" I try to keep the calm voice that Ashley has been encouraging me to use when I'm around animals. But as soon as Daisy walks a few steps and turns her ass so it's facing toward me, I know it's game on.

"So that's how you want to play it then. Right, let's go." Striding with purpose toward her, I try grabbing her with one hand on each side of her belly, but her back legs kick up at me, hitting me hard in the shins.

“Fuck, that hurt,” I exclaim as Daisy jumps a few times and then trots across the kitchen toward the fridge. She glares at me, as if to say, “*Is that all you got, buddy?*”

“Okay, don’t complain, because this is the way you chose to play this.” Walking while dodging the smashed eggs and bread on the floor, I hear Ashley belly laughing like this is some comedy skit, but I can assure her it’s far from funny.

I’m now three feet in front of the goat, and she starts backing up a little. Every step back she takes, I take another one forward. She’s playing straight into my hands and backing herself into a corner, surrounded on either side by cupboards.

“I’ve got you now.” Taking the last step, I reach out to grab her horns, but my foot slips on some mushed banana and I can feel myself falling sideways. At the same time, the horns I was reaching for slam into my chest, changing my direction and pushing me backward until I’m lying on the floor where she jumps over me and runs out of the room.

Staring up at the ceiling, I can hear Daisy’s hooves on the floorboards heading in the direction of the front door, and feel the moisture seeping through the back of my shirt from the smashed eggs and who knows what else is on the floor.

“Great, just great,” I mumble as I try to sit up, but each time I put my hand down to push myself up, it slips, making an even bigger mess.

“Shit, do you need help, Jake?” Ashley is just out of my vision, and her giggle is muffled as though she’s trying to hold it in.

“No!” I grumble, just lying on the floor, annoyed and embarrassed. When I finally manage to push myself up and turn around, Ash has the biggest smile I have seen all night plastered across her face, and I can’t help it. A deep chortle rumbles from inside me, and I’m laughing with her. “I must look ridiculous.” Standing and wiping my hands on my jeans, even the back of my head feels damp as I run my hands through my hair, and they come out with bits of eggshell.

"Ahhh . . . what makes you say that?"

I walk toward her ever so slowly with my sticky hands out in front of me, and a look of panic crosses her face.

"You wouldn't. I'm a poor injured woman just sitting here innocently watching you wrangle a harmless little goat." She pushes her chair as far back as she can and reaches out her hands to fend me off, which is truly no use.

"Harmless my ass. That thing is a terror. And you wonder why I don't like animals." I wave my hands in the direction of the mess. "Maybe you should have Daisy on that town welcoming committee with you. There is no way anyone would move here if she was greeting them."

"Oh my God, you are such a baby." She coughs into her fist.

I crouch down to the floor and drag my finger through egg yolk. "Baby, huh? I'll take that name." An image flashes in my mind of her moaning my name while she begs me to take her. I shake my head to get that thought out of it.

"Okay, let's see who complains louder." I'm leaning over her and her backside slides down the chair as far as she can get, almost hanging off the edge, trying to get away from me. But I'm not letting her off that easy.

"Jake, stop." She turns her head away from me.

"Oh, now it's not so funny." I don't want her to fall off the chair, so instead of egging her, I wrap my other arm around her waist and pull her up against me. I'm careful to make sure I'm not going to slip and drop her, making myself look even more stupid than I already have tonight.

"Jake!" she cries out as I lift her and secure her against my chest.

"Yes, Ash? What's wrong?" I look down into her darkened brown eyes that are sparkling with the electricity between us. There is no fear or panic. Her whole demeanor has changed in a split second. My egg-covered finger is hovering above her cheek, but smearing her with it is no longer something I care about doing. Instead, I'm transfixed by the way she's looking at me, and suddenly it hits me. The longer I hold her this close, the more that look across her face becomes something I can't ignore, because I'm feeling it too.

Longing.

Wiping my finger on the leg of my jeans, I carefully wrap my other arm around her back.

Our faces are being drawn toward each other. And in a way that we shouldn't even be contemplating.

Her hands slowly slide up from my chest and hook around my neck. She wants this as much as I do. But if I kiss her again, I am not going to want to stop.

"We can't do this," I whisper as my lips are practically on hers, almost pleading for her to stop me.

"I know," she concedes but doesn't pull away.

"Why did you have to live next door?" Drawing her delectable scent through my nostrils, she's so close I can almost taste her lips.

"Why did you have to rescue me?" she replies as though I'm at fault for our worlds colliding in such a way that we don't know how to stop them.

"Maybe I'm the one that's being rescued," I murmur ever so softly as our lips finally touch, and it's like I'm breathing in the most invigorating breath of fresh air again. Her lips are so soft against mine.

And the moment she starts to move like she wants more, a crashing sound down the hallway has us breaking apart slightly.

"Shit," I snap.

"Daisy," we both state at the same time and reluctantly pull apart.

"I should've made sure she was outside." Cursing myself, just as I take the first two steps into the hallway, Daisy appears from one of the side rooms with something pale pink in her mouth. Stopping and glaring at me, it feels like we are mortal enemies about to charge at each other in combat. But before I can move, I hear Ash gasping behind me.

"No, Daisy, they are my favorite pair."

Looking harder at what is hanging from her mouth, it's clear why Ash is pushing past me to pull the piece of lace from Daisy's teeth as she scolds her. Turning her around and pushing her toward the front door, Ash is still telling her how naughty she is, while Daisy is bleating loudly to show how unimpressed she is at being treated this way. Finally, the door bangs closed against the latch, and Ash slumps against the back of the door.

"How the hell did she get in through the door, anyway." I look toward Ash now pushing herself upright, looking sheepish.

"Um, you're probably not going to like the answer to that question." She gives the door another shove with her hand behind her.

"Ash?" I ask again.

"I might have a sketchy lock on the door that I haven't gotten around to fixing yet." She eyes me, waiting for a reaction, and she's about to get one.

"Are you telling me you can't lock your door at night when you are here on your own, in the middle of nowhere, and now there's the possibility of that prick turning up here too?" I can feel the hair on the back of my neck rising and my fists starting to clench.

"Of course I can. Don't panic. I could lock the door if I had to, it's just the latch doesn't catch properly. It locks fine." She smiles at me, no doubt hoping I won't ask any more questions.

"Okay, let me rephrase that question, Ash. Do you lock the door at night?" I ask, staring her down.

"This isn't the city. Nobody breaks into houses here. Well, except pesky goats, but it's safe in Abbey Falls," she says, trying to reason with me.

"Lock the damn door, Ash, and I'm fixing that latch for you too." I'm trying not to get too heavy-handed, but knowing she's lying in bed at night on her own, not safe from the outside world, has my chest burning.

"Okay, got it, but I have bigger problems right now." She starts walking back toward the piece of stray lingerie.

"Bet you're glad you rescued that one." Stepping toward her, I look at the piece of lace on the ground then focus back on Ash's face.

"No, no, no. Don't!" Ash shrieks as I lean down to pick it up.

She pulls my hand away, and I watch her swoop down and scrunch it into her hand. Her cheeks are red, and she can't look at me, and when she stands up straight again, we are almost toe-to-toe. Then I catch something out of the corner of my eye and turn to look into a small corner of what must be Ashley's bedroom. There is a trail of clothes and underwear from an overturned basket in the corner, toward the door.

"Oh no, I can't believe she has done this. She has never gotten inside before or taken a fancy to my clothes."

Knowing that she's already struggling with the embarrassment of me seeing her underwear, I need to let her deal with this. "You fix this disaster up, and I'll start in the kitchen." I turn to walk back to the initial scene of the crime, and Ash sniggers.

"Sorry, I can't help surveying the state of your gourmet back. A variety of food in the most artistic abstract pattern."

"Here for your viewing pleasure." I keep walking but manage to catch her mumbling a reply, which I'm not sure she meant for me to hear.

"Oh, it's a pleasure alright."

The smile on my face quickly fades, though, as I survey the kitchen. "There was a reason no one wanted that stupid goat." Not wasting any time, I grab the trash can and start picking up what I can before attempting to clean up the raw egg. There must be a trick to doing this, but I have no idea what that is. So, resorting to my hands and paper towels, it looks like I'm making more of a mess than when I started.

"Umm, do you need some help?"

Looking up, I see Ashley leaning against the doorframe with her arms crossed and the cutest little twinkle in her eye.

"Not sure it's ever something I imagined. You on your knees, in the middle of my kitchen."

"Christ, can you stop opening your mouth if you are going to say things like that? Because I'll tell you right now, the next time you see me on my knees for you, it won't be in the kitchen, and you'll be wearing some of those lace things that you were too embarrassed to let me see."

And instead of her cheeks reddening from my words, I can see the fire in her, and I find myself wishing I could be the one to stoke that heat right up. But I know I can't, so I need to pull this topic of conversation back to my egg problem, before I do something stupid—like what I was about to do before I was cock-blocked by a goat.

"Now, do you have any bright ideas on how to clean this floor, other than getting a hair dryer, turning it on to hot, and cooking it to a solid? Because this shit is slippery as hell."

Ashley is still staring at me, with her mouth slightly open.

"It's either that, or we let that hairy garbage disposal back in here and wait for her to lick the floor clean."

The mention of Daisy being back in the house is enough to snap her out of the moment.

"No way! Daisy is banned from this house forever." She waves her finger at me and then drops her hand to contemplate my question. "Ummm, okay, let me get the dustpan and broom maybe and then the mop for when we are finished."

Shrugging, she very carefully heads to the cupboard under the sink, bringing out the dustpan, which has to be better than my hands and a few paper towels.

It takes us a little while, but finally the kitchen looks more like a normal room and less like a war zone. I can't say the same thing for me. The knees of my jeans are covered in various stains, and I have no idea what the back of me looks like. But I don't care because the laughs we just shared over this whole debacle are worth one set of clothes that I'll probably just throw out anyway.

Carrying the bag of ruined food out to the trash can outside, Ash follows me to the corner of the house, then stops and looks toward the barn. The longer summer days make it so beautiful to be outside.

"If Daisy knows what's good for her, she'll be back in the pasture with Gerald or hiding in the barn with Herb, who's unusually quiet now, which is another concern I don't want to think about," she declares like she's trying to convince herself Daisy might do the right thing and stay put, but the reality is that she probably won't.

Stopping behind her, I can't help taking in the vision in front of me. Ashley standing with her back to me, hair falling past her shoulders, and the dwindling light of today's sunshine mixed with moonlight starting to brighten the night sky is all showcasing her body. Streaks of warm shades of brown glisten in her hair in the light, and the gentle breeze has the delicate strands drifting back and forth. Her flowy skirt is fluttering in the cool night air just as she shudders a little with the chill. The thought of her being cold shakes me out of my trance.

"We need to get you back inside, can't have you getting cold." Walking alongside her and taking her hand, I wrap it around my elbow as I escort her up onto the porch.

"Yes, thank you. We both know what happens when I get cold; I go looking for something to warm me up." She steps in front of me so we are facing each other, on the porch blocking the door.

"Some*one*," I reply in a deep husky voice as I feel my cock reacting to the memories of our night in the woods.

Ashley drops her face and looks down, making her hair fall forward and cover her cheeks.

Placing my hand under her chin, I lift her face so she's looking at me again. "Don't do that. Best night of sleep I had in a long time."

Fuck, those lips are like a magnet.

"On the dirt in the middle of the woods," she softly recounts.

"Yeah, with you wrapped in my arms." I know I shouldn't, but I run my thumb over her perfect lips.

The rush of emotions swirling in my chest gets stronger every time I touch her.

"Fuck, I wish this was a different time and a different place." I maintain eye contact as I lean in and kiss her ever so gently on the forehead. I know that if I put my lips on hers again, like I so desperately want to, then we aren't stopping until I have her on that bed, stripped down to some lace and making her feel everything she's been missing.

Her soft little moan tells me she feels the same. I slip my hand into her hair, place my chin on the top of her head and pull her into my chest.

"If only I dated and you weren't leaving," she murmurs into my shirt, and I feel it all the way into my gut.

"If only I was staying," I whisper to both her and the night sky.

Time is irrelevant as we stand together, dreaming of what could be if things were different.

My phone buzzing in my pocket is enough to break the moment. Ashley pulls away, and I reluctantly let her go.

"Answer it." She takes a step back from me, and the connection is broken.

Looking down, I see it's Declan calling, and I send it to voicemail.

"I should be going, leave you to get that leg up and rested," I say, knowing she's seeing the physio tomorrow, and hopefully she will be able to take the moon boot off and start to get back to normal. "Let me know how your appointment goes." Stepping toward the top of the stairs, I pause for one last look at her and then continue toward my truck. As I get to the driver's door and pull out a blanket to cover the car seat, Ashley has walked along the porch a little so she's now directly in my eyeline.

"Jake," she calls.

Drinking in the sight of her, I just nod at my name.

"Thank you." I'm not sure what she's thanking me for. Cleaning up the kitchen mess or for walking away so neither of us make a different mess that will be a lot harder to clean up.

"I've got you." Because I know I can't say *my pleasure*, because sure as shit this is not fun walking away. Besides, I meant what I said. I'm here for her in any way she needs me, even if it's not what either of us wants. I'll still be here and even more so now, with her dickwad of an ex as a potential threat at any time.

"And lock the fucking door!" I yell to her as I pull away in the truck, which has her giggling as she closes the door.

Hitting the asphalt in the truck as I leave the gates of Windemere, I don't feel ready to head home yet, so pushing Declan's name on my phone, I call him as I drive past the gates of Heatherbrae, and then just keep driving.

"Hey, sorry I missed you." As the phone connects and I hear his voice, I know it's the comfort and the distraction I need.

"Hey, Jake, just saw the photos you sent through of the barn rooms. They look fucking awesome, and I can't wait to get up there." The excitement in his voice is rubbing off on me.

"Me too, man, can't wait to have you guys here. Then we can really get into it. Plus, sitting outside around the firepit just isn't the same without you all."

"Bullshit. Be honest, you just need a break from being Gran's sole focus. Not much fun being the favorite, is it?" Declan is already laughing before I join him.

We both know Gran doesn't play favorites, but if she did, it would be Beckett for sure. She's always had a soft spot for my surly big brother, like he needs just a little extra to break down that grumpy, serious barrier he carries around with him.

"All jokes aside, how's Gran doing?" Declan asks.

"Most of the time she's fine, but when I catch her sitting on the porch swing watching down the drive, it's almost like she's waiting for Gramps to come rattling up in his truck, or on the four-wheeler from the vineyard."

To most people, it would look like Gran is just enjoying the fresh air, but to those who know her, the look of longing in her eyes is heartbreaking.

"Man, I can't even imagine what she must feel like. They had the kind of love you can only dream to find." Declan's words send us both into silence for a few seconds.

Stupidly, I thought I had that kind of love with Danika, but I'm starting to understand that it wasn't even close. Looking back, I'd describe it as a comfort relationship. She made me happy, it was easy, we didn't argue that often, but in a way, it was just because we didn't care enough to fight. There wasn't the passion that I'm discovering should happen every time the woman you love walks into the room. Like I want to climb out of my skin when the electricity pulses through my body from just the way she looks at me.

I am so screwed.

I've found a woman who's worth fighting with and for, and the timing is just so messed up.

"Jake!" Declan's voice echoes through my truck.

"Shit, sorry, what'd you say?"

"How is Rosie? I can't believe Gran adopted a dog. I mean, I love dogs, but Gramps was always against them." He's chuckling to himself.

"He wasn't the only one, but I've got to admit she's good for Gran. Drives me crazy, but Gran loves her." With one hand on the steering wheel and running my other hand through my hair, I'm thinking it's not just Rosie driving me crazy but a certain vet that can join that club too.

We talk for another ten minutes before Declan hangs up and my music starts playing through the truck's speakers. I lower my window and lean my elbow on the door as Kane Brown's "What Ifs" starts playing. Turning up the volume, I just keep driving the back roads of Abbey Falls, feeling the cold air rushing through my hair as visions of Ashley play on repeat in my mind, something I want but just can't have. But still, I have that stupid smile on my face that I can't seem to change every time I'm around her, and a cock that is still hard as stone.

I'm in for another long night.

◆ ◆ ◆

It's been two weeks since my battle with Daisy in the kitchen, and I've seen Ashley a few times but not as often as I would like. I'm guessing we both thought that a bit of distance between us might be best right now. I do keep checking in with her every day, though, to see if she has heard any more from Jeremy, but it's been quiet and she has assured me she will call if anything happens. I just don't trust that's the end of it, otherwise why would he have reached out like that?

Her ankle has healed nicely, and she has been busy at the clinic, but I'm now on the way into town to take Rosie for a checkup that Gran insisted she needs. I'm in Gramps's old truck because there is no way the hairy beast next to me is sitting in the front seat of my truck. My truck is the only nice thing I have left.

Gran told me that Ashley asked to see Rosie to make sure that she's all healed properly from her surgery. Said that she couldn't take Rosie today, as she has her weekly knit and natter get-together with her friends. I would not want to be in that room, that's for sure. It would be just one big gossip session, comparing notes and merging stories that just keep growing.

I'm no expert but looking across at Rosie sitting happily in the truck, even I can tell that she's fine. You just have to watch her chasing the birds out in the vineyard, reminding them it's her farm now and they need to go sit on the fence lines someplace else. But I'm not complaining about a reason to see Ashley.

Rolling down the main street, it's like Rosie is royalty in this town already, sitting up tall as everyone calls out and waves to her. I mean, it's not like you can miss Gramps's truck, and I'm sure Gran has introduced Rosie to every local she's come across. It's like Rosie is another grandchild for her to spoil and make a fuss over.

Walking into the clinic, Rosie trots straight over to the reception desk, tail wagging and waiting for a pat.

"Hi, Adi," I call out as I close the front door.

"Hello, my beautiful Miss Rosie. Oh my gosh, you look so healthy now. I think Betty is feeding you too well." Adi looks up from giving Rosie all her love. "Hi, Jake, she's ready for you. You can go on back."

"Thanks, Adi. Come on, Rosie, let's go and see our favorite girl—*your* favorite girl, I mean." I correct myself in front of Adi, but it's too late, as she already has that stupid smirk on her face.

My hand is on the door, and I must be taking too long because Rosie's paws are dancing up and down, and she gives a bark as if to say, "*Hurry up, I want in.*"

"Alright, alright." Turning the knob, I barely get it open before Rosie is through the gap and off running to Ashley.

"Whoa, Rosie, hi, look at you, happy girl." Ashley crouches down, which is probably not the best idea as Rosie plows into her and almost puts her on her ass with her strength. "Did you miss me?"

"You are definitely missed, Ash." And I'm not just talking about Rosie.

Ash stands up and gives me a quick hug, like friends do. She's close to me just long enough for that sweet floral scent to go straight to my head and have my heart thumping a little harder.

"Hi, Jake, Betty called and said that Rosie didn't look well, but she seems fine now. What's been going on?"

I can't help but laugh out loud.

"What?" Ash looks confused.

"I think we have been snookered by sweet little old Gran. I was told you wanted Rosie to be brought in for a checkup on her healing from the surgery." Still chuckling, I lean back against the exam table, and everything dawns on Ashley.

"Oh, the cheeky old thing." She leans down and pats Rosie on her head again. "Well, since you are here, we may as well give you a once-over." Ash grabs her stethoscope from the counter.

"Do you want me to lift her onto the table for you?" I ask.

"No way. She weighs a ton. Here is just fine." Bending over, Ashley listens to Rosie's heart and feels around her abdomen while Rosie relishes the attention.

"If she wasn't so old and the scare might give her a heart attack, I'd be going home from here telling Gran that Rosie really is sick, just to see her face for the moment of panic. Teach her not to meddle."

"Oh, you will do no such thing. She means well."

Groaning at Ash's words, I roll my eyes. "I'm thirty-nine years old and pretty sure I can manage to find someone on my own." My words just spill out before I even think about what I'm saying.

Ash stands up and quickly turns her back to me, then starts to type Rosie's results into her computer. "True, I'm sure you can." She keeps typing, but I'm not sure if she needs to be putting any information into the computer or if she's using it as a way to hide her look of discomfort.

"Rosie is fine. You can take her back to Betty and tell her I don't need to see her any more unless she is sick." Ash now has her vet persona back on as she turns to look at me.

"Thanks, Ash. I'm sorry Gran wasted your time, but we both know Rosie is important to her." Smacking the side of my leg to get Rosie's attention, I say, "Come on, girl, we need to get you home."

Rosie reluctantly makes her way over to me, because we all know if she had to choose, she would rather spend time with Ash than with me.

Just as we are about to head through the door, I look over my shoulder to Ash. "What are you up to tonight? My cousin Chase is arriving. Do you want to grab a meal together, invite Tiff officially this time?" I don't know why I'm punishing myself by doing this. And to be honest, I'm sure Gran will want to see Chase.

"Sorry, I'm busy tonight. Maybe another time."

I can't see one bit of disappointment on her face, and I doubt she has anything organized unless it's work. But my words have been enough to upset her, so I guess she doesn't want to spend time together while thinking about me looking for another woman.

I'm an idiot.

"No worries, yeah, another time. Thanks, Ash. Come on, Rosie."

We walk out of the back room of the clinic, ready to go home and listen to my gran try to deny her little scheme today.

ASHLEY

"Shit, I'm going to be late if I don't get out of here shortly." Looking down at my bloodstained work clothes, I know I can't wear these to dinner.

It might be a work dinner, but it's disgusting to turn up covered in animal blood. Thank goodness I grabbed a clean pair of jeans and a shirt off the chair in my bedroom this morning. They aren't clean, but they also aren't dirty. Perfect for tonight.

I'm not trying to impress this guy I'm interviewing. I just need to make sure he isn't a complete douchebag and then cross my fingers that he takes the job and can start tomorrow.

Grizzly's is too noisy, so I decided to make it a little more formal and told Beau to meet me at Alberto's Restaurant, just down from the clinic. Pulling on my blue jeans and tucking my black tank top into them. I fasten a couple of the buttons in the middle of my black shirt with red roses on it, leaving it open just a little at the neckline, showing the tight tank top, and then take the rest of the shirt and tie it in a knot at my waist. Then I pull on my cowgirl boots that I don't wear all the time, but they complete the look. To be honest, they are comfortable, and I would wear them more often if I wasn't working all the time and actually had more of a social life.

"Hi, Julie." I come rushing through the front door of Alberto's.

"Don't panic, Doc, you're only five minutes late. Your hunky guy is already here and sitting at the table in the middle. Jeez, you really are picking up all the hotties at the moment, aren't you. Good for you, love." Julie, who's our waitress for tonight, starts wiggling her eyebrows up and down.

In my head I'm screaming, "*No, please, no, don't let him be good-looking. Just let him be an average-looking vet like me. Nothing special and just good at his job. I don't need that extra drama.*"

Taking a deep breath, I approach the table, and he looks up, pushing his chair back to stand. His hand is out ready to shake mine, and, shit, his hands are large and he's as tall as Jake. Why do I have to always be the short one?

"Doctor Alleyne, Beau Robinson. Nice to meet you."

Oh, I love the accent already. It will make for a bit of fun around the workplace hearing his voice and all the weird slang words he will probably say.

"Beau, thanks for meeting me tonight, and please, call me Ashley or Doc. Actually, Doc might get confusing if there are two of us." I blush a little, realizing how stupid it sounded.

Beau pulls my chair out for me, and as I'm sitting, I take in everything about him. Tall, dirty-blond hair that is pulled back into a man bun. Oh, I can just imagine the comments on that hairstyle around Abbey Falls. Freckles across his nose and a big mouth. Not sure why I'm even looking at his mouth, but the moment he smiles, I also see dimples. Seriously, what is it with me and dimpled men right now.

Snap out of it, Ashley, and stop checking him out. Be professional. You are here to interview him.

"Let's order and then you can tell me a bit more about yourself, Beau, and why you think Abbey Falls is somewhere you want to work." I pick up the menu to give me a little time to get myself together.

"Sounds like a great idea," he replies.

Both of us quickly place our order with Julie and I get comfortable as he starts the hard sell about himself. And the more he talks, the more relaxed I feel. I don't know what I was worried about, because Beau seems perfect for the job.

He has so much experience and will be a great asset to the clinic. Beau tells me that he grew up on a cattle station in Australia but wanted to get out of the family business and travel the world. The only downside is that he won't stay here forever, but I'll take the couple of years that he has promised me. It will give me time to find another vet before he moves on.

But the thing that I really like about Beau is that he's funny. And when you have a tough day in the clinic, a sense of humor really helps.

My sides hurt from one of his hilarious stories, and I decide not to wait any longer.

"I'm excited to have you come and work for me, Beau." I hold my hand out so we can shake on the agreement. "Can you start tomorrow?"

To which we both crack up at how desperate I am for the help. He continues talking, telling me everything he owns is in his car parked outside, so he's ready to make Abbey Falls his home.

"Great, I can't wait to see you tomorrow." I can feel the smile on my face and relief in my shoulders.

Until I hear the murmur of a few male voices from a couple of tables away, and I look across to see two brown eyes boring into me like a laser.

Jake's here, and he looks pissed.

Chapter Eleven

Jake

"I can't believe Gran didn't want to cook you up a big dinner tonight." I look across at Chase as we park my truck in front of Alberto's.

"She looked tired, and I didn't want her working hard in the kitchen, which is why I suggested we take her out. Obviously, she wasn't up for company tonight, because for Gran to turn down dinner in town, where she can show off her two grandsons, is unheard of. We better check in on her when we get home." Chase stops outside of the restaurant door and turns back to me. "I can't believe that we aren't going to Grizzly's tonight. I mean, a beer and a steak was what I was thinking."

Chase starts laughing to himself. "Oh, shit, I just worked it out. Don't tell me you've already pissed off a few women in this little town. I must say it didn't take you long," Chase jokes as he pushes open the door to enter the restaurant.

"Something like that. Let me assure you, here is safer," I mumble, thinking to myself that I didn't want all the eyes in Grizzly's to be on us tonight. I'm just not feeling it, and with Chase being a new novelty toy for the rumor mill, here looked like the better option.

"You have no idea what you are in for when the women in town find out there's another single man from Heatherbrae on the loose. Apparently, we are a rare species in this place, as I found out at the first town event Gran took me to. But then again, you are supposedly a big stud who knows what it's like to be mobbed by groups of women when you are traveling the world," I say as I'm standing behind him and shove my hands down into my jeans pockets.

"Jealousy looks good on you." He chuckles as he looks at me over his shoulder and then turns back as a woman approaches us.

"Well, hello there, gentlemen, looking for a table for two tonight?" the bubbly waitress asks.

"That would be great, thanks." Chase starts displaying the smooth charm I've seen him pull off many times before.

"Sure thing, just follow me," she sweetly replies, and as she turns to walk through the restaurant, I slap Chase on the shoulder and lean close to his ear.

"Keep it in your pants, she's a bit old for you." I roll my eyes at him as he gives me the cheeky smirk that he perfected as a kid.

Just as I take my seat, I hear a familiar laugh. It's the same one that inhabits my dreams at night.

Ashley.

She said she was busy.

She said she doesn't date.

So, who the fuck is that guy she's with, and why is he getting the smiles and giggles that should be mine?

I can feel the rage of jealousy rising through my body, and I'm struggling to keep a lid on it. I want to storm over to her table and demand to know who he is and then put her over my shoulder to carry her out of here.

The waitress's voice is just a mumble, and I'm not even listening to her when she steps away and I get a clear vision of the asshole holding Ash's hand while she looks happily back at him.

"Buddy, who are we about to kill?"

Chase's voice snaps at me, but I can't look away from Ashley. It's like my eyes are transfixed on a scene that has my heart feeling like it's being crushed under the weight of an elephant and fuck it hurts like hell. This is why I didn't want to let my walls down to experience this again, not that I had a chance of stopping it, because Ashley just pushed straight through them from day one.

"Later," I grunt because I'm not about to tell him everything here and now, especially why I'm seeing red over a woman who isn't even mine. I have no right to be acting like this, but I can't stop my hands from drawing into tight fists and my left leg from bouncing under the table. I silently curse myself for being too gutless to take a chance with Ashley, so now I have to watch her move on with someone else. Someone who can give her what she needs, what she deserves. Someone who'll stay.

"Well, just so you know, I've got your back, but can we eat first? I'm starving." Chase is humoring himself and laughs out loud, which is enough to catch Ash's attention, and she turns to look our way.

Our eyes meet, and I can feel the shock racing through her at seeing me here.

My fists are now clenched so hard that the muscles in my arms hurt. But I can't do a thing. She's not mine. And my jaw is now so tight that I can't speak, so I just give her a chin lift, acknowledging her but trying not to give away how much pain and rage I'm feeling in my chest.

She pulls her hand away from her dinner companion and lifts it to give me a tiny wave.

Nope, I can't do this.

I stand and shove my chair back.

"I'm not hungry. Let's go to Grizzly's. I need a beer or ten!" I storm toward the door and leave Chase to explain to the poor waitress as I pass her. Ashley might be able to move past the chemistry between us and on to someone else, but there is no way in hell I can sit here and watch her do it.

The fresh night air hits me like a slap in the face as I stop and wait for Chase to catch up with me.

"What the fuck was that?" Chase comes out of the restaurant, throwing his hands in the air.

"It's a long story that requires a beer. Let's go."

Walking down to the end of the street, we turn the corner until we're in front of the door of Grizzly's. I open the door and step inside. Thankfully it's quiet tonight.

Chase takes the last mouthful of his second beer and looks at me, just shaking his head.

"Could you have fallen for someone a little less complicated? I mean, she's a neighbor, and apparently this angel of a vet, in Gran's eyes. I hope you know the pain you are going to be living with for the rest of this year. Wait until Declan and Beckett hear this one."

"Don't you dare open your mouth about this. Especially to Beckett. I'm already a disappointment to him. Let's not add to the list." Looking down at my watch, I know we should head back to Heatherbrae and check on Gran before she goes to bed.

"That's because he can be an opinionated prick. But he does love you . . . in his own way, with his heart of stone." Chase picks up the last fry left on his plate, and I realize how nice it is to finally have one of the guys here. Especially Chase, who always manages to make me laugh on the flip of a dime.

"Yeah, whatever. Anyway, we better get home before Gran starts worrying," I say to him and he looks back at me a little confused. "Oh, I forgot to warn you. You might be a full-grown adult but living with Gran is like we're kids again. We're almost back to curfews and her wanting to know where we are all the time. What did you just say about it's going to be a long year living at Heatherbrae? Well, you can add Gran's hovering over us to the list." I laugh as we both start heading out of Grizzly's to the truck to head home.

As my truck rattles up the drive of Heatherbrae, the headlights hit two little beady eyes belonging to a three-foot-tall menace.

"Fucking Daisy!" I yell, slamming my hand onto the steering wheel. "The universe hates me today."

"Who the hell is Daisy? I'm so confused; I thought her name was Ashley." Chase is looking at me like I'm a lunatic.

I pull the truck to a stop next to the barn and point out the window.

"Meet Daisy, another one of the annoying women in my life." Getting out of my truck and grabbing a rope from the truck bed, I leave Chase in the cab, cackling away.

"Come here, Daisy. I don't trust you to go home on your own, or not to destroy Gran's flowers along the way. And I only just finished my bedroom in the barn, which does not need redecorating goat-style." I'm almost in shock when she just stands there and lets me slip the rope over her neck. At least something is going right tonight.

"Can you check on Gran while I take Daisy back? Message me to let me know she's okay," I call over my shoulder to Chase as I head toward the fence between here and Windermere.

The full moon gives me enough light to find my way, wondering how the hell Daisy managed to get through it since it's been fixed. I look up and down the fence line to see where there might be a hole, but I don't have to worry. The gate that Gran insisted we put in between the two farms is wide open.

"How the hell did you get that open, Daisy? Seriously, they should've called you Houdini, the great escape goat." I walk through the gate and close it behind me. "Okay, let's get you into the yard so I can just slip away. Not sure I should see your momma tonight. I might say something I shouldn't."

Ashley's SUV is parked in the driveway, and the houselights are on, so I know she's home. I just don't want to think about whether she's alone or not.

I'm almost to the gate of the yard before I think about Herb the donkey. He's like an alarm system. The closer I get, the louder he is.

"Now stay here this time, you pain in the ass." I close the barnyard gate, hoping I can make it back past the house without being spotted, but the moment I start moving away from the yard onto the open grass in front of the house, Daisy and Gerald join the chorus of animals, and before I can make my getaway, the front door opens and Ashley walks out and hits a switch next to her, flooding the grass in front of me with light.

She hasn't seen me as she looks straight toward the barn.

"Herb, what's wrong?" Her hands are on her hips as she peers into the dark.

My feet are frozen on the spot. I've stopped, and it's not because of the lights threatening to reveal me. Those little cowgirl boots she's wearing are doing something for me. I didn't know I had a thing for cowgirls until now. Her tight blue jeans are tucked into the boots, accentuating her long legs and the curve of her hips—which is exactly where I'd like my hands to be instead of hers, holding on tight and then sliding them up over the black tank top that is hugging her breasts so nicely. The shirt she was wearing at the restaurant is now gone, and that's enough to start me moving toward her.

All rationality is gone, and pure lust is in the driving seat.

"It's me. Daisy was in Gran's garden again," I declare as I get closer to her so she can see me clearly.

"Shit, Jake!" she shrieks. "You scared me."

I'm not even sorry that I have startled her and take the porch steps two at a time until I'm face-to-face with her. I'm done dancing around this.

"Who is he?" I blurt out before I can think properly.

"Are you kidding me? Who do you think you are, speaking to me like that," she spits back.

Oh yeah, here we are, talking to each other like we're back at day one again, and I can't tell you how much the fight in her turns me on.

"Who. Is. He?" I inch my face a little closer to hers.

"Not that it's any of your business, but if you are referring to the man I was having dinner with earlier this evening, his name is Beau. Now go home, Jake, before you embarrass yourself." She turns back toward the door.

"Oh, I'm long past that point." Reaching out and wrapping my arm around her waist, I pull her to my body. Our chests hit each other with a thud, and the look of surprise on her face gives me no indication of fear, thank goodness.

"I'm done fighting this, Ash. I know you feel it too. There is no denying this anymore. You're mine."

Her eyes widen and sparkle as we both feel the electricity between us. Placing my hand gently on her cheek, I try to calm my voice a little.

"Tell me he didn't kiss these lips." I slide my hand down and run my thumb across them.

"He didn't," she whispers, and the relief sinks into my rage, calming my body a little. But the heat from her body touching mine is rising by the second.

My hand slowly feels the skin on her neck as it slides down and onto the soft bare skin above her breasts, caressing her ever so delicately.

"I want you, Ash, like I've never wanted another soul, and I don't know how to stop this burning desire."

"I know."

Finally, as she wraps her arms tentatively around my back, I can feel her falling into this just like I am.

"Are we feeling the same? Because if you tell me no, I'll walk away. Just don't ask me to be your friend, because I can't do that anymore. You are turning my world upside down in a good way, but I don't have that much strength to keep my distance. This is where I want you. Right here, in my arms, and not on the other side of a fence line." I'm sick of holding in my feelings.

"But how will this end? I don't know if I can let myself be with someone who's only going to leave. I've had my heart broken by someone who left me once before, and I don't know if I can do that again."

Her eyes are almost pleading for me to give her some magical answer, but I can't. I have to go back to Sacramento when this is over to fight the court case against my client, and I will need to work while I'm there if I'm in with any chance of affording the legal fees it's going to rack up. Plus the bank sent another email after I didn't pick up the last call, reminding me they have given me a year with regular monitoring to sort this mess out or they will foreclose on the house.

"One day at a time. Let's just see where this takes us. I can't promise you anything more than a good time at this moment, and I don't think you want to promise me more than tonight either. But this connection is special and I don't think we should keep fighting it."

I try to break through her anxiety. "Who knows, I might be so shit in bed that you run away from me as fast as you can."

She rolls her eyes at me as she replies, "Yeah, right, and Daisy knows how to stay in her own pasture. We both know that neither of those statements is even close to the truth."

Her words, hinting she's imagined what we would be like together, are escalating the burning sensation in my body that has me harder than I thought possible.

"Have you been thinking about me in bed, Ash?" Leaning down, I kiss her softly on her neck, drawing out the sweetest moan as I work my way up to whispering in her ear. "Was it good, Ash? Were you all wet from remembering our night in the woods?"

I feel her body weight slump against me. I'm sure the rush of adrenaline I'm feeling right now is running just as fast through her body too, causing her knees to weaken.

"Maybe." She slides her hands back around to my chest, grabbing fistfuls of my shirt. It's so damn hot when she does this. It's like she's hanging on, wanting me to take care of her. But the shock of her jumping and wrapping her legs around me gives me the answer that she wants this as much as I do.

"Well, we can't leave you wondering what might be." I carry her through the front door, making sure I lock it tight behind me so we don't get interrupted by that damn goat. Heading into the room that I now know is her bedroom, I toss her gently onto her bed that looks just like I imagined it would. Although she works in a world of hard physical effort and stress, this room is delicate and feminine. The bedcover is white and frilly, with soft pink, green, and lemon-colored cushions tossed over it. The furniture is made from distressed white wood, and the top of a chest of drawers is covered in perfumes, lotions, and little trinkets. There are also framed photos of people who I assume are her family, and one of her and Tiff. Her house might need lots of work, but this room is clearly all her.

And fuck, don't I want to get to know this feminine side of Ash.

My eyes fall back to where she's lying on the bed, pushed up on her elbows and watching me.

"Please tell me there is some of that lace under those clothes. Like the ones Daisy tried to eat and had you blushing so hard that night." I'm almost pleading to see the visions of my dreams become reality.

"I'll tell you something about me that no one knows." Her tongue swipes her lips before she bites down on her bottom one, and it's enough to have me already kicking off my boots and pulling my phone from my pocket.

JAKE: Don't wait up.

CHASE: Fuck yeah!

"I love sexy secrets, especially ones that come out of those lips." One by one I undo the buttons on my shirt and then shrug it off my shoulders, onto the floor.

"A few years ago."

I know that she means when he left her, but she's not saying it out loud.

"I gave up on dressing for anyone else but myself. So, every day, no matter what, there is always lace hiding underneath whatever I'm wearing, even my operating scrubs."

"Fuck, you can't do that to a man. Now every time I look at you, I'm going to be hard as steel picturing you under your clothes." I flick the button on the top of my jeans, and the zipper undoes from the pressure on it, giving me some welcome relief.

"Show me." I'm almost growling at this point as I push down on my cock to try to soothe the pain. I reach over and slip the first and then second cowgirl boot off her tiny feet before dropping them to the floor. Then I watch her pull that little tank top out of her jeans and drag it up over her body, exposing her bare stomach and making me twitch with a desire to reach out and touch her there.

Pushing herself to sit up, she continues removing her top but stops again just under her breasts, just far enough so that I can see a hint of black lace. Like a moth to a flame, I move onto the bed. Crawling over her legs, I hold myself on my knees above her. My hands over top of hers, I want the feeling of stripping her bare. There is no guarantee that I'll be here again, so I'm not letting this opportunity slip through my fingers.

"I'm man enough to tell you, without a doubt, this vision is what I've been getting off to every night." I'm now pushing her hands away and dragging the top over her head myself. My eyes focus heatedly on her alluring naked body, and I'm not looking away or even blinking for a second. I don't want to miss one moment of seeing her like this for the first time.

But it's not enough. "Jeans, now," I demand, wriggling back a little with my hand on the middle of her chest and then pushing her back onto the bed. Not once has she looked hesitant, and the moment I demand it, Ash's hands are unzipping her jeans. As she pushes her hips up off the bed to shimmy out of them, I grab her bare waist and feel that the heat of her skin is just how I remember her against me that night in the woods.

I'm not prepared for the moment her jeans disappear and my view of her body is no longer blocked by clothes, but just her skimpy underwear. She takes my breath away when I spot the skin of her pussy through the black mesh lace covered in hearts.

"So beautiful." I lower her to the bed again, and without even thinking about it, my head drops and I kiss the skin along the top of her panties. I need more, though. I stop the kissing when I get to the middle of her stomach just below her belly button, and my gaze catches hers to make sure she's in this same moment with me as I go down on her. Running my tongue over the lace that is soaked through with her arousal, the flavor lights up my taste buds.

As her hands hit my head, I feel my hair in her fingers, and her nails, even though they're short, still sharply pressing into my scalp, sending shudders through me to the point where I can feel my cock leaking.

"Yeah, gorgeous, I knew you would love it like this." The way she responded just when I touched her over her panties last time is no comparison to the way she already wants more from me tonight. "Don't hold back. I want all of you. Tell me what you need, and I promise I'll give it to you, plus a whole lot more."

"That," she shrieks as I run my tongue over her slit again. "And words, all the words."

Good to know.

This lace turns me on, but I've been wanting to taste her since that night, and I'm not waiting any longer. Taking the top of her panties in my teeth, I drag them down, pulling at the sides with my fingers.

"If you change your mind, we can stop, or if it's not what you like, you tell me. I will never assume anything with you." I want to make sure she understands that she has all the control here. I would never take more than she's prepared to give.

"Mhmm," she replies as I run my hands up her calves and push her knees apart. We both should be thankful that I didn't see her naked like this in the woods, otherwise she might've come out of that night with a bark rash on her back from how hard I would've taken her.

"Hot as fuck," I mumble as I start to swipe my tongue through her wet pussy, and this time, I don't stop. My hands rise to her breasts, and I push her lace bra up and out of the way so I can stroke my thumbs over her hard nipples. The moment I take them between my thumb and finger, pinching them, Ash is panting and getting wetter by the second. Pressing my tongue firmly on her clit has her screaming out and pushing her pussy into my face.

"Jake." Ash lets out a strangled moan of my name, telling me that she's hanging on the edge but also wants more. It's the same way her voice sounded as it echoed through the quiet woods, but this time I want her first orgasm on my tongue. I want to own every orgasm she will give me. I would love to say forever, but I'll take every one she'll give me.

"That's it, gorgeous, feel every single touch. Take the pleasure I'm giving because nobody has ever turned me on as much as you. I want your orgasms tonight to be better than you have ever experienced in your lifetime."

Burying my face back between her legs, I run one hand over the inside of her leg, and the moment I feel her quivering, I move two of my fingers to find her opening and push inside her while my thumb teases her engorged clit.

Ash floods my mouth with her juices as she screams out her orgasm, and I feel the sting of her nails in my scalp, knowing I will have wounds to treasure tomorrow.

"Oh, oh, oh, oh shit, oh shit, Jaaaaake."

Hearing her literally losing it all for me makes me desperate to get relief of my own.

I gaze up to see her eyes locked on me, and in that moment, it's like we have crossed a line we can no longer hide behind.

And we have only just begun. By the end of tonight, that line we have been trying not to cross will be so far in the distance behind us that we won't even be able to see it.

With absolutely no regrets.

ASHLEY

I can't breathe.

My body is too busy trying to process that explosive orgasm that just ripped me apart. I don't know what previous men have been doing down there, but it wasn't that, and good Lord, I had no idea that's what it was meant to feel like.

I'm not going to survive this man. I know it already.

His sweaty chest is now hovering over me, and this time I'm touching every inch of it. The smattering of his perfect amount of black chest hair is now wet from sweat. I'm running my hands down his toned stomach muscles that I know come from him just working physically hard every day and that gives him extra sexiness, in my eyes.

A real man.

And like a road map to the promised land, the small tuft of hair just above the line of his underwear that is peeking out from his open button tells me that there is plenty more to see to reinforce this rugged-man image.

"If you keep looking at me like that, I'll come before I'm even undressed."

And before I can answer him, his lips are on mine, sharing with me the taste of what had him groaning the moment I reached the peak of my pleasure.

This isn't the type of kiss we've shared before. It's not rushed or desperate, but instead it's soft and tender as his tongue strokes inside my mouth. It's a sweetness that I'm not sure I was ready for from him. This is not supposed to be a forever thing, so I don't want him to treat me as preciously as he is now.

But I can't deny that I could happily live every day with this kind of affection.

Cupping him over his jeans and squeezing his very large erection is enough for all that tenderness to leave him quickly. Pulling back from my mouth, he's now on a mission. I'm happy to lie here and watch the show as he steps off the end of the bed, finally dropping his jeans to reveal a pair of dark navy boxer briefs with a large wet patch from the tip of his throbbing cock. There is no hiding the size of it, and I squeeze my legs together in anticipation of what it will feel like being pushed inside me.

And now I can't stop thinking what it would feel like to slide that same big cock down my throat and taste every drop when he can no longer hold back from the pleasure I'd be giving him. These raw sexual thoughts are not like me. I have no idea where this frantic feeling of wanting to taste him is coming from, and I don't want to wait a moment longer to experience everything he's promising.

"Don't stop there." I chew my bottom lip as I watch him remove his boxer briefs, and all I can think is that Jake is all man. It's a ridiculous thought, but my brain is so scrambled from taking in all his naked perfection that I can't find the words to describe him. He looks strong and rugged and sexy as hell, but all I blurt out is, "Holy shit."

My words bring a devilish smile to his face. "Glad you approve," he grunts as the bed dips, and he starts crawling over top of me again.

"Do you understand how beautiful you are, Ash?"

I can't answer him honestly because when I look in the mirror each day, all I see is a tired woman who just wasn't enough. But when he looks at me, I just might believe it.

"I can tell by the look on your face that you need reminding, and I intend on doing that all night long."

He slides his body to the side of mine, lying beside me so as not to put his weight on top of me. His big strong hands are now roaming all over my skin, exploring me. Every touch drives my arousal higher, and I'm already so sensitive after he took me to the moon and back a few moments ago that I'm not sure how long I'll last.

I can feel his cock pushing against my thigh, letting me know that he's as heightened as I am.

"Let's get this off."

He rolls me away from him, running his finger ever so slowly now along the edge of my bra until he reaches the clasp. Expecting him to unclasp it quickly, the sensation of his tongue on my lower back instead has me shivering all over. He drags his tongue up my spine and then softly kisses me above and below the clasp before he takes it and unhooks my bra using only his mouth. The sensation of his mouth on me has me softly panting.

"Do you know how often I have been checking out this perfect little ass every time you walked away from me?" he asks, running his hand over my ass.

Glancing over my shoulder, I can see his eyes transfixed on the ass cheek he's caressing.

"Are you an ass man?" I ask as he rolls me onto my back so I can watch him while I pull off my bra and throw it to the floor.

"No. I'm an Ash man. Every. Single. Inch. Of. Her." His mouth closes over my nipple, laving it with his tongue as he takes control of my body.

Every part of me that he touches sparks up with a scorching sensation, making me desperate to stroke more than his chest. Reaching for his cock and then wrapping my hand around it, he responds with a deep hiss, holding his breath as his eyes roll back in his head.

I've never felt power over a man like I do in this moment.

It makes me wonder if Jeremy was ever really into me, because he never reacted to me the way Jake is right now. Jake looks at me like he wants to devour me. And I'm so ready for it.

"Does that feel good?" My insecurity of whether I'm doing it right still hovers in my thoughts, even after Jake's obvious reaction.

"Fuck yeah, but if you keep going, this will be over in thirty seconds. I have been wanting this, even if I didn't realize it, from that first day you started yelling at me, so I'm barely hanging on here, beautiful."

I can't help giggling. "So, you want me to yell at you like a crazy woman so you can get off." I'm still gently stroking up his cock, and twisting slowly on his engorged head has him leaking into my hand.

"Right now, you can do whatever the hell you want, Ash. You literally have me in the palm of your hand, and I'm about to lose it."

I run my thumb over the slit, then coat more of his precum down his length, and it's turning me on just as much as it is him.

"I want to taste you," I blurt out in response to him telling me I can do whatever the hell I want. My inner woman is fist-pumping the air at my confidence to take what I want.

"Do it. I just won't last long." His jaw is clenched, like he's barely holding on anyway.

Pride swells in my chest, and with my other hand, I push him so that he rolls to lie flat on the bed next to me. Pushing up to my knees, that's when I really get to see his body.

Thick toned thighs that I already know are strong by the way he carried me out of the woods. His abs are far more than just a six-pack, and his chest, oh it's just how I remember it. Sexy as hell.

His cock standing tall with my hand wrapped around it is a sight I never thought I was going to get the chance to see. But Jake is right—it was getting way too hard to fight against this sexual energy between us.

I'm done with fighting it too.

Crawling on my knees, I move between his legs and lower my mouth over the tip of his cock, taking it as far down as I can.

He's unbelievably big.

"Aaassssssshhhhh."

Jake's long deep groan has me dripping wet, and I'm not sure I'll last long either.

But I'm determined to drive him as crazy as he drove me.

Lifting my mouth off him and looking up into those darkened eyes that are almost black with arousal, I feel so much power.

"I'm going to make you wish that when you're getting yourself off from now on, it's my mouth you are fucking instead of that hand," I murmur before taking him all the way down my throat again and swallowing around him.

"Fuck that, I'll be thinking of your tight pussy around my cock. Just like this."

His hands are on me, and before I have time to wipe the saliva off my mouth, he has dragged me up, and I'm now on my knees, straddled over him.

"Ride me, cowgirl, give me the best fuck of my life."

I knew this man was going to be the death of me, but what a way to leave this world, riding Jake like I've never ridden a man before.

"Challenge accepted," I reply.

Chapter Twelve

Jake

"As much as I want to fuck you bare, I won't tonight. And not until we are both at a place to feel ready for that commitment." Stopping her just as she's about to sink down onto me, I hope like hell I have a condom in my wallet. It's been a while since I've needed one. I start reaching for my jeans, even though I don't want to move from this position and lose this moment.

"Don't worry, Tiff has got you covered." Ash leans across me to the drawer next to the bed and pulls out a box of extra-large ones. "I told her they would never get opened." She shrugs as she sits back on my thighs, tearing open the box with no finesse, pulling out the strip and then ripping open the first one with her teeth. "So don't you dare tell her we used these, or I'll never hear the end of it."

Smiling, I can't help but say, "Okay, but I'm buying her a beer next time I see her."

The moment she places the condom on the top of my cock and starts rolling it down me, I'm right back on the very edge of the cliff, and I'm about to jump off. "Make it a whole case of beer," I murmur as Ashley reaches the bottom of my cock and then lifts herself onto her knees again, so that she's above me.

I know I'm large, so I give her the control to take it slow.

"Ohhh." Watching her mouth drop open as she inches onto me, I try not to think about how amazing she feels stretching around me. I'm holding back as much as I can, but my balls are getting so tight that the pain is excruciating.

Reaching forward, I start circling her clit with my thumb. "That's it, breathe through it and take my pleasure to get you through the pain."

Inch by inch she drops down on me, and she's so tight that she's almost strangling my cock, and it feels like I'm in heaven.

"I knew you'd be perfect." This is better than any vision I had imagined. Watching her sitting astride me, naked, with her plump tits. Her raised hard nipples are erect from being so turned on.

Every time I circle her clit, it helps her to take me deeper.

"Jake . . ." Her pleading almost has me letting go.

"You need me to move, sweetheart? You want it all?" My hands move to her waist, and as she nods frantically at me, I pull her down hard as I push up into her.

"Fuck," I shout at the same time as she lets out the most beautiful moan of my name. Both of us are panting from the pleasure that is racing through every limb. And just as I get myself under control, she starts moving.

"Oh yeah," I groan. "Ride me, baby, ride me hard." Because if she keeps up with these slow and sensual movements, I'm not going to be able to take it much longer. The look in her eyes tells me that she knows exactly what she's doing to me. This is pure torture in the best possible way, and she loves it.

"You want me to ride you, Jake? I was expecting you to take control here. This must be killing you." She starts to lift herself up off me, ever so slowly, and as I start clenching my jaw, the twinkle in her eyes and devilish grin let me know what she wants from me.

"Be careful what you ask for, beautiful, because if you want it like that, I'm more than ready." Grabbing her hips tighter, I thrust hard up into her, and hearing her gasp is like lighting the fuse on an explosive.

"Yessss." Ash throws her head back, her soft, flowing hair hanging freely as she reaches out with her hands and grasps my forearms. The way she arches her body has her breasts on show for me to admire as I thrust into her again and they bounce with my power.

"More, yes, Jake, oh God, more . . . more . . . harder."

Her screams are like fuel to a fire that is raging out of control in my body.

"Hang on tight, my little cowgirl, this is going to be the best ride of your life."

Letting loose, our bodies are now in complete sync as I pound up into her tight wet pussy and she grinds down on me just as hard. We are taking it just how we both need it. Hot, hard, and ferocious. And as much as I try to convince myself that we can't be like this forever, the deeper she takes me in, the more I know I'm never going to be able to let her go.

This feels so right.

It's as though every woman in my life before her was just holding space for me, waiting for Ashley to walk into my life and seal my soul to hers.

I can tell from the goosebumps on her arms and the sheen of sweat all over her body that she's getting close again—and I want that. To feel her come all over my cock. Reaching one hand up around her neck, I pull her down to me.

"I want all your screams. They're mine now." Her clit and breasts rubbing against my body as I fuck her is all she needs. My lips are on hers, and I'm kissing her like my life depends on it. Grunting and moaning into my mouth, I feel her contract around my cock as the effects of her orgasm hit with force this time, and her waves of pleasure are like a ripple effect.

But I'm not stopping and need to keep her riding me while I race to my own orgasm finish line. Powerful and explosive, it hits me, and finally the relief of coming inside her rushes all the way through me. My body jerks until I know there is not one ounce left in my balls to empty into her.

Ash flops down onto me like a limp doll, exhausted and sated. I wrap my arms around her, just taking a moment to let my heart calm to a normal speed. Not that I think it will ever happen around her.

"I don't want to move," she murmurs into my chest.

"Then don't." I'm not done with her for the night, but I need to give her time to recover and make sure she's not too sore.

"I should've rephrased that. I don't think I *can* move." Her little giggle sounds so beautiful while I stroke my hands down her back and then over her ass. But as much as I want to stay like this, I need to clean us both up so we can spend the rest of the night under these covers, continuing to explore our bodies as we get to know each other.

The harsh sound of a phone ringing has us both tensing up, and the worst part is that I know it's not my ringtone.

"Please, no. Not tonight." Ash rolls off me, stands, and then takes the few steps to where her phone is on top of the dresser. "Ughhh." And that's enough for me to know it's a callout.

"Good evening, Mrs. Thomas."

Listening to Ash use her work voice on the phone seems so strange when I'm lying here naked and enjoying the view of her beauty from behind.

"How long has she been laboring?"

Hearing those words, I know that's my cue to get out of bed and clean myself up. Ashley is going to have to go to work. She keeps talking on the phone as I walk down the hallway through the center of the house, searching for the bathroom and a washcloth. Disposing of the condom in the trash can and running the warm water in the sink to wet the cloth, I head back to her room where I can hear her winding up the conversation.

"Yes, just try to keep her comfortable and I'll be there as soon as I can." Her ear is pushed to the phone as she moves around the room and pulls work clothes out of her closet. "No, it's not a problem. That's what I'm here for. See you soon."

Dropping her phone onto the bed, Ash then looks at me with such regretful eyes. But I won't let her feel guilty for doing her job.

"Don't even say a word. Let me clean you up. I'm not having you leave here smelling like sex. What will the good people of Abbey Falls think if they know their precious doc slept with a man?" I pull her close to me and wipe the warm washcloth between her legs with such care, because I know she will be tender.

"Not just a man, but the grumpy neighbor." She looks up at me with a cheeky grin.

"Hey, enough of the *grumpy*, thanks. I thought we were past that." I tap her on the nose with my finger.

"Me too, but he made another guest appearance tonight," she corrects me as she reluctantly pushes away from me and starts getting dressed. "Jealousy looks good on you, Jake Davis."

"I beg to differ, but now that you bring it up, we haven't finished discussing your date from earlier tonight." My words leave a nasty taste in my mouth.

As I pull on my boxer briefs and jeans, Ashley stands in front of me, barefoot in only her jeans and black lace bra that I just had the pleasure of taking off her. It does something inside of me, knowing she's leaving this house with it on underneath her clothes. But before I have time for this thought to eat me up inside, she steps into my space and loops her hands around my neck.

"If you didn't storm out of Alberto's tonight, I would have introduced you to Beau, the new vet I was interviewing, and who I had just hired when you arrived."

I didn't realize just how much I needed that clarification until she said it. But I'm not going to admit to her that I'm still not happy about her working so closely with such an attractive man. I can tell from the short time watching him at the restaurant tonight that he obviously has a thing for her, even if she can't see it. But that's a thought to keep to myself for now, because I don't want another argument to start before she has to leave for work. And I know my jealousy is my problem to work through, not hers.

"As much as I would've loved to string you along about my dinner with my mystery man, the gossip will be all over town by tomorrow. Especially since he's staying at the B&B tonight. So, there was no point, and now at least one of us gets to have a good night's sleep." Confidence looks good on her.

"Thank you. But I'm not about to sleep tonight, after what we just did. I'll be playing it on repeat in my mind." I lean down so close to her that my lips are almost touching hers. "I had big plans for you tonight, beautiful." I take in a small breath before I continue. "So whatever animal you are leaving me to help, it better be grateful that I'm letting you go." I softly kiss those lips that bring me to my knees every time.

"This is my life, Jake," she says as we part. "I know you get it, but it's not always convenient for . . . this." She's not giving us any sort of title. "Hopefully by hiring Beau, it will help to give me some sort of normal life, but that doesn't mean it will be perfect."

My heart beats a little harder that she's talking about the future and us in the same breath.

"I don't need perfect. Having you in any way that you let me is all I need. All I'm asking is for you to give me a chance. We need to talk more but now is not the time. You have some cow, horse, or random farm animal to deliver by the sounds of that phone call." I run my fingers through her hair and then down her bare back, resting on her jean-covered ass and giving it a squeeze to let her know I understand.

"Puppies, actually. Want me to get Mrs. Thomas to keep one aside for you? They are Australian shepherds and one would make a great friend for Rosie."

I gently smack her on the ass for tormenting me, but it's enough for us to break apart and continue dressing.

"You could stay here if you want to," Ash says, grabbing her jacket from the hook at the front door as we both stop and look at each other.

"As much as I would love to be here in your bed waiting for you to come home, I think it's best I go home tonight. One step at a time." And if I'm being honest with myself, I need a bit of time alone to sort through all the emotions that are raging inside me right now. I know what I want, I just don't know how to make it happen just yet, or even whether it's possible. I need to work out my own plans before I try to match them to Ashley's life.

Gran has dropped in conversation a few times over the last few weeks that she has friends who have asked if she would hire me out to do some handyman work for them. The man who used to do all these sorts of jobs is getting ready to retire and there is no one to take over.

Although I'm used to much bigger jobs, would this be enough income to sustain me in Abbey Falls since my cost of living would be so low? I just don't know and I'm scared to ask too many questions and give both Gran and Ashley false hope if it's not the answer.

Do I even want to be in business anymore, or be a builder? It all just seems tarnished now after what's happened. This is my first thing I need to sort out to find a direction from here.

Why is it that when you find the right person, it's in the wrong place and at the most confusing time of your life? Or is it the right place and I seriously just need to find a way through this confusion?

"You're right," Ashley replies, reaching up on her toes to kiss me, and we both know we have unfinished business here.

We walk to her car, and she offers to drive me home, but I don't want Gran knowing where I've been and I could use the walk.

"Drive safe. Message me when you get home. I'll be awake." I wink at her as she starts the engine and the car roars to life. Closing her car door, I lean in through the window to steal one last kiss.

"Jake," she calls as I'm walking away.

I turn to face her again.

"Thank you, for tonight, for understanding my life, and for not pushing me too hard."

I just nod, then turn and keep walking home, toward Heatherbrae.

"Rise and shine, sleepyheads, breakfast is here." Gran's voice echoes through the barn as she comes in with a basket in her arms.

"You should know by now that I'm up with the sun, Gran. I've already been for a walk with this guy, who needs a bit of fitness training, I think." I point my thumb at Chase, who's sitting on the wooden bench seat at the small table that I built into the common room, near the bedrooms.

"Hey, I kept up with you. I just wasn't ready for the hike into the woods when you said we were going for a casual walk at sunrise. Thought you would've wanted a sleep-in after your little adventures last night." He smirks at me as he takes a sip of his coffee.

"Asshole," I mouth to him behind Gran's back, before she turns from Chase and looks intently at me.

"Where *did* you get to after dinner, Jake?" Gran asks, and I feel like I'm back under the scrutinizing eye of my school principal when he lined up half the football team and tried to get one of us to confess to stealing the team mascot from our rival school. It was never me, because that would involve being around an animal, and I would've had no idea how to even capture it, let alone muster up the desire to kidnap it.

No point lying to Gran, though, because she could always see right through every one of us grandkids whenever we tried to hide the truth.

"Daisy got through the fence again, so I took her back home before she got into your garden." Holding Gran's stare, I try not to give away that it was more than a little five-minute visit.

"How did she get through your perfect new fence?" Gran asks.

"Somehow the gate was open. She's either a very clever goat or someone gave her a helping hand . . ." And as I say it aloud, all the pieces start coming together. The look on Gran's face changes to one of fake innocence. She can't hide the guilt on her face any more than her grandkids can.

"Who would do that?" She quickly places the basket on the table and starts to make her escape. "Got to run, things to do, cleaning, and um, yeah, cleaning." And with that little hurried remark, she's gone, leaving Chase and me looking at one another before we both start cracking up.

"Gran, you little matchmaker." Chase shakes his head as he picks up one of the egg-and-bacon rolls that smell divine.

"You have no idea. Shit, you better watch out or you'll be next. Lock up your women, Abbey Falls, Betty is on the hunt for wives for her grandsons."

When I take my first bite of one of Gran's rolls, it always takes me back to my childhood when she would bring them out after we spent a night camping under the stars with Gramps. Along with a hot chocolate to "warm the bones," she would say. Carefree times that I would jump back to in a heartbeat, so I could stop thinking about this bank crap.

"I'm not husband material. We all know that. Plus, I don't stay in a place long enough to get attached." Chase says it so matter-of-factly.

"Preaching to the choir, buddy." Yet here I am falling hard for a woman in a town that I don't plan on living in and she doesn't plan on ever leaving. So, thanks, Gran, for the help in pushing me into a mess. I take another sip of the strong coffee. It was what I desperately needed after a night of very little sleep. It felt good to get the fresh morning air into my lungs, to try to clear my head.

"You can't blame Gran about Ashley. It wouldn't have mattered what Gran did if you didn't find her attractive. Then you would just be polite every time Gran sent you on a wild-goose chase. Not having sleepovers at the neighbor's house." Finishing his roll, he screws up the napkin and throws it at me. It's like we have reverted to being teenagers.

"What are you, ten? I mean, who describes having sex with a woman as a 'sleepover'? Besides, I didn't get to sleep, and there were no naked pillow fights either." I get up from the table and take the empty coffee cups to wash in the small sink in the kitchenette.

"Now who's the child?" He slaps me on the shoulder and places the basket of fruit and muffins for later into the fridge to stop them from being attacked by ants. After all, we are still in a barn.

"I'll meet you out in the vineyard when you are done and you can start talking me through the plans you've drawn up for the buildings and what needs to be started next. I want to get a head start on trimming the leaves on the vines like Gramps taught us. At least Gran won't have to pay anyone to come in and tend to them this year. Surely we can juggle both the building and trimming them in preparation for harvest time in September," Chase states as he takes his water bottle and camera with him.

He never goes far without his camera, and I can't wait to see what he comes up with for the special project we assigned him at the last board meeting: to document the next twelve months on Heatherbrae into a photo book for Gran. I'm sure any memories he captures will also make great photographic art to hang in the new buildings, maybe even the gallery.

"Yeah, it's going to be a big job but when Declan gets here, it will make it easier with the three of us. I'll be there in ten."

I wipe the cups, feeling thankful that I have work to do today to take my mind off Ashley. When she got in at 2 a.m. this morning, she sent a message telling me she was home but exhausted and needed sleep. Surprisingly, I had already crashed by then. When I eventually saw it, I didn't want to reply until I had been up for a while, just in case I woke her up. When I finally did, our messaging was brief. She told me that she would be busy all day showing Beau around the clinic and getting him settled in.

I know it's a good thing he's around to take some pressure off Ashley, but I just wish we had time to talk last night to define what we are before she spends all day with Mr. Handsome-Animal-Lover.

Maybe I need to address this awkwardness I have around animals. She wants an animal lover, so I'll do my best. If I need to make peace with that ridiculous goat with the stupid name, then that's what I'll do. But I'll be damned if I let this new guy get the better of me.

My phone is vibrating in my pocket, and I pull it out with a smile, thinking it's Ashley, but my stomach lurches when I see the name *do not answer* lighting up on the screen. It's the fourth time this week the number has called me, and there have been countless emails that keep flooding into my inbox, even though I thought that I had time to pay down the debt. By the sound of the last email there is some new person looking after my case and it's probably just my luck they see it differently than the manager before them. I just can't bear explaining it all again. And although I'm ignoring it, the one thing it does is remind me that there is more that needs to be sorted out before my life can move forward.

I didn't want my time here to be clouded by this, so once again, I delete the message before I even listen to it and shove my phone back into my pocket, pushing it all out of my head as I stride out to the vines.

ASHLEY

"Ooohhh, look at the glow on those cheeks this morning. Come, sit down and tell me everything." Tiff claps her hands with excitement.

"How can I be glowing with only four hours' sleep? Are you delusional?" I plonk myself onto the stool in the teahouse. "None of that fancy tea this morning. Just give it to me straight, black and strong." I want to keep what happened last night with Jake to myself until I have time to breathe and think it through properly. But having met Tiff before, I know the chances of that happening are slim to none.

Tiff leans across the counter and whispers to me, "When are you going to get it through your beautiful little head that you can't fool me? I can read your aura, and that red-colored energy swirling all around you this morning tells me you've been getting down and jiggy with Jake."

Smacking my forehead, I can't control laughing at her. "Okay, start at the beginning. What does red aura mean? And what exactly do you see? Red cheeks? That's just from rushing here this morning so I can make it to the clinic on time." I try putting her off the scent, even though I know it's useless.

"How are we even friends? Your aura is the light around your body. What you are emitting is your energy field. The color red represents passion and vitality, so you either got jiggy with him or your vibrator was working overtime last night," Tiff whisper-lectures me, staring at me like I should know this shit.

"What makes you think it was Jake?" I whisper-hiss back at her, because there are way too many people in here for us to be having this conversation out loud.

"Oh shit, the Aussie vet. No!" She gasps and looks at me like I've done something terribly wrong. "Don't tell me you cheated on

Jake with the new guy before he even worked a day in the clinic. Didn't you learn your lesson with that ex-dickhead of yours? Don't fuck where you work."

"I'm about to lose my mind in this place. Not you too! Firstly, how can I cheat on Jake when we aren't together, and secondly, Beau is my employee, so why would I even look at him like that? Seriously, you're as bad as Jake, the way he turned up at my house last night demanding to know if I kissed Beau at dinner." I realize that I've spoken way louder than I should've by the way people are now looking our way.

"Oh, thank goodness it was Jake. I knew it. You wouldn't do that to that sweet, sexy man." She leans her elbows on the counter and props her chin in her hands, her face mere inches from me. "Is he big? I bet he's big, isn't he. Oh, and does he know what to do with it? Of course he does, don't even bother answering that. Otherwise, why would you be all aglow this morning?"

Standing up tall again, she jumps up and down on the spot, clapping her hands. "I'm so happy for you, and maybe a little jealous. It's been a while since I've done the horizontal tango with a man. Now tell me about this new vet."

She finally makes my tea, and I know it's not what I asked for by the way she takes tea leaves from several different jars before tipping them all into my cup. Who knows what potion she's mixing up for me today.

"No, no, no, no, no! You stay away from Beau. It took me long enough to find another vet. Don't you scare him off with your woo-woo and crazy ways. Nope, off-limits. Promise me." I point at her with conviction.

"Who said anything about using my spiritual greatness? I just want a good fuck, and he's a fresh target." Tiff looks at me like I took away her lollipop by banning her from checking out Beau. Placing my tea on the counter and taking a brown paper bag, she then puts three cookies inside it. "One for you, one for Adi, and one for the hot man from Down Under. Because if Jake is worried about him touching what's his, then he sees him as a threat, so he must be hot. Sister, life around here just got so much more fun. Now drink up so I can read your tea leaves." Tiff is talking fast and bursting with excitement.

"What the hell did you put in your own tea this morning, Tiff, because you are off this planet," I tease her as I take a sip. The combination of flavors is new and tastes nothing like she has made me before. But I decide that I'm probably better off not knowing. I've asked questions this morning and look where it's gotten me. My mind is more jumbled than when I walked in here.

Thankfully more customers pour into the teahouse, and while Tiff is tied up serving them, I finish my cup and deliberately walk behind the counter, tipping the soggy tea leaves down the drain.

"I hate you," she mouths at me as I pick up the bag of cookies and head to work.

"Love you too," I call out, blowing her a kiss and leaving with a smile on my face, happy that I've managed to get out of there without giving away too much.

When I get my life straight in my head, then Tiff will be the first to know. But for the moment, this is just between Jake and me, and that's where I want it to stay. Not in another tea leaf reading.

"Well, you managed to survive your first day in the clinic, but be forewarned that the moment you step out the front door tonight, the eyes of the town will be on you," Adi jokes with Beau as we clean up the exam rooms at the end of the day.

"It's okay. I've lived in a few small towns in my time. I like to give them something to gossip about." Beau chuckles as he restocks the disposable gloves.

Luckily, I had a box of the larger-sized gloves for him, because my medium gloves were never going to do the job.

As thoughts of his hands run through my head, Tiff's stupid tea leaf reading starts swirling to the front of my mind.

Good with his large hands, and dimples—or did she say a single dimple? I can't remember. Staring at Beau, I can see he has dimples just like Jake does. Both men have large hands, which I definitely know that Jake can use to perfection. Oh my God, why am I even entertaining her stupidity?

Beau's words shake me back from my crazy thoughts.

"Wait, what do you mean that you like to give them something to gossip about? Please tell me that I'm not about to be in the middle of some town craziness over you." The last thing I want is a practical joker whipping the town up into a frenzy.

"Don't panic. It's all good fun. Like, I may have checked myself into the bed-and-breakfast last night as Lord John Moreton, the Australian cousin to the King of England."

Adi and I both stop what we're doing and look at him in disbelief.

"You didn't," I gasp. "Lorna-Jean will have sent that gossip through the grapevine within minutes of showing you to your room. And then every person who came through the front door today will be out there telling people about the new Australian vet that we have in town, named Beau Robinson—that is your name, right, that wasn't another one of your jokes?" I ask, feeling a little nervous that I've hired a scam artist but within seconds I know I'm panicking over nothing.

"Wait a minute." I put my finger on my chin. "Tiff didn't say one word about this earlier today, so I'm calling bullshit on your story." There is no way Tiff wouldn't have heard about some lord that had checked into town.

"Oh, you're quick. I've got to give you that. We're going to have so much fun working together." Beau winks at me, and I can't help but burst out laughing, before he and Adi join in.

"It's going to be interesting, that's for sure." Adi starts mopping and ushers us out of the room and into the reception area so the floor can dry.

Beau and I then start wiping over the waiting room chairs with antiseptic, and even though the CLOSED sign is in the window, the front door swings open anyway. People know that the sign means nothing if they need help with a critically sick animal.

"It's only me, Adi," Jake announces as he walks through the door, and I watch as his whole demeanor changes at the sight of Beau standing next to me.

"Ash." Jake looks at me before continuing, "And you must be Beau, the new employee." His shoulders are pulled back as he walks directly to Beau with his hand outstretched. "I'm Jake, Ash's *boyfriend*." He stares him down, making sure Beau understands.

"Jake," I groan, but before I can say another word, he steps sideways so he's now in front of me and puts his hand around the back of my neck, pulling me into one hell of a kiss. It takes the air from my lungs, leaving me speechless and completely stunned.

"Hi, beautiful, how was your day?" Now standing to the other side of me, he links his arm around my waist.

Smacking him on the chest with frustration, I demand, "What the hell was that?"

Jake just looks back at me with a very satisfied grin.

"That was him coming in and cocking his leg to piss on a tree the way a dog does to claim his territory." Beau answers my question. "Hey, Jake, I get it, buddy. The storming out of the restaurant last night sort of gave it away. Ash is off-limits." Beau takes the packet of wipes from my hand and heads to the door leading to the back of the clinic. "I'll leave you two to sort this out. Nice to meet you, Jake," he calls over his shoulder as he goes.

I turn to Jake and throw my hands in the air. "What happened to us talking about this? I'm not your girlfriend, Jake." And as much as I want to be, I just don't know if it's going to work between us if he keeps getting jealous like that.

He steps in front of me so we're looking at each other face-to-face. He slips his hand around my waist, pulling me toward him so our bodies are touching.

"Well, you tell me who you are, because, Ash, you sure as hell aren't my fuck buddy. We are more than that—and you know it. So, call us whatever the hell you like, just as long as he knows you're mine. And if that means I need to go piss on his leg or a tree or whatever so he understands it in doggy language, then I'm happy to oblige."

"Why are men such boys?" I mutter as I drop my forehead onto his chest.

"Better than being assholes."

His reply has my head whipping back up and looking him dead in the eyes.

"You're that too!" I try to push away from him, but his arms are locked tight around me.

"Only for you, beautiful. You bring out the best in me."

And as aggravating as this situation is, he's right. The spark inside him is so damn sexy that I know I'm in real trouble here.

I'm deep in heartbreak territory, and it's already too late to back out.

"We need to have that talk. Time to go home." This time he lets me go, but I take his hand and drag him out the back so we can swear Beau and Adi into complete secrecy. They didn't see or hear a thing.

Yeah right, I give it an hour before it's hot gossip around town.

Chapter Thirteen

Ashley

I send Jake for some takeout pizza while I drive home to Windermere to feed the animals. The time on my own gives me a good idea of having a picnic outside. Grabbing a blanket, some glasses, a bottle of wine, and a couple of beers, I set it all up on the grass out front of the house. Hearing his truck rattling up the drive, I kick off my work boots and take a seat on the blanket, waiting for him to notice me.

Seeing me through the window, Jake's whole face lights up and that one dimple that always makes the butterflies in my stomach take flight.

"I hope you're hungry. I couldn't decide on which topping to get, so I ordered two pizzas with different half combinations. So you have four to choose from." Taking the pizza boxes from the front seat of his truck, he places them on the blanket and drops down next to me. "And before you say anything, I know I was out of place in the clinic tonight, so I apologize—but I'm not making any excuses for being protective of you." Flipping the lids on the pizza boxes, he avoids looking up at me.

"Thank you, and yes, it was out of place because Beau doesn't think of me that way." Not wasting much time checking out the choices because I'm starving, I take a piece of my favorite pepperoni, and the first bite tastes amazing.

"Mhmm, okay." Jake glances at me. "You just keep thinking that. You haven't noticed the way he looks at you. There is no way that guy doesn't think his new boss is hot. I mean, he's not wrong, but now that he knows you're spoken for, he'll go looking elsewhere."

I raise an eyebrow as I reply, "He needs to be careful where he goes looking. Tiff already has her sights set on him, and she hasn't even met him yet. He won't know what's hit him if she gets her hands on him."

"How are you two friends? I mean, she's great and a lot of fun, but you aren't alike in any way," Jake points out as he grabs a slice.

"When we were buying the Abbey Falls clinic from the old vet who was retiring, he told us about a house that was for rent in town. Turns out it was Tiff's. She had already decided to move into the back of the teahouse and from the moment I met her, she claimed me as her friend, kind of like kids do on the first day of school. To be honest, I never would've made it through the last few years without her. She got me out of bed and back into the real world while fending off all the nosy nellies in town and making sure I was eating properly. I love her, and every one of her quirks.

"Besides, I think that it's a good thing we're different. You don't want to be the same personality as everyone, otherwise life becomes boring. I mean, look at us." I wave my finger between us as I take another bite. "You hate animals, and I hate the woods, especially at night."

"I don't hate animals. I never said I hated them. You all just keep saying that," he mumbles through his mouthful. "I just don't have any connection with them, and my first introduction to farm animals was with a very annoying goat named Daisy, a female cow with a very male name of Gerald, and then there's this donkey named Herb, who never shuts up. But hey, I'm trying."

He stops to take a breath before locking eyes with me. "I'm only going to admit this secret out loud just this once, and then I will deny that I ever said it, but . . . Rosie is pretty cool, most of the time. And I can see what having her around has done for Gran in her grief. Besides, she found you when you were lost and look where that's led us . . ." Reaching out and grabbing my hand, he lifts it to his lips and kisses the top of it. "Right here." Then he drops my hand again to grab a beer.

"I knew Rosie would get you to love her. There's just something special about that dog." I raise my glass of Moscato to the beer bottle that he has just opened to cover up for the thumping of my heart. No one has ever kissed my hand over a pizza box before. Either that was incredibly romantic or I need to get out more.

We eat in silence for a few minutes, and I know that we are both trying to avoid the hard conversation that needs to happen.

Being so hungry before means I have eaten way too fast, and now I lie back on the blanket, looking up at the sky and admiring the orange-and-pink glow of the sunset.

"I love it when the days get longer, giving us the extra hours of light." It's that weird time of night where there's still daylight yet you can see the faint moon and the stars begin to twinkle.

"Can you pick out the Big Dipper constellation that I showed you that night in the woods?" Jake asks as he stretches out next to me, crossing one ankle over the other, and links his hands underneath his head.

It's the same way I remember him lying down in the woods that night.

"Is this a test to see if I was listening? Or do I get let off since I was in pain and it was difficult to concentrate?" I reply, knowing full well the only reason I was having trouble was because Jake was so close to me.

He looks up at the sky and smiles. "I'll let you off this time, but looks like I need to give you some more lessons, and there will be tests afterward." Happily pointing the Big Dipper out to me again. "When we were kids, we would all camp out under the stars with Gramps, glued to the sky as he taught us about the stars, in a line of little bedrolls filled with boys who wouldn't stop talking and asking questions. The girls tried outdoor sleeping once but decided a sleepover inside with Gran was more their style."

He sighs as he continues. "I thought my gramps knew everything, and no matter who got scared during the night, he would just pull them close and whisper a little story to them until they fell back asleep. I think it's where I got the love of the great outdoors from."

I can hear the love in Jake's words for a man he hasn't really given himself much time to grieve for.

"I bet you miss him." Turning my head to look over at him, I see he's still transfixed with the sky above.

"More than you can imagine. And mixed in with that is the guilt of not visiting over the last few years. It's been a hard time to process, but by moving here and working in his barn, sitting around his firepit at night, I can feel him close." He stretches out his hand and links it with mine. It feels right.

"Why did you stop visiting?" I don't know if I'm doing the right thing by prying, but I feel like he's finally opening up to me and might need to talk it through.

"Danika didn't like coming here. She's a city girl and told me that she hated how quiet it was, that it was dirty, with nothing around to entertain her." His chest rises, sucking in a deep breath before letting out a deep sigh. "I should've just come on my own but something always seemed to get in the way, and then it was too late."

"Is that why you're here now, to make sure you don't miss that time with Betty?" I can feel the regret radiating off him as he nods his head.

"Yeah, that, and to find myself again. To feel grounded. To start fresh."

There's something more he's not saying, but if he's anything like me, I know he can't be pushed to talk about whatever that is until he's ready.

He rolls onto his side, propping his head up on his elbow before looking at me. "But we have gotten off topic here. This chat is about us, not my sadness or regrets."

He's right, and even though I want to help him carry the weight of sadness in his heart, I'll let him keep that tucked away until he's ready.

It's like his words give me permission to open the door too.

"I'm so confused," I blurt out suddenly as I roll my whole body to face him, tucking my hands under my cheek.

"Tell me what's going on inside that cute little head of yours," he says sweetly.

"How long have you got?"

"All night." He smiles at me, and I know he'll be here all night if I need him to, that I can take all the time I need.

"Alright, here goes." I pause for a second, trying to get my thoughts in order, but it's no use because I've been trying to make sense of things for days and it hasn't made any difference.

"I like you . . . *really* like you." And there's that dimple in his smile from my declaration. "We can't deny the sexual chemistry between us is off the charts." I feel my cheeks blushing slightly.

"If you think last night was good, you just wait until we get a whole night together." He reaches out, tucking away stray wisps of my hair that a slight breeze has blown onto my face.

"Confident much?"

"Tell me I'm wrong," he replies, knowing I have no comeback.

"Anyway, moving on." I roll my eyes at him in a playful way before I continue. "But there are so many obstacles between us. And it's not like we are in our twenties anymore. Time is ticking on these ovaries, and I can't afford to put the energy into a relationship that has an expiration date or is heading nowhere." I can see him taking all my words in and imagine him trying to sort through his thoughts.

"I can't do city life again. My home and my heart are here, in Abbey Falls. And if I've learned one thing from my last relationship, I know that I can't ask you to change your life for me. It doesn't work. Jeremy obviously didn't want to be a small-town vet; he just didn't have the balls to say it."

Jake sits up abruptly. "Hang on, let's get one thing straight. Leaving was his choice. You didn't tie him up, put him in the car, and force him to come here. So don't you take that guilt. Plus, he had plenty of opportunities to tell you he wasn't happy here. That's all on him." It's as though Jake's voice becomes a growl every time he talks about Jeremy. "And that's why that call from him begging for a job and that he wants to come back to you here was just pure bullshit. He was just using you as a last resort because he was desperate."

"Maybe so, but I still won't ask you to move here just for me, because I will be constantly living with the fear that you will eventually leave like he did." There is something about Jake that makes me comfortable enough to lay my true feelings and fears out between us.

"I understand how you feel, and I agree. I don't think you should ever do something so major as to pick up your whole life and move it for someone else. That's something you need to do for yourself. But that's not to say your priorities and future can't change direction because of someone in your life." His hand settles on my hip and just that simple gesture calms me.

"Did I love my life in Sacramento? Yes. But things change, and I came here to help Gran and give myself time to sort some things out. Since I've been here, things have changed a bit. For one thing Sacramento doesn't hold me like it once did. One of the reasons I thought I needed to go back there vanished the moment I met you. And while I'm not sure what my future looks like anymore, leaving temporarily was what I needed to do. My life there is complicated. I spent all day thinking about it, and right now my biggest question is, could I stay here and make a living as a builder? That's the unknown right now."

My heart skips a beat at the thought he's even contemplating staying here, but almost immediately, I squash it down.

Both of us take a few minutes to absorb what each of us has laid out. Really search the soul of the other person. We look so deeply into each other's eyes to see if we can discover what we need in that soul to feel comfortable in any decision we make.

"Ash." Jake's husky voice breaks the silence. "All I'm asking from you right now is to give me a chance to discover where my life is heading. And I know that's a lot."

His hand moves to cup my cheek, and I can't help but lean into it, rubbing against his rough hand.

"But what I can tell you is that there is a very large organ in my chest that wants you to be a major part of whatever life I decide on." He lets go of my face, taking my hand in his and pressing it so hard over his heart that I can feel it beating strongly against my palm like a promise.

"I want that too," I whisper, hoping like hell I'm not going to regret this. "Because as hard as I've tried to resist it, you've managed to work your way into my heart."

Our bodies fall into each other, and the rawness of our kiss seals the choices we are about to make, which our hearts already knew long before we were willing to accept it.

"So about earlier, I'm now officially asking you to be my girlfriend." Jake laughs as we break apart breathlessly.

"Jeez, Jake, we aren't in high school. But if it makes you feel better, yes, you can call me your girlfriend, as long as you don't go making it a big deal."

And before I can say any more, he jumps up, standing at the front of the blanket with his arms outstretched, yelling, "Ashley Alleyne is my girlfriend!" He makes so much noise that all the animals join in, and, of course, Herb is braying loudest of all. "See, they're all happy about it too." He turns back to look at me, face flushed, eyes glowing.

Pushing myself up into a sitting position, I watch him carrying on, and I don't think I've been this happy and relaxed with anyone in a long time. Just letting go and having fun.

"You know, if you're my boyfriend, then you have to make friends with all of them." I laugh, nodding to the noisy barn.

Jake stops his craziness and looks at me. "The deal we made was that I would tolerate having animals in my life, and you would come hiking in the woods with me. So, gorgeous, guess where we're going on your first day off. And I can't wait." He reaches out for my hand, and the moment I place mine in his, I'm being lifted off the ground and into his arms. "Pack your swimsuit and I'll take you swimming at the base of the waterfall. You'll love it."

"That's debatable, but a deal is a deal." Wrapping my arms around his neck and rising onto my toes, I whisper into his ear, "What if I don't own a swimsuit?"

"Even better. Skinny-dipping in the water hole is a great fucking idea." He smiles, kissing me on the tip of my nose. "But an even better idea is that we get naked right now. We have something worth celebrating."

Lifting my feet from the ground, Jake twirls us around in circles, and I'm in fits of laughter at his playfulness. I don't know if he was just in the throes of grief when I first met him, or if being around me is bringing it out more. Either way, I like it a lot.

He starts carrying me toward the house when I ask, "Wait, what about our picnic?"

"I'll clean up later," he replies without stopping.

"Not a chance! Unless you want to deal with a drunk goat when she finishes off the Moscato." I'm giggling now.

"That damn goat! Seriously, I don't know how I'm expected to be friends with such a pest," Jake complains as he places me down and marches back to clear up.

"Welcome to farm life, Jake. If you want me, you get all of them too." I wave my hands toward the barn. "We come as a package deal."

I hear him mumbling as he passes by and heads up the porch stairs to the house. "I think I'd rather have ten kids."

"I assume you mean the human variety," I call after him as the screen door on the house slams, and I can hear him stomping down the hallway to the kitchen.

But it's good to know that children are something he's receptive to. It's probably another conversation we need to have, but I think we have broached enough big emotions for one night.

There's always tomorrow.

JAKE

"That's two nights in a row you've been sneaking in after midnight. Whatever will the neighbors think you've been out doing? Oh, that's right, it's the *neighbor* you *were* doing." Chase looks up at me from the book he's reading, sitting on the couch we have in the little living room in the barn.

"Hilarious as usual." I drop down next to him. "And if I had my way, I wouldn't be here. I'd still be over there in the neighbor's bed, but she got a work call." As much as I don't trust Beau, I can't wait for him to start taking over some of the night callouts and weekend shifts. Then I can get Ash to myself with no interruptions.

"Must be a hard life, being a vet," Chase replies, putting his book down.

"Yeah, but she loves it, and from what I've already worked out, the town loves her too. She's an amazing vet." I rest my head on the back of the couch.

"Seems to me it's not just the town in love with her." Chase smirks at me.

"Not there yet, but I'm definitely falling harder than I was expecting." I'm surprised that admitting it to Chase doesn't scare me as much as I thought it would.

"Oh crap, I wasn't anticipating that answer, but good for you, man." Chase pushes himself up off the couch. "I'm going to hit the hay for the night. And just a heads-up for tomorrow, Gran is calling a family meeting, so don't make any plans with Ashley."

"Should I be worried about what this meeting is about?" I stand up too, because it's late and I could use some sleep. Great sex will do that to a man.

"How would I know? I'm just delivering the message. Night," he calls over his shoulder as he disappears into his room and closes the door.

Standing in the silence for a moment, I consider taking a shower, but weirdly, I'm not ready to wash Ashley off me just yet. So I head to my room, strip, and fall into my bed with a warm feeling in my chest that I know Ashley put there.

I've got a lot of thinking to do, because I don't want to fuck this up with her. And that's when I hear Gramps's voice in my head. Whenever he was teaching me anything, he would say, "*Don't rush this, that's when mistakes happen. If you take your time to think it through, then the whole thing will turn out perfect. So slow down and stop trying to get over the finish line when you are just beginning the race.*" It was usually in relation to a woodworking project in this very barn, but I'm starting to understand that so many of his words were meant for more than just a moment; they were life lessons.

Gramps may not have his feet in his old work boots anymore, but he's still here walking among us.

"Thanks, Gramps, I'm listening. Love you," I whisper as I turn out the bedside lamp and shut my eyes.

Kicking off my boots at the front door of the house, I wander inside for dinner before our "board meeting" as Gran calls it.

"Smells good in here. What's on the menu?" I walk over to Gran, who's at the stove and stirring what looks like meatballs—Gramps's favorite meal.

"Meatballs, roasted vegetables, and mashed potato." She doesn't look up, but I notice the little quiver in her voice. One of Gran's love languages with Gramps was always food, so I understand how hard this is for her.

"It's been a while since we had meatballs around here." Placing my arm on her shoulder, I give her a little squeeze.

"Yeah, it's the right time for them." She straightens herself up and stands a little taller before shooing me out of the kitchen to set the table. Chase comes through the front door with his hair still wet from his shower after our long day out in the vines weeding and making sure they're looking healthy.

I hear a vehicle approaching and Chase calls out, "Are we expecting anyone?"

"Just Doc. I ran out of sugar and asked her to pick me up some on her way home, save me driving into town," she answers him nonchalantly.

"What?" When I walk back into the kitchen, she's taking the vegetables out of the oven, and I place my hand on the lid of the sugar bowl. "There was plenty of sugar when I made you a cup of tea this afternoon."

"Oops, silly me, I spilled it all over the floor earlier." But I'm not buying her story as she looks at me with a sheepish grin.

"What about the spare bag or two in the pantry?" Gran could almost be called a doomsdayer with the way she hoards food. We could easily live here for a month or two and never have to leave the property.

"Yes, dropped that too. Must be getting clumsy in my old age. Maybe I'm getting arthritis in my hands." She continues prepping the dinner while she talks. There is no way this woman has arthritis; not with the way she crochets at speed.

"Gran, you can't have Ash delivering groceries. She's busy enough saving the animals of the world. I could've done it for you."

She just shrugs her right shoulder while draining the potatoes.

I want to call her out on all this bullshit, but I can hear Ash's car come to a halt and the engine turn off, so I head to the front door instead.

"Hey, are you back already?" Ash smiles as she walks up the steps toward me.

"Hi." I lean forward and give her a quick kiss on the cheek, even though I want to give her way more than that. "Back from where?"

"Betty told me you and Chase were out hiking so she was having dinner on her own and that she ran out of sugar for her cup of tea. I was just about to leave the clinic anyway, so it was no trouble."

And this is another reason Ashley makes my world a better place. The way she looks out for Gran has nothing to do with being with me. She would've been doing it whether I was here or not.

Before I can say a word, the screen door hits me in the back, and Gran pushes me out of the way.

"Ashley, dear, thank you so much." Gran takes the bag of sugar out of her hand. "So very sweet of you. We're just about to have dinner and there is plenty, so come, come. Chase, set another place at the table," she yells as she links arms with Ash and drags her inside.

I'm left holding the door open while Ash looks back at me, wondering what the hell is going on, and all I can do is chuckle as I follow.

Gran leaves Ash standing in front of Chase and then rushes back into the kitchen to finish mashing the potatoes.

"Chase, this is Ashley Alleyne, Gran's neighbor and the town vet." Pulling Ash to my side and wrapping my arm around her waist, I lean in closer to Chase. "And my girlfriend, but if you don't want me to hurt you, best you keep that from Gran for the time being."

Chase knows what's going on, but Ash asked for no fuss, so I wasn't planning on telling Gran just yet anyway. It will be fun to string her along for a little while, teach her a lesson for her meddling matchmaking. I kiss the top of her head as Chase starts laughing at us.

"Nice to meet you, Ashley. I've heard all about you. Now get your grubby hands off her, Jake, so I can welcome her to the family."

He pushes my shoulder and gives Ash a hug, just because he knows how much it will piss me off.

"Right, you have had one hug, but don't think you will be allowed near her again. I don't trust you, cuz." I place my arm around her shoulder, feeling very territorial even though we are family. I really need to get this jealousy under control.

"Well, I'm almost afraid to ask what he has told you about me, but whatever it was, I'm sure it's all story and there's no truth to it." Ash lightly smacks me on the stomach which has us all cracking up.

"Well, apparently you're staying for dinner." Chase looks at Ash and then leans in closer, whispering to us both, "So, I would run while you still have a chance." He winks at her before disappearing to grab another set of cutlery and a glass.

"You know I wasn't hiking, right?" I say, turning her to me. "I'm sorry about this. She means well."

"I was starting to work that out. It's fine, but you know if you told her about us, then she wouldn't be trying so hard with her matchmaking."

"No, it serves her right to be kept in the dark. I want to string her along a little first as punishment for her meddling." I know that I won't last longer than tonight's dinner before I put Gran out of her misery, but I at least deserve a little fun.

Ash slips her fingers into the front pockets of my jeans and pulls me close. "You didn't need her help; your irresistible grouchy personality hooked me from the beginning," she teases.

"And now who's making up stories, hmm?" Tapping her on the nose, we separate as we hear Gran approach.

"Sit, sit." Gran is carrying two mountain-sized plates of food.

While I'm pulling out the chair for Ash to sit next to me, Gran places the plates in front of us both while Chase stands behind her with the other two plates.

"Jeez, Gran, I hope you aren't expecting Ashley to eat all that. Damn, even I'm going to struggle." And I eat a lot.

"Oh, shush, you. Doc works just as hard as you do—she needs a hearty dinner. Now eat. Start with the meatballs, Doc, they were Noel's favorite."

Chase smirks across the table at me for being scolded by Gran.

The conversation is kept minimal as we eat. We were all hungry, and there's no disputing what an amazing cook Gran is, so everything tastes delicious.

"You know, Jake, now that Chase is here, you could help Doc with the renovations over at her place. She's barely had time to sleep lately, but with that new vet, she'll have more time to spend at home getting things fixed up. You would both make a good team." Gran sits up in her chair at the head of the table, looking at us both.

"Oh no, I'm fine. Jake already did so much with the fence. I'll get there eventually. All good things come to those who wait." Ash looks down at her plate and pushes around a few of the meatballs with her fork.

I know that time is not Ash's only obstacle; it takes money to renovate. And even if I spent all my time over there, she'll still need to buy materials.

"Gran, with all the work you want done here, I'm going to be fairly busy myself. It's not like Chase knows anything about construction. I've got major works to start this week, if the council gives us the approval they promised after you went in and bullied them about it."

"I didn't bully anyone, young man. I just went in and told them to start doing their job, otherwise I would be bringing my friend Mayor Johnson in next time to see what was holding them up. And then I dropped some of the mayor's favorite cupcakes to his office, which he loved, of course." She crosses her arms over her chest, like she's defending herself from my accusation.

"Gran, if that's not bullying, it's certainly bribery," Chase says, teasing Gran. "You know that no one can resist your cupcakes. Poor Mayor Johnson will end up with diabetes at the amount of sugar you keep delivering. He'll think you have a thing for him."

Gran shoots Chase a glare. "Mayor Johnson thinks nothing of the sort. I'm a married woman. Why would I even be looking at him like that?" Her sentence catches us all off guard, and a silence falls over the table because we all know that's not technically true anymore. "Anyway, it worked. Everything is now approved, and we will be starting next week. It doesn't matter how I got it done, just that I did."

"Well, that's good news about the plans." Ash speaks up with a sweetness she always shows Gran. "And Jake and I have some news for you as well. We're together now, so you can rest easy and stop trying to push us into the same place all the time. We get that you think we would make a good couple."

Gran almost jumps out of her seat with excitement.

"I *knew* the love meatballs would do it. Because you two were taking your sweet time. Someone needed to give you a little nudge."

And I can't help but laugh at Gran thinking it was all her meddling that got Ashley and me together.

"I'm not sure a sledgehammer is what you would call a little nudge, Gran. It's not like you've been subtle with your little schemes. But we love you anyway. Now what's for dessert? Because I know you'll have something out in the kitchen, even though you were '*out of sugar.*'" I raise my fingers and make air quotes, because we all knew how untrue it was.

"It sounds like you need to put these boys to work, Betty, so they aren't just here for a holiday and to give you cheek." Ash reaches out and takes Gran's hand, giving it a reassuring squeeze to let her know she doesn't care about all her little games, and that she'll protect her from her grandsons.

Little does Ash know that Gran has no problem handling us on her own, and she has since the day we were born. I'll be thanking Ash later for changing the subject so easily for Gran. We all need to live in our grief, but by having family and friends around us, it makes the journey a little easier. Ash just helped Gran come through that hard moment.

"Umm, do we get a say in this hard work you're talking about?" Chase mocks annoyance at Ash.

"Nope, not at all. It's why you are here, isn't it?" Looking proud of herself, Ash reaches over to rest her hand on top of mine, and it feels amazing.

"Oh, you are going to fit into this family just nicely, Doc, not that I ever doubted it." Gran gets up from the table to get the dessert, chuckling to herself as she heads to the kitchen.

"Thanks, Betty, but you might regret that statement down the track." Ash is only joking, but I don't like the way it feels like a barb in my heart.

"Never," I growl at her, but she's ignoring me.

"Now, Chase, surely you have some embarrassing stories about Jake that you can share with me. I already know he can't sing in tune. What else is he bad at?" Ash changes the subject and turns to Chase, who's sitting across the table from us with a devilish look in his eyes.

"Don't you dare, or karma will come back and bite you on the butt one day." I'm pointing my finger at him and Chase knows what I really want to say is, "Karma's a bitch, buddy," but we're in Gran's house, so I can't. And I know full well that no matter what I say, nothing will stop him anyway.

"Well, there was this one time . . ." Chase relaxes back into his chair, and I know this is going to get ugly real quick.

"Here we go." I roll my eyes at him and get ready for the onslaught.

Chapter Fourteen

Jake

"I can't believe you told Ash about that girl at the fair. It was hardly my fault that the ride spun so much I puked on her. Seriously, you had to pick that story over all the dumb shit we did together." Both of us are standing at the sink while I wash the dishes and Chase dries them.

Ash left to go home and feed the animals, and we insisted that Gran take a seat to relax while we cleaned up.

"What, you think I was going to give her any stories that involved me? I'm not that stupid. Suck it up, princess. She still wanted you to walk her outside to her car, where I assume you kissed the hell out of her. So, she's not too turned off you yet. There's still time for that." Chase whips my leg with his wet dish towel.

I grind my teeth together from the sting and mouth to him, "Motherfucker." Technically I didn't say it, so hopefully Gramps won't strike me down with lightning.

"Chase, stop whipping your cousin and hurry up and finish. We have that face video thingy meeting. I don't want to keep Becks waiting," Gran calls from the living room.

"How the hell did she know what I was doing?" Chase starts wiping quicker.

"Oh, I've given up trying to work out how Gran knows everything. Now get moving. We can't keep precious little Becks from his solo gym session because he has no friends and then home to a shower with his hand." I smile at my own joke.

"You're cruel, and don't pick on him just because you have a girlfriend now. We've all been through those droughts—so did you just a few weeks ago. Well, not me, but the rest of you old boys have, I'm sure."

Maintaining a straight face, I just roll my eyes at him calling me old. He's not that much younger.

"So full of yourself. They say it never happened unless there is evidence, but I've seen all the photos you've posted from your travels. There's no way you haven't slept with half those models from the way they look at you through the lens." I finish washing the last pan and place it on the drainboard.

"What can I say. I'm a chick magnet." Chase holds his arms out, trying to show me why women are so attracted to him.

"Sorry, can't see it." Wiping my soggy hands all over his shirt before leaving the kitchen earns me a balled-up wet kitchen towel in the back of my head. I flip him the bird as I walk through the door.

I take the chair next to Gran, and Chase joins us while the video call starts connecting with Declan and Beckett.

"Hi, Gran." Declan's face appears, smiling like always.

"What are we, chopped liver?" Chase asks jokingly.

"Gentlemen," Declan replies as Beckett's face appears on the screen too.

"Good evening," a grumpy Beckett says while looking to another one of his computer screens.

"Hello, my boys. How are you both?" Gran's eyes light up.

"I'm great and counting down the weeks until I'll be there. Feels like I'm missing out," Declan replies, and I can tell he means every word.

"Fine. Busy," are the only words Beckett answers with, and it's obvious that he's doing two things at once.

"We won't keep you long, Becks, I know how important your work is to you." Gran panders to the arrogant asshole.

I hear Chase groan beside me, and it's clear from their facial expressions that the other guys heard him too. Declan is trying not to laugh, while Beckett stares at Chase with a look that could strip paint off walls. It never gets old, pushing Beckett until he explodes. I guess this childish side of us will never grow up. And if I'm honest, part of me misses my brother, no matter how grumpy he is.

The more I spend time working here, it's like the memories of our childhood together are flooding back, not only visiting here with Gramps and the boys, but from home too. Beckett might have always been a perfectionist but he used to carry it less rigidly. I wonder if we will ever be able to get back to that happier relationship we used to share, but I just don't know if too much water has passed under the bridge, and if there's any chance of coming back from the distance that's now between us.

"It's okay, what did you want to talk about?" Beckett now looks into the screen like we have his whole attention. I want to say, "Nice of you to finally join us," but I bite my tongue instead and keep that opinion to myself.

"Jake has already let you know that we got the council's approval, but there are going to be a couple of stipulations. It's something Gramps and I always talked about but we never got around to, and that's putting in a dedicated water tank and installing sprinkler systems on the roofs of all the buildings, just in case we ever get a fire out here. Should be simple, I'm guessing." Gran looks around at us all, and when no one comments, I guess it's left to me.

"No problem. I can organize it once we see what specifications the council gives in their approval. What else?" I ask.

"Make sure you add that into the budget when you get the price, Jake," Beckett grunts.

"That would be in the spreadsheet I built and have been maintaining since we started." And he wonders why we clash these days. Guess I know now that the answer is yes, to the question whether too much water has passed under that bridge between me and the arrogant prick.

"Yes, the same one I reconfigured so it made more sense." He looks me in the eye, and I can tell he wants me to get back in my box; finance is his world.

Gran gives us the look and we all stop squabbling. "Moving on, we also need solar panels, you know, all the necessary environmental things that people talk about. We have to look after this world for my future great-grandbabies."

We all ignore her not-so-subtle comment. Bless Gran, she believes she's running this project—and I would never tell her anything different—but I have already factored that into the costs.

"Okay, now that I've told you all that, I want to get onto talking about the restaurant. I've got a manager who's also a chef. So, you don't need to worry about looking for one." She sits with her hands in her lap, looking quite pleased with herself.

"Wait, we haven't even started building yet, and you're already hiring people?" Beckett looks like he's about to blow a fuse. "You can't do things like that, Gran. I knew it was a bad idea to let this happen without me being there. Please tell me you haven't asked them to sign anything yet, before I've had a chance to review the contract." He may be trying to say it patiently, but he's not even in the same zip code.

"You're welcome to join us, Becks," I spit back at him, using Gran's nickname for him to piss him off further.

"Oh, Becks, I haven't hired them yet, I just know who it will be. That's all." She shuts down Beckett before he can get more wound up. "Remember, I'm the general manager, so I get the final say."

It's not even worth the battle with Gran now. Anyway, whoever she has lined up might be perfect for the job. I mean, Gran is the only local among us, so she knows more people than we do and has all the connections in Abbey Falls.

We are all waiting for the next bombshell when she pulls out a painting from down beside her chair. And boom, there it is.

"Here is the first painting for the gallery. I painted it especially." She looks so damn proud of the canvas that she's holding up, but it just looks like a blur of colors to me. It's atrocious, but how do I say that? Thank goodness Declan the peacemaker is the first to speak.

"Wow, Gran, I didn't know you had taken up painting. I can't see through the computer properly—where is that scene from?" Good call, Declan, blame the computer.

"Oh, I've been painting for years, which is why I wanted Gramps to build me a gallery, but he never seemed interested. This is the view from the house out over the vineyard, and I'm only going to show you this one; the rest are a surprise for later."

Shit, this is going to be a disaster. No wonder Gramps didn't want the gallery. He obviously didn't want to hurt her feelings.

"That's great, Gran. Well, put that one safely away, and we look forward to seeing them all when the time comes," Declan says as Chase kicks my foot, and we both start panicking at how we're going to handle this.

"Yes, I have a secret storage area, so don't go peeking. I don't want anyone to ruin the surprise." Her smile is so bright.

"Wouldn't dream of it, Gran," I say with a little cough at the same time.

Beckett's phone rings, and he glances down at it, frowns, and then picks it up. "Sorry, must take this. Bye, Gran." And his face is gone.

"He works so hard. We need to get him to Heatherbrae for a while so he can relax a little and breathe some of this good clean fresh mountain air." She puts her painting down beside her before straightening back up. "Bye to you, my Declan." Blowing a kiss to him, he takes the hint.

"Bye, all, talk soon." And with that, he's gone as well.

"Feel like a beer?" Chase looks at me as we put the dining room chairs back.

"You have no idea how much." I sigh. "Good night, Gran, we're heading out to the barn." Leaning down, I kiss her on the cheek and then Chase does the same.

The moment we are both out the front door, boots on and far enough away from even Gran's supersonic hearing, I look over at him and explode into laughter. "Fuck me. Gramps is probably up there howling with laughter at the mess he has left us."

"Yeah, it's our punishment for not visiting more often before he died. This is going to be one long fucking year." Chase kicks a stone on our walk back to the barn, and we both keep chuckling at how bad the painting was.

"It was just smudges of color on a canvas. You can't call that art." I look at him as he opens the door to the barn.

"Oh, you would be surprised what people call art these days. Some of the things I've seen in galleries around the world just baffle me. Gran could be sitting on a million-dollar fortune with those blobs of paint. You just never know." He snorts as he grabs two beers out of the fridge.

"Find me a canvas and some paint then, because I could use that kind of money."

Chase laughs at me not knowing the truth behind that statement. I really could use the money, that kind of cash could fix everything.

ASHLEY

Waking up in Jake's arms is the best way to start the day.

Well, weekend, actually. It's the first weekend of summer and my first official one off. After yesterday's Fourth of July fireworks celebration in town, I've never been so glad we don't have to get up early. Last night was a long and tiring one, and after trying to settle all the animals who were spooked by the fireworks that went off incessantly, I'd been more than ready to crash.

Jake has spent the last month with Chase, working hard to get all the land at the vineyard back into perfectly fertile paddocks. Making sure all the wires that the vines run along on were fixed and ready to hold the heavy crops as the grapes start to grow. Trimming and pruning season has begun and it's a lot. And in the meantime, doing all the maintenance on the outside of the barn and Gran's house ready for when Declan arrives in three days' time, so they can start the next big project, which is the cellar and winemaking room.

But the best thing about the last month has been watching Jake find his happy place on Heatherbrae. I can see him falling more and more in love with the place as he starts to bring it back to life. I'm not sure he's noticed that at the same time it's bringing him back to life too.

I can't believe it's been four weeks since Beau started working at the clinic, fitting in far better than I could've hoped for. He's a good vet, so I don't have to worry about my patients. They are in safe hands. At times making me think back to the kind of vet Jeremy was. How he would complain about everything from aggressive animals to the late hours. Beau's humor and laid-back attitude are going down well with the town, and of course, half the single women in Abbey Falls are after him. I did try to warn him what it would be like as the new piece of man meat in town, but he just responded with "Bring it on."

That Aussie guy is going to be breaking hearts all over town.

Thankfully Beau and Jake are getting along, now that Jake's jealousy has settled. I wouldn't say it's disappeared altogether, though, by the way he makes sure to kiss and touch me in front of Beau. But we are starting to feel like one happy little family at the clinic. Hell, Beau has even told me to head home from the clinic, that he's got the last few patients handled so I could get some rest before I was on call for the night and to give me time to see Jake. Jeremy never offered, not even once, to take any workload off me and complained profusely about callouts at night, so it was usually me that would do them. How life can be so different with the right colleague! But I hope it continues.

The early-morning light is streaming through the bedroom window where we left the curtains open last night to look up at the stars. It's easily becoming one of my favorite things to do.

My head is resting on Jake's chest, and I can feel him starting to move at the same time, when his arms start to hug me that little bit tighter.

"Morning, beautiful." That morning rasp in his voice is like turning the switch on for my body. It gets me every time.

"Good morning." I raise my head to look up at him so I can kiss him. His stubble around his lips gives it that little bit of ruggedness.

"Oh, it's good, alright. Your first weekend off, and what better way to start it than with morning sex." He rolls us so he's now on top, pinning me to the bed.

"You're insatiable. Twice last night wasn't enough?" I tease him, running my hands over his bare ass.

"Are you sore?" The softness in his voice shows me how much he cares. "I wasn't gentle last night," he asks with a sense of concern.

"No, you weren't." Biting down on my bottom lip, I can't help but blush a little. "But I loved every single minute of it."

"I aim to please." He leans down, placing soft kisses on my neck, and I can feel myself getting wet already.

"There's no denying that you please me, over and over again." I sound breathy and already know I'm going to regret this. "But if you want me to be able to hike all day today, you need to rethink your morning wake-up ideas."

"Ughhh." His head drops onto the bed next to my neck, and I can't do anything but laugh at him. "Looks like we aren't going hiking then."

"Oh my God, you're ridiculous." Pushing him off me, I scramble from the bed and stand naked with my hands on my hips.

"Yes, I am. But while you get to hike pain free, look at what I'll be suffering with." His hands frame his cock that is ready for a good time, standing straight up and looking for attention.

"And that there is why we aren't fucking this morning. Look at the size of it."

Now he's not even trying to hide how much he likes hearing me say that as he gazes up at me with a proud look on his face.

I turn and walk toward the bedroom door, swaying my hips just a little more than usual before looking over my shoulder. "But I didn't say oral sex in the shower was off-limits." Opening the door, I start to run for the bathroom as I hear the creaking sound of the bed and then his feet hit the floor.

"Hell yeah!" he bellows at the top of his voice as he follows me.

I fumble as I try to get the hot water up to temperature in the shower before feeling his chest against my back and then his hands cupping my breasts. He licks up my neck, and the nibbling on my ear makes it so hard for me to concentrate.

"Fuck, you taste so good." Jake proceeds to drag his lips over my shoulder and down my back, nipping and licking at my skin that is covered in goosebumps. Electricity is coursing through my veins, escalating every time he squeezes my breasts and grazes over my nipples.

The water running over my hand is finally hot enough, and I can't wait any longer. Being an old farmhouse, the shower is over the bath, and I haven't had the funds to renovate it yet. Stepping in and pulling him in with me, our bodies collide under the warm water. Jake's hands are in my hair, and our mouths seek each other out like we have been starved of contact. Hands roam, lips devour each other, and the water cascades down through all the crevasses of our molded bodies.

It's my turn to take the lead, and after last night's awesome sex fest, with the way he made me feel so treasured and wanted, Jake deserves to be worshipped too. I drop down onto my knees in the bath where his body protects me from the water as it pours down onto his back. I'm now eye level with his cock that I've come to understand how skillful he is at using.

"I should be feasting on you first." He runs his hand over my head and down through my hair that is all plastered onto my back. His other hand is under my chin, tilting my head to look up at him.

I shake my head. "Let me do this. You won't regret it, I promise."

"You on your knees begging to suck me off is a fantasy I didn't know how much I was longing for until now." Running his thumb over my wet lips, he stops in the middle of my bottom lip. "Open up for me like a good girl."

He might have just had a lightning-bolt moment of a fantasy, but that same bolt of electricity just went all the way through me too. Jake standing above me and demanding that I do what he wants has just given me a new desire.

Dropping my lip, his thumb then enters my mouth, and I can see the darkness descend in his eyes.

"Suck it," he demands in a tone that sends shivers through me.

Dragging my lips back and forth over his thumb, I can't help pushing my thighs tighter against each other to stem the need to touch myself. Jake wraps my hair around his hand, pulling tighter. Spurring me on.

My hands, that were resting on his thighs to stabilize myself, I'm moving now to wrap one around his cock, and the other to slide down and cup him around his balls. They feel so full as I roll them in my hand while I continue sucking on his thumb.

"Fuuuccckkkk," he growls as I drag my hand to the tip of his engorged cock, twirling my fingers around it and then back down to the base.

"Open." His hand is back on my chin, pulling my mouth open as wide as it will go. He's pushing his hips forward until the tip of his cock is on my bottom lip and my tongue is already out to take the first taste of the precum that is leaking profusely from him.

"You hungry for this cock, beautiful?"

I can tell he's holding himself back and is close to losing his load before I even take him.

"Ravenous." I kiss the tip before opening my mouth again, ready to take him.

"Then take what you want from me," he growls.

Rubbing my thighs together, I try so hard not to come just from his words.

With my hand, I feed his cock into my hungry mouth, running my tongue along the vein protruding on the underside of it.

Warm water from the shower pools around my knees, and I realize Jake has placed his heel over the drain so the tub is starting to fill. He doesn't need to worry about keeping me warm, because I'm burning up with sexual heat.

The harder and faster I suck, the more his body takes over, pumping in and out of my mouth, using me just how he needs to get off, and I'm here for it.

"Spread your knees," he groans demandingly. "Touch yourself."

Although I'm desperate to make him come, I'm so turned on that the moment I part my knees the small amount I can in the bath, it's enough to let the cool air hit my clit. The erotic feeling of being told to pleasure myself while he watches and gets off is enough to take me to the edge of an orgasm, even before I've touched myself. So, the moment I move my fingers and start circling my hard clit, I'm moaning on his cock.

Both of us are now frantically racing toward our orgasms, and Jake can't hold it any longer.

"Shit! Ash, I'm coming," he mumbles as I taste the first shot of cum hitting the back of my throat and then swallow it down.

I rub my finger faster and harder now as I reach my climax, moaning louder around his cock. He continues to unload inside my mouth, and I lap up every last drop while I continue to ride through the high.

I did this. Made him lose his mind so much he couldn't hold back, coming before me. He's never done that before, and I feel proud that I managed to unravel him like that.

I slide slowly off him, licking him clean as I do, and the moment I look up into his eyes, it's like something has changed. I don't know what it is, but he's seeing me differently.

"Jake," I gush.

It's as though the sound of my voice has snapped him out of the place his mind had taken him to. He quickly reaches his hands down under my arms and lifts me to my feet. Thankfully he doesn't let me go, because my legs are still weak from the explosive orgasm that just wracked through my body.

His foot shifts to let the water run down the drain, and he spins us to the side so that we're now both in the warm spray of the water.

Whatever thoughts are in his mind, he starts expressing what he's feeling by letting loose in the kiss he's now devouring me with. It's hard but sweet at the same time. Like he's trying to tell me how he feels but can't say it in words, and I feel every part of that same feeling too. We are past the stage of keeping things simple between us.

Simple is the first step to complicated, and we're already there. But what comes after complicated?

Right in this moment, in the deepness of a desperate kiss, complicated feels like it is racing toward love.

"Ash." He calls my name in such a breathy, desperate way.

"I know," I whimper, trying not to cry at the thought of the pain I know is going to come later, when he leaves. Because he *will* leave, they always do, no matter what he says, and I can't make him stay, I won't.

I drop my head onto his chest to find comfort and conceal my face. We're standing together with the water falling around us, hiding my tears.

Our breathing starts to slow, and I pull myself together because I don't want to waste the time I do have with Jake by feeling sad. There will be plenty of time for that after he has gone.

I smack my hand playfully on his tight ass. "Are you taking me hiking or what? It's my first proper weekend off in over three years. Let's not waste it."

"Oh, I wouldn't call blowing my mind a waste of time." His smile is back, and before I have time to reply, he pulls me into the shower stream that is starting to get cold.

"Shit, we need to hurry, the hot water is about to run out." We scramble for the soap, then lather up and rinse off, panting as the water becomes icy.

"Well, that's one way to kill a boner," Jake grumbles as he shuts off the water. Climbing out of the tub, he reaches for the towels and hands me one as he says, "We need to fix that problem."

"What, the boner or the shower?" I laugh as I step out of the bath to dry off.

"Both," he complains.

I finish drying the water off my body, then wrap the towel around my wet hair before walking toward my bedroom to find some clothes. And then it hits me: I would never have done this with Jeremy. We were never comfortable enough to walk around naked together in any of the places we lived. Yet Jake is different; he gives me this inner confidence with my body that I didn't know was missing.

It's the feeling of allowing myself to be beautiful in my own skin.

If I learn one thing from this relationship that I will keep forever, that's it.

"On second thought, scrap fixing the shower if I get to see this view every time we finish." He chuckles as he follows behind me.

Turning to face him, I walk slowly backward, with my hand up in front of me.

"Stop with that thought, right now. You are taking me hiking, remember?" Stopping at my bedroom door, he's two feet away from me, stark naked too. It's a sight I will never get sick of seeing.

"Oh, I will be taking you, alright." The glimmer in his eye has me running into the bedroom, squealing as he chases me until we both fall onto the bed together, laughing.

I could love a life like this.

Days filled with happiness and love.

I'm falling in love with Jake Davis, and there is nothing I can do to stop it, so I tell myself that the pain of losing him will be worth the bliss and fall deeper.

JAKE

I'm torn between whether I should be walking in front of Ash to protect her from any danger or walking behind her so I can catch her if she falls. But I must admit, the choice to walk behind her is giving me an amazing view of her ass climbing up the trail.

I thought this would be fun, and even with the sexy view in front of me it's the most stressful hike I've ever been on. Normally it's just me and I don't have to look out for anyone else. But Ash isn't just anybody.

That feeling that slammed into my chest this morning is something I can't ignore. Since the first day I met Ash, it's a feeling that's been building gently, and I've been happily letting it. But this morning, it felt like a tidal wave of emotion swamping me, and there was no chance to run from it. I couldn't breathe when the realization hit me. I've crossed the line of just falling, and I'm now firmly on the ground in the land of love.

If I'm honest with myself, I always knew where things were heading with Ashley. Now, I need to dig deep and do some serious thinking on where my life is heading and how I can deal with some of the ghosts of my past. Or not so much ghosts, more very alive and persistent problems . . .

But that's not what today is about, so I push those thoughts aside and try to concentrate on showing Ash the beauty of the woods. I want her to see that connecting with nature can take away the pressure and stress that builds up in our everyday. I want her to love it as much as I do.

"When you get to that fork in the path ahead of us, we go to the right so we can head for the waterfall, but just stop for a minute so we can take a breather." I reach for the water bottle on the side of my backpack, getting it ready for Ash, and then I'll take a drink too. We have been hiking for just over an hour, and it's been on a steady incline. Once we turn this corner it's going to get steeper for a bit, but the reward of the view when we get there makes it all worthwhile.

I offer her the water as I set the pack down and let my eyes rake over her to make sure she's doing okay and not feeling too fatigued. I don't doubt how fit she is with the hard work she does every day, but hiking like this requires a different type of fitness.

"How do you feel?" I ask, kissing her on the forehead as she finishes her drink and then passes me the bottle.

"I feel good, surprisingly. The only thing that feels sore are my eyes from focusing on watching out for snakes."

Her reply has me spitting out half my water with laughter.

"Hey, don't waste that water. We might need that later. You never know when you might get stuck in the woods." She starts patting me on the back as I begin choking on the other half of the water that went down the wrong way.

"You're ridiculous, you know that?" It feels like I've almost coughed up a lung, but I finally get my breathing under control.

"The stomping of our feet through the woods will be enough to scare the snakes away. Yes, you still need to pay attention, but there is not going to be a snake every four feet. I know you have a fear of them, but really, the only snake you should be scared of today is mine." I thrust my hips at her and watch as she leans forward, holding her sides with laughter.

"Should I be worried that you find my trouser snake that funny, offended even? If I remember rightly you were gagging for it this morning." My smirk gets her attention straight away.

"You did not just say that." She gasps at me.

"What, you don't like to hear the truth?" I'm waiting for her to bite, and she has no idea I'm doing this to take her mind off the fear of what is crawling around in the woods.

But what I didn't count on was for her to outwit me.

Throwing the bottle of water at me, she walks up beside me and picks up the pack, shoving it at me to put on my back and then pushes me to go first.

"I was gagging *on* it actually," she whispers in my ear from behind me. "Now move so you can be the one that the snake attacks, since you are so confident that we are safe."

With another push in the back from Ash, I start up the trail and can't stop smiling.

"Where have you been all my life? I've never met anyone who could take a joke like you and give it back just as quick."

"Hiding away in Abbey Falls, waiting for someone to bring out my humor," she cheerily replies. "And I kind of like having this sort of fun. I think I've been taking life too seriously."

"Yeah, me too. Maybe we both deserve this kind of relationship. The last few years have been heavy for us, and it's time to start living again."

"I like that plan."

Her words stop me in my tracks, and I turn to face her before taking her face between my hands.

"Me too, beautiful. Damn, there is so much I need to tell you." Emotions are flooding forward, and the words are on the tip of my tongue.

Her finger lands on my lips and shushes me. "Shhh. I know, but not now. Today is just about having fun. Save it for later when the time is right."

Her words throw me off guard.

Maybe she doesn't feel the same. And that's okay, but I don't know how much longer I can hold it in.

I love you, Ashley Alleyne, and if you aren't ready to hear it yet, that's okay. I'll just show you instead.

If it means picking up my life, moving here, and burying all my past mistakes, I'll do it. He might not have picked you, but I'm not that stupid.

I'll pick you first every single time.

Now I just need to work out how.

Chapter Fifteen

Jake

"Wow. I had no idea how beautiful it would be." Ashley stands, taking in the view, sweaty and dirty, with a smudge on her forehead where she has wiped away the effort of the steep ascent.

But I can see a different view to the one she's talking about.

The beauty I see is in the slightly disheveled woman standing in front of me.

In all my previous relationships, the women needed to look perfect all the time, even when there was no one around. Don't get me wrong, I love to see someone taking care of themselves, but after meeting Ash, I now know that can mean different things to different people. And watching her find the beauty in something I enjoy means more to me than any pretty dress or perfectly styled hairdo. I don't care if the purse matches the shoes or whether diamonds from a certain designer are the only ones acceptable.

I fell into that materialistic trap with Danika, and it became a slippery slope of trying to keep her happy. One that has me in the trenches of financial hell, trying to claw my way out, and it was all for nothing. Looking back now, I know it was really just about me trying to hang on to her when she was already gone long before she left.

"I can't believe I've lived in Abbey Falls all these years and my fear of snakes has made me miss out on this."

The emotion in her voice pulls me to her. I walk up behind her and wrap my arms around her so we can just take a moment to soak in the spectacular view in front of us.

"This is not the Abbey Falls that the town is named after. I've been there, but I believe this waterfall is more special because not many people know it's here, and it's on the land that my family owns. So, to me that means something."

"What's this waterfall called?" Ash wonders.

"Welcome to Peace Falls. The name's kind of fitting, don't you think?" Listening to the sound of the water hitting the rocks at the bottom of the falls, a peacefulness settles in my soul. "I used to come here as a teenager on my own, when things got hard trying to live up to my brother's high standards and my sister was being a moody teenager. Gramps had brought us up here enough times we were allowed to hike on our own because he knew we were safe."

Memories of those years come flooding back from a place I had obviously buried them. I love my family, but sometimes growing up as the youngest was tough. So much expectation from so many angles. But never from my grandparents. They were always a safe place. We were all equal in their eyes.

"So perfect." Ashley is in awe, like I was the first time I came here. "I can imagine sitting here for hours just taking it in. How deep is the water at the bottom of the waterfall? Can you really swim in it, is it safe?" Ash looks over her shoulder at me like an excited child.

"Deep enough to dive right in. The water is so clear most days that you can see the rocks on the bottom." Leaning close to her ear,

I ask, "Did you bring your swimsuit or are we skinny-dipping?" I feel her shiver all over at my suggestion.

"You wish. Of course I brought a swimsuit, and you know that because you were the one who sorted out your precious pack. I hope you at least brought better food this time, rather than cardboard snack bars," Ash quips back, taking a few steps forward onto the rocks and glances into the rock pool.

"Oh, my wounded heart. Those so-called cardboard bars you speak of saved you from starvation when you were the stranded damsel in distress." Placing my pack down on a high rock where it will stay dry, I start setting up our lunch. "I think you'll take back your harsh words when you see what I prepared for you today."

Knowing I was going to be at Ash's in the morning, I sent a message to Gran and asked her to make me some of her famous ham sandwiches, as well as some raspberry and white chocolate chip cookies. They are to die for.

"Oh wow, you aren't taking credit for Betty's cooking, are you?" Ash stands beside me as I lay a towel on a large rock next to us.

"Technically I prepared them, when I took them out of the pack and laid them out here for you." Passing her a sandwich, I help her to sit beside me. "But I'd be kidding if I tried to pass off my cooking skills to be as good as Gran's."

"You did okay with those steaks the other night." She smiles as she takes her first bite and then moans as the food hits her taste buds.

"I can grill, make a basic roast, and cook some pasta successfully, but anything harder than that and it's takeout for me." My first mouthful takes me straight back to summers up here with Gramps. There is some special homemade chutney that Gran puts on the sandwiches that makes them extra delicious, but she won't tell anyone the recipe.

"Well, we make a great couple then, because I can boil eggs, make an omelet, heat up frozen meals, and cook instant noodles. It's how I got through college, and then life became too busy to learn to cook anything more than that. Most nights I'm still at the clinic, so I just pick up something on the run on the way to a call. Or heat up a meal that Tiff has put in my freezer because she claims I'm going to die from malnourishment if she doesn't keep me well fed. Always overreacting."

Ash rolls her eyes, but it reminds me that I need to thank Tiff one day for how good a friend she has been to Ash.

"All I can say then is we are doomed." I nudge her with my shoulder, and we both giggle.

A comfortable silence settles over us as we enjoy the sounds of the woods blending with the splashing of the water hitting the rocks.

But there is one noise that has us both pricking up our ears in shock.

"Rosie!" Ashley pushes up in a panic as the dog comes ambling out of the woods behind us, her nose to the ground like she's following our scent.

"Shit, is it Gran?" I reach into my pack for my phone, which I deliberately put on silent because I didn't want to be disturbed while Ash and I were spending time together.

"What are you doing all the way up here, my beautiful girl?" Ashley is down on her knees patting Rosie and giving her all the love while checking her over to make sure she isn't hurt in any way.

CHASE: Rosie started carrying on after you left. Barking and howling, looking up into the woods where you walked. Couldn't do anything to calm her down, so Gran said to

let her go. Hope she finds you and I
haven't done the wrong thing.

"It's okay, Chase said she dashed after us." I pass Ash my phone for her to read the message.

"Oh no, were you worried about us, Rosie?"

Watching Ash with her, she's completely settled now, sitting calmly and her tail wagging.

"Damn, I've got it. I think she was worried you might hurt yourself again. She wanted to make sure you were safe. Nice to know you trust me, Rosie. I can take care of Ash all by myself, you know." I lean over and pat her on the head because I will never forget her help in rescuing Ash that night, and look where it got me.

"Rosie, come." I call her to where there is a little pool of fresh water between some rocks. "Grab a drink, girl." I know she must be thirsty from her long trek.

"I think you have been hiding your inner animal lover from me." Ash pulls her swimsuit out of the backpack. "If you can become the man who has conquered his fear of animals, then I can be a little bit more adventurous for you." She starts to undo the buttons on her shirt and says, "Turn around while I change." She then flashes her sexy smile at me.

"Not a fucking chance. Get it all off, baby." I pull my shirt over my head with full intention of snatching that swimsuit out of her hands the moment she's naked, scooping her up, and jumping into the rock pool together.

If Ash is going to get the full experience of this amazing place, then the best way to do that is naked and in my arms. Not even Rosie can protect her from me this time.

Pushing my boots and socks off, I drop my shorts and underwear onto the rocks. Then I'm standing naked, watching her while trying not to laugh at her turning her back on me as she strips.

Like it turns me on any less looking at her profile, with that perfect little ass on full display. Stepping as quietly as I can, I move with stealth as close to her as possible as she steps out of her underwear and trousers. She made the rookie mistake of taking her shirt and bra off first, so she's now naked and getting ready to step into her one-piece swimsuit.

Taking the opportunity, I pounce on her from behind.

"Jakeeeeeee." Her scream echoes all around us, bouncing off the rocks.

Within a few steps, we launch into the air and then break the surface of the water with a huge splash. Not letting her go, I kick forcefully to send us back up to the surface until our heads pop up for air.

I'd forgotten how cold the water is up in the mountain and straight off the waterfall.

I let Ash go so she can get her balance in the water and suck in a bit of air that I'm sure whooshed out of her the moment we were airborne.

"I can't believe you did that." She splashes water at me, half annoyed at taking her by surprise, but I can tell that the other half of her is trying to hold back laughter.

"Just giving you the full nature experience. There is nothing purer than the water in this swimming hole." Lying on my back, I float, enjoying the sun warming my face.

"So pure it's straight off a glacier somewhere, it's so freaking cold." I can hear her shivering.

"Come here, baby, and I'll warm you up." I reach out to pull her to me.

"I don't know if I can trust you to just warm me up." Ash swims back one stroke for every stroke I swim toward her. "You are trouble." She splashes me again as I match her strokes. "With a capital *T*."

"Yeah, and you love me for it." I lunge for her as she freezes, staring at me. Pulling her close and kicking my legs to keep us both afloat, the words I just said come racing back to me. I can feel the panic in her as her body stiffens, which has me quickly fumbling over what to say next.

"You know what I meant. Being an idiot makes you laugh, and you know you like it." I sound like a high school kid trying to dig himself out of a hole.

If she hadn't reacted the way she did earlier today, shushing me and telling me, "*not today,*" I would've just blurted out the words that are sitting so close to the surface. But I'm holding back so I don't spook her any more than I already have.

"Anyway, I should be the one worried about the cold water again for the second time today. Shrinkage is not flattering to the male ego, you know." Changing the topic as quickly as I can, I run my hands down over her ass and lift her legs so they're wrapped around my waist, making it easier for me to keep us afloat.

"I'm not sure that's even a thing, because what I can feel right now still can't be considered small." Her face begins to relax again as we move past my dropping of the *L* word.

"Besides, I should be the one panicking. What if someone else arrives here and I'm naked. Like, full butt naked. Do you realize I've never been naked outside in the open before? And now I'm in the middle of the woods, a place that freaks me out, with another human being . . ."

I interrupt her rant to add, "And a dog."

"Fine, and a dog, plus a million creepy crawlies that I don't even want to think about that might be swimming inside my hoo-ha right now. For fuck's sake, how do I let you get me into these stupid situations?" The way she's pushing her pussy so hard against my stomach, I'm guessing she thinks she's sealing it off from danger, and that's what's got me now absolutely losing it.

I struggle to hold us both above the water. My concentration is lost from laughing so hard at her comment.

"It's not funny!" she exclaims, slapping me on my shoulder. "I'm a vet, I know about animals. There is weird shit that lives in water."

I kick my legs and propel us toward the rock ledge so I can hang on to it with one hand.

"Okay, let's get a few things straight so we can relax and enjoy the rest of the swim." I was not picturing that she would freak out this much.

"Firstly, the only thing that will be inside your hoo-ha while we're in this water is me—if you're lucky. Secondly, Peace Falls is on Heatherbrae property, so the only people who could be here today are me or my family. Gran can't walk up here anymore, and Chase is not stupid enough to gatecrash our date. That's why he let Rosie go and didn't bother chasing after her. It's guy code not to interrupt private time with your girl. So, slow down that breathing and just enjoy this." I kiss her softly on her wet pouty lips.

"Trust me, Ash. I would never put you in a position to be hurt or embarrassed. I will always be here to protect you. For as long as you let me." Her hands, that have been around my neck and hanging on for dear life, start to loosen a little, and I can see her shoulders droop a bit.

"I do, it's just all new to me." She reaches forward and kisses my lips gently.

"What, having someone protect you, or swimming naked?" I won't let her get too much inside her head.

"Both," she admits.

"Then I'm glad to fix those problems for you." I let go of the rock and start to drift out to the middle of the pool. "Now stop gripping me like a monkey and lie on your back. Just float and enjoy the sun on your skin. Look around at the picture-perfect scenery . . . and just breathe. I have a feeling you have forgotten how to just . . . be." Keeping my tone calm and gentle, I bring her back to the serenity of the moment.

Her body is still rigid, but it doesn't take long before her limbs stretch out and her muscles begin relaxing.

"I've got you." Holding her hand, we float alongside each other in the current of the water created by the waterfall. A very fine mist settles on our faces from the spray. From the corner of my eye, I see Rosie has settled on the big rock in the sun, her eyes lowering as she takes a nap.

"The water doesn't feel so cold now," Ash says quietly, trying not to disturb the tranquility that has finally descended.

"Your body is acclimating to the temperature, and we are on the top of the water where the sun heats it more. But for me, the cold refreshes and rejuvenates my soul." I turn to look at her and see she has finally been overtaken by the magic of this place. Her eyes are closed, soaking in the sun and just enjoying the moment.

The sheer beauty of the woman next to me, naked, with her face above the waterline and her hair spread out like a fan while different parts of her body float just above the surface. Perfect brown nipples and half of her plump breasts point to the sun, a small sliver of her stomach around her belly button, a strip of skin down the tops of her thighs and the tips of her toes. It's a picture in my mind I'll never forget. A moment of peace captured in the pure beauty of the light flickering on the water, the shadows of the trees, and the unspoken love between us.

That thought of moments like this, just us and the love we share, has sealed it in my head. She's it for me, and now I need to face some tough decisions to make sure she will always be the one beside me in the future.

I need to tell her *everything*.

ASHLEY

Who even am I?

This is not something I could imagine myself doing, even in my college days. I was never one to take a risk, so now, at my age, I'm surprising myself even more.

But Jake is right.

As I give in to being just in the moment, I feel this kind of peacefulness wash through my body. Is this why he brought me here and made sure I ended up naked in the water?

Just floating with no confines is a totally new experience and one I don't want to end just yet.

It's healing. I lost trust in every man after Jeremy, but now, in a way I can't explain, I trust Jake. He's open with me, and I feel like I can lay my soul bare to him, knowing he won't crush it.

I don't know how long we have been floating in the sun, but it's something that I will treasure long after Jake has gone back home. If it wasn't for him, I would never have made it this far into the woods and up to the falls. Looking to my side, I see him watching me with a look of pure desire on his face. It makes an inner burn run through my body, and this time it's not lust but something I can only describe as love.

His eyelids start to open wider, like he's surprised. He places his finger to his lips and then points to the opposite side of the pool to where Rosie is sleeping. I turn slowly and at the same time drop my body into the water in case someone is there who will see me.

I gasp with shock at the sight before me. Standing on a small dirt patch that leads into the water is a fawn taking a drink. But not just any fawn, it's *my* fawn. The one I tried to save that night. I can see the scar on her leg and the facial markings that I remember so well after watching and trying to get close to her for what felt like hours.

I was sure she would've died from an infection or been attacked by a bear or wolf drawn to her by the scent of her blood running from her wound.

"I can't believe it," I whisper to Jake, who's now also upright in the water, pulling me back against his chest and helping to keep me up.

"She's beautiful. Seeing an animal like this in her natural environment, I can understand your passion for them."

And if I wasn't already in love with him, that would seal the deal.

"She's not just any animal, she's my fawn from that night. The one I tried to help." I'm transfixed by her, watching her drink as though she isn't threatened by us being so close. There is no way she doesn't know we are here. Animals are too smart for that.

"Holy shit."

His freak-out sounds so funny as just the faintest whisper.

"Maybe Tiff is right, that the waterfalls in this town have magical powers." I watch her take her last drink and lift her head to look directly at us.

"Do you think she's trying to tell you thanks for attempting to help her, or sorry you were so clumsy and hurt yourself, but at least you got a Prince Charming out of it?" Jake never ceases to bring humor to my world.

"I just think she's here to show me she's fine and healing from her injury." For the first time I sound like Tiff in my head, hoping this is the sign to me that I'm healing too. Every minute I spend in Jake's arms, more of the weight I have been carrying over the years is breaking away.

"What a gift from the universe," Jake whispers as he kisses my cheek.

"Yes, it is." My words mean more than he will ever understand.

A crash behind us wakes Rosie up, and she lets out a loud bark, scaring the fawn into scattering back through the shrubs.

Panic races through me as Jake and I both turn quickly in the water, only to see a branch that has fallen from a tree landing just behind Rosie. She's now standing on her rock, fully alert and growling a little to let us know how unimpressed she is as she watches the leaves of the fallen branch drift slowly to the ground.

"It's okay, girl," I call out to Rosie to get her attention.

"I should get out and reassure her," Jake says, pushing us toward the edge.

"No, she's fine, she'll settle. You have something far more important to do." My heart celebrates seeing his concern for Rosie.

"What?" He turns us face-to-face and kicks us back out into the pool a bit farther.

"Fuck me under that waterfall." I can't believe I just said that.

"Now *that* I can do. It will be my pleasure. Rosie, you're on your own," he yells to her and then spins me around his body so I'm hanging on to him from behind, arms around his neck. "Told you skinny-dipping was a great idea. I knew you'd come around." He laughs as he starts swimming breaststroke toward the side of the waterfall.

"Hmmm, coming, what a great idea." I giggle as he starts swimming faster.

"I'm full of them, Ash, let me assure you." As we get closer to the spray, he calls over his shoulder to make sure I can hear him above the noise of the water. "Close your eyes and hold your breath as we break through."

With no time to ask questions, we are already below the waterfall, and I can feel the power of the falling water as it hits my skin. Before I know it, we are through, and the view that greets me when I open my eyes was worth it.

"Oh my goodness, Jake, this is so special." It's like we are in a tiny room that has a waterfall curtain, and nothing exists outside of here. It's just Jake and me.

He pulls away from me and hoists himself up onto a flat rock that is almost like a seat just beneath the water level.

"As special as you." Lifting me up, he sets me to straddle his waist. My face is now level with his, and he doesn't need to say the words. I can see it in his eyes.

Jake has fallen in love with me too.

Deep, soul-binding love.

I just can't bring myself to say those words yet. And I hope he understands why I'm not ready to hear them yet either.

"I know we talked about us both being clean, and I'm not pushing you for anything, and I know you have birth control, but we don't have protection, so you can change your mind," Jake warns.

"No, it's time. I want to feel every part of you, and this is just perfect. We will never forget this moment." Not waiting for him, I drop my hand and line him up, taking him in one motion.

"Fuccccckkkk!" we both cry out in unison at the pleasure and pain of him filling me.

As he starts to move, I know I'm never going to be able to let him go.

Then every conscious thought leaves me as he makes raw, sweet love to me under the veil of Peace Falls.

So perfect.

"Tiff will never believe me when I tell her I spent time lying naked on a towel-covered rock in the sun today, tanning parts of my body that haven't seen sunlight since I was a baby." I giggle. Jake is driving us into town to meet up with Chase and Tiff for dinner at Alberto's Restaurant.

"Maybe don't share that story in front of Chase, though. I don't want my cousin thinking about my girlfriend naked. I kind of like him and don't want to have to make a scene in the restaurant again," Jake says while squeezing my hand that he has sitting on his leg as we drive.

"Oh, your cousin is going to have more than that to worry about tonight. Tiff is annoyed we haven't introduced him to her yet. I just hope he knows what he's in for." I smile at him, looking so handsome in his blue jeans and plain black shirt. Simple but enough to get my hormones whirring.

"Damn, what is she going to be like when Declan arrives in three days' time and there are three of us in town?" He shakes his head with a stupid smirk on his face.

"Do you still think Beckett will stay away, and just try to micromanage you all from Los Angeles?" I still can't get a read on the relationship between Jake and his brother. He obviously loves him, but it seems like he has spent most of his life trying to seek his approval.

"We can only hope." His demeanor changes a little at the mention of Beckett, and we sit holding each other's hand for the rest of the drive, just listening to the music on his truck's stereo.

As soon as we get out, you can tell that summer has really hit us. There is a breeze that's not as fresh as usual, so I'm glad I could wear bare shoulders, showing off the glow of today's tan. It's the part I love about summer, flowy thigh-length dresses like this one, with little spaghetti straps tied up over my shoulders.

Seeing sweat beading on Jake's brow, I feel for him in jeans. "Don't worry, Alberto's is air-conditioned." I take his hand and we head straight into the restaurant because if we stay outside much longer, the little amount of makeup I have on will be running down my face with sweat.

As Jake opens the door to the restaurant for me, I can feel the cool air hit me.

"Enjoy it while it lasts. My house is not much fun in the summer, and it holds the heat." I glance to my side where I see him smiling before leaning in toward me.

"That's fine, we can just sleep naked under the stars. May as well finish the day as we started it." He wiggles his eyebrows up and down at me.

"You are incorrigible. Stop corrupting me." I roll my eyes at him.

"Then stop begging me to do naughty things with you."

A shiver travels all the way down my back from his words as we are greeted by Julie.

"Well, hello again, Doc. Different date tonight? Watch this one, he's a bit skittish." She chuckles to herself at her little joke.

"Just needed a good woman to tame me." Jake pulls me closer, tucking me under his arm.

"Well, it seems you picked one of the best from what I hear. Table for two?"

"No, for four, please." I don't elaborate. Julie doesn't need any encouragement to keep talking.

"Okay, let's put you down the back then. Follow me."

Jake is busy pulling out my chair and getting me comfortable when we hear Tiffany arrive. It's not like she's quiet and doesn't know every person in town.

"Oh, sorry I'm late. There was this customer who wouldn't stop talking even though I was almost pushing him out of the teahouse. You know, places to go, people to see."

Although Jake was just about to sit, he's now back standing and pulls out Tiff's chair for her.

"Love a man with manners, thanks. So, where's the hot cousin?" Tiff blurts straight out, and I just groan.

"We talked about this, Tiff—behave." I hit my forehead with my hand as I hear the front door open again and look up to see Chase making his way toward us, quickly brushing past Julie, which I'm sure she won't be happy about.

"Me? I'm always on my best behavior." She proclaims her innocence.

"I call bullshit, like I do with most things that come out of your mouth," I reply as Chase joins us.

"Evening, all. You must be Tiffany, the spooky lady." Chase holds his hand out for her to shake, and I can see she's sizing him up.

"Not spooky. Maybe a little mystical, but not spooky. I'm not a witch. Jake, what did you tell him?" Huffing, she looks our way as she shakes Chase's hand.

"Hey, it wasn't me, I didn't say anything," he professes as Julie arrives at the table next to ours to take their drink order.

"Well, I know it wasn't Ashley because she doesn't believe in anything I tell her anyway. But hello, Exhibit A." She waves her hands up and down in front of Jake.

"Shh. Don't you dare say any more in here where there are so many ears." I slap my hand over her mouth.

"This sounds like a story I need to hear." Chase is already encouraging her, and this is not a good sign.

"Me too." Jake sits back in his chair, folding his arms like he's waiting to be entertained.

Before Julie gets a chance to turn and take our order, Kimberly, the manager of Alberto's, walks out from the kitchen and stops at our table.

"Can't hide that you've arrived in the room. Hello, everyone." Glancing around the table, she makes eye contact with us all.

"Oh, come on, why is everyone picking on me tonight? Lucky I love you, Kimba." Tiff stands and hugs Kimberly.

"Hi, Kimberly, this is my boyfriend, Jake, and his cousin Chase." The two boys are both staring at Kimberly in a strange way.

"Oh wow, as in *little Kimberly* who used to play at Heatherbrae with us sometimes as kids when your gran was visiting ours," Jake pipes up as both he and Chase smile like some happy memories are running through their minds.

"I didn't think you would remember me. It was such a long time ago." Kimberly shrugs.

"And you were so little that the girls used to smother you with attention like you were their own living doll. But I remember you for sure." Chase now joins in. "I forget how small this town is. Well for us anyway."

"Yeah, no need to remind us that you guys got to get out of here, lucky you. Some of us were born here and will die here." Kimberly smiles.

"Nothing wrong with that. I'm here with you, Kimba." Tiff reaches out to take her hand and squeezes it.

"It was different obviously than living here, but we loved being up here because we were holidaying together," Chase says as he picks up his napkin to lay it in his lap. "But yeah, small-town life is not for me. I don't really settle anywhere for that long. But I'm going to enjoy this time with the guys and Gran, that's for sure."

"What about you, Jake, is small-town living your vibe?" Tiff pins him with a stare.

"I think it's time to order some drinks, and I don't know about anyone else, but I'm starving," I announce, changing the topic of conversation, not ready to go there.

I rattle off my drink and meal order to Kimberly as the others scramble to choose.

As she heads to the kitchen and passes the drinks order to the bar, Tiff and Chase get into a conversation while Jake's head hangs a little low.

I don't want today wrecked, so I'm determined to pick the mood back up. Placing my hand on his thigh under the table, I give it a gentle squeeze. "It's okay, let's just enjoy a good night." I lean closer to him to finish. "And if you're lucky, it might end up under the stars . . ."

"Naked?" he asks, a naughty grin spreading across his lips.

"Maybe." I wink, and he reaches toward me to kiss me on the cheek.

"Thank you." His voice is gravelly with emotion.

"I trust you. We'll work it out when the time is right."

And we both understand this is neither the time nor the place for any big deep and meaningful conversation, especially when we have company.

"Yes, we will." This time, Jake kisses me hard on the lips, then turns back to join in the conversation, and Tiff looks at me with concern.

I just shake my head gently.

I know the time for that conversation with Jake is getting closer. And the closer it gets, the more I'm scared of what the outcome will be. I know he still has months here yet, and a year is a long time, but the harder I'm falling I know I won't be able to wait that long to know if he's staying or going. Already I know I don't want to let him go, so even though we agreed to take it one day at a time, I'm not sure I'm cut out for that.

If it becomes my only option, could I cope with being a vet in a city again?

I suppose time will tell.

Chapter Sixteen

Jake

I've been trying all night to keep a smile plastered on my face, but deep down, Tiffany's question has rocked me.

Not because I don't think I can live here. I know I can.

I just don't know how to clean up the mess I've left in Sacramento.

"So, when Declan gets here in a few days, you girls need to come out to Heatherbrae, and we can have a big cook-up. Don't worry, I'll be doing the cooking, because Jake here is no chef. I'm not sure how a grandson of Gran's can be so useless." Chase takes great delight in throwing me under the bus for my lack of chef skills.

Tiff throws her hands over her face in despair. "Oh, they will make a fine pair. Looks like I'll be cooking freezer meals for both of you now. Seriously, Jake, you were supposed to be the savior that Ash needs to make sure she eats properly. Her terrible cooking skills would have her surviving off instant noodles if it wasn't for me providing her some home-cooked nutritious meals."

"Hey, I can't excel at everything. I'm a great builder, and I have it on good authority that I also have some other special skills . . ."

I say, wrapping my arm around Ash's shoulders and pulling her closer to me.

"Do share with the class." Tiff, as usual, is trying to encourage a conversation about our sex life.

"Please don't. I can do without stories of my cousin and his escapades. Remember, I'm sharing a shower with him, so I don't want to know what he's doing in there all on his own." Chase responds to Tiff with his own humor.

"I can assure you, he's not in there doing that all on his own," Ash replies with the straightest of faces, which makes Chase and Tiff break into fits of laughter and leaves me shocked at her confidence. Even though it's just a joke, it has me thinking about taking her there, when no one is around, of course.

"That's it, you two are banned from the shower in the barn. It's a no-go zone. I don't care how smelly this guy gets, I refuse to shower after him."

We all start laughing at Chase's panic.

"What you don't know won't hurt you." I sit smugly in my chair as Kimberly walks by and places our check on the table.

This is the part of the night that always makes me nervous; hoping that my credit card won't be declined. It puts a cold shiver through me every time. I can't wait until I get back to a point in my life where I don't have to worry about an empty bank account. But until the phone calls stop, I can't move on. And while carrying this stress all on my own makes it even harder, the shame of it makes me hide it deeper.

I reach out to grab the check off the table, but Chase grabs it out from under my hand. "I've got this one, buddy. You can get the next one." I want to argue, but the relief that runs through me has me accepting his offer.

"Time to take my weary little body home to bed so I can get some sleep before an early start tomorrow." Tiff stands, and we all follow her out.

"And you complain I work too hard," Ash says.

I step outside the restaurant and the breeze has cooled somewhat, which makes the heat of the evening more bearable.

"No, no, no, I don't like that." Tiff stands still, wrapping her arms around herself.

"What's wrong?" Ash asks, giving her a hug.

"There has been a shift, and not in a good way. No, I need to do something about that. I must go. It needs fixing now. I'm not letting that darkness gain traction." Tiff shivers and is now talking to herself like we aren't even here.

"Can we walk you home?" Chase looks as concerned as I am.

"Nope. I don't want it to touch any of you. Go. Go home." Tiff turns on her heel and hurries off down the street toward the teahouse before anyone can say another word.

"What the hell was all that about?" Chase asks, turning to Ash.

"I don't know, and I've given up asking because I usually end up just as confused as I was before she starts explaining it. Tiffany is a very spiritual being and feels all sorts of things that none of us have any idea about. Well, that's what she tells me, anyway. I don't really believe any of it, but I'm not game to completely discount it either. If I've learned anything in all the years I've known her, it's better just to let her go do what she needs to do. If it's something she wants to share with you, she'll let you know."

"Okkkaaay thennnn." Chase looks at Ashley like she's the one who's insane. "I understand what you mean by woo-woo now. It's similar to cuckoo." He twirls his finger in circles next to his head. "Well, I'm heading back, so I guess I'll see you both tomorrow." Already chuckling, he leans in and kisses Ash on the cheek and slaps me on the shoulder.

"I thought we might spend the night at the barn tonight," I tease Chase as he starts walking to Gramps's truck. I don't need to wait long before he quickly flips me the bird and yells out, "Be careful the games you play, Jake, karma is a bitch."

Jumping into the truck, he starts the engine and backs out of the parking space as Ashley and I both laugh and head to my truck.

"Is Tiff really okay?" I ask as we drive back to Windemere. The breeze is still strong enough to throw sticks across the road but nothing too major. "I know she can be quirky, and some of the stories you've told me are a bit out there, but she seemed a bit distressed."

"I think so. She does things like that occasionally, but I'll admit she was freaking me out a little tonight too. I'll message her later to check in," Ash replies, looking out the window.

While she's distracted, I'm trying to think of a way to bring up my life before I came to Abbey Falls and what led me here. I know she hates secrets, and I should have told her from the beginning, but it never felt like the right time. It's not really a secret, though I haven't really told anyone . . . I wish I'd told her that night in the woods when we were sharing about the hurt from our prior relationships, but we agreed to just be friends.

And now I'm so deep in this mess of not telling her that I don't know how she's going to react. But it's only fair that I lay all my cards on the table, she should know the man I really am.

"Looks like your naked night under the stars will have to be canceled with this wind." Ash's playful voice pulls me out of my thoughts as we rattle up her drive and the farmhouse comes into view.

"Don't act like you ever intended to go through with it." I poke Ash in her side where she's a little ticklish. All those little spots, those little things I now know about her.

"I thought about it . . ."

Pulling the truck to a stop at the side of the house, we both climb out, and I hang back a little to watch her walk up the porch steps without a care in the world. It's like I'm soaking in every single moment now. I know it's time. I have to tell her.

In her living room, Ash kicks off her sandals and flops down onto the couch. "Who knew that a day of hiking and swimming would take so much out of me? You don't look half as exhausted as I feel." She lifts her arms up into the air, beckoning me over to lie down beside her, but instead, I lift her legs and sit on the end of the couch.

"Are you okay?" She looks concerned and wriggles backward to sit herself up next to me.

"We need to talk, Ash." I'm aware that these are words that no woman ever wants to hear from their boyfriend.

"Oh, Jake, if it's about what Tiff asked you tonight, don't worry about it. We both knew what we were walking into. We were honest with each other." She rests her hand on top of mine.

"Not entirely." I feel sick saying the words as I watch her retreat from me a little.

"What do you mean?" The worry and hurt in her eyes almost kill me.

"There is something I need to tell you. It explains why I'm here." I can feel the sweat building on my hands, and the dinner I ate begins to churn in my stomach.

"You are here for your gran and Heatherbrae, right?"

"Yes, that was always my main intention, but something else was driving me to move here." Gulping, I stop, then, taking a deep breath, let it all pour out.

"I also came here to hide from my mistakes. I ran from Sacramento because it was the easy solution. But I know now that I should've stayed and faced things head-on."

"Jake, you're scaring me," she confesses and then is asking, "Are you in danger? Is that it?"

"No, Ash, nothing like that, but I am running from something that I need to sort out before I can be the man you need me to be." I rub my sweaty hands on my jeans, but it's not helping.

"Jake, for fuck's sake just tell me, before I get sick." She's already hugging her arms to her belly like she's on the verge of having a meltdown. A feeling I share with her right this minute.

"I'm broke, Ash. When Danika left and took all our cash, she also left me with a house that is mortgaged to the hilt. I was working so hard just trying to keep the roof over my head. My business was going well for a while, but when one big client didn't pay, I took a heavy financial hit and things started to snowball. A friend of mine suggested I invest the little bit of cashflow that I did have into crypto. He told me about a friend of a friend who had tripled his money in three weeks."

Running my hands through my hair, I can see her shutting down before my eyes. And saying this out loud reminds me how desperate I was.

"Stupidly I took what I had and invested it all, hoping it was the break I needed. But of course, it wasn't, and then I was left with nothing to pay the suppliers at the end of the month. So, I sold off my furniture, rented out my house, paid off my suppliers and the bank with what I had left. I'm still paying off the mortgage and my overdraft as the rent payments come in." I can't sit still any longer and start pacing her living room.

"Please understand, I would never run from my responsibilities, and I am paying every single cent that I owe. But I don't want to be the man who walks into a relationship with nothing to offer. You have already lived through that and spent years struggling to get on top of your debt. I can't do that to you again."

Water is pooling in her eyes, and she can't look at me as she curls into a ball on the couch.

"Say something, Ash. I need to know what you are thinking," I plead with her.

Instead, she's just shaking her head and continues to look down at the floor.

"I'm not telling you this now so you help me—that kind of pity would almost kill me. I just don't want anything between us anymore. I asked you to trust me so that I can take care of you, and I will, but I just need time to be in a position to do that. If you want the truth, my hesitation to be with you was never about my feelings or any fears about being hurt. I knew you would never do that. It's the shame I carry every day of not being able to be the man you need me to be. The man you deserve."

Ash's phone starts ringing on the coffee table and the moment we both see whose name is on it, I want to turn it off and throw it out the window, but I can't.

Reaching out, she picks up the phone, and I can see her putting on the armor she needs so she can answer the call.

"Hey, Beau, what's up." She listens to what he's saying and then replies, "No, it's no problem at all. It's what happens in our job." Ash stands and looks straight through me before moving to the front door where her clean set of overalls are always hanging, for just this reason. "Yeah, you take the case at the clinic, and I'll head out to Hannigan's and pull the calf."

Undoing the straps on the top of her dress without a care in the world, she continues to undress while she talks on the phone, standing in her cream lace underwear like I am not even there. Stepping into her overalls and pulling them up, her words cut through me. "No, Jake won't mind. He was just on his way home anyway. He understands how everything in my life comes second to my job. I made that clear from the beginning when we discussed our future. We were on the same page." And that's the moment I understand how badly I've fucked up.

"Yep, I'll call once I'm done and fill you in. Call me if you need help. Thanks, talk later."

Hanging up the call and placing her phone on the hall stand, she zips up the front of her overalls, then pulls some socks on and slips her feet into her boots by the door. Grabbing a hair tie off the table in the little bowl she keeps on the stand, she rolls her hair into one long strand then expertly winds it up into a bun on the top of her head so it's out of the way.

"Ash." I reach out for her.

"Don't. Just don't touch me right now. I need to go and save a cow and its calf, and that's all I can think about." She looks at me with no expression at all.

"Can I wait here for you so we can finish this?" I'll get down on my knees and beg if I have to.

"I think you've said enough. Go home, Jake, leave me to be on my own for a bit." Taking her car keys off the hook just inside the front door, she pushes the screen door open and then turns.

"I don't care that you have nothing, Jake, I'm not that shallow. But what hurts is that you didn't think all those times before now when we've talked so openly and deeply that I was worth sharing your whole life with. I just never seem to be good enough."

Before I can even open my mouth to tell her that it's me who's not good enough to be with her, she pushes out the door and is gone.

By the time my feet think to move and I scurry after her, her car is already halfway down the drive, gravel spraying up, and making enough commotion to set off Herb and the rest of the barn animals.

"Sorry, guys. I've pissed off your mom big-time tonight. So maybe be on your best behavior, including you, Daisy." I walk back inside the house and see the two rocks I had picked out of the waterfall today and given to Ash as a keepsake. I wanted her to have something she could show our grandchildren one day and I could tell them about the day I understood how much I loved their grandmother, but she just wouldn't let me say the words out loud.

I pick up the two smooth rocks, roll them over with my thumb, and hold their weight in my hands.

"Now I may never get the chance." I close my eyes to stop the tears from falling.

Pulling myself together, I put the rocks down and walk out the front door, locking it behind me and knowing what I need to do now.

What I should've done in the first place.

ASHLEY

I feel like the weight on my chest is heavier than anything I've ever carried before, even after Jeremy left.

Pain, hurt, but more than anything, it's the crushing disappointment.

Jake asked me to trust him, and I did, but he obviously didn't trust me. And that's what hurts the most.

I was glad the call from Beau came when it did last night, but it didn't make the problem go away. I still need to face Jake and talk this through. But I'll be damned if I let this derail me like Jeremy did.

In the back of my mind, I always knew things with Jake were too good to be true. But today, I still feel deep in my soul that I'm also not completely ready to give up on us either. We all make mistakes, and Jake's is a total grade-A fuckup, but it doesn't mean I shouldn't hear him out.

Dragging myself out of bed, I manage to shower, but I can't eat. My stomach is too churned up. I don't even bother driving, thinking instead that a walk over to Heatherbrae will do me good.

The fresh air and summer sun warming up for the day and hitting my face is what I need.

As I come across the pasture and around the side of the barn, I notice Jake's truck isn't in the driveway, and I can feel my emotions deflating. I had worked out in my head what I wanted to say to him, and now it feels like it was all in vain.

With a glimmer of hope, I knock on the barn door.

"Ashley, since when do you need to knock?" Chase is looking at me confused as I fight to hide my disappointment.

"Morning, just wondering if Jake is here?" My voice is a little hoarse, probably from the lack of sleep and tears during the night.

"Ummm, I thought he was with you. Didn't he stay over last night?" Chase steps back from the doorway, waving for me to come inside.

"I had a work call, so I sent him home." I'm trying to keep my voice light without saying too much, but he can see it in my face.

"Ashley, what happened? Should I be worried he didn't turn up here after he left your place?" Chase grabs his phone from his back pocket.

"I don't know, I just expected he would be here. We were in the middle of an intense discussion last night before I had to go to work, so I wanted to talk it out with him today." My hands are shoved into the front pockets of my jeans, and I shift nervously from foot to foot.

"Hey, where the fuck are you? Ash's here, and we are both worried." The sound of Chase's stern voice speaking into his phone gives me relief that Jake answered. Maybe he has just gone hiking to clear his head.

"What the hell do you mean you are almost in Sacramento? Somebody needs to tell me what the fuck is going on!" Chase's anger is obvious, and I can feel my despair now turning to anger too.

"He's running again," I mumble to myself and turn to leave.

"Ashley, wait," Chase calls after me, but I need to get out of here before I say something I can't take back. My breathing speeds up as I stomp toward the fence between our properties. I should've stayed on my side from the beginning and used it to keep out the pests.

I thought I knew Jake.

But knowing every time things get hard for him that he just runs is not a trait I want in a man. He left Sacramento because his life fell apart and he couldn't face it, and now he's running from me because things got difficult. I mean, I could've done the same and left Abbey Falls when Jeremy deserted me the way he did. I could've sold the clinic and run home to my mother, not that I would've wanted to be there, but it is still always an option even if we aren't that close. More than once, I wanted to move anywhere to get away from the endless hard work and town gossip. But I didn't. I dug deep and worked through it, got my life back to where I wanted it—until Jake came bowling in.

Stupidly, I was even thinking about shifting my whole life for him. I should've stayed true to my mantra of never living my life for a man again.

"Ashley!" I can hear Chase chasing after me, as my home comes into view.

My safe haven that Jake has now infiltrated, and I won't ever be able to get those images of him spending time here out of my head. Most of them are naked. And they are good fucking images!

Chase grabs my arm as he tries to stop me.

"Jeez, woman, you're fast when you are pissed." Sucking in a few deep breaths, Chase doesn't let go of my arm.

"What do you want, Chase? Because I'm not in the mood for any more bullshit." Turning to face him, I yank my arm out of his grasp, and my hands are now on my hips.

"Oh, I can see it now," he says with a smirk.

"See what?" I demand.

"Jake told me about the first day he met you, but I didn't believe him when he said you get scary when you're angry. But yep, he's right." His humor is not wanted right now.

"Well, I suggest that unless you really want to see me at my finest, you say what you need to say and then head back over to your side of the fence." I'm grumbling at him, when really, I shouldn't be taking it out on Chase, but he's here and the closest thing to the man I want to yell at.

"Look, Ashley, I don't know what happened between you two. Jake just told me he needed to go and fix something and that he would explain it all to me soon. But he did give me a message for you."

I shake my head because Jake obviously hasn't learned his lesson, keeping the people who love him in the dark.

"Oh, this will be good," I huff.

"He asked you to trust him and just wait until he's back. He doesn't want to do this over the phone or in a message. He needs to be here face-to-face with you."

I can see Chase is trying to calm me down, but it's not working.

"Trust him!" I yell. "I did that and look where that got me. With a boyfriend who runs when things get hard. That message was a waste of his breath. I'm sorry, Chase, that you got caught in the middle of this. I just need to be on my own." Turning and walking away, I hear him behind me.

"Jake's a good man, Ashley. I don't know how he fucked this up, but what I do know is that he loves you in a way he has never loved another."

"Well, he's got a funny way of showing it," I reply without looking back.

"One last thing I think you should know," he calls out to me. "He took Rosie with him. Now, if that doesn't tell you how much you've gotten under his skin, then nothing will."

Chase's words stop me at the bottom of my porch as they sink in. Two thoughts are now racing through my mind.

First, that Jake drove six hours through the night with a dog that he claims to find annoying.

And the second is the thing that really has me trying to process how I feel about what Chase said. If he took Rosie, then it means he is coming back. There is no way he would take his grandmother's dog and then not bring her companion back.

Stomping up the stairs and lifting my hands to my mouth, I yell at Chase, who's now heading back toward Heatherbrae.

"Well, I hope she shits in his precious truck!" I smile to myself at my retort and then feel utterly crushed by my childish comeback.

Tiff is the only person I can turn to right now. I don't care if she's working this morning. She can close the teahouse for all I care, but I need to talk to her. Someone needs to help me make sense of this whole mess, and although she probably isn't going to give me the rational advice I need, she's never steered me wrong before.

Maybe she'll have some magic tea for an angry heart.

Damn you, Jake, now you have me turning to Tiff and her woo-woo and acting like I believe in it.

"Shit." Tiff looks at me as I come storming through the front door of the teahouse.

"Out the back. Now," she says, grabbing my arm and dragging me behind her without me even saying a word. "Sit, don't move and don't scream when the room goes black."

As she rushes past me, I see her flick the main fuse on the power box, and the shop descends into darkness.

"Oh no, the power has gone out. Sorry, everyone, I'll have to close up for the day. Let me pour your drinks into to-go cups." I can hear Tiff ushering everyone out of the shop. "Yes, I know, Ethel, it's okay. Rita will give you a lift to church, won't you, Rita. I hear they have great cups of tea and biscuits there."

I slap my hand over my mouth to stop myself from losing it at her bossiness. Luckily, it's a Sunday, so the old ladies have somewhere to be anyway.

Slowly, the noises lessen until I hear the front door being closed and the bolt being slid into place and the light switches flicked off. As Tiff heads toward the back again, she turns the mains back on and the light above me comes to life.

"Sometimes I worry about how quickly your brain reacts. Remind me if I ever need an alibi to call you."

"Like you'd call anyone else." Pulling over one of the food crates, Tiff sits herself down next to me. "What happened?"

I sigh, and the tears I have been holding off all morning finally start to fall.

Tiff's eyes harden. "Jake better be scared. I don't know what he did, but I'm coming for him. Now start talking, woman, because I've got a hole to start digging." She hugs me tight and makes me giggle just enough to slow down the tears.

"I can't tell you everything because it's not my story to tell, but what I can tell you is that he fucked up, and he fucked up good." I wipe the tears off my face.

"No shit, otherwise you wouldn't be here. And I felt it in my waters last night. I knew something bad was coming and I tried to stop it, but I obviously wasn't quick enough. Now start at the beginning." Tiff takes my hand, giving it a squeeze and me the strength I need to talk.

"I have no idea what you just said, but anyway, here goes." Taking a deep breath, I start at the beginning—if you can call it that.

JAKE

"Block your ears, Rosie, because I can tell you now, there is about to be a lot of yelling and plenty of swearing." Lifting her head off the center console she has been using as a pillow, she looks confused, and I don't blame her. I've had hours to get this conversation right, and I know within the first minute, it will probably all go to shit.

The phone call connects, making my stomach clench as my blood pressure rapidly rises.

"Jake." Beckett's gruff voice echoes around me.

"Hey, Beckett, how are you?" I'm trying to keep my voice as upbeat as possible.

"Fine. Why are you calling me at 3 a.m. on a Sunday morning? What's happened? Is it Gran?"

It always baffles me how this man manages to talk in such a monotone voice, devoid of emotion.

"No, Gran is fine," I reply and then take a deep breath before continuing, "I'm calling because I need your help."

"You." He coughs. "You haven't wanted any help from me since you were about ten years old. And the last few years since I told you some home truths you didn't want to hear, you've hardly spoken to me. So I can't imagine that this morning will be any different."

"Which is why I didn't ask for help earlier, and my pride has come back to bite me on the ass," I grumble.

There is a noise in the background, and then his voice gets clearer and louder.

"Fuck, you weren't joking when you said you needed help. I'm sorry, I wasn't expecting that. Are you okay?" And for the first time in a very long time, his voice sounds different, less robotic, like a person who genuinely cares.

"I will be, but I think I need your help to make that happen."

"Okay, talk to me."

I must admit this wasn't the reaction I imagined, but I'll take it.

"Have you got a few minutes? And promise not to lose your temper until the end, where I'll give you exactly five minutes to let loose and tell me how stupid I've been. But after that, what I'm about to tell you stays between us, and you don't hold it over my head for the rest of my life." I'm trying to set down some ground rules, but I already know it's not going to make any difference.

"What the fuck have you done, Jake?"

"Now *that's* the Beckett I was expecting," I reply, and then, not giving him a chance to say another word, I start talking and lay it all out for him. By the time I finish, I have heard him growling and sighing at the appropriate places, but just like I asked, he hasn't said a word.

"And I can't lose her, Beckett. I love her, and this time I know it's forever. I just need to fix this." The weight I have been carrying for the last year all of a sudden feels like it's starting to shift.

The silence hanging between us is unnerving, but I can still hear him breathing, so I just wait.

"You're lucky we aren't in the same room."

If he thinks I would be that stupid, then he doesn't really know me at all.

"Understood," I reply.

"And besides being furious with you, I'm kind of hurt that you didn't think you could come to your own brother with this earlier. But I think that's a conversation for another day, because we both know it's time to sort this shit out between us, but not now."

His words settle in my chest, and I silently agree that we need to talk, like really talk about everything I have let build a wedge between us all these years, and I'm sure he has the same list of things that he needs to air.

"I've just booked a flight. Pick me up at the airport in five hours. Nobody rips off my baby brother and gets away with it. And don't worry, we will have you back on the road to Heatherbrae as quick as we can, then you can go and grovel on your hands and knees to win back your girl."

I can hear him moving and assume he's packing his computer and whatever else he needs.

"Beckett." There is a slight quiver in my voice.

"I know, brother. I don't need your thanks. A video of you on your knees begging for forgiveness will be payment enough." He starts laughing in a way I haven't heard in years.

"Asshole," I murmur before throwing my head back and joining in, and shit, it feels good to let go.

"It's in our genes. Now get some sleep and I'll see you soon."

He ends the call and I don't dare tell him that I'm just coming into Sacramento now and the only place I'll be sleeping is in this truck, in the airport parking lot with my trusty guard dog, Rosie, while I wait for him. I don't want to give him another reason to yell at me.

I take a deep breath now step one, opening up to Beckett, is done. I've survived, so far.

And funnily enough, I already know that step two won't be as easy as this, and that's saying something after step one involved dealing with my brother.

Step two, explaining all this to Ashley, is going to be the hardest thing I've had to do, and I don't think it will be pretty.

But that's one of the things I love about Ashley.

Her strength to stand up and fight, even if it's with me.

Chapter Seventeen

Ashley

"Have you heard from him?" Tiff asks me as I take a seat at the counter in the teahouse.

"No, but I'm not expecting to." Which is total bullshit because I have slept every night since he left with my phone right next to me.

"It's been four days and still nothing. You wait until I see that big arrogant dickwad." She's busy pulling out my iced tea cooler from under the counter.

"What are you doing?" Because how stupid am I to think that I get to choose what I want to drink in the morning.

"It's too hot for tea this morning, or coffee for that matter, so iced it is." She's distracted today and busy with her jars of tea leaves, concocting some mixture that I'm sure is supposed to heal all my hurt, but nothing has worked the last few days, so I'm not sure today will be any different.

"Yeah, summer is here. I can't believe how hot it was last night, and this morning isn't any better. They are talking about a thunderstorm later today, but sadly, not much rain to go with it. Which means all it does is annoy the animals while leaving us no water for the grass."

In these storms I have to lock all the animals up in the barn, otherwise I spend hours having to round them all up, usually from the pastures at Heatherbrae.

The loud noise of Tiff mixing the iced tea in the glass cooler is driving me insane.

"Could you do that any quieter?" The words slip out of my mouth, and I regret them immediately. The death stare I get from Tiff could make a baby cry.

"Just because you're touchy doesn't mean you can take it out on me. I'm just as tired as you from lack of sleep. This bad vibe that is hovering over the town is scaring me, and I just can't get it to move on. I have tried everything I can think of, including dancing under the moon, and even that didn't work. I don't know what's coming, but it's freaking me out."

Banging my iced tea down in front of me, she then turns away and clears up the containers of tea leaves that she keeps spread across the shelf behind her. Which, as soon as I notice the tea leaves strewn everywhere, it hits me that she's never that messy with her precious brew mixes.

What an awful friend I am, wrapped up in my own selfish dramas that I haven't noticed my best friend is in a spin.

"Tiff, whoa, come here." I stand and rush around the counter. "I don't understand what you are talking about, as per usual, but you look like you are at breaking point. What can I do to help?" I notice the black circles under her eyes and that she doesn't have her usual sparkle. How did I miss this?

"You can find that stupid man of yours and sort this shit out. Then maybe the universe will go back to normal."

Pulling her toward me and wrapping her in a big hug, I try to reassure her that everything is okay. "I'm fine, Tiff, you don't need to worry about me."

She pulls back and looks me in the eye with daggers as I continue.

"I'm serious, I'll be fine. And as for Jake, I'm sure he will be too, eventually, after I castrate him or something to the equivalent." And my stupidity finally brings a weak smile to her face.

"I suppose that's better than digging a hole for him." Tiff pushes me away and starts shooing me back to my side of the counter.

"Better for whom, him or his balls?" I smile as I take a seat and sip today's brew. "Oooh, that's sweet."

"Yeah, well, I figured you could do with a bit of an energy boost for what's to come, whatever that may be." She's now concentrating on wiping down the counter.

The bell on the front door dings, and I can hear her before I see her.

"I knew I would find you here. How is my girl?" Betty is beside me quicker than I was expecting for an older lady, with two ladies tagging along behind her.

"I'm doing great. How has your morning been, Betty? Hello, Lesley, Margie." I give Betty's friends a wave as they hover nearby.

"Find a table, girls, I won't be too long." Betty waves them away, and I try not to laugh as they sit at the closest possible one to Betty and me. Obviously, they don't want to miss a thing.

Betty sits down next to me at the counter, and I'm about to tell her I must get to the clinic for an early appointment, but the moment I make the slightest move, her hand is on my thigh, and I'm anchored to the stool.

"I'm sure you have time for a cup of tea with me, sweetheart. I've been calling you on the telephone over the last few days, but you must be so busy that you haven't had time to call me back." Betty knows full well I've been avoiding her. "Anyway, it's all good, you're here now, so we can chat. Now, Tiffany, be a good girl and go clean a table or something over in that back corner of the store."

Trying not to choke on my tea, I watch Tiff's face at being told what to do in her own teahouse.

"Surrreee, Betty. No problem," Tiff says, rolling her eyes. "It's not like I need to serve customers or anything."

But in true Betty fashion, she gets her way, and Tiff does as she asked. I love that she doesn't care if her friends are listening in on our conversation, but mine can't.

"I just wanted to check in that you are okay. I know what it's like when your man is away. It can get mighty lonely. But he is due back today, so I expect you both home for dinner tonight. I'm sure he won't want to let you out of his sight either."

Oh no, she has no idea there is a problem between us. I don't know where she thinks he is, but it doesn't sound like she knows the truth.

"Sorry, Betty, I'm on call tonight, but thank you for the invitation. I'm sure Jake will be looking forward to one of your home-cooked meals." This woman is so sweet and important to not only her family but this town as well, I don't want to upset her.

"Of course he will, but he will be looking forward to seeing you more. That's okay, I'll wait until tomorrow night for family dinner. I'm making meatballs. I think you will both enjoy them again. And it's time for you to meet Declan, Jake's other cousin, who arrived yesterday. I'm so happy to have most of my boys home with me for a while. Not that I think Jake will be living on Heatherbrae for much longer." Betty winks at me.

I need to get out of here.

"How are you coping in the warm weather, Betty?" Yes, if all else fails go to the weather.

"I'm okay, dear, but I don't want it much hotter because it's not good for the grapes. And this will be the first good harvest in a few years. Declan is going to try to make our first batch of wine instead of selling the grapes to another winemaker, which we've had to do since we bought the place, which has been a real shame. But it's time for a new beginning, so I hope for his sake that the weather is kind to us, and he can try his hand at wine making."

Her face lights up when she talks about any of her grandsons and I soften toward her again. God, this is how this woman gets everything she wants around here.

My phone starts buzzing in my pocket, and when I pull it out to see Tiff's name, I look over to where she's pretending to clean a table that is already sparkling. She gives me a hand signal to answer my phone.

"Hello," I say tentatively.

"I'm pretending to be Beau and need you," she whispers into the phone, and I can only just hear her, so there is no way Betty will be able to.

"Hi, Beau, do you need me in the clinic already?"

Tiff is trying hard not to laugh on the other end of the call.

"No, that's no problem. I'm just at the teahouse so I'll be right there. See you soon." Ending the call, I stand and look at Betty.

"I'm so sorry, Betty, I must run. Duty calls. But enjoy dinner with your boys tonight, and I will see you another time." I avoid promising to be there tomorrow night, or ever, depending on what happens when Jake returns.

I take my iced tea flask with me because I could use a bit more of Tiff's calming sweet mixture. "Thanks, Tiff." I wave to her as I pretend to rush out of the door.

As I walk around the corner toward the clinic, Betty's declaration that Jake is due home today rocks me. I'm not sure I'm ready to see him, but on the other hand, I want to finish our conversation. Because the fact that he raced off to Sacramento without speaking with me first is really playing with my head, and my heart.

With Jeremy, I was never given the chance to have it out with him and tell him how much he hurt me when it happened. He just disappeared from my life, and while I'm glad I got my chance to say my piece to him on that phone call when he came groveling back for a job, it would have done so much for my mental health if I could have done it at the time. So the fact that Jake is coming back to face the music, to talk this through, well, I have to give him points for that.

Off in the distance I can hear the first rumbles of the thunderstorm heading our way. It won't be long before it's time to batten down the hatches.

Both literally and figuratively, since there are two storms brewing. One in the town of Abbey Falls and the other on Windemere Farm.

And I'm ready for both of them. Bring it on.

JAKE

Rosie's nose is pressed against the passenger window as she flinches at every flash of lightning and jumps with the loud bang of thunder that follows it.

"It's okay, girl, we'll be home soon, and you can cuddle up with Gran. I know she will have missed you."

Turning her head, she looks at me and barks in agreement.

"Looks like the storm has passed over Abbey Falls, so we will be driving out of it soon enough." Laying eyes on the hills in front of us, I can see the sun peeking through the clouds and, like most storms, it is passing as quickly as it came.

It's one of those annoying dry storms where it's one big light show with loud bangs and just a few spots of rain that are almost gone before they hit the ground.

As I get closer to town, it's all sunshine and blue sky, but I don't like the look of that thin plume of smoke rising from the valley behind Heatherbrae. And I jam my foot down that little bit harder on the accelerator and then push Chase's name on my truck screen to call him.

"Hey, buddy, how far away are you? Did you miss the storm?" Chase asks.

"I'm about ten minutes, but we've got a problem. I can see smoke over the back of Peace Falls in Riversdale Gully. Tell Gran to call the Wildlands firefighters. I think we might have a lightning strike that has sparked a fire."

As I'm talking to Chase, the stream of gray smoke gets thicker and higher into the sky.

"Shit, hang on the line." Chase relays the orders to Declan, and I can hear them both moving.

"Fuck, can you remember any of the woods around here burning since Gramps and Gran bought Heatherbrae?" Chase is back talking to me, and I know we're both fearing the same thing.

"No, and that's what scares me. There will be so much dry undergrowth that if a fire takes hold, Abbey Falls is in trouble. I've got to go. I need to call Ash and tell her to get home to Windemere." My gut sinks at the thought of losing both farms if we can't stop this fire in its tracks.

"Let me do it. You and I both know there's not a chance in hell that she'll pick up the phone to you right now."

Chase's words hit me hard because it's the truth, and I smack my hand onto the steering wheel in frustration.

"Then tell her that we will help her. There are enough of us to prepare both the farms as best we can. And don't take no for an answer. She's as stubborn as I am," I grumble to Chase as I drive through town and squeal onto the back road leading to Heatherbrae.

"Oh, two stubborn-ass people in a relationship? That always ends well."

"Fuck you, asshole. Look at Gramps and Gran. Two of the most stubborn people I've ever met. Go. Call her!" I feel myself becoming more frantic the closer I get to home, and as I roll down my window, I can smell the woods burning.

"Sorry, Rosie. But don't worry, we'll make sure you are safe. I just need you to do your job and keep Gran safe too. Got it?" It's not lost on me that I've gone from being a man who couldn't even bring himself to go near an animal to now talking to Rosie like she's a human. "Yeah, don't look at me like that. I admit when I'm wrong. You've won me over." I reach over and give her a few pats on her head and down onto her back, which she loves.

The moment I throw the truck in Park, I'm out of the driver's door, the smoke thick in the air now. I race around to the passenger side where Rosie's sitting, open the door and clip her leash on her. She jumps down from the truck, and we run up to the house.

"Gran!" I yell as I clatter through the door, still wearing my boots.

"Here!" she yells from the living room where she's stacking boxes of family photo albums. "Leave her with me. Go help Ashley. The boys are prepping the property." She's in full evacuation-plan mode, grabbing the things she can't bear to lose.

"You sure?" I check with her, although my feet are already walking back toward the door.

"Go, go, go. And don't agitate her any more than you did before you left. You boys are as stupid as your gramps sometimes." She's now talking to herself as much as me as she keeps pulling things from cupboards.

"That's the plan." I close the front door behind me to make sure Rosie doesn't get spooked and take off.

Running toward the barn, I can see Chase and Declan moving logs from the woodpile into the building so there's no chance of an ember landing on them and bringing a fire quicker to us than we are prepared for.

"You good?" I yell as I get closer. "Wet down the house before the barn. I can rebuild this, but losing that house would kill Gran."

"Got it," Declan hollers back before disappearing inside with his arms full of wood as Chase passes him on his way back for more. "Wildlands firefighters are on their way into the gully. Go, get out of here. Ashley was almost to Windemere when I got hold of her."

Without another word, I'm running across the pasture toward Windemere. The breeze is coming at me from the direction of Riversdale Gully, which is the worst thing that could happen right now. It's just going to push the flames toward us faster.

As I come through the gate in the fence, I can see Ash running around in the pasture by the barn, chasing all the animals. Adrenaline pushes me harder, and I call out as I get closer.

"Ash!" She can't hear me over the noise of Herb, Daisy, and Gerald, who are all running in different directions. "Ash!" I scream as I get to the fence and climb over with ease and land on the other side.

"Go home, I don't need you, Jake!" Yeah, she's still pissed and has every right to be, but that can wait until later. "I can do this on my own!"

"Hate me later, but don't be so damn stubborn. Let me help." Running around behind Gerald, I try herding her toward the barn door.

"Ugghhh. Fine!" she growls at me, as she's trying to put a lead around Herb's neck. "You get Gerald inside." Which, if things weren't so serious, would be laughable because neither of us can control any of these animals. They are completely spooked and uncontrollable.

Finally, Ash gets Herb inside the barn, but Gerald and Daisy are making me look useless as they keep running from me. But I'm determined to win because they are too important to Ash to let anything happen to them.

Seeing her running back toward me, I know we need to split up.

"Go hose down the house and the barn. I'll get these two in." The wind that is in front of the fire is getting stronger, and it's bringing tiny embers with it.

"No! They are *my* responsibility; I don't care about anything but the animals."

And I'm not stupid enough to spend valuable time standing around arguing with her.

"Fine, I'll do it, but be careful." I look at her one last time before I take off toward the house, and I hate what I see in her eyes. She's scared as hell, but it's anger that overrides her fear when she looks at me. I know the animals are her priority, but I don't want her without a house either. She has fought so hard for her home. I'm not about to let her lose it.

I can hear sirens in the distance, and I know they will be fighting hard, but that's rough terrain over the back of the mountain. Even with the fire trails, it's still full of steep hills and rocky ground.

In the back of my mind, I can hear the discussion we had about installing fire safety systems at Heatherbrae, and I'm furious at myself for not doing it straight away, but I know that it wouldn't have helped here on Windemere. Ash doesn't have the money to buy that type of equipment, and my fucked-up situation meant I couldn't have sorted it out for her either.

The hose is no more than a garden hose, and the pressure coming from the pump on the tank is not strong enough for the water to reach the roof of the barn. But I know that's where she would want me to start.

The ash and embers falling around us are getting bigger, and the air is getting thicker with smoke. But the thing that is freaking me out the most is the sound of fire—the crack of timber and the roar that people talk about in forest fires as it races up the mountain.

My phone in my pocket has been vibrating constantly, but I don't have time to check the messages.

I've tried my best to wet down the barn and have now turned my attention to the house. The water is making it onto the roof, but I'm not sure it's going to be enough by the time the fire peeks over the top of the ridge and starts racing down toward both properties.

It feels like we are fighting it blind because of the mountain behind us, and with the speed it will come over the top, it will be on us before we know it. The truth is, we won't know it's too close to us until it's actually too late and we've run out of time to evacuate.

Out of the corner of my eye, I see Gran's car speeding up Ash's driveway with Chase driving, Gran in the passenger seat, and Declan and Rosie in the rear. The back of the SUV is jammed full of boxes.

As the car screeches to a stop, Declan jumps out and runs over to me.

"Get the girls out of here. The emergency alerts say it's time to leave. Did you get them on your phone?" Declan is yelling, as the noise of the fire gets louder with every minute. He grabs the hose out of my hand and throws it to the ground.

"Ash will never leave." We both run toward her where she's still struggling with that stupid cow.

"Then you need to make her!" Declan jumps the fence and tries to cut off Gerald, but she scatters again, running and darting all over the place. And instead of trying to help Declan, I rush to Ash and grab her around the waist as she tries to follow Gerald for the millionth time. I lift her off the ground with her feet still in motion.

Ash's clenched fists start beating on my arms.

"Let me go, Jake!" she screams at me, and yet it's still hard to hear her over the noise around us.

"It's time to go, Ash. They have issued a level-two warning. We need to evacuate." I'm still holding her tightly because I know if I let her go, there's a chance she'll take off again.

"I don't care!" she bellows at me.

"Ash, listen to me!" I scream as I spin her in my arms so that she's facing me while I lower her feet onto the ground. I use all my strength to hold her in my arms while she continues to fight me.

"You need to get in the car with Gran and get out of here. We are running out of time." She stops fighting as hard and starts listening. "You take Gran to safety. Get her out of here." I know she'll be as worried as I am about an old lady breathing in all this smoke that is starting to settle in all our lungs.

"I need you both out of here and safe. I'll stay and fight to protect the animals. But I can't concentrate when I know the two most important women in my life are here, in the thick of danger." It's then that she really looks at me properly.

"No, Jake, you don't understand. I can't leave them. When no one else loved me, they did." Tears spring to her eyes.

I get it, but she needs to know the truth of why I'm here.

"Let me help you. You are not alone in this life anymore, Ash. You will never be alone again, because I love you!" It's not how I imagined telling her, and regardless of whether she's ready to hear it or not, I need her to know.

Ashley shakes her head, and my panic is getting greater every second we stand here and argue.

"No! I can't rely on you, Jake. You're going to leave, just like everyone else. You told me the first time we met that you didn't come here to stay, and I'm never going to leave."

"I'm staying for you!" I bellow.

"But that's the problem. I'm not the person you need to be staying for," Ashley replies sadly. And I can't help but reach out to take her face in my hands, forcing her to look me in the eyes so she hears me this time and it sinks into that stubborn head of hers.

"You're wrong, Ash. I need to be staying for you." I rest my forehead on hers. "Because you're not just enough for me—you're more, you're my everything." With red glowing embers and ash falling around us and in the craziest of places, it feels like time stands still as I lay myself out for her in my rawest form. "I'm staying for you, Ash, because without you, I'm not the real me that has been lost for so long. Without you, I'm nothing."

Gerald lets out a distressed moo as Declan finally gets her into the doorway of the barn, which has all the other animals calling out in a chorus of fear. Both of us look across to where the noise is coming from.

"I can't lose my dream." Ashley is now crying. Her hands land on my chest and hold on to my shirt as if for dear life.

"And I can't lose you." I grab her and kiss her so hard but for only a mere second. "I know I don't deserve to ask this, but please, just trust me. Let me prove to you the kind of man I really am. I'm not running. I'm here for you, and I'm here to stay. But right now, you need to go."

Before she can say a word, I pick her up and throw her over my shoulder, rushing down to where Chase is sitting in Gran's car. The motor is still running, and as I get closer, he opens the driver's door, jumps out, and stands aside. I put Ash down in the driver's seat Chase vacated and Gran's talking at breakneck speed while Rosie is barking, and it's pure chaos. Ash is trying to get back out of the car, but I hold her in there as I swing her legs in and struggle to get the seat belt on her.

"I'm trusting you to keep Gran safe. Now drive and don't stop until you get to town. We will find you once this is over. Go!" Kissing her one more time, I can't bear to think that it could very well be the last. Then I pull back and slam the door.

Both my cousins are now beside me, and we all start yelling at her to go as we motion for her to drive. Then I see Gran reach across and place her hand on Ash's arm and say something. Whatever she said works, because the car starts moving, and there is no time to watch them as they disappear down the driveway.

Patches of grass are starting to smolder from the pieces of burning debris falling from the sky.

"We need to get these animals out of the danger that is heading for us." I grab them both by an arm. "But I don't expect you to stay. This is my battle to fight."

"Like fuck we're leaving. One in, all in, that's the rule. Stronger as a wall of strength, Gramps would always say, remember?" Declan yells back at me.

"But didn't you just get them in that damn barn? What's Plan B?" Chase is right beside me as we move to where the commotion is coming from.

"It looks like the fire is about to come over the hill on the west side. Let's herd the animals over to Heatherbrae and into the dam. The water is their best chance. Declan, you round up the little animals and get them in Ash's car. The keys should be in the ignition. Chase, grab some wire cutters and get that fence down. I'll start pushing the bigger animals toward you, which I think they will naturally do because it's away from the fire."

Everyone's moving as I pull open the main door, and the barn erupts into chaos.

It all happens so fast as I open each of the stalls to release the animals and push them down the pasture toward Chase. I pause as I see that damn fence that was the beginning of my life changing in such a big way fall to the ground, and I've never been so thankful for the barrier between the farms to be gone. For someone who knows nothing about animal behavior, I'm just glad my lucky guess is working.

"I'm loaded," Declan yells to me from Ash's car.

"Get to Heatherbrae," I shout as I run back into the barn for the last two animals which of course are Gerald and Daisy.

Rummaging on the workbench, I find a rope, because I'm not leaving anything to chance with these two. I make a noose on each end of the rope and struggle to get it over both their heads.

"Just this once can you two please cooperate so we can all live happily ever after?" With the rope firmly in my hand, I open the stall and exit the barn and then start running toward Heatherbrae, praying they won't have any other option but to follow.

To my surprise there is no weight on the rope, and it's not because it's slipped off Gerald or Daisy. It's because they are keeping up with me.

It looks like I've finally gained their trust. And if I can just keep them safe from this fire, then there's a chance I might win back Ash's trust too.

I spot Chase waist-deep in the dam as he drags Herb in with him, and I'm pushing on even though it's getting harder to breathe because of the smoke.

And the moment I get to the edge of the water, Declan comes driving into the pasture like a madman and pulls up next to us, before a strange noise, louder than the sound of rushing wind and fire, has us all looking skyward.

"Water drop!" we all yell in unison as a huge orange helicopter flies straight overhead to where the smoke is the worst.

And for the first time since I drove into town earlier today, I feel hope.

Chapter Eighteen

Ashley

The town hall is full of people, all talking at once, with fear and panic written all over their faces.

"Ashley." I hear my name spoken over and above all the other noise, and I've never been so thankful to see Tiff in my life.

With Rosie on her lead, I pull Betty across the room faster than I should be dragging an old lady, but I need to get to Tiff as quickly as I can.

"I told you. I knew there was something bad about to happen, but I just thought it was you and Jake being idiots and trying to give me a heart attack." She pulls me to her and gives me the biggest hug, but I don't have time for this.

"You and me both, Tiff," Betty pipes up from beside me, "but don't you worry, I'm cooking up a batch of my love meatballs as soon as this is all over."

And although she's trying to put on a strong face, I can tell she's rattled. There is a fire heading straight for her home, and I've just left her three grandsons in the direct line of danger as they try to save my animals and my home—not hers.

As soon as Tiff releases me from her grasp, I place Betty's hand in hers. "Take care of Betty and do not let her or Rosie out of your sight. She needs a cup of your calming tea." They both look at me, confused.

"Wait, where are Jake and the boys?" It now dawns on Tiff that we are here on our own.

"At Windemere," Betty answers at the same time as I plead with Tiff.

"I need your car keys. Betty's car is full of her treasures." Holding my hand out to Tiff, I can tell by the look on her face that she's about to launch into one of her big speeches, but I stop her before she gets started. "Now!" I yell louder than I should. In fact, I don't think I've ever yelled at Tiff like that before.

She doesn't say a word and just pulls out her keys and places them in my hand.

"This negative energy I feel better be connected to the fire, because I swear, if you do anything stupid and get yourself hurt or killed, then I will come find your spirit, wherever it might be, and annoy the shit out of you for eternity. Do you understand?" She squeezes my hand so hard it hurts.

"I love you too. And I mean it, don't let her out of your sight." I point to Betty because I don't trust her not to follow me.

I push my way through a crowd of people holding on to their small animals and calling out to me for help. I reassure them that Beau is in the clinic and that he will take care of them. What a welcome to Abbey Falls poor Beau has had, and weirdly the thought jumps into my head that I know he will be coping with today far better than Jeremy ever would have. It's quite likely that Jeremy losing his job had nothing to do with his ex-girlfriend. He was never a very good vet, and I carried him in the clinic for so long, but I never said anything at the time. I'm now grateful every day for Beau being here.

Running across the park and around the back of the teahouse, I jump into Tiff's old yellow Volkswagen Beetle. Revving up the engine and kicking it into gear, I tear out of the back alley and head toward Windermere. Peering through the windshield, I can see smoke so thick it's darkening the sky over the farms, so I push down on the accelerator and race into the fire.

I'm almost there when I see a huge orange helicopter carrying water toward the smoke and watch as it flies over the ridge behind both farms before disappearing out of sight into Riversdale Gully.

I hope like hell this is the answer to our prayers and that it will slow the fire down on the mountain.

Turning so sharply into my driveway that I almost tip over Tiff's little car, I correct my steering then race up the gravel, screeching to a stop in a spray of pebbles and dust. I start to panic when I can't see anyone and then fling the barn door open, but every stall is empty.

"Shit." Dashing back out, the smoke is thicker than when I left, making me cough. I look around me, trying to see any signs of where they have gone, but my gut tells me there is only one possible place and I take off across my front lawn and past the house until I spot Gerald's deep hoofprints in the ground. The closer I get to the boundary between our farms, I see the fence that Jake and I once stood and argued over is now lying broken on the grass, and the hoof marks continue on to the Heatherbrae side of it.

Running with so much smoke in the air is hard on my lungs, but I push my body harder than I ever have before. As soon as I come into the first pasture of Heatherbrae, the smoke gets a little thinner and visibility is slightly better. There, in the distance, I can see my car down near the dam, and it all starts to make sense. As I come up over the hill, I see something that makes me stop.

Jake standing in the dam, hanging on to a rope that is attached to Daisy and Gerald. And beside him is Chase, arm around Herb's neck, while my sheep, pigs, and horses stand around them in the water.

Both Jake and Chase are drenched and not looking particularly happy at their current situation. That's when I notice the wind shift to the south and push back toward the hills.

"Wind is changing direction," Declan calls out from beside my car, full of chickens and ducks. He pulls his phone out of his pocket as I feel mine vibrating in my jeans. "Alert says the water bombing hit the fire front and that the firefighters have it under control. Advice is to still watch and wait for further updates, but this wind shift will help blow the fire back on itself, hopefully running out of fuel."

And that's when it starts, deep in my belly as the relief pours out of me in the most ridiculous way. Standing with my hands on my hips and looking at the most absurdly precious thing I've ever seen, I'm doubled over with laughter and can't stop.

Trying to suck in some air, I yell at Jake, "When you told me the first day we met that it was about to start raining asshole men around here, I didn't think you meant like this."

I drop my butt onto the grass, feeling giddy with relief. And just as I let myself fall to the ground, Daisy begins jumping around like crazy, splashing water all over the boys, and I'm starting to understand how they got so wet in the first place.

"I think these belong to you," Chase calls back at me, tilting his head in the direction of Jake and the rest of the animals.

"Yeah, I think they really do." Every single one of my lost souls, including Jake, are all standing huddled together. And even though I'm still angry at him and we have some things to sort through, there is no denying that his soul is the one imprinted on my heart until the day I die.

As the firefighting helicopter flies overhead with another load of water to drop, Declan takes a seat on the grass next to me.

"We were a little rushed before, but hi, I'm Declan, and I'm guessing one of the so-called *asshole men* you speak of."

He holds out his hand for me to shake, but that doesn't feel right, so I throw my arms around him instead. "Thank you for saving my family," I mumble into his shoulder. He's so gentle and comforting as his arms wrap around me.

"You're welcome. That's what we do for family, and you will be family, there's no denying that." Pulling back from my hug, Declan's hands remain on my arms. "Because there is no man who hates animals as much as my cousin, but for you, he's standing in the middle of a dam, soaking wet and trying to keep your menagerie safe . . . Yeah, so I guess, welcome to our crazy family!"

"Get your hands off my woman!" Jake bellows from the dam, and Declan just laughs.

"See?" he says, pointing at Jake with his thumb. But those two words "*my woman*" make me feel a little warm and fuzzy.

"Maybe we should go rescue him?" Declan suggests.

"Nah, let him suffer just a bit longer. He still has a lot of groveling to do, so he may as well start now."

Both of us turn back toward the dam, and Declan puts his arm around my shoulders while I drop my head onto his. I've got a feeling Declan and I are going to get on just fine.

My phone is vibrating again, but this time it's not just a message; someone is trying to call me.

The moment I see the screen, I smile and answer the FaceTime from Tiff, but it's not her face that fills the frame.

"Betty." I'm glad I didn't answer with some smart-ass comment.

"I made Tiffany do one of them timing of the face calls."

Declan lets out a little groan next to me at Betty's description, but at least she was close to getting it right.

"You know, so I could see you all. I want to know you are all okay and safe. Where are my boys?"

"I'm here, Gran, and we're all fine," Declan answers her. "And besides some charred patches of ground where some embers fell, there is no damage to Heatherbrae. We were lucky this time."

I pull the phone out in front of us a little so she can see us both.

"Lucky, yes. Good, now where's Chase and Jake?"

She's trying to look behind us, expecting to see them, but instead, I reverse the camera on the phone and call out to them, "Wave to your gran, boys."

To which they both reluctantly lift a hand and wave at her from the dam, but I can tell they're trying to cover that look of wanting to kill me. I'm sure they don't want me snapping a screenshot to capture the moment so I can laugh about it for a long time to come, but too bad, because I'm framing this picture.

"Oh my, how clever of them. Farming suits my boys." She looks so proud.

Switching the camera back onto me, I smile at Betty and say, "I'm not so sure about that, Betty, but yeah, they didn't do too bad under the circumstances."

"Right, now let's talk about you, my dear. Are you okay?" She looks at me intently, and for the first time since I've met Jake, I realize where he gets his soul-piercing gaze from. The one you can't hide from even if you try.

"Everyone's safe, and that's all I care about." I smile at her with relief and notice that the air around us is becoming clearer the longer we sit here talking.

"That's not what I asked you, young lady. I asked if you were okay. It's been a rocky few days, but you need to know he is a good boy. Please just give him a chance to fix whatever he broke."

And I can feel through the phone how much Betty loves her family. It's not that long ago she lost Noel, and she's still more fragile than she lets on. I don't know what to say without getting her hopes up, because as much as I want this to work out, there are no guarantees it will.

"I promise we'll talk," I reassure her.

She looks happy enough with my answer and gives me a nod before the image on the phone starts bouncing all over the place, and I can hear her muttering at Tiff.

"I've finished talking to their faces now. How do I make her go away?" Betty's muffled voice is gone, and before I can hang up, Tiff's face fills the screen.

"Proof of life," I gulp, knowing I'm about to get an earful from her.

Tiff leans closer into the phone, and I try not to laugh as she hisses at me through gritted teeth, "You owe me! Like big-time, woman. I love Betty, and I know she's old, but fuck me, this has been a lot."

"I'm sorry, but you were the only one I trusted with her. I'll bring your car back soon, okay, after I've gone fishing."

"Fishing? What the hell are you talking about." Her voice rings out as I turn the camera again to point at the boys, because I figure Tiff will enjoy the joke.

"I take it back; it was worth looking after Betty to see that image. Yeah, go fish lover boy out of the dam and then call me later."

The camera is now on me as I blow her a kiss, and she ends the call.

"I've got a feeling that I'm going to enjoy meeting whoever that was." Declan stands up off the grass and extends his hand to help me up.

"You might think that now, but maybe ask your cousins to tell you about Tiff before you decide." I grin up at him as I take his hand, and he helps me stand.

It surprises me how much clearer the sky looks now, but the smell of smoke and wildfire will stay with us for a few days yet, I'm sure.

"You might want to move a little," I tell Declan. He looks at me, confused, while I turn my attention back to the animals in the dam.

"Come ooonnnn!" I yell at the top of my voice and watch with delight as Herb, Daisy, Gerald, and all the other animals hear my familiar call and start rushing out of the water toward me, leaving Jake and Chase flat on their faces in the dam and Declan roaring with laughter beside me.

Turning to move back as my four-legged family starts following me up the hill toward our home, I feel a sense of calm settle over me.

"Tell him to bring my car, ducks, and chickens back once he's showered," I shout to Declan.

"Will do," he calls back, and I can hear Jake and Chase carrying on as they try to get out of the water, complaining about how much they stink like shit.

I smile to myself as I lead my animals home.

JAKE

"Yes, Gran," I reply as I walk out the front door of the house, but I can hear her footsteps following closely behind me.

"I'm serious, Jake. I think I should come with you to make sure you don't mess this up. The men in this family are useless with words. You all take after your gramps, who didn't have one bit of swoon in his handsome body. Lucky he was good with his hands . . ."

I swirl back around to face her at the top of the stairs before she can go any further with this conversation.

"Gran." I gently place my hands on her shoulders. "I've got this. And just so you know, I like to think I've got plenty of swoon that has gotten me this far. Now, can I go fix this?" Leaning down and kissing her on the top of her head, I pull her into a tight hug.

"Okay, but don't come home until you do." She huffs and walks back inside as Declan marches over the field from Windemere.

"Man, she's going to have fun cleaning out all the chicken and duck shit that car is covered in. I figured there was no point in you driving Ash's car back after you showered. Not sure you want to be smelling like shit, when being down on your knees groveling is going to be embarrassing enough." Declan slaps me on the shoulder and then keeps walking toward the barn. "I need a long shower and a cold beer, because that wasn't quite the welcome to Abbey Falls I was expecting, but it got the heart started, that's for sure."

"Yeah, I think we can all agree we don't want another day like this one anytime soon. Thank you . . . for everything, and tell Chase the same for me, will you."

Declan just waves at me from over his shoulder as he enters the barn, and I set off on the short walk over to Windemere.

I already knew what I wanted to say to Ash. I'd been replaying it over and over in my head on the long drive home from Sacramento. I practiced how I would apologize, explain to her where I've been and why and—most importantly—that I love her deeply. But every part of my carefully rehearsed speech was thrown out the window, and instead, I ended up blurting it all out in the middle of a crisis.

And she didn't say it back.

No matter how many times I keep telling myself it's because there was too much happening around us, I can't shake the doubt that I read this situation all wrong. Maybe she just doesn't feel the same. But no matter what happens today, I'll wait.

I'll wait until she forgives me.

I'll wait until she loves me.

And I'll wait until she's ready to spend the rest of this life together.

Because I'm not leaving.

Stepping over the broken fence makes me chuckle. I couldn't get it built quick enough to put a barrier between me and her and those ridiculously named animals. But today, I couldn't tear this fence down fast enough to save those same annoying four-legged pests that are starting to grow on me. Although Daisy and I still have a long way to go before we are at the friends stage.

As I approach her house, I see Ashley take a step out onto the porch wearing a long flowing dark green dress, and my thoughts automatically jump to what she's wearing underneath. I'm a long way from finding out, but that doesn't mean her beauty doesn't take my breath away every time I see her.

My heart is banging against my chest, and my blood pressure is rising just like I knew it would.

In her hands she's carrying two bottles of beer that I've never been more thankful for in all my life. She makes herself comfortable on her porch chair that has a blanket thrown over it, probably so we don't sit in all the soot and ash that has been floating around in the air.

I stop myself at the top of the porch steps and just take a minute to really look at her. I knew from the moment she stood tall and challenged me on the day we met that I was in trouble. And as much as we have both fought it, we are here now on the edge of the cliff, and we need to decide whether we are ready to hold each other's hand and take a leap of faith.

"Hey." She signals for me to take a seat next to her.

"Hi," I reply as I sit, resisting the urge to lean over and kiss her. "Thank you, you must have read my mind." I take the ice-cold beer from her.

"Well, I figured I owed you at least one drink for rescuing my animals and saving my farm." We clink our bottles together, and the first mouthful tastes like pure heaven.

"You don't owe me a thing, Ash." I'm still sitting up straight, as I just can't seem to relax into the chair like she has. She definitely has the upper hand here, and I don't know where to start. It's like all my carefully rehearsed words have left on that wind that swept through here this afternoon.

"You're right, I don't, if we are talking about you leaving without a word and not one single form of contact for days, but this afternoon, what you did, putting yourself in danger for my animals, that's something I need to say thank you for. I just need you to know how grateful I am."

I can see the emotion in her eyes and the words she hurled at me in the middle of the crisis come back to me now.

She said her animals loved her when no one else did. I always knew she loved animals, especially her own, but I understand now that they are more to her than that. They have been her support when she felt she had no one. They don't judge her, and in return for her kindness of a home, food, and treatment for whatever ails them, they simply love her back. It's all she ever needed. To them she was always more than enough.

"It's me that owes you for the hurt of being lied to. Although I never lied. I just didn't tell you everything." Her steely glare tells me that she doesn't agree with me, but I push on anyway. "I know it's a technicality, but to me it's important. Because I promised that I would never lie to you."

"Jake, just move on." Ash takes another sip of her beer and stares at me.

"Okay, okay. It's not like this is easy." I'm trying to gather my thoughts together as they scramble around in my head.

"Oh, and ripping my heart out was? Leaving without speaking to me, not calling or texting or even sending a damn carrier pigeon to let me know you were coming back. That you had to sort your shit out. But. That. You. Were. Coming. Back! Because being abandoned by a man is not a trigger for me at all."

Oh yeah, she's still angry, and now that the fire has passed, it's all coming back to the surface.

"No! I never wanted to hurt you, and if we'd had the opportunity to finish talking that night, then I'm sure things would've ended differently." I can feel myself getting annoyed by her shortness with me. But I need to curb my frustration because I know I'm in the wrong here. So, taking a deep breath, I try to start again. "But I couldn't talk to you unless it was face-to-face, and all I could think of was that I needed to sort my problems out as quickly as possible and race back to you. In the hope that you will understand and forgive me."

"Why are men so dumb, seriously," she mumbles to herself, looking out past me to the yard.

"I know I fucked this up, but all I'm asking is a chance to explain. And if at the end you want me to leave, I'll walk away." I nervously run my hand through my hair as I wait for her response.

Ash looks at me and sighs. I don't know if she's still trying to decide whether she's prepared to give me that chance or if she's just making me wait to punish me a bit more.

"Okay," she says calmly, and I'm starting to think it was the latter.

"Thank you." Agitated, I stand and walk to the post on the porch steps and lean my back against it so I can see Ash's reaction.

"I told you how I got myself into financial trouble, but I didn't get to explain the role Danika played in this whole mess. You already know that when she decided to leave me, it came as a shock. But what I didn't tell you was that she had obviously been planning it for a while, because without me knowing, she had been slowly siphoning money out of our joint billing account and into another one in her own name. So, when she eventually said she was leaving, I did everything I could to convince her to stay. My desperation played right into her hands." Sighing, I adjust my weight onto my other foot.

"She said she needed time to clear her head and suggested we take six months apart. Since I would be staying in the house, she would need money to live off, so I agreed that she should take the cash we had in our joint savings account, and I would keep paying the bills and the mortgage while she was gone from our billing account. I was hoping like mad that she would come back to me after our time apart and that we'd finally get married. I didn't look after any of the home finances when we were together; Danika did all that, while I just ran my business account. So, she did as we agreed, and when she moved out of the house, she took all our savings with her. I had thought we would be using that money for an engagement ring, but she obviously had different plans." As much as I'm over Danika and everything that happened, it still hurts telling the story.

"Mhm," is all Ash says while waiting for me to continue.

"But there were two things I didn't know; one was that the money I thought was in the billing account was nearly all gone, and the second was the moment she got the money, she left the country and started screwing her way through Europe. And she so kindly chose *not* to delete me off her social media accounts, and I know I could've deleted her but I was still stupid enough to hope that she'd realize her mistake and come back to me. Instead I got to see it all play out in front of my eyes. It was her last *fuck you*."

This time I wait for Ash to say something, but she continues to sit silently.

"The rest you know, about me working to try to get myself back on top, and I was almost there until I got ripped off by a customer who thought I was an easy target. And to be honest, at that time, I probably was. I was vulnerable and didn't have the strength to fight them, but I was also too embarrassed to ask for help from Beckett. Until now."

At that, Ashley sits up straighter in her chair, looking shocked. "You went to Beckett for help?"

"Yes, I did. For one reason and one reason alone." I look into her eyes. "I did it for you."

"Why?" she asks softly, and I can see some of her anger has dissipated.

"Because I love you, and I can't lose you, Ash. I needed to fix my past so I could have a future with you. I wasn't running away like you thought I was. I had to go back to be able to move forward. And now, with my brother's support, he's helped me do what I should have done back then. I know I tease him about his finance job, but that man knows what he's doing. He's what I would call a ballbreaker when it comes to money." And I can't help but smile because it was actually interesting to watch Beckett in action.

"I don't think I really appreciated how good he is at his job until now. Being a man who works with tools in my hands, I didn't respect that he works just as hard behind a desk. But I do now. And although we need to work on it, I think spending a few days together has brought us closer as brothers and wanting to be more in each other's lives. We have talked and yelled through all the things that have pushed us apart and tried to see it from the other person's point of view. Don't get me wrong, there are still things we will never agree on, but we have decided to bury them and move forward. An unexpected benefit of my shit show, I guess and I can't tell you how good it feels."

Walking back to her and sitting down, I reach for her hand and am thankful when she actually lets me hold it.

"Beckett loaned me the money, and I have cleared all my debts. I will need to pay him back over time and with interest, because I wouldn't have it any other way. You should have seen the way he marched into Jeff Peters' office—the guy who refused to pay—and serve him with a notice to pay in thirty days or we would see him in court. When Jeff started rolling off bogus reasons why he didn't have to pay, Beckett walked up and stood over him. He very quickly made him understand how he would make sure his legal fees would be three times more than what he owes me by dragging out the court orders, oh, and making sure that it became known around town that he was a business risk because he couldn't pay his debts. I just stood and watched as Jeff crumbled and agreed he would pay me within the next seven days. Beckett knew exactly what to say to get the right result.

"I know the crypto money is gone, but we also reported that guy to the authorities for illegally trading without a financial license. At the very least it made me feel good to know that no one else will fall for his scheme the way I did." I'm rubbing my thumb over her hand, and I can't stop now.

"But the biggest thing I did was instruct a real estate agent to sell my house. There is nothing in Sacramento for me anymore. My life is here now, in Abbey Falls. And although the money I will get when it sells won't be much, I was hoping to find some farmland to invest it in. Maybe I can find a place that will take on a man who's useless with animals but willing to learn. Although, he's good with his hands and handy with his tools. Of course, all in good time, but if you hear of any place that is looking for someone, then let me know."

"I've heard my neighbor has a room in her barn that is free to rent. Apparently it's quite comfy and the landlord is such a softy," Ash jokingly suggests.

"Tell that to Gran, who told me when I was about to head over here that tonight I'll be sleeping outside with Rosie if I don't fix up my relationship with you. I don't think she understands that's not a punishment for me, but still, she believes I need her help. Which could mean anything, so I'm just warning you in advance that you may want to put me out of my misery sooner rather than later."

Watching Ashley's facial expression change, I can tell she's trying hard to not let her guard down just yet.

"So, you're staying then?" She isn't scared to ask this time.

"Until the day I die, and then they will bury me right up there on the hill next to Gramps under the white oak tree we used to climb as kids. I plan on becoming the next Abbey Falls handyman, working for people like my grandparents who are getting on in age and need help. Gran tells me she already has clients lined up. I know you are surprised by the fact she is meddling"—I pretend to cough twice into my hand—"helping again." I lift her hand to my mouth and kiss it, more serious now.

"This is home, Ash." Looking out over the land and the view stretching as far as Heatherbrae, I can feel the warmth in my chest spreading.

"A place with a goat that has a cow's name, a female cow that has a man's name, a chatty donkey who won't shut up, and all their furry friends. But most importantly, there is this farmer who has made me love her even when I tried my hardest not to.

"You, Ashley Alleyne, are my home. Now I just have to wait until you feel the same about me, that I'm enough for you too. Every day, I'll ask you one question. Do you love me?" I desperately want to take her in my arms and kiss her, but I know I can't, not yet.

"And on that magical day when you finally answer '*Yes,*' that's when I'll know I'm your home too." Standing and letting her go is hard, but it's what I need to do. I walk to the top of the stairs and look directly back at her.

"Do you love me?" I smile at her, knowing her answer already.

Her lips don't move, but her eyes tell me all I need to know. I nod.

"Good night, Ash, I'll be back again tomorrow." I walk away like I said I would.

Tomorrow is a new day.

Chapter Nineteen

Ashley

I've been tossing and turning in bed for what feels like hours but when I look at my phone, it's only 11 p.m.

Lying on a pillow that is imbued with the comforting scent of Jake should be relaxing, but it's not anywhere near the same as the real thing. Being here alone just feels so wrong right now. I keep questioning over and over again why I let him walk away tonight.

I love Jake.

I know it and he knows it. So why didn't I just blurt it out.

All my life all I've wanted is someone to fight for me.

Sitting up and looking out my bedroom window at the night sky, with my animals safe in the barn, the gravity of today really starts to hit me.

I could've lost all of this, including Jake. Everything I worked so hard for, gone in an instant. Yet something heavier is weighing on me now, and that is that Jake stood up when it counted. He left his family to help me and then pushed me away to keep me safe, putting his own life in danger and that of his cousins too. That has to be the ultimate sacrifice for someone you love. He didn't just say it tonight, he *showed* me the only way he knew how, in the biggest of grand gestures that will be hard to ever top.

I know what I need to do.

Picking up my phone and ignoring the time, I call Tiff and put her on speaker as I jump out of bed and start getting dressed.

"You better just be calling me because you've run out of condoms with Mr. Studley and you need a home delivery, otherwise I don't want to know." Her muffled voice comes out of the phone.

"Oh my God, you crack me up, but just for future reference we're way past the condom stage," I reply but with excitement in my voice now.

"Then you better not be about to fuck us, all over again. I was finally getting the best night's sleep I've had in days. The negative energy is almost gone from Abbey Falls, and you are the only one who can mess it all up again. So you better not be punishing Jake for his male brain fart and stupidity that he has more than made up for, or are you about to do something stupid? Because I think it's your civil duty to make things right for the town too. Well, not really the town, just me. Put me out of my misery and just tell me you told him you love him."

I can't help but start laughing.

"Almost. But, Tiff, I need you to tell me I'm doing the right thing. You've seen me at my worst—"

"And at your absolute best. The last few months you have been glowing with the most beautiful red aura." She cuts me off.

"But he hurt me so bad, can I trust he won't do it again?" Standing still in just my panties and bra under one of Jake's plaid shirts he left here, I ask her what I've been chewing over in my head for the last few hours.

"No, you can't. Because I promise you, he'll hurt you again, and you'll hurt him too. But it's how you take ownership of that and both get through that hurt together that will define your relationship. Growing and making your bond stronger. That's what love is."

And that's the honesty I need to hear from my best friend. She's not telling me it will be perfect from this day forward. Because that's not who we are.

Is it really who any of us are in this world? The beauty of life is the perfectly imperfect inside all of us. It's called being a human being.

I've had a long time to decide what I want in a man. I want someone who will protect me enough that I can be safe to feel vulnerable with him but at the same time allow me to still be my strong stubborn self and ask for what I want in this life. To stand up and not be afraid to tell him how I feel and know that I will hear and feel the same in return.

I want a man who's my equal.

And that man's Jake, who's just finished laying his heart on the line for me.

"Thanks, Tiff. Couldn't do this life without you. Love you," I yell excitedly to her as I finish buttoning up the oversize shirt that hits my thighs before pulling on my jeans and cowgirl boots for the quick run across to Heatherbrae.

"Seriously! Don't tell *me* that—go tell Jake that! Put that poor man out of his misery and let the universe finally rest, so I can then stop worrying and sleep too," she screams.

"I am," I reply with determination and pick the phone up, taking it off speaker.

"He's the one I've been waiting for," I try to say through the emotion that is now boiling up and out of me.

"He was always the one. You just had to wait until your stars aligned," Tiff replies softly.

"Exactly." The tears are falling now as I open the front door and step out onto the porch with a smile.

"Good night," she says as the phone goes dead and I'm left looking out at Jake, asleep on his bedroll on the lawn in front of my house with Rosie curled up beside him. Wow, Betty wasn't joking when she said she'd kick him out if he didn't make things right with me.

I hurry down the steps and across the lawn toward him, and Rosie's already lifting her head, giving a little bark to alert Jake.

"Sshh, we don't want to wake Ash," Jake mumbles, half asleep, as his hand reaches out to stroke her head.

"I couldn't sleep without you," I gulp as I reach him.

Jake sits bolt upright, now fully awake, "Ash, are you okay?" He's fumbling with his bed roll, trying to get his body out of it and up on his feet without tripping over.

"Yes. Yes, I really am. I need to tell you this and it couldn't wait." It's like my chest is about to burst with every emotion that I've been holding in there for weeks. I've been frightened to let myself truly lean in and fully open my soul to him, but I'm not afraid anymore.

Jake steps to me and takes my hands in his, holding them so softly, running his thumbs over their backs, and the calmness of him is now flowing through to me.

"I heard everything you said earlier tonight, and I appreciate your honesty and vulnerability. But I want to make one thing clear. I was never upset about your situation. My hurt came from you not feeling you could trust me with your greatest worries. Because if we are going to do this, and not just a half-hearted relationship, but like a happily-ever-after thing, we need to trust one another with every part of our souls. I need to know you are all-in, Jake. That you trust me, will talk to me and tell me everything no matter how bad it is. We carry those burdens together. Do you understand what I'm trying to say?"

The nervous excitement I had earlier has gone and instead is fully replaced with the love that I hold for this man. I finally understand what people say when they talk about that feeling in the depth of your heart that you're right where you are meant to be in this world.

He nods at me, understanding I have more to say, and I don't want him to interrupt me until I get it out.

"You asked me to trust you, and I do, but I need you to trust me too. Otherwise, as good as this is, it's not going to work. I've been in a one-way relationship before, and I'm not prepared to do it again."

I feel so calm, and I see Jake almost about to break down in tears. I'm feeling that my strength and the emotion in my words are resonating with him. I've grown so much in the short time I've known Jake, and so has he. I'm so proud to be standing up for what I deserve, like Jake told me to that night in the woods. That I should never accept anything less.

"So, do you trust me with your heart and your soul, Jake?" I squeeze his hands tighter now, waiting for his answer.

"From now until eternity, you have me. You are in the deepest part of my soul and have owned my whole heart from the day I met you. I trust you with it all. Because like I told you, the biggest lesson I've learned is that, without you, there is no me."

As he finishes, there are a few stray tears trailing down both our cheeks.

Nodding my head at him and taking in a deep breath, I step closer.

"Ask me again, Jake." And I can hardly speak as the enormity of what is happening descends on me.

Now it's him moving closer until there is no distance between us, his arms around me pulling me into his body, our chests touching and I look up to him with all the passion in my eyes that I need him to see.

"I love you, Ashley. Do you love me?" Jake holds his breath, waiting for my reply.

"Yes, Jake, I love you, and as much as I tried not to, I discovered it's impossible to do anything but love you, fiercely."

There are no more words needed, and my hands are on his cheeks, pulling him to me. Our lips collide and seal our bond.

I will remember this moment for the rest of my life.

We are finally home, together, here on Windemere.

Our safe place to be ourselves in all our crazy happiness.

I pull back from our kiss that is getting totally out of control.

"Are you ready for sex in the wild?" he asks as he looks into my eyes and I see that spark in his that was dulled the night he opened up to me is now finally back and burning bright.

"Promise me, Ashley, that no matter what happens in life from now on, when things get hard, that you will always meet me out here under these stars. Together, where we belong."

"It's my new favorite place to be, thanks to you." Pulling him down to the ground, on top of his bed roll, I crawl into his lap, and it's like my life is finally how it's meant to be.

"When all my dreams had disappeared, you loved me back to life. I will forever be grateful you took a risk on me," he says as he wraps me so tight to his body, where I fit against him perfectly, burying his face in my neck and taking in a deep breath. And as he slowly lets it out his lips are on my ear, and he drags it through his teeth.

"You're wearing your cowgirl boots and my shirt. You know what they both do to me." He growls in my ear.

"Mhmm." I giggle as I get to my feet. "I was counting on it."

Taking off running for the stairs with Rosie at my heels and Jake right behind me, I've never felt freer.

"Stay, Rosie," Jake's deep voice commands and as I make it into my bedroom, I hear the front door close and the loud click of the lock engaging, making sure he keeps Rosie out, which has me smiling.

I watch Jake striding into my room and stop in front of me. His dark eyes are raking over me and his heated stare is giving me goosebumps.

"I thought I lost you," he whispers, taking my face in his big hands and his dimple appears at the side of the smile of pure relief on his face.

"Look for the North Star. You'll always find home in our love that's written in the stars . . . oh and my tea leaves." I step into his arms and we finally just let ourselves become one.

And as crazy as it sounds, he knows I'm right.

"Just don't tell Tiff I said that," I mumble into his shirt and we both dissolve into laughter.

"Tiff is the last thing on my mind right now." He growls in the way that sends my body into a wet mess, knowing what's coming, as he pulls back and rips the shirt I'm wearing open in one go, sending buttons flying.

"Time to saddle up, cowgirl. I'm about to give you the ride of your life."

There's no sleep happening in this house tonight, but we're about to rock the universe back into its peaceful place.

"You talk the talk, but can you walk the walk?" I'm taunting him with my words as I'm taking a step backward, closer to my bed.

"Watch me," he replies with that sexual rasp in his voice that tells me he's on the edge. He pulls his shirt over his head and is kicking his boots off. They land with a thud on the floor at the end of my bed.

"Welcome home, Jake." I'm pulling him on top of me as we both fall onto the bed.

And the world around us slips away as he makes love to me, with not one inch of fear between us, finally.

Showing me the kind of love I've always longed for.

◆ ◆ ◆

"Hurry up. I am not explaining to your gran that we are late because you were fucking me stupid in the shower, again," I yell down the hallway at Jake, who's just drying himself off.

"Did she say why she needed to see us so urgently this morning? Is she about to lecture us? I mean, I can't believe she really kicked you out of the barn to sleep outside when you tried to go home last night without me." I'm giggling to myself.

Walking into my bedroom, Jake just rolls his eyes at me. "I can't believe you've known Gran all these years and haven't worked out that you don't cross her. That woman is as sweet as apple pie, until she's not. You have been warned," he says, picking his jeans up off the floor from where they landed last night. He quickly throws them on along with his shirt and boots.

Jake's reaching down and kissing me on the cheek. "You okay to walk across to Heatherbrae?" And his asshole smirk appears on his face.

"Barely, and I blame you, Jake Davis." I smack him in the middle of the chest as we head out the door.

We are walking hand in hand past the newly renovated barn at Heatherbrae when Betty comes bustling out the front door of the house.

"About time, otherwise lunch will be late. Come on, come on."

We both look at each other confused, because it's only ten thirty in the morning.

Betty ushers us into the kitchen where she has all these random ingredients lined up on the counter and starts pushing aprons into both of our free hands.

"Time to learn the art of making love meatballs, since *I* fixed your relationship finally." Patting us both on the cheeks, she starts going about showing us what to do, and I feel every bit of the welcome to the family she's trying to give me.

◆ ◆ ◆

As we step back from plating the love meatballs and get ready to call Chase and Declan inside, Betty takes both our hands in hers.

"You are now part of the secret society and must never reveal this recipe. Because people think there is some secret ingredient in the sauce, and they aren't entirely wrong, but it's not what they think. It's that the dish is made with love for the person you want to feel that love. That's what makes them so special. They fix everything and I have a feeling you two might need the extra help along the way." Gran stands and lifts her head up for us to lean forward and kiss her cheeks.

"Thanks for the vote of confidence, Gran,." Jake chuckles.

"Oh it's not like that. I see so much of Gramps in you that I know there will be many a time you will need to apologize. These will help."

I love this woman. Betty is the heart and soul of this family that I'm blessed to be a part of now.

JAKE

As Gran and Ash sit on the porch swing, enjoying the fresh air of the afternoon after what was a beautiful lunch, Declan, Chase, and I stand on the site of where the winery and cellar are about to be built.

I roll out the plans on the ground and we all crouch down in wonder at what we are about to create.

"Today feels like the start of new beginnings. Who feels like marking this out and breaking ground?" I glance up at them both.

Declan has been doing all the research and wants to be the one to take on the task of trying to make our first Heatherbrae original vintage, so I see his eyes light up.

"I'll go grab the string line and stakes." Chase jumps up and is back from the shed in minutes.

It doesn't take long before the foundations are marked out, as we all stand back and take it in. "Who wants to break ground on the winery first?" I look at both Declan and Chase.

"Since it's going to be Declan's baby, I think he should be the one to take the first step into our next adventure," Chase replies.

"I agree. Okay, Declan, pick up the shovel and push it in nice and deep. Let's see what trouble you can dig up, because let's be honest, if the last few months are any indication, nothing this year is going to be smooth sailing." I pat him on the back and he strides forward to sink the shovel into the soil.

"Great, now you've jinxed us." Declan laughs when he hits a rock only halfway in. "Awesome, just what we need. Great start."

Looking over at Ash with my heart overflowing, I know nothing is ever simple at Heatherbrae. But complicated doesn't mean it's not going to work out exactly how it's meant to be.

And we wouldn't have it any other way.

Epilogue

Three Months Later

Jake

"Really? You think another goat is a good idea?" I'm standing looking at the trailer. "I didn't purchase that trailer when my house sold so we could accumulate more animals." Like the one on the back of it that's eyeballing me. We definitely won't be friends.

Stupidly I thought getting us a trailer with a cage around it would be a good idea in case we ever need to move the animals in a hurry again. But instead, all it's done is give Ashley a way to bring another stray home.

"But she needed someone to love her. Look at her, she's been neglected. It's not like we don't have room, and she will make a great friend for Daisy." Ash starts backing her off the trailer as Herb calls all the others to the fence.

"I'm sure she does, like every single one of this noisy menagerie." I point to the group, who are calling out their greeting. "Do I dare ask what her name is?" I walk toward Ash to help close the gate on the trailer.

“Well, since you were the last stray to move into Windemere, maybe you should get the honor of naming her.” Ash pats the goat’s head to calm her for a moment.

“You are lucky there is an animal between me and you, because otherwise I would have you over my shoulder and take you into the house to remind you just how much you love having *this* stray calling Windemere his home. And let’s be honest, I was virtually living here anyway.” Stepping around the back of the goat, leaving plenty of distance between me and its hind legs, I wrap my arms around Ash and kiss her forehead. “Hi, beautiful, how was your day?”

“Long, and you are never going to guess what happened today.” She looks at me like she can’t believe whatever it is either. “A letter arrived in the mail at the clinic, which is weird in itself because nobody sends letters anymore. So, when I opened it and saw it was Jeremy’s handwriting it took me by surprise.”

I can feel my whole body tensing up.

“The contents of it totally blew me away, though. He apologized for what he did to me when he left and for the phone calls. He has a job now and has started therapy and drug counseling to help work himself out. Can you believe it, drugs. I never would’ve picked up on it but it just goes to show we didn’t really know each other, even though I thought we did. He wished me well and a happy life. Like what the hell.”

She throws her hand that isn’t holding the rope into the air. “He actually sounded like the guy I fell for in college.” She takes a deep breath before finishing. “I didn’t know how much I needed closure on that relationship and that he wasn’t just going to turn up here one day, until I read it.”

And I can see the relief on her face, and deep down I feel the same.

“After that I’m just so thankful it’s now officially the start of my weekend off, and I can’t wait to lie around and do absolutely nothing." Ash is reaching up on her toes to have her lips touch mine, and she tastes just perfect.

"Well, I suggest that after you get this new family member in the barn that you go have a shower, because as much as I love you, you stink like cow shit, woman." I tap her on the ass, bringing a little giggle.

"Only if you plan to join me. That double shower has so much room to . . . get clean." She looks at me with that cheeky grin I love seeing on her these days.

"Like you even need to ask. Why do you think I installed it, and with the extra-large water tank? Not for you to shower alone, that's for sure." I step back to give Ash room to start walking the goat to the gate on the yards at the barn.

"So, what's her name?" Ash looks at me.

"Well, in true Windemere style, if she's a girl, she gets a boy's name, so how about Billy?"

"Okay, not very imaginative, but I'm sure you'll get better at this," Ash calls to me over the fence now that she's in the yard with Billy.

"Why would I need to get better at it? It's not like we are getting any more pets." I lean on the railings and smile to myself that the piece of wood is perfectly secure since for the past few months we have been working on fixing everything up. My days are spent at Heatherbrae with the guys, and then I do a few hours here, either with Ash or on my own if she's on call.

And then on her weekends off, we usually spend a bit of time on the farm but always make sure we have at least one day just for us. We call it date day, and it can be whatever we want it to be, as long as we are together and there is no work involved.

"It's cute that you think that's the case. Just because you live here, it doesn't mean the animals will stop coming." Ash slips the harness off Billy and watches her get sniffed by Daisy. They check each other out and then start walking farther into the yard and through the open gate out into the pasture.

"Just can we make a no more goats rule? They don't like me. I mean, look at Daisy; it's been months, and we still aren't friends. I swear that goat is jealous that I get more of your attention than she does." I lean my arms on the top railing of the fence where Ash has just climbed up and sat so we can make sure that Billy is accepted by the Noah's Ark family.

"You do realize we are having a conversation here about you competing with a goat for my affection. And you think Tiff is the crazy one?" She places her arm around the top of my shoulder, when we look at each other and reply at the same time.

"She is." And then laughter fills the space around us.

We stay outside for a while until Ash is happy that the family is getting along, and then it's time for a shower, which is exactly what we both need.

But I have plans for us both.

Keeping Ash busy helping me cook my love meatballs, I have tasked Declan and Chase with setting up my surprise.

After we finish devouring our dinner and then clean up, I pull a white blindfold from my pocket. I hold it up for Ash to see.

"Jake, what is that for?" she asks nervously.

"Do you trust me, Ash?" I take a step toward her so our toes are touching, and she nods.

"Of course I do." And I lean in and kiss her gently after her reply.

"I'm just going to put this over your eyes, as I have a surprise for you." I slide it on her head and make sure it's secure, because I don't want anything ruined. And before she's got time to think about it, I pick her up in my arms and carry her outside. She shrieks the moment her feet are off the ground, but I'm not taking the risk of her falling as I try to walk her out while blindfolded.

Opening the front door, I can see everything looks perfect. Just like I imagined.

Spread out on the grass is our blanket that we use every time we picnic out here or lie out looking up at the stars. So far we have never managed a whole night as yet, but tonight's the night.

Around our blanket is a huge heart shape of little tea lights in jars, because nobody wants another fire started.

Then there is a double sleeping bag in the middle of the blanket and a couple of pillows. Beside it is a basket of snacks and a bottle of champagne on ice with glasses. White rose petals are scattered around, which I figure Daisy and Billy will just eat off the ground tomorrow.

As I carry her in my arms into the middle of the candles arranged like a heart, I slowly place her feet back on the ground and make sure she's balanced. Releasing her, I move one step back and take one last moment to soak in the scene before me.

Ash had no idea what was about to happen tonight when she slipped on her favorite long green strapless dress that she also wore the night I poured my heart out to her and asked her if she loved me. Every time she wears it, it's a reminder of how fragile a relationship can be if you don't nurture it with good communication. It's something I work hard on every day.

Her hair is flowing over her shoulders with a slight curl in it from letting it dry naturally after our shower, and peeking out from the bottom of her dress are her pink-painted toenails. It's something new she has started since we met. She likes to do little things for herself that make her feel feminine, so on those hard workdays where she looks down at her clothes and she's covered in some sort of animal byproduct, underneath it all there is something pretty. As much as I appreciate the lace underwear and painted nails, I love the fact that she isn't doing it for me, but for herself.

Ashley sets the bar of how she wants to be treated in this world, and now my job is to make sure that I'm always aiming above it.

"Jake." Her soft whisper sends goosebumps all over my skin.

"I'm still here," I reply as I lower one knee to the ground and pick up the wooden box I carved out of a branch from the white oak tree on Heatherbrae. "You can take off the blindfold now but don't open your eyes just yet."

She pushes it up over her head and lets it drop to the ground. Her hands are by her sides, and she rubs her fingers together with nerves.

"Slowly open your eyes, beautiful, and take it all in." I watch her eyes focus on everything around, and her mouth drops open as she does.

"Oh, Jake." She gasps as her hands land on her mouth, and already there are tears building in her eyes as she sees me on my knee, holding out to her a flat round diamond ring set in a gold band. We had talked about jewelry one day and how for her she will never be able to wear anything that is big and showy. But she was okay with that because it's not who she is. Instead, she wanted something that even when she was working, she could still wear every day under her gloves.

I thought I would be as nervous as hell today, but I'm not. Instead, excitement is buzzing through me.

This is the beginning of sealing our lives together.

"I arrived in Abbey Falls to fall into the arms of my family, hoping that they would put me back together. But that's not what I really needed. It was to find the woman who would push me with her no-nonsense words and not take excuses for the things I did wrong. To challenge me to be a better man, every single day. To open my heart again to not only her but to the animal kingdom as well."

Ash lets a little giggle out in between her tears that are falling freely now as I continue. "And as much as I tried to tell myself I wasn't ready, the magic of this place already had other plans for us." Taking a deep breath, I'm trying to hold back my own tears now.

"Ashley Alleyne, you complete me, you are my home, and I want you to also be my happily ever after. I promise to be by your side when things are perfect and never to run when things get hard." I take the ring from the box and place the box down.

"I love you with all that I am and all I will ever be. Marry me so we can live our forever together." I hold my breath just watching her look from my face to the ring and back again, with a smile so bright it shines through the tears.

"Yes. A thousand times yes."

She's holding out her hand and I slip the ring on her finger. I then jump to my feet, wrapping my arms tightly around her. I twirl her in the air, with the beautiful sounds of her happy laughter echoing around us.

Slowing, placing her feet back on the ground, I lean into her, whispering, "You said yes." The reality of the moment overtakes my emotions.

"I said yes," she whispers back at me, and it's the perfect time to kiss my fiancée.

And of all the times I have kissed her before tonight, this one feels the sweetest, filled with such pure love that is binding us as one.

As I open my eyes, it's then that I see my forever looking back at me.

Sometimes you need to weather the storm to see the stars come out again. But the most important thing is it's not about the storm or when it's going to clear, it's who you choose to ride it out with.

Ashley will always be my storm-and-stars girl.

"Can you let your cousin who's hiding over in the bushes taking photos know that it's time to leave now? Because I really want to get naked with you to celebrate."

Ash's words hit me exactly as intended, lighting every spark in my body.

"Absolutely." I start kissing her hard and the electricity is tingling on both our lips. It was meant to be a quick touch, but this is not stopping anytime soon. So instead of yelling to Chase, I just hold my hand in the air, waving for him to go, and thankfully he gets the message.

"Congratulations, and yeah, I don't need to see this. I'm out," he calls out to us as the flashes stop, and he disappears off toward Heatherbrae. Hearing the gate close in the distance, I pull my black T-shirt over my head and stand in front of Ash, with all the signs of arousal building on her cheeks and the fidgeting movement of her legs under her dress.

"Naked, now!" I growl at her.

"Make me." The challenge in her eyes is all I need.

"Challenge accepted."

Eighteen Months Later

ASHLEY

"I swear if I have to get up one more time to go to the toilet tonight, you are being evicted." My bare feet hit the floor as I hear Jake's grumble from the bed.

"You better not be talking about me." His drowsy voice tells me he's getting as little sleep as I am.

"No. *Your* son, that is kicking my bladder like crazy because he's obviously running out of room. If he lasts another two weeks in there it will be a miracle." I'm now yelling from the hallway as I waddle in the dark to the bathroom.

When we talked about having kids on our many nights lying under the stars, it all sounded so beautiful and something dreams are made of. But no one prepared me for this part of the journey, where I feel like my body has been taken over and is no longer my own. Or that because my husband is a big man that his baby boy will also be a man child before he's even born. I swear I will be so much nicer to every pregnant animal I see going forward. Because these last few weeks have sucked.

We are so lucky that Abbey Falls has grown on Beau, and he's found a reason to stay. Jake and I have talked about after the baby is born and my brain is operating at least on some sort of logical capacity that it might be time to sit down and talk to Beau about buying into the clinic with me. I will never give up my life as a vet because it's who I am, but I want to step back a little now and add the title of Mom to my name.

And this new job is going to be both the most important and the most challenging I will ever do in my life. Because let's be honest, any son of Jake's is going to be a handful and will want to spend every moment he can outside. And on the nights I'm uncomfortable and can't sleep, I imagine visions of this little boy sneaking over to Heatherbrae to Gran to get a cookie or sweet when I have said no more. Or following Rosie as she wanders between the two houses. We gave up trying to keep her at Heatherbrae all the time; she has a bed at both houses now, and the bigger I have gotten in this pregnancy, the more frequently she sleeps in the living room in her spot.

She didn't just claim Gran as her human—Rosie claimed the whole family, and we love her for it.

I'm waddling myself back into the bedroom and Jake is now standing next to the bed on my side with the covers thrown back.

"Here, baby, let me help you back into bed and try to get you comfortable." He takes my hand and lowers me, picking up my feet and helping me swivel to lie down. He then collects all my pillows that I have stuffed between my legs and under my belly to help with the constant backache and pulls the covers over me before kissing me softly on the lips. He walks back around the bed, climbs in, and wraps his arms around me, running his hand in circles over my swollen pregnant belly. And there's something about his touch that seems to soothe his son, bringing calm to him and sending him back to sleep. Which in turn helps me drift off too.

"That first cuddle will make all this work worth it. As much as I love you in all your pregnant glory, I know you are going to be the most amazing mother, and I can't wait to see it."

Jake's soft words fall in the darkness as we sleep, but all I can think is, yeah, well, tell that to my body that is getting ready to push out an oversize watermelon. Thankfully I'm so exhausted that the worry of that disappears as I fall asleep.

But as I wake again with that constant feeling of needing to pee, this time it's joined by some pain that has me a little worried. I reach back and tap my husband, who's still wrapped around me.

"Jake, I don't feel well. Can you help me to the bathroom?"

And he was already moving before I even got the whole sentence out.

"Ash, what's wrong?" My big strong man is already in panic mode.

"I don't know, but this pain at the same time as the need to go to the toilet is not normal, and my vet brain is telling me that something isn't right here." And as much as I don't want to think about my son as an animal, it's all the same process in theory. "Either that or my mother's intuition is kicking in early."

And almost like I brought it on by talking about something not being right, my water breaks halfway down the hallway, and the first sharp contraction hits me, almost bringing me to my knees.

"Jake!" I scream as I grab hold of him before I fall to the floor.

"Shit, is it supposed to start that hard?"

He's worried, but I can't actually answer him right now as the pain rages through my body and it takes every bit of my energy to keep breathing.

As it backs off, I look up at him and see my poor husband with fear in his eyes.

"No. Get me to the hospital because this little guy has decided it's time, and he's not waiting."

As Jake loads me into his truck, I'm rubbing my belly before the next contraction hits. Talking to my little boy, trying to reassure him it's all going to be okay, but I think it's a pep talk for both of us.

"Just hang in there, little one. I don't want to be trying to talk your dad through delivering you on the side of the road." Because it's the problem of a small town. The hospital is thirty minutes away, and full of bumpy country roads.

And as we screech into the hospital, they rush me through triage while Jake is trying to shout details at the poor nurse filling out the paperwork. But the moment I'm in the labor room and I finally see the doctor's face, it's like I check out and let it all just start to happen, because I don't need to be the medical expert here anymore. I'm just a woman who's about to give birth, and the sooner the better, because I feel like I'm being ripped in two.

"Jaaaaaake!" I scream so loud I'm sure they will hear it back in Abbey Falls as my son's head crowns, and before I can take a breath, his little body follows, and the doctor is lifting him onto my chest.

Tears rush from me as I look down at my little boy's mushed-up face, covered in muck, and think he's the most beautiful sight I've ever seen.

Jake kisses my forehead as we both wrap our arms around our son, who lets out his first cry to signal his entry into the world.

"Welcome to the family, our little Brock Noel Davis. We've been waiting to meet you." And looking into Jake's tear-stained face, the love he has inside him is bursting already.

It's like Jake can feel his gramps in these ten tiny fingers and ten tiny toes, and I will thank Noel every day. We lost a great man, but in turn he brought Jake to me and gifted us the next generation of men to walk the soil of Heatherbrae.

And for that, I'm eternally grateful.

Read on for a sneak peek at the next romance in the *Abbey Falls Series* by Karen Deen, *Falling Back to You.*

Available by Spring 2027

Extract

Lauren

Sometimes you need to go backward to move forward, no matter how painful that may be.

"What would ten-year-old Lauren say if she could see her life now?"

I almost groan out loud at the words coming through the speaker on my computer. I look pointedly through the screen at my college mentor turned friend, Celia. The Florida moonlight is streaming through her window behind her.

"Seriously, that's like asking, 'So, Lauren, has your life been all apples or did it turn to shit?' No medical school undergrad is going to want to listen to my boring life," I grumble back at her. I can't believe I agreed to this interview.

"This podcast is for more than just medical students. You never know who will be listening and needs to know that it's perfectly acceptable to be a small-town doctor and not chase the big bucks as a specialist in a city or want to be on a research team in a major hospital," Celia says with pleading eyes.

"Fine," I moan, adjusting myself in my chair, sitting up straighter and then putting on my sweet, professional doctor face to answer this last question.

"Ten-year-old Lauren had a dream of being a doctor in the town she grew up in. Seeing my brother live with chronic asthma all his life and my parents often having to drive long distances to get him the help he needed, or even to see a doctor, I knew I wanted to help the people in my town back home. After college I became a qualified family doctor, moved back to Rocky Cedars and I haven't left. Since then, the community has built a new, better-equipped hospital and, although it's not in the same league as one of your major city hospitals, like Johns Hopkins, we can still cope with most crises here and in the surrounding small towns. So, looking back, I would tell young Lauren to follow her dream regardless of what others say, and don't give up. Some people may look down on you for going back home like it's some kind of failure, but just know they're wrong, and I'm living proof of that. Because going forward is not always in a straight line. Your step back may be the best possible way to move forward to bigger and brighter things. Life will throw some hard times at you, and you will feel like the mountain you are climbing is just too high, but that moment when you stand on top of it, it will all be worth it." I smile, with my most professional mask.

"Okay, got it," Celia replies as I drop back into my chair sighing, the fake smile gone.

"Now, what the hell is wrong with you today? Why the long face?"

"How good's your basketball knowledge?" I ask offhandedly.

"The men are tall, rich, and have big feet, and you know what they say about big feet . . ." Celia leans back in her chair, laughing out loud at herself.

"Well since we are both doctors and know the feet thing is bullshit, that's not the question I was asking. I need to know, like, the rules and how the game's played. Have you got anything that's moderately useful?" I snap back at her, rubbing my forehead, already feeling out of my depth.

"I can replace a heart valve with my eyes closed, but sport? I don't do sport. You know that. So, what's this with the need for basketball knowledge?" She picks up her glass of red wine that she poured before we started to film the little podcast snippets.

"You know me, I can't say no to my niece, Fia, but this one is a doozy." Curling my legs up under me on my chair and taking my wineglass in hand, I take a much-needed sip. It's 8 p.m. and I might be wearing a beautiful blouse on my top half, but underneath the table I've got my trusty purple sleep shorts on. So, I may as well get comfortable now the interview is over.

"Oh, do tell, I love a good Fia story. Is your sister-in-law talking to you yet, over the whole giving her the birth control pill saga?" She rolls her eyes at me.

"No, but she will be thanking me when she's not a grandmother at the age of forty-two. Anyway, moving on, so Fia's school basketball team has no coach. The boys' team has a coach and gets the majority of the school funding, even though it should be evenly split, but no surprise it doesn't happen that way in a small town. So the girls were getting desperate. Fia comes into my office after school with those big puppy-dog eyes that she has used on me since the day she was born, begging me to help. She said they don't need much, just for me to turn up to practice two afternoons a week and on game day of course." I lay my head back on the chair and close my eyes.

"And what did you say, no, wait, let me guess . . ." She starts to chuckle.

"Well, no guesses needed. I started two weeks ago, and we have our first game coming up soon." I stop talking because there is no point going on when Celia is now laughing so hard that she won't hear what I'm saying anyway.

Tears are still rolling down her cheeks as she tries to talk.

"You . . . a basketball coach . . . Oh this is gold . . . I can't . . . Oh my sides are hurting."

I watch her trying to suck in air after her outburst.

"Bitch, you are supposed to tell me that I can do this, you know, be my cheerleader or support staff, or whatever they call them." I huff at her, even though I totally agree.

"I will. I'll turn up on your first game day with pom-poms and yell 'go Lauren' from the bleachers. And bring you little cut-up oranges to eat during the zone-outs . . . is that what they call them—no wait, hang on, time-outs, that's right," she rambles while continuing to shake her imaginary pom-poms above her head.

"Ughh, this is not helping. And no, you aren't coming anywhere near my embarrassing disaster. Anyway, I need to go. I have back-to-back appointments all day tomorrow before I leave for basketball practice, and I need to watch some more YouTube videos on how to be a basketball coach." I drop my feet off my chair, back down on to the floor. "Because that's a winning formula if ever I heard one."

"Well at least you're tall enough to look like a basketballer." She smiles and shrugs.

"Like I haven't heard that a thousand times over the years. Apparently being a six-foot-tall woman means everyone assumes that I play. Little do they know it couldn't be any further from the truth. Basketball and I are like oil and water; we do not mix," I tell her.

Celia sits up closer to the screen with a serious look on her face. "Look, jokes aside, at the end of the day, it doesn't actually matter how good you or the team are. All that matters is that those girls know that someone gives a shit about them and that they are just as important as the boys. You never know what each of those girls are going through in their lives, so this might be you helping a child that would otherwise fall through the cracks. And we both know in this social media age any activity that has them off their phones for a few hours a week is a huge win."

Her words sink in, and I realize that I have been so caught up in my head with questions like how many steps can you take between each bounce that I didn't even think about the positive-role-model aspect of coaching.

Thinking back to my college days when I first met Celia, I was an absolute mess, and if I didn't have her to look up to, and at times be my sounding board on life, I'm not sure I would've gotten through it.

"Thanks, hon. I needed that. Talk next week. Love you." Blowing her a kiss, she does the same as we disconnect and I sit looking at the blank screen in front of me.

I might be helping the girls' mental health by just showing up for them, but no one knows how much it's also screwing with my head every time I walk onto the court.

Because all I see is him.

Declan Rogers.

Six foot five of jaw-dropping sex on a stick.

And every time I think about him, the memories of that summer come flooding back.

I used to watch him on the court as he practiced his shots over and over again, because basketball was his whole world. It was the only time I cared about a sport, so I would turn up on time and watch him and his ridiculously hot body run up and down the court and shoot hoops. All the while I sat there, I knew our dreams would take us in different directions—I would go on to become a doctor and his life as a basketball star was just beginning.

Why didn't I learn anything about the game? That would have helped me a lot more now. I still remember his kisses though, and how gentle he was with me. The way I loved him as though I couldn't breathe without him, and then the feeling of despair as it all slipped through my fingers. We discovered a world of firsts together, and for that I will always be so grateful it was with him. No regrets.

But as I click the YouTube icon on my computer, trying to work out what the hell to teach the girls tomorrow, I can hear in my head, as clear as day, his deep laughter. He would think this was the funniest thing he's ever heard, and I'd agree with him.

◆ ◆ ◆

"Shit, what did that YouTube guy say again?" I almost trip over my feet climbing out of my Audi because I'm rushing as usual and have fifty different things on my mind—none of which are basketball related.

"*Fake it till you make it. They don't know you are an inept idiot.*"

Fia is already running into the gym because she hates when we are late for practice. My head is pounding with a headache after a long stressful day in the clinic, and I've just dropped my water bottle. Great! The only positive is that Fia hasn't got shitty with me since the first day we were late, especially when I just told her that she should feel lucky we made it here at all. So as I scrabble to pick up my water bottle, she at least isn't complaining. As I get closer to the gym doors, I can hear my niece before I see her. She inherited her father's loud voice.

With my bag slung over my shoulder, water bottle under my arm again, and my coach's folder in my other hand, at least I look the part even if I'm nowhere close. My footsteps echo loudly through the gym, which is probably because I'm stomping as per usual. Clearing six foot, I'm not a little woman so it's hard to walk like a delicate fairy.

As I approach, I can see that all the girls are huddled in a circle, giggling and looking down at something.

"Okay, ladies, sorry I'm late. Start your warm-up laps, please."

The giggling stops and they fall silent as they turn to look at me. At the same time, a man pops up from nowhere, standing in the middle of the girl's circle and towering over them with his height.

And my world stops.

I look into the eyes that still frequent my dreams and stare at the lips that I have never forgotten.

"What the hell are you doing here?" My internal panic makes the words slip out before I have time to stop them so they sound harsher than I meant.

Declan's smile instantly disappears and that spark that I saw for a split second is snuffed out, only to be replaced by a darkness that tells me he's not happy to see me either.

"Coaching my team," he sternly replies, as though it should be obvious, and then the death stare he gives me feels like a warning for me to leave.

Well, fuck you, buddy.

"Correction, my team," I tell him, and I know in this moment that as much as I complain profusely about being their coach, I'm not giving up my girls without a fight.

Meanwhile eighteen-year-old Lauren is inside my head screaming with excitement that he's here.

But I'm not that girl anymore and there has been a lot of water under the bridge since then, and not all of it good.

DECLAN

The moment I lay eyes on the old coach, every reasonable thought leaves my body and a hate I had long buried comes rushing to the surface.

So many emotions run through my head at lightning speed, but the one that cuts the most is a pain that I never wanted to feel again.

Because Lauren Gregory might be standing right in front of me, ready to tear strips off me, but there is no way I'm giving her another chance to break me.

She was the love of my life who vanished without a trace.

You don't get a second chance at breaking my heart. And she's about to learn that I'm not the soft young guy she walked away from.

Because twenty years of carrying this hate will harden a man.

"No, sorry, miss, but as of 5 p.m. tonight when practice started fifteen minutes ago, they became *my* team, and your services are no longer required. So please close the door on your way out," I state dismissively, hoping she'll take the hint.

It's not like she knows anything about basketball . . . and I clench my fist as hard as I can to make the memory of her laughing questions as she stared at me like I hung the moon . . .

Bang!

Her bag drops to the floor and before I know it Lauren Gregory is standing one foot away from me, hands on her hips as if she's squaring up for a fight. And the past I've buried deep down might not be deep enough. Because my body is already reacting to her being so close.

"You might be taller, stronger, and more knowledgeable than me, but these are *my* girls, and I'm not going anywhere, so deal with it." She rams her finger into my chest to accentuate her point with a final, "Jerk!"

And I hate the way her words and a single touch have my cock twitching. She always was my kryptonite.

Damn you, Gran, volunteering me for this job is one cruel setup.

But I guarantee it will be ending before it even begins.

I straighten my shoulders and allow myself to take full advantage of my height and fix her with a stare that could freeze lava.

Because I only have one heart and Lauren doesn't have the key.

Not anymore.

ANOTHER ROMANCE BY KAREN DEEN

Read on for the first chapter of one of Karen Deen's bestselling books, Gorgeous Gyno, available to buy now.

GORGEOUS GYNO

Chapter One

Matilda

Today has disaster written all over it.

Five fifty-seven a.m. and already I have three emails that have the potential to derail tonight's function. Why do people insist on being so disorganized? Truly, it's not that hard.

Have a diary, use your phone, write it down, order the stock—whatever it takes. Either way, don't fuck my order up! I shouldn't have to use my grown-up words before 6 a.m. on a weekday. Seriously!

Standing in the shower with hot water streaming down my body is no relief. I feel like I'm about to draw blood with how hard I'm scrubbing my scalp, while I'm thinking about solutions for my problems. It's what I'm good at. Not the hair-pulling but the problem-solving in a crisis. A professional event planner has many sneaky tricks up her sleeve. I just happen to have them up my sleeve, in my pockets, and hiding in my shoes. As a last resort, I pull them out of my ass.

I need to get into the office to find a new supplier that can have nine hundred mint-green cloth serviettes delivered to the hotel by lunchtime today. You would think this is trivial in the world.

However, if tonight's event is not perfect, it could be the difference between my dream penthouse apartment or the shoebox I'm living in now. I'll be damned if mint napkins are the deciding factor. Why can't Lucia just settle for white? Oh, that's right, because she is about as easy to please as a child waiting for food. No matter what you say, they complain until they get what they want. Lucia is a nice lady, I'm sure, when she's not being my client from hell.

Standing in the bathroom, foot on the side of the bath, stretching my stockings on, I sneak a glance in the mirror. I hate looking at myself. Who wants to look at their fat rolls and butt dimples. Not me! I should get rid of the mirror and then I wouldn't have to cringe every time I see it. Maybe in that penthouse I'm seeing in my future, there will be a personal trainer and chef included.

Yes! Let's put that in the picture. Need to add that to my vision board. I already have the personal driver posted up on my board—of course, he's sizzling hot. The trains and taxis got old about seven years ago. Well, maybe six years and eleven months. The first month I moved to Chicago I loved it. The hustle and bustle, such a change from the country town I grew up in. Trains running on raised platforms instead of the ground, the amount of taxis that seemed to be in the thousands compared to three that were run by the McKinnon family. Now all the extra time you lose in traffic every day is so frustrating, it's hard to make up in a busy schedule.

I slip my pencil skirt up over my hips, zip up and turn side to side. Happy with my outfit, I slide my suit jacket on, and then I do the last thing, putting on lipstick. Time to take on the world for another day. As stressful as it is and how often I will complain about things going wrong, I love my life. With a passion. Working with my best friend in our own business is the best leap of faith we took together. Leaving our childhood hometown of Williamsport, we were seeking adventure. The new beginning we both needed. It didn't quite start how I thought. Those first few months were tough. I really struggled, but I just didn't feel like I could go home anymore because the feeling of being happy there had changed thanks to my ex-boyfriend. Lucky, I had Fleur to get me through that time.

Fleur and I met in preschool. She was busy setting up her toy kitchen in the classroom when I walked in. I say hers, because one of the boys tried to tell her how to arrange it and her look stopped him in his tracks. I remember thinking, he has no idea. I would set it up just how she did. It made perfect sense. I knew we were right. Well, that was what we agreed on and bonded over our PB&J sandwich. That and our OCD behavior, of being painfully pedantic. Sometimes it meant we butted heads being so similar, but not often. We have been inseparable ever since that first day.

We used to lay in the hammock in my parents' backyard while growing up. Dreaming of the adventures we were going to have together. We may as well have been sisters. Our moms always said we were joined at the hip. Which was fine until boys came into the picture. They didn't understand us wanting to spend so much time together. Of course, that changed when our hormones kicked in. Boys became important in our lives, but we never lost our closeness. We have each other's backs no matter what. Still today, she is that one person I will trust with my life, is my partner in crime, my bestie.

Leaning my head on the back wall of the elevator as it descends, my mind is already running through my checklist of things I need to tackle the moment I walk into the office. That pre-event anxiety is starting to surface. It's not bad anxiety. It's the kick of adrenaline I use to get me moving. It focuses me and blocks out the rest of the world. The only thing that exists is the job I'm working on. From the moment we started up our business of planning high-end events, we have been working so hard, day and night. It feels like we haven't had time to breathe yet. The point we have been aiming for is so close we can feel it. Being shortlisted for a major contract is such a huge achievement and acknowledgment of our business. Tapping my head, I say to myself, "touch wood". So far, we've never had any disaster functions that we haven't been able to turn around to a success on the day. I put it down to the way Fleur and I work together. We have this mental connection. Not even having to talk, we know what the other is thinking and do it before the other person asks. It's just a perfect combination.

Let's hope that connection is working today.

Walking through the foyer, phone in hand, it chimes. I was in the middle of checking how close my Uber is, but the words in front of my eyes stop me dead in my tracks.

Fleur: Tonight's guest speaker woke up vomiting – CANCELLED!!!

"Fuck!" There is no other word needed.

I hear from behind me, "Pardon me, young lady." Shit, it's Mrs. Johnson. My old-fashioned conscience. I have no idea how she seems to pop up at the most random times. I don't even need to turn around and look at her. What confuses me is why she is in the foyer at six forty-five in the morning. When I'm eighty-two years of age, there is no way I'll be up this early.

"Sorry, Mrs. Johnson. I will drop in my dollar for the swear jar tomorrow," I mumble as I'm madly typing back to Fleur.

"See that you do, missy. Otherwise, I will chase you down, and you know I'm not joking." I hear her laughing as she shuffles on her way towards the front doors. I'm sure everyone in this building is paying for her nursing home when they finally get her to move there. I don't swear that often—well, I tell myself that in my head, anyway. It just seems Mrs. Johnson manages to be around, every time I curse.

"Got to run, Mrs. Johnson. I will pop in tomorrow," I call out, heading out the front doors. Part of me feels for her. I think the swear jar is more about getting people to call in to visit her apartment. Her husband passed away six months after I moved in. He was a beautiful old man. She misses him terribly and gets quite lonely. She's been adopted by everyone in the building as our stand-in Nana whether we like it or not. Although she is still stuck in the previous century, she has a big heart and just wants to feel like she has a reason to get up every day and live her life.

My ride into work allows me to get a few emails sorted, at the same time I'm thinking on how I'm going to solve the guest speaker problem. Fleur is on the food organization for this one, and I am on everything else. It's the way we work it. Whoever is on food is rostered on for the actual event. If I can get through today, then tonight I get to relax. As much as you can relax when you are a control freak and you aren't there. We need to split the work this way, otherwise we'd never get a day or night off.

The event is for the '*End of the Cycle*' program. It's a great organization that helps stop the cycle of poverty and low education in families. Trying to help the parents learn to budget and get the kids in school and learning. A joint effort to give the next generation a fighting chance of living the life they dream about.

Maybe if I call the CEO, they'll have someone who has been through the program or somehow associated with the mentoring that can give a firsthand account of what it means to the families. Next email on my list. Another skill I have learned: Delegation makes things happen. I can't do it all, and even with Fleur, we need to coordinate with others to make things proceed quickly.

As usual, Thursday morning traffic is slow even at this time of the day. We are crawling at a snail's pace. I could get out and walk faster than this. I contemplate it, but with the summer heat, I know even at this time of the morning, I'd end up a sweaty mess. That is not the look I need when I'm trying to present like the woman in charge. Even if you have no idea what you're doing, you need people to believe you do. Smoke and mirrors, the illusion is part of the performance.

My phone is pinging constantly as I approach the front of the office building. We chose the location in the beginning because it was central to all the big function spaces in the city. Being new to the city, we didn't factor in how busy it is here. Yet the convenience of being so close far outweighs the traffic hassles.

Hustling down the hall, I push open the door of our office.

'FLEURTILLY'.

It still gives me goosebumps seeing our dream name on the door. The one we thought of all those years ago in that hammock. Even more exciting is that it's all ours. No answering to anyone else. We have worked hard, and this is our reward.

The noise in the office tells me Fleur already has everything turned on and is yelling down the phone at someone. Surely, we can't have another disaster even before my first morning coffee.

"What the hell, Scott. I warned you not to go out and party too hard yesterday. Have you even been to bed yet? What the hell are you thinking, or have the drugs just stopped that peanut brain from even working?! You were already on your last warning. Find someone who will put up with your crap. Your job here is terminated, effective immediately." Fleur's office phone bangs down on her desk loud enough I can hear her from across the hall.

"Well, you told him, didn't you? Now who the hell is going to run the waiters tonight?" I ask, walking in to find her sitting at her desk, leaning back in her chair, eyes closed and hands behind her head.

"I know, I know. I should have made him get his sorry ass in and work tonight and then fired him. My bad. I'll fix it, don't worry.

Maybe it's time to promote TJ. He's been doing a great job, and I'm sure he's been pretty much doing Scott's job for him anyway."

To be honest, I think she's right. We've suspected for a while that Scott, one of our managers, has been partying harder than just a few drinks with friends. He's become unreliable, which is unlike him. Even when he's at work, he's not himself. I tried to talk to him about it and was shut down. Unfortunately, our reputation is too important to risk him screwing up a job because he's high. He's had enough warnings. His loss.

"You fix that, and I'll find a new speaker. Oh, and 900 stupid mint-green napkins. Seriously. Let's hope the morning improves." I turn to walk out of her office and call over my shoulder, "By the way, good morning. Let today be awesome." I smile, waiting for her response.

"As awesome as we are. I see your good morning and I raise you a peaceful day and a drama-free evening. Your turn for coffee, woman." And so, our average workday swings into action.

By eleven-thirty, our day is still sliding towards the shit end of the scale. We have had two staff call in sick with the stupid vomiting bug. Lucia has called me a total of thirty-seven times with stupid questions. While I talk through my teeth trying to be polite, I wonder why she's hired event planners when she wants to micromanage everything.

My phone pressed to my ear, Fleur comes in and puts her hand up to high-five me. Thank God, that means she has solved her issues, and we are staffed ready to go tonight. It's just my speaker problem, and then we will have jumped the shit pile and be back on our way to the flowers and sunshine.

"Fleurtilly, you are speaking with Matilda." I pause momentarily. "Hello, Mr. Drummond, how are you this morning?" I have my sweet business voice on, looking at Fleur holding her breath for my answer.

"That's great, yes, I'm having a good day too." I roll my eyes at my partner standing in front of me making stupid faces. "Thank you for calling me back. I was just wondering how you went with finding another speaker for this evening's event." I pause while he responds. I try not to show any reaction to keep Fleur guessing what he's saying. "Okay, thank you for looking into it for me. I hope you enjoy tonight. Goodbye." Slowly I put the phone down.

"Tilly, for God's sake, tell me!" She is yelling at me as I slowly stand up and then start the happy dance and high-five her back.

"We have ourselves a pilot who mentors the boys and girls in the program. He was happy to step in last-minute. Mr. Drummond is going to confirm with him now that he's let us know." We both reach out for a hug, still carrying on when Deven interrupts with his normal gusto.

"Is he single, how old, height, and which team is he batting for?" He stands leaning against the doorway, waiting for us to settle down and pay him any attention.

"I already called dibs, Dev. If he is hot, single, and in his thirties then back off, lover boy. Even if he bats for your team, I bet I can persuade him to change sides." Fleur walks towards him and wraps him in a hug. "Morning, sunshine. How was last night?"

"Let's just say there won't be a second date. He turned up late, kept looking at his phone the whole time, and doesn't drink. Like, not at all. No alcohol. Who even does that? That's a no from me!" We're all laughing now while I start shutting down my computer and pack my briefcase, ready to head over to the function at McCormick Place.

"While I'd love to stay and chat with you girls," I say, making Deven roll his eyes at me, "I have to get moving. Things to do, a function to get finished, so I can go home and put my feet up." I pick up my phone and bag, giving them both a peck on the cheek. "See you both over there later. On my phone if needed." I start hurrying down the corridor to the elevator. I debated calling a car but figured a taxi will be quicker at this time of the day. Just before the lunchtime rush, the doorman should be able to flag one down for me.

Rushing out of the elevator, I see a taxi pulled up to the curb letting someone off. I want to grab it before it takes off again. Cecil the doorman sees me in full high-heeled jog and opens the door knowing what I'm trying to do. He's calling out to the taxi to wait as I come past him, focused on the open door the previous passenger is closing.

"Wait, please . . ." I call as I run straight into a solid wall of chest. Arms grab me as I'm stumbling sideways. Shit. Please don't let this hurt.

Just as my world is tilting sideways, I'm coming back upright to a white tank top, tight and wet with sweat. So close to my face I can smell the male pheromones and feel the heat on my cheeks radiating from his body.

"Christ, I'm so sorry. Are you okay, gorgeous?" That voice, low, breathy, and a little startled. I'm not game to look up and see the face of this wall of solid abs. "You just came out that door like there's someone chasing you. I couldn't stop in time." His hands start to push me backwards a little so he can see more of me.

"Talk to me, please. Are you okay? I'm so sorry I frightened you. Luckily, I stopped you from hitting the deck."

Taking a big breath to pull myself back in control, I slowly follow up his sweaty chest to look at the man the voice is coming from. The sun is behind him so I can't make his face out from the glare. I want to step back to take a better look when I hear the taxi driver yelling at me.

"Are you getting in, lady, or not?" he barks out of the driver's seat.

Damn, I need to get moving.

“Thank you. I’m sorry I ran in front of you. Sorry, I have to go.” I start to turn to move to the taxi, yet he hasn’t let me go.

“I’m the one who’s sorry. Just glad you’re okay. Have a good day, gorgeous.” He guides me to the back seat of the taxi and closes the door for me after I slide in, then taps the roof to let the driver know he’s good to go. As we pull away from the curb, I see his smile of beautiful white teeth as he turns and keeps jogging down the sidewalk. My heart is still pounding, my head is still trying to process what the hell just happened. Can today get any crazier?

GRAYSON

‘I’m just a hunk, a hunk of burning love

Just a hunk, a hunk of burning love’

Crap!

What the hell!

I reach out to grab her before I bowl her over and smash her to the ground. Stopping my feet dead in the middle of running takes all the strength I have in my legs. We sway slightly, but I manage to pull her back towards me to stand her back up. Where did this woman come from? Looking down at the top of her head, I can’t tell if she’s okay or not.

She’s not moving or saying anything. It’s like she’s frozen still. I think I’ve scared her so much she’s in shock.

She’s not answering me, so I try to pull her out a little more so I can see her face.

Well, hello gorgeous one.

The sun is shining brightly on her face that lights her up with a glow. She’s squinting, having trouble seeing me. She opens her mouth to finally talk. I’m ready for her to rip into me for running into her. Yet all I get is sorry and she’s trying to escape my grasp.

The taxi driver gives her the hurry along. I'd love to make sure she's really okay, but I seem to be holding her up. I help her to the taxi and within seconds she's pulling away from me, turning and watching me from the back window of the cab.

Well, that gave today a new interesting twist.

One gorgeous woman almost falling at my feet. Before I could even settle my breathing from running, I blink, and she's gone. Almost like a little figment of my imagination.

One part I certainly didn't imagine is how freaking beautiful she looked.

I take off running towards Dunbar Park and the basketball court where the guys are waiting for me. Elvis is pumping out more rock in my earbuds, and my feet pound the pavement in time with his hip thrusts. I'm a huge Elvis fan, my music tastes stuck in the sixties. There is nothing like the smooth melodic tones of the King. My mom listened to him on her old vinyl records, and we would dance around the kitchen while Dad was at work. I think she was brainwashing me. It totally worked. Although I love all sorts of music, Elvis will always be at the top of my playlist.

"Oh, here's Doctor Dreamy. What, some damsel in distress at the hospital that you couldn't walk away from?" The basketball lands with a thud in the center of my chest from Tate.

"Like you can talk, oh godly one. The surgeon that every nurse in the hospital is either dreaming about fucking, or how she can stab needles in you after she's been fucked over by you." Smacking him on the back as I join the boys on the court, Lex and Mason burst out laughing.

"Welcome to the game, doctors. Sucks you're on the same team today, doesn't it? Less bitching and more bouncing. Let's get this game started. I'm due in court at three and the judge already hates me, so being late won't go well," Lex yelled as he started backing down the court ready to mark and stop us scoring a basket.

"Let me guess, she hates you because you slept with her," I yell back.

"Nope, but I may have spent a night with her daughter, who I had no idea lives with her mother the judge."

"Holy shit, that's the funniest thing I've heard today." Tate throws his head back, laughing out loud. "That story is status-worthy."

"You put one word of that on social media and I won't be the one in court trying to get you out on bail, I'll be there defending why I beat you to a pulp, gossip boy. Now get over there so Mason and I can whip the asses off you two glamour boys." Lex glares at Tate.

"Like you even have a chance. Bring it, boys." I yell to him as he waves at me to come at him.

Game on, gentlemen.

My watch starts buzzing to tell us time's up in the game. We're all on such tight work schedules that we squeeze in this basketball game together once a week. These guys are my family, well, the kind of family you love one minute and want to kill the next. We've been friends since meeting at Brother Rice High School for Boys, where we all ended up in the same class on the first day. Not sure what the teachers were thinking after the first week when we had bonded and were already making pains of ourselves. Not sure how many times our parents were requested for a "*talk*" with the headmaster, but it was more often than is normal, I'm sure. It didn't matter we all went to separate universities or worked in different professions. We had already formed that lifelong friendship that won't ever break.

Sweat dripping off all of us, I'm gulping down water from the water fountain. Not too much, otherwise I'll end up with a muscle cramp by the time I run back to the hospital.

"Right, who's free tonight?" Mason is reading his phone with a blank look on his face.

"I'm up for a drink, I'm off-shift tonight," Tate pipes up as I grin and second him that I'm off too. It doesn't happen often that we all have a night off together. The joys of being a doctor in a hospital.

"I can't, I'm attending a charity dinner. It's for that charity you mentor for, Mason," Lex replies.

"Well, that's perfect. Gray, you are my plus one, and Tate, your date is Lex. I'm now the guest speaker for the night. So, you can all come and listen to the best talk you have witnessed all year. Prepare to be amazed." He brushes each of his shoulders with his hands, trying to show us how impressive he is.

We all moan simultaneously at him.

"Thanks for the support, cocksuckers. My memory is long." He huffs a little as he types away a reply on his phone.

Mason is a pilot who spent four years in the military, before he was discharged, struggling with the things he saw. He started to work in the commercial sector but then was picked up by a private charter company. He's perfect for that sort of role. He has the smoothness, wit, and intelligence to mingle with anyone, no matter who they are. He's had great stories of different passengers over the years and places he's flown.

"Why in God's name would anyone think you were interesting enough to talk for more than five minutes. You can't even make that time limit for sex," I say, waiting for the reaction.

"Oh, you are all so fucking funny, aren't you. I'm talking about my role in mentoring kids to reach for their dream jobs, no matter how big that dream is." The look on his face tells me he takes this seriously.

"Jokes aside, man, that's a great thing you do. If you can dream it, you can reach it. If you make a difference in one kid's life, then it's worth it." We all stop with the ribbing and start to work out tonight's details. We agree to meet at a bar first for a drink and head to the dinner together. My second alarm on my watch starts up. We all know what that means.

Parting ways, Mason yells over his shoulder to us all, "By the way, it's black tie."

I inwardly groan as I pick up my pace into a steady jog again. I hate wearing a tie. It reminds me of high school wearing one every day. If I can avoid it now, I do. Unfortunately, most of these charity dinners you need to dress to impress. You also need to have your wallet full to hand over a donation. I'm lucky, I've never lived without the luxury of money, so I'm happy to help others where I can.

Running down Michigan Avenue, I can see Mercy Hospital in the distance standing tall and proud. It's my home away from home. This is the place I spend the majority of my waking hours, working, along with some of my sleeping hours too. My heart beats happily in this place. Looking after people and saving lives is the highest rush you can experience in life. With that comes rough days, but you just hope the good outweighs the bad most of the time.

That's why I run and try not to miss the workouts with the boys. You need to clear the head to stay focused. The patients need the best of us every single time. Tate works with me at Mercy, which makes for fun days and nights when we're on shift together. He didn't run with me today as he's in his consult rooms and not on shift at the hospital.

I love summer in Chicago, except, just not this heat in the middle of the day when I'm running and sweating my ass off. It also means the hospital struggles with all the extra caseload we get. Heat stroke in the elderly is an issue, especially if they can't afford the cool air at home. The hospital is the best thing they have for relief. My smart watch tells me it's eighty-six degrees Fahrenheit, but it feels hotter with the humidity.

I don't get the extra caseload, since I don't work in emergency. That's Tate's problem. He's a neurosurgeon who takes on the emergency cases as they arrive in the ER. Super intense, high-pressure work. Not my idea of fun. I had my years of that role, and I'm happy where I am now.

Coming through the front doors of the hospital, I feel the cool air hit me, while the eyes of the nursing staff at the check-in desk follow me to the elevator. The single ones are ready to pounce as soon as you give them any indication you might be interested. Tate takes full advantage of that. Me, not so much. When you're an intern, it seems like a candy shop of all these women who want to claim the fresh meat. The men are just as bad with the new female nurses.

We work in a high-pressure environment, working long hours and not seeing much daylight at times. You need to find a release. That's how I justified it, when I was the intern. I remember walking into a storeroom in my first year as an intern, finding my boss at the time, Leanne, and she was naked from the waist down being fucked against the wall by one of the male nurses. Now I am a qualified doctor who should hold an upstanding position in society, so I rarely get involved in the hospital dating scene anymore.

Fuck, who am I kidding? That's not the reason. It's the fact I got burned a few years ago by a clinger who tried to get me fired when I tried to move on from her. Not going down that path again. Don't mix work and play, they say—well, I say. Tate hasn't quite learned that lesson yet. Especially the new batch of interns he gets on rotation every six months. He is a regular man-whore.

Am I a little jealous? Maybe just a tad. And my cock's now firming up just thinking about getting ready for some action. It's been a bit of a dry spell. I think it's time to fix that.

Pity my date for tonight, Mason, is not even close to who I'm thinking about to break the drought. My cock totally loses interest now, and I can't say I blame him.

But on my way back up to my office upstairs, I start picturing the enchanting woman from today, and my whole focus changes. The way she sparked something inside me, and I remember the feeling of her body against mine and how quickly it affected me.

It was the briefest encounter, yet she captivated my mind with her stunning beauty and those spellbinding eyes, leaving me wanting more.

I just wish I knew who my mystery woman was.

ACKNOWLEDGEMENTS

Words are only words, until they become a story.

A story is only enjoyed if there is someone reading it.

To all my readers, thank you will never seem enough for the chance you took on me. Whether you have been with me from my first book or are just joining me now, I will always be grateful to you, for giving me the opportunity to live this life every single day.

They say it takes a village, and that applies to publishing books too.

My PA Lee is the most amazing woman who I can't function without. Nothing is ever too much for her and I wouldn't be where I am today without her. I'm so blessed to have her on my team. Thank you for putting up with me and all my crazy.

To my beta readers, Lee, Christine, Lisa, Di, and Lindsay, you are all so important in my life. Thank you for being patient with me, and for just making my books better.

To Bekah, Sammia, Hannah, and Victoria at Amazon, and all the amazing staff who work behind the scenes, thank you for all you have done for me. For guiding me on this new adventure and being part of my team now. I'm grateful that Amazon gives me the platform to publish my books, but now working with you all, it takes that gratitude to a whole new level. Thank you for believing in me.

My Deen's Diamonds girls, thank you for all the support and love you show me. You stand behind me and share my books with the world. You are all awesome.

To my dear friend who keeps me grounded, picks me up when I fall, and cheers the loudest with every win no matter how big or small. Love you from the bottom of my heart.

There are four people I get up every day and do this for. To my husband and three kids, you are my world. Your undying love and support is what keeps me going on the hard days. You are the air I breathe and the reason my heart feels so full.

Happy reading and until next time, where I'll see you between the pages.

Love
Karen xx

ABOUT THE AUTHOR

Karen Deen is a bestselling romance author known for character-driven love stories filled with emotion, tension, and heart. Her novels explore connection, healing, and the pull of relationships that refuse to stay at a distance. Writing across contemporary and billionaire romance, she creates immersive worlds where attraction sparks, walls fall, and trust is hard-won. Falling Under the Stars brings her signature emotional depth to a small-town setting, where love grows through vulnerability, choice, and courage.

Follow Karen on Amazon for all her releases and stay in touch with her on the following links to talk books, check reading order, and any upcoming events:

Website: www.karendeen.com.au
Instagram: @karendeen_author
Facebook: karendeenauthor
Facebook Reader Group: deensdiamonds
TikTok: @karendeenauthor

Follow the Author on Amazon

If you enjoyed this book, follow Karen Deen on Amazon to be notified when the author releases a new book!
To do this, please follow these instructions:

Desktop:

1) Search for the author's name on Amazon or in the Amazon App.
2) Click on the author's name to arrive on their Amazon page.
3) Click the 'Follow' button.

Mobile and Tablet:

1) Search for the author's name on Amazon or in the Amazon App.
2) Click on one of the author's books.
3) Click on the author's name to arrive on their Amazon page.
4) Click the "Follow" button.

Kindle eReader and Kindle App:

If you enjoyed this book on a Kindle eReader or in the Kindle App, you will find the author 'Follow' button after the last page.